A

FINE

LINE

AN ENDS WORLD NOVEL,
BOOK 3

MERCYANN SUMMERS

To the fractured. The anguished.
The abandoned. The wronged.
I see you.
Take my hand.

Foreword

Dear Reader:

Welcome to Book 3 of the Ends World.

While *A Fine Line* (AFL) is considered an interconnected standalone within the Ends World, I do believe it is a better reading experience to start your Ends World journey at the very beginning with the *Ends Duet: Ends of Being* and *What Doesn't Kill Us.* AFL is the story of a new couple, however, there is a bit of an overlap in part of the story, and the whole crew is back, ready to fuck around, per usual.

AFL is classified as romantic suspense with dark themes and, yes, I'm still here with all the jokes. Lots and lots of jokes. And yes, as most of you know, I am unapologetically not funny.

If you have no triggers and have zero issues reading any kind of questionable content, please skip ahead to the prologue to not risk any type of spoilers. Even if you are seldom triggered, please read this note in its entirety, and make a conscious decision on whether this book will be a good choice for you. Your mental health is important. Always choose wisely for your own personal well-being.

TW/CW: While there are no graphic scenes of child abuse there are implications and discussions of child abuse, neglect, trauma, suicide, and claustrophobia. There is human trafficking, and implications and discussions of noncon and drugging though NOT between the MMC/FMC and not on page. There is organized crime and vigilante fuckery, as well as trauma healing, trauma redemption. There is kidnapping, breath play, spanking, FF curiosities, and perhaps other various forms of kinky fuckery. And let's not forget, more naughty words and graphic depictions of sexual acts and violence than I would care to count (697 fucks (a new record!), 66 cocks, 53 dicks, 28 pussies, and just for good measure, 14 cunts).

This book is not suitable for persons under the age of 18.

Thank you for reading. Now let's fuck around.

—Mercy

Prologue

Tony

LOOKING BACK ON MY life, it's difficult to determine where the darkness began. It seems unlikely I was born with it, and I can't even say it's a result of my fucked-up upbringing because, all in all, my upbringing wasn't all that messed up. If I allow myself time to sit back and reminisce on the highlights that have been imprinted upon my existence, the majority of them are drenched in darkness. Because, in some ways, darkness feels like home.

By the time I met Darius Hughes and Mathias Shields, I was already firmly cloaked in shadows. It was with them I learned how to hone this armor into a persona that suited me.

Don't get me wrong, Dare and Matt both harbor their own shades of depravity, though Dare's has currently been tempered by the love of a woman.

Fucking choke me.

As if any amount of love could temper that pitch-blackness entirely.

I don't recall many moments after adolescence when the light would call to me. Once puberty set in and whatever good intentions I could have had were overwhelmed by testosterone and impulsivity, it was pretty much a downwards slide that I rarely cared to lift my head from.

This doesn't mean I don't know right from wrong. This doesn't mean I'm not capable of being a kind and generous person. This doesn't mean I'm never conscientious, loving, or forgiving.

Okay, maybe *forgiving* is too far.

What I'm trying to say here is I'm not a completely unrepentant, bloodthirsty fucklicker. I care about my people. And yes, that's a very short list, but once you're on it, you're on it until I die.

If I had not met Dare and Matt, my life would've gone in a completely different direction. They caught me when I was teetering at the precipice of a downward spiral. They grabbed onto my hands tightly, and even as I fought, kicked, and screamed, they did not relent. They still hold on, keeping me suspended in the air, my toes almost touching that pool of pitch-black. And even as I feel it crawling up my legs, attempting to pull me in, they won't let go.

And this is why we have our people.

When things feel out of control, when our minds are steeped in darkness, and our hearts stutter with coldness, our people are there to keep us grounded. Our people are there to bring light to any situation, with their facts and cold, hard truths, and to throw hands if necessary to keep us in the gray.

But all this makes losing one of them all the more difficult, even the ones who came later in life. The ones you've had less time with. The ones you may not even be sure would be able to go the extra mile to become your people because you didn't have time to find out for sure.

And maybe that's what makes it so infuriating—the unknowns. The what-ifs. The should've-could've-would've mentality of never knowing what might have been.

It's these atrocities that sometimes trigger that headfirst plummet into the pitch-black. Losing your what-if as you're choking on that should've, could've, would've.

And I think that's what led me to the first time I've ever lied to my people. The first time they ever asked me a direct question, and the truth didn't automatically spill out. That should've been my first red flag; that should've been my first indication that maybe I should take a step back. That maybe I should rewind and confess that I'm not cool. I'm not alright. I'm fucking pissed, and someone better tie me down.

On the other side of that, though, they most likely didn't believe me. Darius probably ended that call and immediately muttered to himself some variation of "that lying motherfucker" which means the clock is winding down on my current mission.

And I won't kill her. That wasn't a lie.

But that doesn't mean she won't wish she was dead.

Chapter One

Tony

I SHOULDN'T BE HERE.

Dare told me again and again to leave it alone, to let it go, to leave it be.

But here I am, doing none of that.

Dare and Matt only understand my anger to a point, and I don't understand their lack of response toward the situation.

For her to have so deeply entrenched herself in the lives of other people that they began to care about her, knowing that she meant to do them harm is unforgivable. The fact that they don't feel the same way boggles my mind, and though I did promise not to kill her, I have a feeling it's going to be a difficult promise to keep.

I'm a cut-and-dry kinda guy. I don't deal well with gray areas, and the fact that she thinks she can live all high and mighty in her gray area pisses me off.

I managed to ignore that festering rage in my gut for a short period of time before it finally boiled over and I felt inclined to do something about it. It really should've taken me longer to find her than it did, but once I had my sights on her, time was ticking.

I've been on her balcony every night this week, and she hasn't noticed. Sometimes, she comes out in the evening, and I lean against the wall right behind the open door, but still, she hasn't noticed me. A few times, it appeared as if she knew someone was there and I was going to be caught, but then she'd shrug and shake her head with a laugh and go back inside.

Surprisingly, she hasn't had any visitors. Nor has she left her apartment. Food has been delivered. And as far as I can tell, she's had no contact with the outside world—no phone or computer. She reads books, watches television, and does half-ass exercises, but mostly, she stares off into space.

Now, I've seen enough to know she's been up here living in her high-rise luxury while a friend of mine lies in her grave, and the injustice of it all boils my blood.

Maybe if we had never met before, maybe if she was just another nameless face, I wouldn't take it so personally. But to me, it is personal.

And I'm tired of waiting.

She always closes her balcony doors but doesn't bother locking them, which makes sense, given it's not an easily attainable area. I wish I could say it had been more difficult for me to get up here than it was, but frankly, anything's easy if you have the mind for it.

I wait for her to leave the living room, then slowly make my way after her. So far, she has run the same routine, day after day, and it appears that tonight will be no different.

She disappears into the bathroom in the main hallway leading to the bedrooms, a habit I find off, considering she has a very nice ensuite bathroom that she rarely uses. I also find it odd that she always closes the bathroom door and locks it, but I suppose there's a story behind it.

Done hiding, I lean against the wall next to the bathroom door. The door opens, and she exits the bathroom, so preoccupied with whatever is on her mind that she doesn't see me.

She turns down the hallway toward her bedroom, walking a few steps, and then she stops, her head tilting in concentration as she listens. I don't move an inch—I don't even breathe. Instead, I wait to see what she'll do, and after a few moments, she slowly turns, so she's standing in the middle of the hallway, her eyes focused on my face.

She says nothing, but the look on her face is an odd mixture of resignation and sadness but no fear.

This pisses me off even more, that I went so wrong in my handling of her that she doesn't even fear me because she should fucking fear me. She should fear for her life for her deceit and malice. I scowl at her, and she winces minutely, but I see it.

I walk toward her, and she doesn't move, her eyes never leaving my face as I lean in close and whisper, "She's dead, you know. All because of you."

She flinches at my words, her sadness changing to regret, but that's not good enough for me because no amount of sadness or regret changes the fact that her actions lead to the death of someone I cared about. As if I'm supposed to believe anything about her, given her ability to lie and pretend.

I move a little closer, asking a little louder, "Was it worth it? Did you get what you wanted?"

She frowns, stepping back and narrowing her eyes at me as she hisses, "Are you fucking kidding me? I never wanted any of this."

I snort, my lips twisting as she tries to step away from me. I reach a hand out and grab her by the hair at the back of her head, yanking it until she gasps in pain. With my other hand, I stroke along her neck as I ask, "Did you do the same thing to Darius that you did to me? Distract him with your body to hide your fucking lies?"

She pulls against my grip, but it's unrelenting, so she stops and sputters, "Of course not. You're fucking crazy!"

I laugh at her humorlessly, almost cruelly, and reply, "Oh, I'm fucking crazy, sweetheart. You seemed to have forgotten that fact when you decided to try to pull one over on me. As if I'd let you get away with it."

A glimmer of annoyance passes over her features, and then, it's gone as quickly as it arrived. "I didn't forget. How could anyone forget how insane you are? Maybe I just don't fucking care."

I tighten my hand in her hair until she flinches again, but there's a little spark in her eyes that sends a flare of heat down my spine. I turn us, pushing her back against the wall, pressing right up into her until her breath hitches, then I skate my nose along her jaw to her ear. "Still playing games, huh? Do you think you can distract me again with that hot body and beautiful face? Do you really believe that I'd be duped twice by you?"

"I didn't dupe you, Tony," she says breathlessly. "I have never duped you."

I give her a little shake, my fury renewed that she'd attempt to lie to me again. As if she thinks I'm so fucking stupid that I'd fall for it twice. "I don't think so, sweetheart. Fool me once, that's all you're going to get."

I release my grip on her throat, stroking my hand down her front, reveling in the catch in her breath as my hand caresses over her breast and down her stomach. I cup between her legs, feeling the unmistakable heat there, and I curse. "Your body tells me you like being in trouble. Do you like the danger? Do you like knowing you can use your body as a weapon?"

Her hands come up, and she pushes at my chest as she whispers, "No. Never."

"Don't you fucking lie to me," I spit out, my hand pressing between her legs more firmly, my palm grinding against her clit. Her hands move down, gripping my wrist and attempting to pull me away, but I'm stronger. I yank her head back again, my lips and teeth going to her neck. At first, she freezes, the shudder going down her body giving me a little thrill of victory that I'm correct in my assessment of her deceitful ways.

I push closer, consumed by anger and bitterness that she managed to play me so perfectly that I missed all the signs that she was a two-faced viper.

It takes me a few moments to realize that she's no longer emitting breathless moans. She's gone completely lax in my arms, her face turned away. My hands are still in her hair and between her legs, my gaze fixed on the hot trail of tears on her cheek as she whispers, "Stop it. Please. Please stop."

I remove my hand from between her legs and tighten my grip in her hair, forcing her to look at me as I say, "Is this what you do? Feign victimization to get your way? Pretend you don't want it long enough that you can turn the tables?"

Her face twists with emotion, and suddenly, her hands are fisted in my shirt, and she screams, "No!" Then she yanks on me and pushes me away as if she's trying to shake me as she comes back even louder, "No!"

Her sudden change in demeanor startles me enough that I loosen my hold on her hair, and then she goes wild on me. I step back, staring at her in shock as she loses control, screaming, "I never asked for any of this! I never wanted any of this! I've been forced, coerced, and blackmailed my entire fucking life. I've been used as a tool and a weapon for other people's gain. I'm so fucking tired of it, so fucking tired of being blamed, of being the scapegoat for something I have nothing to do with. So tired of having the people I love used as leverage to keep me in line, to keep me on track, to keep me a prisoner of other people's fucking greed!"

I narrow my eyes, hesitant to believe anything that comes out of her lying fucking mouth. "Why should I fucking believe you? After what you did. You played Darius like a fiddle. He still believes your bullshit, even going so far as to make me swear on a stack of fucking Bibles that I won't kill you. Don't forget, sweetheart, I don't actually answer to Darius Hughes or any other motherfucker out there. I answer to me, so don't think you're safe for one second just because you're now crying wolf on your own deceitful bullshit."

Her eyes bug out of her head, her hands fisting and then flying at me, pounding against my chest. "I fucking hate you! You don't know anything, you miserable fucking asshole. You think you know everything, but you don't know anything about me, my situation, or the lengths I've gone to protect people I love! Maybe you wouldn't know what that's like because you've never actually loved anyone other than yourself!"

I grab onto her wrists and yank her hands off me, shoving her back up against the wall again as I shout, "Don't you fucking try to tell me about love, sweetheart. What the fuck do you know about love? You seem to live your life one mark to the next to see how far ahead you can get by constantly screwing people over. They fall for your bullshit, even begin to care for you, and then you lead them to their own fucking death trap. So, fuck you if you want to try to tell me about love."

"Everything I've ever done has been for love. Every sacrifice I've made, every hurt I've withstood, my entire existence has revolved around protecting those I love. Don't try to talk to me about understanding collateral damage and making hard choices to protect those you care about. You don't fucking know anything, Tony. If I could've found a way out, I would've. There is no way out. I'm trapped in this fucking prison forever!"

"We all have choices. You have a choice every fucking day between being a good person and screwing over people that care about you. And even after all you've done, you still sit up here on your fucking pedestal in the lap of luxury, doing as you please while all the people that you have betrayed lie in their graves. Fuck you and your choices."

"There's no way out of this prison for me!" she yells. "How the fuck would you like me to leave? I'm stuck here with no way out until the next time they come for me and give me a job. Another 'do this or we hurt someone you love' vicious cycle."

I snort and grit out, "There's always a way out, sweetheart. If you're so sick and tired of your life, maybe you should've gone off the fucking balcony like you deserve. Taken a fucking swan dive to paradise."

I regret the words as soon as they're out of my mouth, but I'm so fucking pissed off that I'm spewing whatever nonsense I can come up with.

She grabs at me for a moment and clenches her teeth so her scream is stuck vibrating in her chest. The sound is so guttural and animalistic that I immediately release her and step back entirely.

Then, as quickly as she started, she stops. An eerie calmness surrounds her as she steps toward me, tears streaming down her face, all the light gone from her eyes as she whispers, "You're right. You're right. I shouldn't be here. I should've done that years ago when it all began. None of this ever would've happened. This entire existence wouldn't have happened, and everyone I've hurt would be fine."

She says nothing further; she just brushes her fingertips along my cheek and down over my chest, and then she turns and walks away from me down the hallway. Her change in demeanor is so swift that I'm briefly startled, and I stand there for a few moments in confusion as she disappears into the living room, out of sight.

The click of the balcony door snaps me back to the present, and I yell, "No!"

I'm running down the hallway, sprinting through the living room, leaping over the sofa on my way to the balcony doorway, where I see her on the other side, climbing up onto the railing.

I'm shouting, "No! No. *No!*" all the while, in the back of my mind, I'm questioning what the fuck I've done.

It's all in slow motion, me watching her as if she's already suspended in the air, and I'm running through the doorway and out onto the balcony. She steps onto the edge and leans over, and I know I'm gonna be too late—that I won't be able to get her in time to pull her back to safety, to save her, to stop her.

So, I don't think. I don't stop. I run harder, using the balcony furniture as steppingstones to propel me forward so when I step up onto the ledge, I'm launching myself up and out, pushing myself off the wall, so as I fly through the air, I run right into her, snatching her out of the void, the force of my body pushing her out and away.

And then we're falling.

Falling.

Falling.

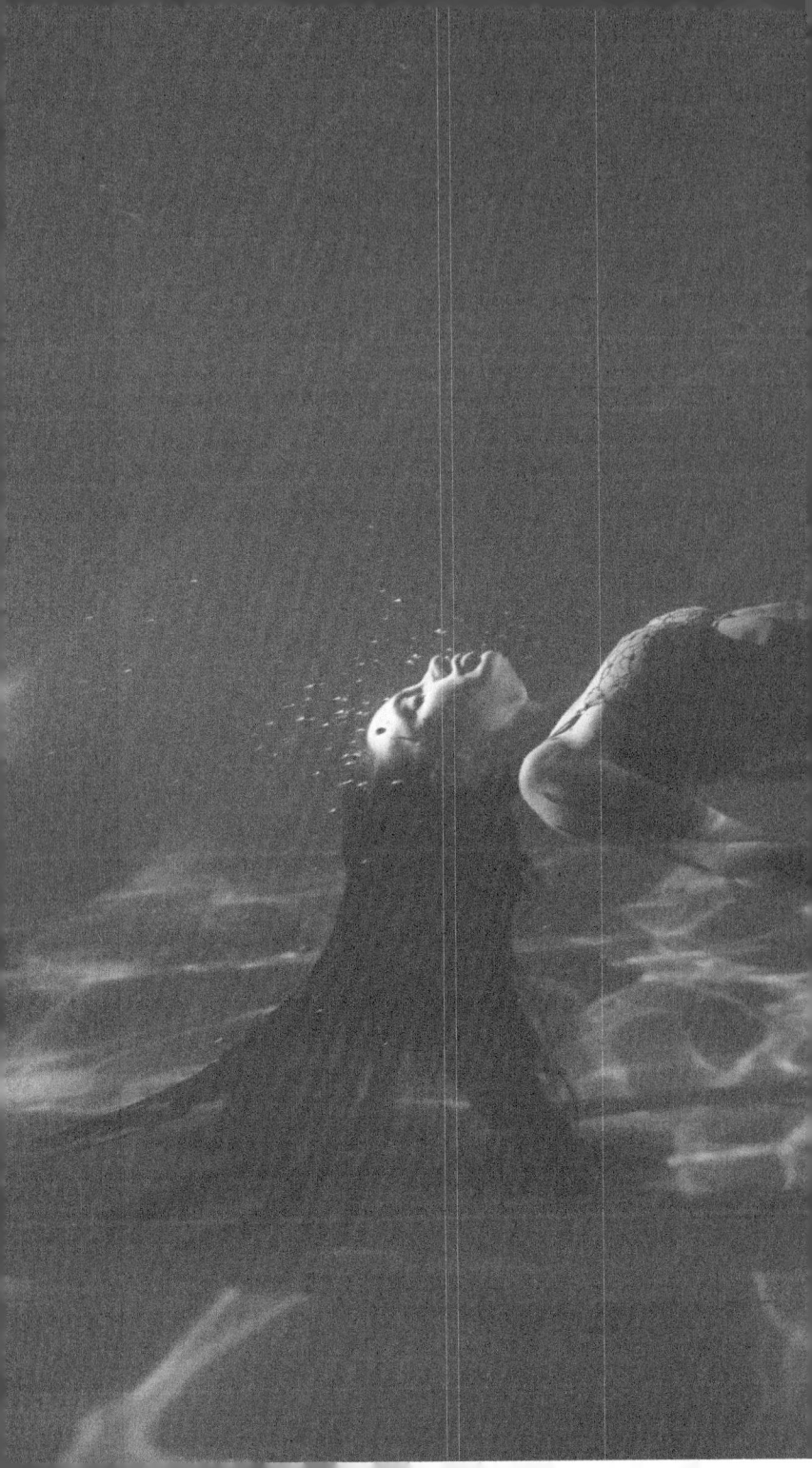

Chapter Two

Carolina

How DID I GET here?

A seemingly simple question that many of us ask at random points in our lives, though likely not when actively headed to their doom.

I'm in a trance, my body moving of its own volition, but I have this niggling cadence in the back of my brain that can't quite squeeze through the darkness of the right now. It can't shove aside the pain I've learned to numb throughout my entire life. The chronic emotional turmoil, the suffering, the agony, all of it spews up from my being, washing away reason and pushing aside years of reinforcing walls needed to withstand my reality.

And now I'm left here, hemorrhaging internally, every bad thought, every terrible thing done to me, as every scream and tear that's festered within me boils over, blinding me to...something.

I'm forgetting something.

There's something.

Someone.

I've taken this path down the hallway, through the living room, and out to the balcony door. If my eyes were shut, now that I open them, I see I'm suspended in the air, and I remember something.

My why.

My who.

I freeze on the edge of the ledge, my arms circling, pinwheeling frantically, though it feels as if I'm swimming through sludge rather than air as I try to force myself backwards. It doesn't work; momentum and gravity have me in their clutches, so I try to use force to jump in order to propel myself backwards, but it's no use. As I flounder on the cusp of the fall, I gasp, "Flora."

Shouting breaks through, and then, suddenly, I'm jarred violently, a force hitting me so hard from behind that my breath is forced from my lungs, and steel bands tighten around my torso. There's a gruff cursing in my ear as everything drops from beneath me, and I'm falling.

Falling.

Falling.

I don't scream, cry, or question; I allow my arms to fly and wait for the end, only to have cold snap me out of it. And when I attempt to pull in a long overdue inhalation, icy fire infiltrates my lungs.

Water.

I try to swim, attempting to kick my feet and move my hands through the water, but my limbs are lead, completely unmoving, and a small part of me laughs because I'm the only person that can jump from a building and then die of drowning.

I remain suspended, my eyes growing heavy, but then my arm is yanked, and those steel bands are beneath me, yanking, pulling, and pushing me, rolling me free of my crystalline tomb.

But I still can't breathe.

My lungs are so full of water that I'm incapable of spitting it out, meaning I can't breathe in until I manage to breathe it out.

There's that shouting again, incoherent due to the ringing in my ears, and I open my eyes to light and shadows. I try to swallow, but my tongue feels too big in my mouth, and then I'm being rolled onto my front, and there's a pounding on my back and more cursing as I choke out a dribble of water, but it's not enough.

I'm rolled onto my back again, there's a pinch on my nose, water dripping on my face, and I blink against the sting in my eyes as cold envelops my mouth, forcing an excruciating pressure into my chest once—twice. The third time is more vicious than the rest, and I'm immediately rolled onto my front, and the pounding hits harder as I choke and choke and choke, coughing and vomiting until there's nothing but an empty burning.

I hiccup a tiny breath, then another and another, until I'm pulling in air through my wide-open mouth for what feels like eons, but I know it's only seconds. I lie there on my front, my cheek pressed against scratchy, wet concrete, and blink until my vision clears, and the ringing in my ear dissipates.

I hear the cursing coming from the body lying beside me. "You goddamn fucking crazy-ass women. Throwing yourselves off fucking buildings as if you've got nine fucking lives. What in the ever-loving fuck is wrong with you? I'm too old to deal with this fucking shit."

I blink, my lips curving up as I watch Tony lying half on his back half of his side, his eyes looking in my direction as he curses a blue streak, still gasping for air, and I choke on a laugh.

His eyes meet mine, and he glares at me, shaking his head, but he says nothing. I'm certain he'd like nothing more than to actually throttle me right now, and I can't say I blame him.

He continues to mutter to himself until I ask, "Am I really not the first?" I pause and take a shuddering breath then manage to whisper, "The first woman you've known to jump off a building?"

His lips press together, and he shakes his head, making a frustrated sound in his throat as he mutters, "No, and you better be the fucking last."

"Did you save the other woman?" I ask quietly, still lying there, completely incapable of moving.

His laugh lacks humor as he replies, "Dumb fucking luck saved her. And I'm certain a third time wouldn't be the charm."

"Probably not."

We lie there for a few more minutes, staring at each other, not speaking, until slowly, I start to get feeling back into my body. My lungs are still on fire, but my arms and legs are functioning, so I slowly push myself up onto my hands and knees.

I get a foot beneath me, wobbling a bit as I attempt to stand, and Tony rolls to his feet in one motion, moving beside me and putting his hands on my waist to steady me as I attempt to rise.

He's staring down at me with such an odd look that I suddenly feel uncomfortable, foolish even, so I open my mouth and say, "I'm so—"

"Don't you dare apologize, sweetheart," he interrupts harshly. "I wanted to hurt you, not realizing how damaged you already are. In my mind, there's no excuse for what you did, but that's also no excuse for what I said that pushed you off that building."

"Well, if you truly wanted me dead, that would've taken care of the can't-kill-me clause," I reply rather flippantly.

"That's not how I operate. If I want someone dead, then I kill them. I don't use psychological warfare to get them to do the dirty work for me. If I want you dead, I'll be looking you in the eyes when the life drains from them."

He's not kidding. The look in his eyes tells me his words are true, and I shiver, not just from the cool night air on my wet skin.

Then he blinks and says, 'I guess I don't have to figure out how to sneak out of your apartment now."

"What do you mean?"

He raises his brows at me like I'm an idiot and replies, slowly, "Since you're already down here we'll head out straightaway."

"I can't leave!" I exclaim, the idea of losing my only connection to the entire reason I exist sending me into a panic.

He narrows his eyes at me—clearly unhappy with my words—takes a step closer, and points his finger at me as he says, "You can and you will, whether on your own two feet or over my shoulder."

Anxiety overwhelms me, and I sputter, ready to duke it out if necessary. "You don't understand!

"Then make me fucking understand!"

The words get stuck in my throat, and I snap my mouth shut, grinding my teeth together in frustration. I don't know how to explain my entire existence without putting someone I love in danger, so, finally, I decide to keep it generic and say, "I can't go do whatever I want with my life. People's lives depend on what I do and how I act. I can't live a life knowing I didn't do whatever I could to protect them."

He waits a few moments, eyeing me suspiciously, and then he glances away and rubs his hands over his face. He turns back to me and asks, "What's the point in living your life in a cage if you don't get to see the results of your sacrifices?"

"My life doesn't matter. The people I love, those lives matter."

"That's where you've got it all wrong, Carolina," he replies. "And that's what you need to change in your mind. We care about other people, we love them, and we do our best to take care of them, but we do not live for other people. We live for ourselves. You need to learn to live for you."

I blink rapidly against the burning behind my eyes. "I don't know how to do that."

"Well, maybe it's time you learn."

"I can't," I yell, panic overtaking me at the thought of moving away from the only existence I've known for most of my life. "I can't fucking do it. Put me back in my prison and walk away, Tony. That's what you need to do."

He smirks at me, and I groan, knowing what's coming before he opens his mouth. I don't wait for him to speak. I take off, sprinting back toward the entrance of my high-rise prison. He's right on my heels, his boots slapping heavily on the concrete, and I quickly recognize that there's no chance I'll outrun him, but I continue to try.

A few feet from the doors, he grabs me from behind, and the doorman raises his brows at us questioningly as Tony lifts me off my feet and spins around. "Now, now, darling," he says sweetly. "Let's not get too excited with our little chase game. You'll get those spankings soon enough."

The doorman cracks a small smile and averts his eyes, and I scream internally and thrash in Tony's embrace so he sets me onto my feet, only to turn me to face him and shoving his shoulder into my stomach as he stands, hefting me up in a fireman's carry.

He turns away from the building and stalks across the parking lot, and I yell, "Where the fuck are you taking me?"

He pauses, stooping down and picking up a duffel bag he had hidden in the bushes, then starts walking again, completely ignoring my question.

A car alarm system beeps, doors click unlocked, then a trunk lid releases, and I'm being dumped off his shoulder. I fall into the trunk with a thud and immediately attempt to get out, but his hand on my chest pushes me back down, and he leans into me, forcing me still as he says, "I'm only going to say this once, sweetheart. Either you come with me willingly, or I take you by force. You choose."

"I can't co—"

He doesn't let me finish, instead shoving something into my mouth, and I struggle, shaking my head in an attempt to spit it out, but it's too late. I bring my hands up behind my head to undo the buckles of the gag, but he grabs my wrists, quickly flipping me onto my front and shackling my arms behind my back.

He rolls me onto my side so I'm not lying on my cuffed hands, then looks me over. He adjusts the gag in my mouth only enough where I can pull air around it if needed but not enough that I can remove it, then he straightens. "We're going to take a little trip, sweetheart," he says almost pleasantly. "When we get where we're going, we can discuss your past, present, and future, and also how you plan on repenting for the death of someone I care about."

I scream behind the gag, thrashing about to no avail, and eventually, I calm down, lying there panting through my nose.

And the fucker smiles at me, obviously pleased with himself, as he leans in close and whispers, "Don't think just because I saved your life that I don't still hate you."

Then he jerks back and slams the lid of the trunk shut, leaving me in darkness.

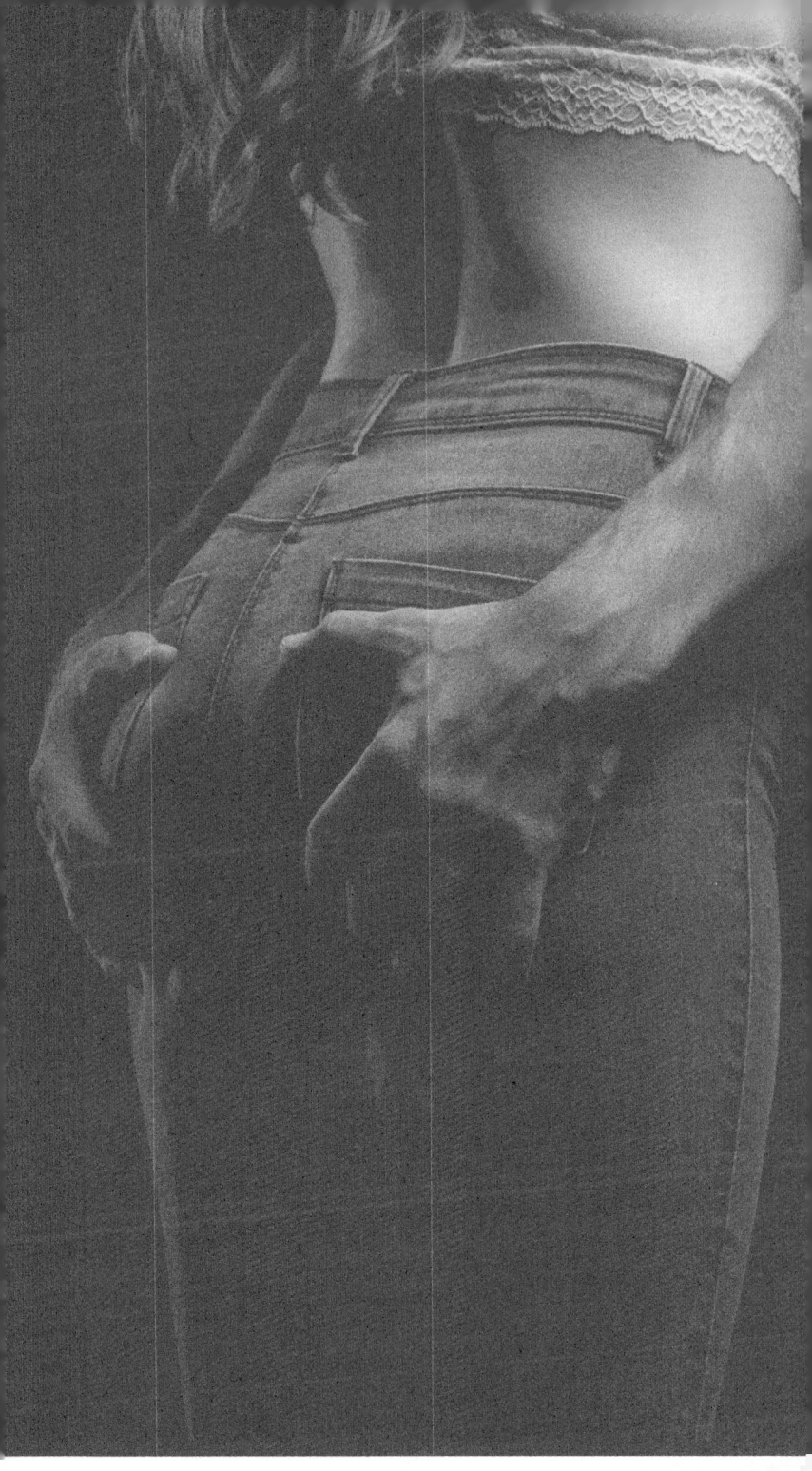

Chapter Three

Carolina

IF I WAS ANY other woman, I'd likely be freaking out to find myself in what appears to be a wooden box—crying, blubbering, and begging to be released, even.

But that's not me.

I mean, it helps that I know who put me in this box. And while he may be considered a scary motherfucker to most people, he doesn't scare me.

Not that he doesn't have the capacity to make me fear him, but I'm at the point in my existence and our relationship where I understand that there are far worse things than death. I suppose, if he felt inclined, he could break me with pain. But there really isn't anything left to break. The one thing he could've used to hold over my head is the one thing I can't locate.

Hindsight being what it is, his stealing me from my fancy prison is likely doing me a favor. Now, if I can stay out of that prison while also getting out of this prison, I might be able to make some headway in locating that missing piece of me.

One thing is for sure: he can't kill me. Today, anyway.

He may not know that I know this, and he may believe I'm lying in this box, wallowing in the idea of my imminent demise, but as I've already explained, death is easy.

And I know Darius Hughes. Regardless of how things ended up, he said that someday we'd sit down with a bottle of whiskey and come to terms, and he's a man of his word.

Antoinette may want to slap the shit out of me, and rightly so. But I don't believe she would go against Darius. She may not let me off the hook easily, but at some point, she would.

Then there's Tony Andersen; the man spent time locating me and ended up putting me in this box, knowing he can't kill me. Lilith Ferro was a huge force within the criminal world, and finding out that she was also Antoinette's mother right before her death threw everyone into a tailspin.

After months spent chasing the ghosts of those who were out to get Antoinette, they finally manage to put it all to rest, only to be left with countless unanswered questions.

And yes, I am partially to blame.

They may be under the false impression that I don't care. For all I know, they assume that their loss didn't affect me. But it did. Knowing that I'm partially responsible for the loss of someone they cared about rips me apart.

I didn't know Lilith that well, but from what I did know of her, I understand how the loss of her reverberates throughout their existence. Even if there was no love lost between some of them, I still feel that vacancy in the landscape of their future.

When Tony got to the airstrip, he allowed me to get out of the trunk of his car, and even removed the gag and cuffs and allowed me to put on dry clothes. But that was the end of his charitable nature, and he gave me the option of either sedating myself or enduring a long flight in a closet. My first inclination was to argue, a new tendency I'm not quite accustomed to, and after a few moments of inner dilemma and his promise that I would remain untouched, I decided I'd take the nap.

And now, I'm not sure how long I've been in this box, but from the pressure on my bladder, I think it's been a while. Pretty soon, all it'll take is one good sneeze, and I'll have an embarrassing moment on my hands. That will really tick me off because this dumb fuck will assume I pissed myself scared.

I don't fucking think so.

Heavy footfalls sound nearby. They stop when they're right next to me, and then there's silence for a moment. And then there's metal scraping on metal and the distinct sound of metal snapping against wood. Next, I'm moving on the smooth roll of wheels, and then I'm blinded by a light.

I squeeze my eyes shut and then blink rapidly until a shadow falls over my face.

And there he is, once again. Tony fucking Andersen.

I glare up at him, and he gives me a self-satisfied, somewhat creepy smile that has me suppressing the urge to roll my eyes.

He kneels down, his hand coming out to rub his knuckles down my cheek. I flinch away, and he leans in close and says, "Are you ready to play?"

I laugh. I can't help it. Don't get me wrong, it's a pretty well-known fact that Tony Andersen is a *bad* guy. He may not be the mythical legend of the beast, but he's a mythical legend in his own right. And under different circumstances, I might be inclined to be worried.

My laugh is cut off by his hand gripping my face, his thumb digging into one cheek, and his fingers digging into the other as he squeezes. I try to wipe the smile off my face, although it's difficult, but I finally manage to squeak out, "I really gotta pee."

He shakes his head at me and barks out a laugh as he yanks his hand back in annoyance. Then he sighs. "Why can't you fucking women at least pretend not to enjoy being in danger?"

I shake my head and half-shrug as I reply meekly, "Oh, no. Please don't hurt me." When all he does is give me a bland look, I continue in a more serious tone. "I am a little scared that I might piss my pants. Does that work?"

Tony purses his lips at me as he stands, crossing his arms over his chest as he replies, "If you piss in that box, I'm gonna be in trouble. Darius will never forgive me."

He drops his arms and then turns away from me as he continues, "Come on. The bathroom is downstairs."

I squirm around, making sure all my limbs are working before I sit up and slide over to the edge. I ignore the pins and needles in my feet, flopping myself over the side and slowly standing.

It takes me a few moments to scramble down from the loft on my tingly feet, and by the time I stand in the middle of the living area, I ask emphatically, "Bathroom?"

He points behind me, and as I scurry across the room, I'm already unfastening my pants and don't even take time to close the bathroom door before I sit my ass down on the toilet seat. "Oh, thank god. Holy shit, that was close."

A shadow appears in the doorway, and I glance up to see Tony standing there, frowning at me. He shakes his head as he grabs the doorknob and yanks the door closed with a bit more force than necessary.

I laugh to myself, this new feeling of freedom to poke the bear already growing on me. I quickly finish up in the bathroom, washing my hands before I head back into the living area, where Tony is standing in the middle of the room waiting for me. "What is this place?"

"Dare's little hideaway out in the middle of fucking nowhere, so don't get any ideas."

"Oh. Is this the place Antoinette escaped from?"

"Nettie didn't escape," he scoffs, his face twisting in annoyance. "Dare didn't secure her properly. If he hadn't been such a besotted fool, she never would've escaped. And since I'm definitely not besotted with you, there's zero chance you'll escape."

"Well, that sounds like a challenge."

I only manage to take one step back before he's on me. Maybe it's too soon for jokes.

His breath is hot against my face as he says, "The only reason you're still breathing is because of Darius. You should be dead for what you did."

I stare straight into his eyes as I nod in agreement. "You're right. But in the end, at least I tried to make it right."

"You tried a little too late. And you ended up with blood on your hands."

I narrow my eyes, my jaw clenching as I place both of my palms against his chest and shove him backwards. "Do you think I don't fucking know that? Do you think that I don't look back and wonder if there was something I could've done to prevent Lilith's death?"

He steps back into me but doesn't push me back against the wall. His eyes search mine as he says, "I don't see why you would care."

"How could I not care?" I shout as his ridiculous assumptions make my blood hot in my veins. "Stop making snap judgments about something you know nothing about. I may not have known Lilith that well, but she's the closest friendly connection I've had in years, and god knows I needed that connection. I needed a friend like her in my corner. A friend that's..."

Tony's face twists as he considers my words, and then he responds, "Gleefully murderous?"

I nod, my laugh a touch watery as I say, "Yes. I could definitely use a gleefully murderous friend right now." I pause for a moment, then meet his gaze. "Look, Tony, I'm really sorry about Paris. I should've told you the truth when you asked—"

He raises his hand, the furious look on his face cutting off my words as he spits out, "I don't wanna fucking hear it. I don't give a fuck about any of it, least of all some stupid interlude that meant less than nothing."

Yeah, that stings, but I don't bother responding. He's obviously more bitter than I originally thought, so talking about the past is out.

He presses his lips together, his eyes assessing me, but I don't miss the spark of heat in their depths, and, annoyingly, my pussy clenches in response.

I swallow back the spontaneous cackle that attempts to erupt from my mouth, and instead, I end up choking on what is likely an obviously inappropriate laugh. He inclines his head at me in interest and asks, "What could possibly be funny right now?"

I laugh again, the blatantly inappropriate undertone entirely obvious this time, and the corner of his lip curls up knowingly. He takes a step closer to me, then another, and another until he's standing only a few inches in front of me. He leans down a bit, so his face is directly in front of mine, searching my eyes as he asks, "Are you seriously fucking checking me out right now?"

The smile I give him is more of a grimace, and I shrug rather awkwardly. But my reply is clear. "You're fucking hot, and I'm prone to clearly inappropriate thought processes at the completely wrong time."

He shakes his head at me, his eyes looking up to the sky as he mutters, "What the actual fuck?"

I laugh awkwardly again as my hands come up, hovering over his well-defined pectoral muscles under his Henley. His gaze drops to my hands and then back up to my eyes, and he raises an eyebrow at me questioningly.

I drop my hands, quickly moving them behind my back, where I clasp them together. I give him that same uncomfortable grimace that I can't seem to get rid of.

He steps closer to me, and this time, I step back. He raises both eyebrows at me, and the smile he gives me is feral as he continues to move forward. I continue to retreat.

I can't even pretend his little chase game doesn't have me panting, and I find it exhilarating and confusing at the same time.

"Well, well, well. Isn't this an odd turn of events?"

I press my lips together, knowing that any sounds likely to slip out are going to be equal parts anticipatory arousal and awkward embarrassment. He continues, "What do you have to say for yourself, Carolina?"

My first inclination is to not respond, but it also feels as if I don't have any choice, and I now seem to be predisposed to word vomiting whenever stressed, something I never would've done in my previous existence. So, I do. "I don't see any shame in me wanting to climb you like a tree. Sure, you kidnapped me and stuffed me in a box under a bed, probably with the idea that you're going to do terrible things to me, and I'm sure now, you're confused because you don't understand that there isn't anything terrible you can do to me that hasn't already been done or would even bother me. So, here we are. You know that I know that you know that you're hot. And who doesn't enjoy some bad-boy ex-military fuckery less than an hour after the danger has passed."

He stares at me, then leans closer until his nose is just shy of touching mine. One of his hands comes up, and his fingers stroke down my cheek softly as he whispers, "I fucking hate you for what you've done and for your treachery that led to the death of one of mine."

Now, my smile brightens, and I nod, refusing to offer an apology that will change nothing. "Noted. But who doesn't love a good hate fuck?" I turn my head, my teeth snapping at his finger sharply, a little thrill running down my spine at my completely spontaneous outburst. I get a tiny nip in, but he pulls back before I can really sink my teeth in, and the growl that rumbles in his chest makes my pussy throb, and that thrill runs over me again.

He steps closer, pressing me back into the wall, his cock pushing against my stomach, and I press myself into him. The hand I tried to bite moves behind me and squeezes my ass before running down the back of my thigh and lifting my leg that he then hooks around his waist.

I can only recall one other time when I've felt that pang of arousal, that deep heat inside me that yearns to be fucked, and it sends my blood soaring.

I don't fight it. I lean closer to him as he presses into me fully, wishing our clothes would disappear and he was balls deep inside my throbbing cunt. I hiss out, "Yeah. That's it, you fucking asshole. Don't you wanna take out that loathing on my pussy?"

His free hand comes up and slaps over my mouth, and he grits out, "Shut your fucking mouth. I don't wanna hear another fucking word out of you, or I'll edge you and then stuff you back in the box with your hands tied behind your back so you can't find relief."

I contemplate my choices, seriously considering calling his bluff to find out if I like it, but I keep my mouth shut because, right now, I need to come. I don't know why; I have no idea if I'm running toward something or away from something, but the painful ache between my legs matches the painful ache in my chest, and I need to assuage it. I need him to gather every ounce of hatred and loathing he has for me and shove it into me so hard and fast that all I can do is scream incoherently.

So, I nip and lick his palm, my eyes boring into his in challenge. He moves his hand from my mouth, wiping my saliva on my cheek before pressing his wet hand against my throat. He squeezes, and all the pent-up desire I've held hidden inside me over the last few years boils to the surface, and I give up any semblance of pretending.

I drop my leg back to the floor, my hands coming between us, and I unbuckle his belt, then unfasten, and unzip his jeans, pushing them down out of the way of my seeking hands. I bite back a groan as my hand touches the hot skin of his hard cock, not at all surprised to find he's commando under his pants.

I don't bother teasing him. I wrap both hands around his cock, stroking firmly up and down his shaft and then rubbing my palm over the tip, smearing the pre-cum around.

I move to drop to my knees, my mouth open in invitation, but his hands on my upper arms stop me. I raise my eyes to his, and he says, "As much as I'd love to stuff that lying fucking mouth with my cock, that's not what you want."

I frown, ready to say otherwise, but he continues, "Do you want me to fill your wet pussy with my huge fucking dick? Do you want me to ram it in until it hurts? Until you're screaming and wailing for me to stop while also begging me to never stop?"

My cunt thrums, the clenching almost painful. I nod. "Yes."

He knocks my hands out of the way, unfastening and unzipping my pants, then wedging his hand inside. There's no soft touch, no hesitation, as he slides his fingers right where I want him. "You're fucking drenched for me. Did you spend all that time in the box dreaming about my dick inside you?"

I choke out a sobbing laugh and gasp, "No. Not at all. I spent all that time thinking about what a stupid fucking asshole you are—"

He glares at me as he slides two fingers deep inside me, cutting off any further insults I might have wanted to throw at him to piss him off. "Stupid, huh? Do my fingers inside your dripping cunt feel stupid?"

I shake my head almost violently, but I can't form any words as he twists his hand, and the base of his palm presses into my clit. He moves his free hand up, grabbing the hair at the base of my skull and yanking my head back so I'm looking him in the eyes. My mouth falls open, and I'm nothing more than incoherent moans and gasps as I gyrate my hips, looking for more friction. The self-satisfied look on his face makes me seethe, but all I can think about is getting off.

Without warning, he pulls his hand out from between my legs, his other hand releasing my hair before he yanks my pants down around my hips. "Are you on birth control?"

My heart stops in my chest for a moment, my arousal suddenly tampered by his question, and I shake my head as I reply, "I can't get pregnant. But you should still use a condom. I haven't been tested in a long time. It's not safe for you." I force the words out as my eyes focus on a spot on the wall behind him.

His body tenses, and his hand grips my chin firmly, forcing me to look at him. "What are you saying?"

I shrug, attempting to pull my face from his hand, but his grip tightens, and I'm forced to look him in the eye as I reply, "Nothing. It doesn't matter."

His grip tightens painfully as he grits out, "Are you saying someone fucked you without your permission?" I don't respond, but my lack of response has the look in his eyes going completely pitch-black as he continues, "Who was it?"

I grind my teeth together, my lips pressed into a tight line. I raise my chin obstinately even as I push back the burning behind my eyes. I shake my head in his grip but say nothing, so he speaks again. "We'll get that list later. But remember, no one touches you without your permission, and that includes me."

The weight on my chest is excruciating, but his gaze on mine is unflinching, and I feel like he's staring directly into my soul as he asks, "Do I have permission to touch you? To fuck you?"

And just like that, the weight on my chest eases, and I manage to take a deep breath. I didn't feel at any point in our interaction that I was being forced, but maybe there was that tiny little voice inside me that was conditioned to accept the inevitable spiral that drives me. So, I say, "Quit your fucking romantic bullshit and fuck me already."

He glares at me, one of his hands grabbing my throat while his other hand grips my pants, and then he's half-leading, half-pulling me around until he pushes me face-first over the arm of the couch. He releases my throat, yanking my pants halfway down my thighs, and then he's yanking on the back of my thong, the lace burning the skin of my hips as it's pulled free. I feel the hot tip of him pressing between my legs, and I squirm beneath him, craning my head around so I can look at him as I say, "Condom, Tony. Please."

He freezes, then shakes his head as if he's trying to clear his thoughts. He eases away from me and grabs his wallet out of his back pocket, pulling out a condom and tossing his wallet to the side. I breathe a sigh of relief and turn my head away, changing my focus to my hands pressed into the cushion of the couch beneath me.

Then he's there again, pressing the tip of his dick against me and sliding it up and down teasingly. I push back against him in invitation. He slides in, just the tip, then stops and says, "You need a safeword, Carolina."

I glance back over my shoulder and frown. "No, I don't. Jesus fucking Christ, Tony. Stop stalling."

He grips my hips with both his hands, pushing me down into the arm of the couch so I can't keep rubbing against him. He stares at me calmly until I'm practically screeching in frustration. I don't know what his game is, but I've already given him too much backstory, too clear of a glimpse into me, and I don't want a fucking safeword. I don't want an out. I want him to use that big dick to drill me right into the sofa until I'm a crying, screaming, blubbering mess. But he keeps staring at me, so I finally relent and say, "Fine. Red. You happy now?"

He doesn't say anything or respond in any way; he drives his cock into me until his balls slap against my clit. My inner walls protest slightly, and I rotate my hips as he remains firmly pressed inside me. He waits a few moments, then pulls back slightly before driving back in, setting an easy rhythm. But I didn't ask for easy, so I taunt him. "I thought you were going to fuck me, asshole. I didn't realize you wanted to make love."

"You're such a fucking bitch. I told you to shut your fucking mouth." He reaches over beside me, then his hand is in my hair again, and he's yanking my head back and shoving something in my mouth. My lace thong. "If you want me to stop while your mouth is full, pinch me. Hard."

I nod and almost cackle behind the lace meant to muffle my words, but then he's pushing my face into the sofa, keeping his hand on the back of my head to keep me there as he pulls back and slams his dick back into my cunt as hard as he can. The slap of his pelvis against my ass stings, the drive of his dick exacting the painful pleasure I didn't know I was seeking.

He doesn't relent, his thrusts forceful and commanding. He leans over me, rubs his face against my cheek, and says, "That's fucking right. Is that how you want it? You want my cock to break you in half?"

I nod my head and sob my confirmation, my words muted behind the lace in my mouth. He pulls back, pulling out until only the tip of his cock is inside me, then he drives back into me so hard the sofa moves beneath us, and the end table scrapes across the floor.

He does it again, shoving into me so hard the sofa jerks against the end table, sending the lamp on top of it crashing to the floor. He doesn't even pause—doesn't slow down—the rhythmic rut of his dick in my pussy and the grit of his voice in my ear, causing the pleasure inside of me to spiral with the chaotic beat of my heart.

"If you want to be my little fucking whore, all you have to do is say so. Put your hand between your legs. Rub your clit while I fuck you. Make yourself come all over my dick."

I do what he says, lifting myself beneath the weight of his body on top of me and wedging my hand between my legs. The position doesn't allow for much movement, but the pinching pressure of my fingers against my clit is enough that I immediately feel the heat building more rapidly. I grind against my hand, each jarring thrust of his dick inside me a rhythmic pulse that has me moaning and cursing behind the lace in my mouth. I sob, grunting with pleasure and effort, my sounds broken and garbled, but I don't give a fuck.

He eases his upper body off of me, bracing one hand beside my head and lifting himself up. He reaches his other hand out, pulling the saliva-soaked fabric from my mouth, and then his hand grips my jaw, and he presses his face against mine. He bares his teeth at me, nipping the curve of my cheek, spittle splattering on my hot skin as he bites out through his gritted teeth, "Let me hear you fucking beg for it. Fucking beg for my cum, you dirty fucking whore."

Pleasure explodes inside me, and I don't bother trying to suppress my broken exclamation of pleasure that reverberates through the room. "Please. Don't stop. Fuck your dirty little whore. Fuck me. Don't stop. Please. Please."

He hammers into me relentlessly, his hand still gripping my face, and then he moves his other hand so he's also grabbing my shoulder, holding me steady as his cock punishes my quivering cunt with pleasure.

And I fucking come.

I scream into his hand, and he removes it, replacing it with his mouth, and he drinks it all in, sucking every pained moan, grunt, and sob out of my very soul. He pushes himself into me, the slap of his body stinging as he shoves in as deeply as he can get, and then his incoherent curse of release mixes with my own, his cock throbbing inside me.

He leans over me, his forehead now pressing against my temple, his lips against my cheek, and his sweat drips into my hair. Our panting breaths are the only sound in the otherwise silent room, and he mutters breathlessly, "Holy fuck. What the fuck?"

I shake my head in silent answer, unable to form words. I squirm as I try to remove my hand from beneath the weight of our bodies, and he eases back enough so I can bring my hand up to lay limply beside me. I'm sure my forearm will be bruised, along with several other places where I was pressed into the arm of the sofa, but I don't fucking care.

I don't care about anything right now.

After a few minutes, he shifts behind me, and after a few more moments, the heated weight of his body lifts off me completely. I groan, getting my hands beneath me to push my upper body up when

I feel his hands on my waist to assist me. I shake him off. "I don't need your fucking help."

He releases me immediately, and I turn and glare at him over my shoulder as he says, "Right back to fucking bitch, I see. I guess I'll have to try harder to fuck that outta you next time."

I push myself up, wriggling around until I am leaning against the arm of the sofa, facing him. "Who says there's gonna be a next time?"

"Your pussy did when it was spasming around my cock like it didn't want to let go."

My lips twist, and I narrow my eyes at him as I stand, pulling my pants up around my hips enough so I can walk. I shove my way around him, muttering, "In your fucking dreams, asshole."

His dirty chuckle vibrates around me as I walk toward the bathroom, feeling him on my heels. I stop in the doorway, turning to face him as I reach for the doorknob with one hand. Then I show him my middle finger and slam the door in his face.

Chapter Four

Tony

WHAT THE FUCK JUST happened?

Not even in any of my wildest daydreams of how my first day with Carolina Tennent would go, did *this* happen.

I can't decide if I'm slipping or if I should add this to my arsenal of tactics to use in the future. No. The majority of the people I have to teach a lesson to are not at all fuckable, so that won't work.

When she flipped me the bird and slammed the door in my face, she was doing me a favor. I walk into the kitchen, remove the condom, and toss it into the rubbish bin. I grab a couple of paper towels to clean myself off with, then shove my half-hard cock back into my jeans, carefully fastening and zipping them.

I move to wash my hands, but I pause, bringing my fingers to my nose and sniffing, the smell of her pussy clinging to them. I groan, my dick hardening fully in my pants again, making me curse.

This isn't fucking good.

What the actual fuck?

I'm not the kind of man who allows his urges to direct his choices, but here I am, reveling in the lingering perfume of pussy on my fingers.

Jesus fucking Christ.

I force myself to wash my hands, annoyed with my idiotic thought process.

I grab my phone off the counter and send Darius and Matt a text message.

Tony: Is there a word for being hyper-focused on a single person?

Boy Scout: Depends. Is this person a man or a woman?

Tony: Opposite sex.

Nettie: Besotted.

Tony: Who the fuck added her to this chat?

Boy Scout: Don't look at me.

Beast: It also technically wasn't me.

Nettie: If you wanna get technical, I added myself.

You removed Nettie from conversation

Beast: Are you trying to get yourself killed?

Tony: She has no business interfering with our bromance time.

Boy Scout: Good luck, man.

Beast added Nettie to conversation

Nettie: Don't fuck with me, Tony.

Tony: I'll start a new chat, then.

Beast: I can assure you, she will continue to add herself.

Tony: And you don't have a problem with this?

Beast: No.

Tony: Matt? Help me out here.

Boy Scout: No can do. It's not like she's not going to find out about everything we say anyway. This is actually less work.

Tony: What the fuck?

Nettie: Why do you feel you have to have secrets from me, Tony? What are you hiding?

Tony: *middle finger emoji*

Beast: That is definitely not going to get her to shut up about us.

Tony: *double middle finger emojis*

Boy Scout: You may want to rethink your strategy.

Beast: Matt's right. And honestly, if you're dealing with a woman, Antoinette is far more equipped to answer your questions.

Nettie: Exactly. You don't need another man-brain leading the charge.

Boy Scout: I can't argue with her logic.

Nettie: *smiling devil face emoji*

Beast: You'll never win, man. You may as well just tell her.

Tony: Never mind. I'm thinking it was a fluke. I'll circle back to this if it persists.

Nettie: You don't do flukes, Tony. That's absurd.

Tony: *heart hands emoji* TTYL.

I close the app and then turn my phone off. I know the next time I turn it on, I'll probably have about a million angry text messages from Nettie, but I can't deal with it right now.

Surely this situation is not as dire as I think it is.

There's a thud from the bathroom, so I walk over to the door and press my ear against it. "Are you okay in there?"

"Goddamn it, Tony," Carolina huffs in agitation. "Give me some space."

I scowl, glaring at the door in a moment of uncharacteristic petulance. This fucking woman. I fucking hate her.

Unfortunately, my cock likes her just fine.

I walk back into the kitchen area and start pulling things out of the fridge. By the time Carolina exits the bathroom, I already have mushrooms and onions sautéing in the pan, and I'm whisking eggs in a bowl. She moves closer until she's standing at the counter, giving me a skeptical look. "What are you doing?"

"Seems pretty obvious to me," I reply blandly.

"I'm allergic to eggs."

"No, you're not," I huff out, rolling my eyes at her attempted lie.

"How the fuck would you know?"

"I know every fucking thing there is to know about you. You're not allergic to eggs."

Carolina raises her brows at me and crosses her arms over her chest, resting her hip against the counter as she replies, "And why would you know that?"

"When I set my sights on someone, I make it my mission to make their life hell, and I tend to know every fucking tiny detail of their existence. And I know yours."

She doesn't say anything for a few moments as she stares at me with a thoughtful expression on her face. Then she says, "Do you excel at finding out things about people?"

It's not so much a question as a statement, and I nod as I carry on with food preparations. "So," she continues. "Say I needed help trying to find out what happened to a person. Can you help with that?"

I nod again, removing the vegetables from the pan, wiping it clean, and adding some butter to it. I slowly pour the whisked eggs into the pan and give her a look as I put the bowl in the sink. She hasn't said anything else, so finally, I ask, "Were you going somewhere with this line of questioning?"

She presses her lips together and inhales deeply through her nose. "I need to find someone."

"Are you gonna ask me to find your boyfriend or something? I'm not fucking doing it." The words come out with more emotion than I'm used to, and it catches me off-guard. I clear my throat, then add, "Unless he's on that list you're going to make for me. Then I look forward to slitting his throat."

"I imagine one or two of those probably would be involved, but they're not who I need you to find."

"Who is it, then? Out with it."

"My daughter. Flora," she whispers, pain crossing her features.

I glance away, allowing her sadness without reproach, and ask, "Is she the reason you've been living your life as a prisoner for so long?"

Her eyes widen, but she doesn't immediately reply, so I press, "I need to know, sweetheart. I need to know why you've been a slave to such evil for so long. What has driven you to make such huge sacrifices that you've given up on your own life?"

She stares back at me for a few long moments, then nods. "Yes. She's entirely innocent in all of this. I'll do anything to keep her safe."

I search her eyes, noting the deep pain there then ask, "Do you have any idea where she might be?"

She shakes her head, the sadness on her face intensifying. I'd heard from Darius that she has a daughter. He'd given me the few details he had before I went in search of her. And I get it, the need to protect those you consider yours, the lengths you'd go to do so. And as fucking pissed off as I am that Lilith got taken out in the crossfire, I can't begrudge her need to protect her own child.

I still fucking hate her, though.

"Do you at least know the last person she was with?"

"Yes. I have a short list of people who are most likely to have information on her whereabouts. I also have a list of less obvious people, but I'm hopeful that the first list will know where to find her because the second list—" She stops talking, obviously choked up by emotion, and I stare at her as the implications hang in the air.

I don't want to ask, but I have to. "Do you have proof of life?"

She winces but shakes her head. "No. Not for months now. And many of the people who would most likely know her are dead. If nothing else, they're in hiding."

I grab some bread and put a couple of slices in the toaster. I slide the butter dish and knife toward her, "You're on toast duty."

She gives me a small, watery smile and nods as she moves closer to me. She waits for the bread to finish toasting, and I divvy up the omelet between two plates. She says from over my shoulder, "For fuck sake, Tony, did you make a twelve-egg omelet?"

I glance at the plates in confusion. "I don't know. Maybe nine. Why? Aren't you hungry?"

"I am. But there's no way I can eat all of that."

I raise a shoulder dismissively, setting the egg pan in the sink as I say, "Eat what you want, and I'll eat the rest."

The bread pops up, and she snatches it out of the toaster, slathering butter across each piece. Then she asks softly, "So you'll help me? I'll do anything." The knife clangs against the counter, and then she's right beside me, looking me in the eyes. She waggles her eyebrows as she says, "And I mean anything."

I turn to face her and lean my back against the counter, my arms crossing over my chest as I look her over. As much as I would love for her to owe me. As much as I would like to have her at my beck and call for literally anything, that's not how I fucking operate. So, begrudgingly, I shake my head and say, "First of all, let's get a few things straight. I don't take sexual favors as payment. I certainly wouldn't use sexual favors as leverage because that wouldn't make me any better than those fuckwits who already touched you without your permission. I won't coerce you or blackmail you to open your legs for me. I'll hate fuck you day in and day out if that's what you want, but not under duress. Do you understand that?"

"Yes. I understand."

"Second, you will give me both of those lists at the same time. You don't decide what I do with them. If you have a gut feeling that someone on that list doesn't deserve to die, don't put them on that list. Because they're all going to fucking die."

Her eyes widen, and she opens her mouth to say something, but I raise my hand to stop her. "Third, I went to great lengths to locate you and bring you back here for two reasons: one, putting you in the box was satisfying, even knowing I couldn't do much with you once you got out of it. And two, I don't believe all this shit with Nettie died with Vincent and Dmitri, and I'm sure you're the link that will get us to the brain of the entire fucked-up organization.

"And finally, I still fucking hate you. I hate what you did. I hate what you represent. I hate the fact that your actions in some way led to the death of someone my people cared about. You hurting *them* is what I find unforgivable."

She waits a beat before responding, obviously considering her words before speaking. "I know it's no consolation, Tony, but I hope you believe me when I express how sorry I am about Lilith. Maybe it doesn't hurt me in the same way it hurts Antoinette or Agatha or even you, but it hurts me in a way that reverberates through my very being because I know, in some ways, I am responsible. I'm a lot of things, but I'm not a murderer. And if I was going to be a murderer, there's a pretty big list of people that I would've taken out before her. Even as fucking crazy as she was, she was good."

"Maybe. Someday. But I wouldn't count on it. I'm not as reasonable or forgiving as Nettie. And I don't have any kind of attachment toward you like Darius might. And don't even get me started on your fucking brother."

She frowns at me, clearly taken aback by my statement as she stares at me and retorts, "My brother? I don't have a brother."

Now it's my turn to stare at her in confusion. "Yes, you do. Jaymé. The other reason I was forbidden from outright killing you."

"I don't know what you're talking about, but I suppose the number of things I don't know about myself is long."

"I'm not gonna get into it with you right now," I say, wishing I hadn't brought it up. "I'll let Jaymé do all the explaining when the time comes."

"And when will that be?"

"I don't know. I'll reach out to Dare to find out what's going on there."

We sit down and eat in companionable silence for a while. She manages to put quite a bit of food away, then she pushes her plate over to me. I place her plate on top of my empty one and then rise and walk to the kitchen. I open a drawer under the counter and pull out paper and a pen before returning to the table and setting it in front of her and say, "You can start that list now."

She looks from the paper to me. "What list?"

"I told you. Make me a list of all the people you think might be involved with your daughter's disappearance."

She picks up the pen and shuffles her chair closer to the table as she starts writing down names. I place my hand over hers, and she stops writing and looks up at me, and I say, "And when you're done with that list, you can make me that other list."

She frowns again, twisting her hand out of my grip. "And what other list might that be, Tony?"

I lean in close to her, staring her straight in the eyes as I say, "Stop playing with me, sweetheart. You write down the name of every person who ever laid a hand on you without your permission. Male, female, I don't give a fuck. I want their name."

She laughs nervously, rolling her eyes before she looks back at the paper and starts writing again. "Don't be ridiculous. None of that matters anymore."

I don't know why those words piss me off, but they do, and my fisted hand slams against the top of the table in response. She jumps in her seat, her eyes wide as she looks at me. "But it does fucking matter. No one should ever lay a finger on a woman without their permission and not pay the price for it. So, you make me that fucking list. Do you understand me?"

She slowly swallows but nods. "Okay. Fine. I'll make the list."

Sure, she doesn't understand why I give a fuck, but she doesn't have to.

The fact of the matter is, I may fucking hate her, but I'm the only one allowed to make her pay.

Chapter Five

Tony

I LEFT CAROLINA SECURED and hidden away in the woods. She said I didn't need to lock her in, but I did anyway. It's not that I believe she's a flight risk at this point, given she needs my help to find her daughter, and I assume she needs my help to keep herself hidden from whoever had her locked away in Europe. I just felt like pissing her off.

I sent a message asking the guys to meet me at our usual location in the city. I also specified that Nettie did not need to be there for this meeting. Specifications that I'm sure will be outright ignored. It's not that I have anything to hide from her, but I like to annoy her, too.

Sure enough, when I enter the warehouse, the first thing I see is her beaming face from across the room. I shake my head, glaring at Darius, who gives me a sheepish look from behind her. Matt laughs from the corner where he's sprawled in what appears to be a brand-new recliner.

I glance around the freshly refurbished warehouse sputtering, "Jesus fucking Christ, Dare. What have you done to the place?"

"I told you. I was sick of fucking warehouses."

"I understand that, but don't you think this is a little overkill? What if we need to torture someone?"

Matt hops up and walks over toward me. "He's got a special room for that, which still looks like a warehouse."

I shake my head, and Nettie laughs. "Don't try to make sense out of any of it, Tony. Next thing you know, he'll get a shag rug and a disco ball to make it a real party pad."

I pull the pieces of paper out of my back pocket, unfold them, and then hand them to Matt. "I've got some people I need you to locate for me."

Matt takes the papers from me, frowning down at them and then looking up and meeting my eyes as he asks, "And who are these people?"

Darius appears behind me, and the next thing I know, he's standing next to Matt, looking over his shoulder at the list. "Please tell me you don't have another kill-spree list. They're tedious to keep quiet."

I snatch the papers from Matt, placing the first list on the counter as I explain, "These are the people who might know where Carolina Tennent's daughter is. We need to locate them and see what they know."

Nettie pipes in from right behind me, "And the other list?"

"I'd rather not say."

Nettie's eyes widen, and her eyes glint as her mouth falls open, and she laughs. "You'd rather not say it? You know that's not gonna work."

I look at Dare and Matt, silently asking for help, but they both stare at me, waiting. Finally, Nettie continues, "Does this have anything to do with the woman you're besotted with?"

I glare at her, placing the other piece of paper on the desk and then leaning back on it with my arms crossed over my chest. "There is no besotted. There is no woman. For fuck sake, Nettie. Stop with the romanticized ideas."

Her lip curls up at me, and she gives me an assessing look, her eyes sparkling as she persists, "I'm not buying it. Spill."

"I'm not touching another list for you until I know what it's for. I trust you, but give me a break," Matt interjects with a rather quizzical look on his face.

I glance over at Dare, who's also waiting patiently, smirking at me knowingly. That motherfucker.

I huff out of breath and then mutter, "Those are the people who touched her without her permission."

All three of them gape at me, and then Dare says, "What was that? You're gonna have to speak up, Tony. We couldn't quite hear you."

I growl, my hands rubbing over my face in agitation. I rest both hands on the counter behind me, and my head bows a bit as I mutter a bit more clearly, "Those are the motherfuckers who put their hands on Carolina without her permission."

No one says anything for a moment, and a glance out of the corner of my eye shows they're all looking at each other in surprise. I'm sure they are genuinely surprised that I'd know anything about Carolina, never mind enough to get a list from her.

I don't know why I came in here thinking I was going to be able to avoid a conversation about any possible acquaintance I might have with that bitch. But I'm in for it now, if the increasingly calculating look on Nettie's face as she sharpens her claws, preparing to attack, is anything to go by.

Finally, she says, "I told you, Darius. Did I or did I not tell you?"

"Oh, you definitely told me. I was a little skeptical, but you really nailed that one right on the head," he replies dryly.

Then Matt asks, "How am I only hearing about this now? We have a fucking group chat, and nobody ever uses the fucking group chat."

Nettie giggles and says, "Well, if you'd like me to include you in our post-coital bliss gossip via group chat, I certainly can do that. Is that like a new type of exhibitionism? Voyeurism?"

Matt shakes his head. "That's not necessary but thank you. At least someone thinks about me once in a while."

Dare walks over to the desk, pulls out a stool, and sits down, his eyes on me as he asks, "So you found Carolina?" I nod. "And you still have her?" I nod. "She's tucked away in the bunker?" I nod again. "She won't try to escape?"

This time, I shake my head and reply, "No. She asked me specifically to help her find her daughter. And I get the impression that in terms of enemies you know, I'm the least of her worries."

Nettie leans against the desk near Darius and asks, "Why would you help her? You fucking hate her."

I raise one shoulder dismissively. "I don't hate her daughter. And I'm sick and tired of seeing kids paying the price for the sins of their parents. Paying the price only because they were born into the wrong family."

She smiles at me, her hand squeezing my forearm as she gives me a close-lipped smile. I shake her off and say, "Stop looking at me like that."

"I don't know what you're talking about."

Matt and Darius both laugh because we all know she's full of shit, and so I add, "Sure you don't, Net. What do you think, guys? She about to go on one of her romance novel trope lectures?"

They both nod, and she takes a moment to glare at each of them individually before turning back to me. "Hey. My romance trope lectures have done a lot of good for us. Admit it."

She's not wrong. And most of the time, it's greatly entertaining, but that's only when it's not directed at you. Having it directed at Darius, Matt, or anyone else for that matter is usually all laughs for me.

I can tell she won't let it go, so I may as well get it over with. "Go ahead. Lay it on me."

She smiles triumphantly, sitting fully on Dare's lap as she claps her hands together. "Definitely enemies-to-lovers. Certainly, some form of suspense, maybe even a little thriller. Not really office, but forced-proximity..." She pauses, obviously thinking over her choices as she continues, "Insta-love. Oh, this is great!"

I frown and shake my head. "No fucking way. Insta-love, my ass. I fucking hate that bitch. If it wasn't for you all, I'd have slit her fucking throat a long time ago and never thought a thing about it."

She's still giving me that smug smile as she retorts, "But only after you hate fuck her, right?" And I kind of want to wipe that superior look off her face. Not that I'd ever actually hit her, but maybe putting her in a rear-naked chokehold until she passes out isn't a bad idea.

As if he can read my mind, Darius pipes up, "Don't even think about it, Tony."

"No, go ahead and do it, Tony," Matt gives his two cents from the other side of the room where he's tapping on his computer. I'm sure he'd like nothing more than for me to try something to give Darius an opening to try to hand me my ass. I'm not sure if either of us could overtake the other one. It's more than likely that it would be whoever gave up first.

I raise both my hands in surrender. "Calm down, Beast. I ain't gonna do nothin'."

Dare narrows his eyes at me. "Don't fucking call me that."

I go to jab back, but Matt interrupts me. "Calm down, kids. Let's not get distracted. Tony was going to tell us what he knows about

Carolina's situation."

"I don't know much. I ran into some complications when I retrieved her from her apartment in Spain, and she didn't really have much to say before I stuffed her in the box."

"You put her in the box?" Nettie exclaims. "Seriously, Tony! What the fuck is wrong with you?"

I give her an incredulous look because she knows everything that's wrong with me, but I tell her anyway, "I fucking hate her. We've already covered this."

She rolls her eyes at me, muttering incoherently under her breath, earning a laugh from Darius.

"Hate to break up the party," Matt interrupts what was likely a lead-up to a tirade from Nettie. "It looks to me like a lot of these people are already dead. It would probably be a good idea for me to bring in Anton on this one. I bet he'll have a lot of insight on most of these fucking assholes."

"Cross-check those names with his crew list first. Make sure he doesn't have any obvious double-crossing motherfuckers in there."

Matt picks up his phone, pressing a couple of buttons before putting the phone to his ear and walking away. I don't believe that Anton would knowingly allow a woman-beating rapist on his crew, but we know how easily snakes hide in plain sight sometimes.

Darius whispers something in Nettie's ear, and she glares at him, then rolls her eyes and whispers loud enough for me to hear, "Fine. You have your bro time." She leans in like she's going to give him a kiss but instead licks the side of his face like a dog, and when he attempts to grab her, she jumps out of reach, laughing.

Fucking disgusting.

Dare catches me giving him a dirty look and asks, "What? What are you looking at?"

"I'm downgrading you from beast to lapdog."

His lips twitch, then he shrugs. "That's fine with me. I never liked that shit name anyway."

He may have never liked it, but it served its purpose well. What I find most amusing about Dare's legendary reputation is that while only 75% of it may have been true, the true highlights reel is part of the 75%. Not that I think Darius has become tame or anything. If anyone wants to get a glimpse of the Beast, all they have to do is fuck with Nettie, and they'll quickly find out what it's like to have their spine ripped out and shoved up their ass.

"What's the story with Carolina?" Dare throws the question out nonchalantly, humor twinkling in his eyes as he watches me.

"There is no story," I say calmly. I lean back against the table, showing him how relaxed I am about the whole situation. "We came to an understanding. Simple as that."

Dare sighs, then leans toward me, his forearms braced on his thighs as he replies, "Simple as that, huh?"

I raise a shoulder dismissively, glancing over at Matt, who's still on the phone having a rather emphatic conversation. I feel Dare's eyes on me, and I can't for the life of me figure out what his goddamn problem is.

He looks like he's going to say something further, but I'm saved by Matt waving us over. I rise, walking across the room toward him with Darius right behind me, and Matt points at a highlighted name on the paper on the table. "Anton said this guy is a good place to start. I managed to cross out more than half of the names as deceased. Anton's gonna follow up on a handful of others to see if he can find out any information."

"What about the other list?"

"A few of those are also listed as deceased. He said a couple of them are high up in the organization, so taking them out won't be impossible, but it also won't be easy."

I scoff and wave my hand dismissively. "I'm not worried about easy. One way or another, they're gonna be dead. And from what I understand about these fucking people, we may need to make an example of them."

Dare chuckles from behind me, and I give him a dirty look over my shoulder as I ask, "Is there something you'd like to say, Darius?"

He shakes his head, but he's still laughing. "Not at all. What could I possibly say about your need to get revenge for this woman that you fucking hate?"

I glare at him and then turn my glare at Matt, who's also laughing. "I can hate someone and still not want them to be violated."

Matt laughs again, then pats me on my shoulder as he gives me an incredibly condescending yet patient look. "Don't worry, Tony. Your secret is safe with us."

"I don't have a fucking secret."

Dare leans closer to Matt and whispers loud enough for me to hear, "I think he doth protest too much," and Matt nods his agreement.

I slam my fist down on the counter. "Can we focus on what's important here and figure out where to start in locating Carolina's daughter, so then she can piss off to live happily ever after far away from me?"

The two assholes have one final laugh at my expense, and then Matt sobers and clears his throat. "Anton said he'll put a team together for us, and we can go over there and make short work of these lists. It'll take a little bit of coordination, but it shouldn't be too difficult."

"Wait. Where's 'over there'?"

"Russia."

I grimace, my face twisting in annoyance. "Fuck my life."

Darius pipes in, "Did you think you'd be able to eliminate these people without leaving New York?"

I raise a shoulder dismissively. "I don't know what I thought. Please tell me you're not gonna make me fly commercial."

"No. Mayhem trips don't allow for unwanted questions or customs. You need to go in under the wire."

"But you guys are coming with me, right?"

Matt points at Darius and says, "He'll go with you. I don't have any more time off."

"Jesus fucking Christ, Matt. When are you going to give up that stupid day job?"

"It's not stupid, Tony."

Darius places a hand on my shoulder and gives it a squeeze. "Come on, Tony. That's not very nice. You know how sensitive he is about his life's work."

Dare's words are only slightly mocking, so I attempt to tone down my disdain as I relent. "Fine. You stay here and miss out on all the fun. At least Dare and I can go over there and fuck around."

"And Antoinette."

"What? Why does she have to come?" I ask in annoyance.

"I'm not even going to bother answering one of the dumbest questions I've ever heard in my entire life," Dare says dryly. "Carolina should come as well. Having her there to give visual confirmation on certain people will be helpful."

"She may not be too keen on going back there."

"Maybe, maybe not. But I think she'll want to be part of the action. If nothing else, she'll want to be as close as she can to her daughter when we locate her. Do you know how long it's been since she has seen her?" Matt asks as he continues typing on his tablet, likely making flight arrangements for us.

"I'm not sure," Dare replies with a sigh. "But I imagine it's been quite a bit of time, considering how long it's been since I first met her. I'm not even sure how old her daughter is—"

"We'll have plenty of time on the flight to get more information from her," I interrupt, giving them my best stern look before continuing, "How about you have Nettie go out to the cabin and retrieve her? Save me the hassle of having to see her face before I'm stuck with her on a fourteen-hour flight."

Matt snorts, and Darius laughs and taunts, "Oh, yes. Lord knows her face is such a hassle."

I glower at him, then turn, and walk toward the door. I hear Matt yell from behind me, "Where the fuck you are going, Tony?"

I don't stop; I just say, "I'm gonna go fuck around and find out. I have my phone on."

Chapter Six

Carolina

When Tony said this place was secure, he wasn't joking.

I'll be honest, I took his statement as a challenge. And I've tried every which way you could possibly dream up to get out of here to no avail. Then I got bored with the whole thing and gave up.

When my snooping didn't come up with much, I started my tour with the box beneath the bed up in the loft, and there really wasn't anywhere to go from there. Not that I snooped too hard, considering I figure most of the personal belongings hidden out of sight probably belong to Darius and Antoinette. Let's say it's not their personal belongings I'm looking to creep through.

I did find a reading device which I assume belongs to Antoinette because the content in it seems rather questionable for the likes of Darius or Tony. Of course, I mean questionable in a good way, and I quickly found an enemies-to-lovers, dark romance that had questionable enough reviews for me to assume it must be good. And I wasn't wrong.

By the time I hear someone at the door, I've lost track of how much time has gone by. I don't bother looking behind me before saying, "It's about fucking time you came back, you asshole."

A feminine voice comes back at me, "I wanna argue, but he is an asshole."

I scramble off the sofa, my legs getting caught up in the blanket, and I end up flopping over the side onto the floor. I lay there for a moment, wedged awkwardly between the sofa and the heaviest fucking coffee table in existence, where I squirm around until I'm able to flip myself onto my stomach. I go to push myself up to stand, but then Antoinette is standing in front of me, so I look up and meet her amused gaze as she asks, "Whatever are you doing?"

I shrug, then push my upper body up until I'm kneeling. She extends her hand to me, and I take it with a much stronger grip than I'm actually feeling. She pulls me to my feet, and she must see something strange on my face because she grips me by my upper arms and leans in close to me as she whispers, "What's wrong with you?"

I don't know what's wrong with me. I try to speak, and a gurgling sound comes out, so I try again. Nothing. Her eyes search mine, and then she releases me and turns and heads toward the kitchen. "I'm getting you a drink. You, come sit."

I follow her silently, sitting in the chair she indicates as she opens the cupboard above the built-in refrigerator and says, "Pick your poison."

I clear my throat and manage to croak, "I didn't realize you all were big drinkers."

She laughs, waving her hand dismissively as she replies, "Oh, we're not. Darius says I only like to buy alcohol. He's not wrong. But it's nice to have a wide variety for the odd chance that I feel like having a taste."

I totally get that. "Surprise me. But only if you're having one."

She reaches up and grabs a large brown bottle, snags a couple of rocks glasses from the cupboard, and then joins me at the table. "Would you like ice?"

"No, thank you."

She pours a good amount into the glasses, then pushes one in front of me. I look at the glass cautiously and then look at her. She's smiling at me. "Something wrong?"

"No. Nope. Everything's fine."

This time, she laughs outright and says, "Oh, for the love of god," as she reaches for my glass and takes a decent swallow before handing it back to me. "Is that better?"

I manage a small smile and nod, feeling silly. "I guess so. I don't know what's come over me."

She returns my smile, but it doesn't quite reach her eyes. "Well, you should know by now that if I was going to kill you, I wouldn't poison you. It's not personal enough."

"Thank you. I haven't had a chance to say that to you yet."

She takes another sip of her drink and frowns. "For what?"

"For everything?" I pick up my glass and take a larger swallow than is probably advised, barely managing to stifle a cough as I continue, "For making me a widow. For taking out an entire branch of a criminal organization. For literally blowing the cock off of my piece of shit father-in-law, for starters."

Then her smile does meet her eyes and she cackles. "Oh, that grenade to the cock was spectacular. And we were fortunate that I didn't take out a bunch of other people at the same time."

I grimace and try to hide my pained expression behind my glass. I take another sip from my glass then put it down, and clear my throat.

"I'm sorry," I whisper. "About Lilith."

Antoinette's face falls, and her hand comes out to rest on my forearm. "That was not your fault." Her words are firm and sincere, her eyes steady on mine, and she squeezes my arm again. "Do you understand me? If we're going to start slinging blame around, not one of us would have a clear conscience. The fact of the matter is, Lilith did whatever Lilith wanted. She jumped into the line of fire to save me, and that was her choice. I'm grateful to be alive, and I'm also sad to have lost her, but I don't think there's anything that we could've done to prevent it. The one thing I do know about Lilith is that she would not hold it against you. We all know you only ended up involved in this shitshow because of events that were outside of your control. Lilith knew that game all too well, and just as you've done whatever is needed for your daughter, she did whatever she had to do to protect me."

I place my hand over Antoinette's and give it a tentative squeeze. She turns her hand over and grips mine, and I immediately feel the sting of tears behind my eyes. This isn't good. I blink rapidly, but a little sniffle escapes, and Antoinette giggles and says, "Don't you hate that? It happens to me all the time."

I give her a watery laugh, and she releases my hand, reaches into her jacket pocket, and pulls out a small tissue packet. She pulls out two, handing one to me and keeping one for herself before stuffing the package back in her pocket. "I keep these on me all the time now, and most of the time, I can pretend like it's not happening. I haven't even hit middle age yet, so I don't know what's happening."

I'm grateful for her words on my random waterworks problem. I don't usually have one, but it's been a long time since I had a moment where I could decompress enough to let my emotions roll. We sit here for a few moments in comfortable silence. Eventually, I say, "What are you doing here? Where's Tony?"

"Oh, I was given the task to come retrieve you. We're going on a trip."

I frown, taking another sip of my drink as I ask, "And where are we going? And who is we?"

"Well, all of us except for Matt. Matt can't take time off right now from his day job," she says with obvious sarcasm, and I laugh, unsure what she means by it. "Apparently, we have some business in Russia. Tony called us all together and gave us the list you made for him. Quite a few of them are already dead, so that's something. I'm thinking if Tony could dig them all up and torture them before killing them again, he would happily do so." She stops speaking and leans in close to me. "What's going on between you two?"

I immediately choke on my own saliva as I attempt to reply. "What? Nothing. There's nothing going on."

Her eyes sparkle, and one side of her mouth curves up knowingly. "Oh, I don't think so. There is definitely something going on."

"Why? What did he say?"

She presses her lips together and shakes her head, and then says, "Nothing. That's how I know something's going on because Tony is the biggest TMI'er in the world. He never says nothing. Spill."

I shake my head, another denial ready to spill out right as she leans closer, her words quiet and serious as she says pleadingly, "Come on, Car. I'm basically surrounded by boys all the time. I never get any girl TMI. Please, please, please, please."

I sigh deeply and sit back in my chair, rubbing my hands over my face tiredly. "Fine. I'll give you a little bit, but only because you know Tony so well."

She claps her hands together in front of her gleefully. "Yay! Anything at all. Give me the details."

I chuckle at her outwardly excited response. "We may have canoo-dled."

She claps again, dancing in her seat. "Ooh! I love that word. Tell me more."

My cheeks flush, and I press my cool palms against my heated skin. I don't know why I'm embarrassed; it's just sex. Hot, animalistic sex with someone who loathes my very existence. It's not like Antoinette doesn't know anything about hot, animalistic sex, given the man she lives with. "That's pretty much it."

Her smile is instantly replaced by a frown, and then she looks a bit crestfallen. "Really? That's it? All I get is canoodled?"

My initial awkwardness is driven by the fact I've never had a close girlfriend before. I've never had a close friend, ever, and I'm not en-tirely sure what she wants me to say. So, I try again. "Technically, he caught me checking him out in the middle of an argument, and I didn't bother trying to hide it because, well, he's fucking hot. There's no way you can even pretend that Tony isn't hot."

Antoinette nods, her hands fidgeting with her glass as she says, "True! Even I know Tony is hot. Disgusting but still hot."

I laugh, unsure where she's going with the disgusting comment and also unsure I want to ask, so I add, "At first, I'm sure he was confused, but it didn't take him long to get on board, as they say."

Her eyes widen, and she smiles saucily as she exclaims, "Ene-mies-to-lovers! *Yes*!"

"What are you talking about?"

She raises her brows and titters, "You know. Ene-mies-to-lovers—one of the best tropes ever."

"I know what enemies-to-lovers is. I don't see how it pertains to me and that asshole Tony. We had a nice hate fuck. End of story."

Antoinette gasps and then squeals in delight. "You got to have a hate fuck? I'm so jealous!"

I burst out laughing, shaking my head at her antics. "You are insane. You are an insane person."

"You have to be an insane person to make it in this life. You've met the people I spend the majority of my time with, right?"

I incline my head at her in acknowledgment. She certainly has me there, but I can't help but be a bit envious of her relationship with those she's close to. My entire life has been made up of one fucked-up thing after another, and I can't recall ever being truly close to anyone.

"But you like him a little bit, right?" Antoinette asks, leaning in close like she's searching my eyes for the secret truth.

I make a face, inclined to immediately deny any possibility that I could ever like him, but something stops me. So, I finally reply, "I don't dislike him, but I wouldn't say I like-like him either. It's a very complicated situation that will likely take some time to work itself out, but I am eternally grateful he's willing to help me find Flora. For that alone, I can't hate him."

Antoinette goes to reply, but then her phone rings. She retrieves it from her jacket pocket, glancing at the screen and making a face before accepting the call and bringing the phone to her ear. "Sup, asshole."

I snicker, probably a little louder than is appropriate, but I can't help it. Sometimes, I want to be her.

She listens intently for a few moments, and then says, "Yep." She pulls the phone away from her ear and ends the call before placing it back into her pocket. She picks up her drink and takes a long sip, humming in pleasure as she swallows the golden liquid. "The best part about not being a big drinker is that on the odd occasion that I decide to, it's amazing. Like my taste buds haven't been deadened to the uniqueness of it all."

I squint as I look between my drink and her a few times. "I mean, it is enjoyable. But I don't think we have the same taste buds."

She freezes in her seat, her mouth falling open in disbelief as she reaches over and pushes my drink closer to me. "You're not doing it right. Take the slightest mouthful, so it barely fills the bottom of your mouth, only to the point where if you open your mouth too much, a little bit might spill out. Then hold it there for a few seconds and roll it around. And swallow it slowly and exhale."

I look between her and my glass a few more times before relenting. I pick up the glass and do as she says, as she watches me intently. I exhale slowly, certain if someone lit a match on my breath, it would be like a small blow torch. I rub my tongue against the roof of my mouth and then say, "I see what you mean. I suppose I'm not normally that mindful about my drink."

Her smile is almost blinding, and I can't help but grin back. I'm shocked things have been so easy with her. I'm also slightly suspicious that it all may be a farce, and she's buttering me up to see what she can get from me so she can cut me down later.

I do my best to abandon that thought process. No good can come of it, and if nothing else, I may as well enjoy a small reprieve in my otherwise tumultuous life.

We finish our drink in companionable silence, and then she grabs our glasses and carries them over to the sink, where she gives them a quick wash before placing them in the dish rack to dry. She places the bottle back in the cupboard and then does a quick tidy of things that are mostly already tidy before she turns back to me. "Are you ready?"

I rise from my seat and push the chair against the table. "What's the plan?"

"Don't you worry, Car. We're a bunch of wily motherfuckers. You're gonna have to sit back and watch."

I frown, following her toward the door and then stopping while she manages the security system. "Sit back and watch what exactly?"

She pushes the door open, and the glaring sun blinds me. I squint against it as it creates a halo around her head. She smiles and says, "You're gonna watch us fuck around and find out."

Then she heads out into the sunlight, and I follow her.

Chapter Seven

Tony

MY URGE TO DRAG her into the cabin lavatory is intense.

So far, she has spent the entire flight commiserating with Nettie and ignoring me entirely, and frankly, it pisses me off. I know I shouldn't care. Maybe I don't care, and it's my giant ego talking, but this is bullshit.

Their laughter breaks through the silence again, and I glance over to find Nettie watching me with a grin, which is entirely indicative of the obvious topic of their conversation. Me.

I show her my middle finger, and she sticks her tongue out at me like the brat she is. Carolina's back is to me, and she turns around slightly, her eyes catching mine briefly before she faces forward again. She reaches over and smacks Nettie on her forearm, and Nettie laughs again in response. Obviously, they're having a joke at my expense. Fucking typical.

"Are you going to stare at them for the whole fucking flight?"

I turn my chair so I'm facing Darius, who's giving me a disgusted look. I mirror his look and shake my head. "I don't know what you're talking about."

Dare throws his head back and laughs so loudly that it reverberates throughout the plane, drawing the attention of both women as I reach across the narrow table and punch him in the shoulder. "Fucking keep it down, man."

He laughs for a few more moments, eventually sobering enough to wheeze out, "I never thought I'd see the day."

"See what day?"

"When Tony Andersen succumbed to something as ordinary as neediness."

I scoff, shaking my head with more vigor as I hiss, "Oh, fuck off. I'm not needy."

Dare laughs even harder, tears pooling in the corners of his eyes as he replies, "But you are. And it's fucking hilarious."

I suppress the urge to roll my eyes, knowing he'll take such a flippant move as an indication that he might be right. And even if he is right, I can't let on that he is, or I'll never hear the end of it. "You could not be any further from the mark if you tried. I hate her, and I spend most of my time daydreaming about ways I could make her pay if only you all weren't so intent on denying me the pleasure. Being denied retribution is having a negative effect on me. So, this is basically your fault because the only need I have is the need for revenge."

He laughs even harder, once again drawing the attention of the two women sitting on the other side of the plane. Then Dare says, "Don't even get me started on that fine line between love and hate thing, Tony. I know firsthand what it's like to dance along that line, and I also know how freeing it was to allow myself to fall onto the other side and accept that I didn't hate her at all because at that moment, I knew if I had to choose between my own life and hers, I would choose hers every time. So be careful how loudly you deny things...you do know what they say about protesting."

"For fuck sake, Darius. I don't have time for your history of verbal anecdotes. I said what I said, now shut the fuck up about it."

He stops laughing, his features turning serious as he asks, "Have you at least had a heart to heart with yourself on why you have such a burning hatred for a woman who was only doing what she had to do to keep her own child safe? Because we both know firsthand the difficult decisions we have to make in order to keep our own safe and also the lengths we will go to in order to ensure their health and well-being. What line wouldn't you cross to save me? Or Matt? Or even Nettie?"

"That line does not exist," I answer plainly, without hesitation.

"So why are you holding Carolina to a higher standard when the person she was trying to protect is an innocent? Lord knows none of us are innocent, and at times, we likely deserve whatever violent end we come to."

I stare at him, unable to come up with a concise answer, so instead, I shrug. "Because you're you, and Matt is Matt, and Nettie is Nettie, and you're my people. Obviously, my people get their own set of rules."

He smiles at me and nods as he replies, "And Carolina is now an extension of your people, and you need to work on giving her a tiny bit of that grace that you give the rest of us."

I scowl, pushing away from the table as I mutter, "Yeah, okay. I gotta use the head."

I ignore his low laugh that follows me as I make my way to the rear of the plane where the lavatory is. I push through the small door, allowing it to automatically close behind me, then I stand in the enclosed space, my hands resting on the counter as I stare at myself in the mirror.

I'm not fucking needy. There's no fine line here. She's not my god-damn people. Before all this went down with Lilith, did I perhaps have a possible deep interest in Carolina and maybe even think there might be a future there? Of course, I did. No one can deny her outward beauty, but once I found out that beneath her beauty was a snake, that interest rapidly changed.

The door slides open, startling me, and there that bitch is, smirking at me with amusement. I huff again and ask, "What the fuck do you want?"

She steps into the room, her body almost touching mine as the door closes behind her. She leans a hip on the counter and shrugs. "Do you want the truth or the bullshit answer?"

"Give me the bullshit answer first."

"I was checking to make sure you're okay. You seemed rather an-noyed with whatever Darius was laughing about."

I laugh, shaking my head. "That is the most bullshit thing I've ever heard, but that's a good one. Now, give me the truth."

"Antoinette dared me to come in here and blow you."

My cock immediately hardens in my pants. My brain wants to tell her no fucking thanks, but my body does not give a single fuck about propriety, ethics, or a good manner. I reach my hand out, wrapping her ponytail around it a couple of times so I'm holding onto her tightly, then I ask, "And you're not bothered by the fact they're gonna know what you're doing?"

She pauses for a moment, obviously considering my question, and then says almost in awe, "Shockingly, not at all. It's actually quite freeing to be able to make the choice. It's been a long time since that was in the cards."

I frown, my hand tightening in her hair at the implication of her words. "Are you saying this isn't your first time in a plane lavatory?"

She shrugs and shakes her head at the same time. "It doesn't matter. I'm only concerned about this time."

I release my grip on her hair, straightening as she steps closer to me. I turn so my back is against the door, and she sits on the toilet lid, waiting for me to close the short distance between us. "You want to lead or follow?" I ask clearly, wanting her to make as many choices as she can since she brought up the topic.

She tilts her head to the side, then replies, "Lead. To start anyway."

I sidle closer, and her hands grasp my hips and pull me closer in the cramped space. I brace one hand on the wall to my left and the other above my head as she goes right for my belt and then the button and zipper of my jeans. She yanks the material to the side and pauses, her lips curving up slightly as she sees I'm not commando this time. She giggles, her eyes raising to meet mine as she asks breathlessly, "Whatever are you wearing, Tony?"

I barely manage to suppress my own laughter as I give a nonchalant shrug, as if it's no big deal. "Do you like it?"

She giggles again, her eyes sparkling with amusement, and an uncomfortable warmth blooms in my chest. Then she says, "I'm genuinely surprised. I'm not sure if I should feel offended that you did this with the assumption that I would be seeing them or flattered you thought of me when you decided to wear them on the plane."

She pushes my jeans and outrageously colorful boxer briefs down my hips, and I hiss out a breath as her hand grips my cock firmly. "Definitely the latter," I whisper, my eyes closing as she strokes me.

She pauses in her stroking, and I peek one eye open to find her staring up at me, wide-eyed, likely startled by my admission. She's not nearly as surprised as I am, and my breath catches a bit as she whispers, "You really thought of me? When putting on your underwear?"

I don't respond with words, only nodding briefly and then saying, "Quit stalling. You're supposed to suck my dick."

She ducks her head, her tongue rolling over the tip a few times before she sucks me into her mouth, and my head falls back on a groan. It's everything I can do not to grab her by her head and throat-fuck her, but I told her she could take the lead, and I won't go back on my promise.

I let her suck me off for a few minutes, enjoying the feel of her tongue, lips, and hand on my cock before I reach down and grab onto the hand that she has resting on her thigh. She pulls back a little, her eyes questioning as I move her free hand to my hip and say, "It'll be impossible for you to talk with your mouth full of my cock, so if you need me to stop for any reason, pinch me right here as hard as you can, do you understand?"

She nods, so I continue, "Give me the words, sweetheart."

"Yes. I understand," she says. "Now, stop trying to butter me up and fuck my mouth already."

I growl deep in my chest, my hand releasing hers and delving into her hair. I tighten my grip, pulling her head back until her eyes meet mine, and her mouth falls open, her lips glistening with saliva, and I ask, "Is that what you want? You want me to fuck your face like you're my little whore? You want me to show you how to please me?"

She nods in my grip and whispers, "Yes. That's what I want. Please."

"Fuck," I groan, my other hand moving so I'm gripping both sides of her head firmly. "That's my fucking good whore. Open your mouth wider."

She opens her mouth wide and sticks her tongue out as I lean in closer, allowing saliva to pool in my mouth. I bend down, dribbling my spit onto her tongue, and she doesn't flinch or try to pull away. Her breath hitches, a little whimper escaping as I adjust my hands and the angle of her head, pulling her closer so I can easily slide between her lips and into the back of her throat.

She relaxes in my grip, allowing me to maneuver her easily, and I inhale deeply through my nose, reveling in the slide of my dick gliding through our mixed saliva. I push all the way in until the tip pushes against the back of her throat, and then I pause, waiting to see what she'll do: if she'll protest or gag, give me a pinch, or ask me to stop. But she doesn't; instead, she swallows, and for a moment, I fear I might come down her throat right then and there.

I bite the inside of my cheek, withdrawing about halfway before sliding back in, pushing against the back of the throat a bit more forcefully. She swallows, and I push my dick against her swallows until the vibrations of her restricted moan force me to pull back before this comes to an end too quickly.

My heart pounds in my chest, and I shake my head in an attempt to clear the lustful fog that has me on the cusp of coming prematurely. I'm no unseasoned boy, and this is borderline embarrassing, but there's something about her giving herself over so willingly that has me on edge.

I shove into the back of her throat a few more times, then pull out, yanking her head back so I can look into her eyes. Tears stream down her face, saliva drips down her chin, and I choke out, "Fuck. You're so fucking beautiful when you cry for me." I pause to dribble more saliva into her mouth, and she moans again, her hands coming up and gripping my wrists as I continue, "I wanna come down your throat, but not nearly as much as I wanna come inside your wet cunt. Would you like that? Do you want me to fill you up?"

She appears to shake her head and nod at the same time, and I laugh, "You're gonna have to be clearer than that, sweetheart. Try to form some words with that cock-drilled mouth."

She swallows, then sniffles and says, "Yes, I'd love for you to fill up my wet cunt." She pauses for a moment, swallowing again. "But that will have to wait until you don't need a condom anymore. So not today."

I groan, my hands on her head tightening. I forgot about the need for a condom. Part of me doesn't give a fuck, but I respect her wishes more than my foolish thought process, so I meet her gaze again and say, "The throat it is."

Her lips curve up, and another soft moan slips out as she opens her mouth wide again. I don't waste any time before shoving my dick back inside, and this time, I don't play with her. I face-fuck her like I mean it, just like she asked me to.

She pushes my hands away from her head, and I release her, bracing myself once again on the wall beside and above me. She grips both my hips, licking and sucking my cock until I'm groaning deep in my throat and thrusting my hips forward. She takes me deep, pulling me into her until my cock is down her throat, then she pulls back and starts the licking, sucking, and teasing all over again before unceremoniously deep-throating me.

I curse, my hands fisting against the wall as I force myself to let her keep control, to take the lead, but I already feel the tingling in my balls, the heat in my pelvis indicating that she won't have to wait too long.

Her hand on my hip moves, and she grips my balls, squeezing to the brink of too hard and giving a little tug, and I'm fucking done. "Fuck. That's right, sweetheart. Worship that fucking cock. Suck all my sins out and swallow them down like the whore you are."

I've been looking down, watching her suck me off this entire time, so when she looks up and her eyes meet mine, I'm surprised by the power that burns in them. Tears trickle down the sides of her face, smudged mascara framing eyes that burn back at me with such force that I fear she's getting a glimpse into my soul.

I don't blink. I swallow past the ache in my throat and the heat in my chest and thrust sharply, pushing the tip of my dick into her throat as my dick throbs and releases—deep. She swallows around me, her gaze still unflinching, and I remain frozen in place, my dick in her mouth and my heart pounding in my chest as I attempt to catch my breath.

After a few moments, she pulls away, her lips wrapping around my shaft and dragging down to the very tip of me, where she flits her tongue, then sits back. She brushes her finger along her bottom lip delicately, and then as she looks me directly in the eye, she licks the side of the same finger.

"You are a dirty fucking girl," I grit out breathlessly, shaking my head on a small laugh as I mutter, mostly to myself, "I guess it's a good thing I fucking hate you so much, or else I might think this could go somewhere."

She gives me a brilliant smile that matches her eyes and replies, "Sometimes, hate is better fuel than love. You never have to worry about disappointing someone."

I bark out a genuine laugh and nod in agreement, then turn away to fix my clothing and put my dick away. I turn back to her, but she's still seated on the toilet lid, appearing nonplussed by the entire situation, so I ask, "Are you okay?"

"Sure," she replies. "I'm good."

I cock my head and narrow my eyes as I look her over. She appears to be fine. She seems quite relaxed, given she's not the one who had an orgasm. She must sense my hesitation because she continues, "Really, Tony. I'm good. I appreciate you allowing me to use you in such a manner."

Now, I frown. "Use me? I'm not following."

She sighs, her shoulders rising and falling as she explains, "I've had a lot of terrible things in my life. I haven't had a lot of time to process most of it, but I'm slowly adjusting to this new mindset and learning who I am without being told who I have to be." She pauses, her eyes moving to the wall over my shoulder as she gathers her thoughts. After a few moments, her eyes meet mine again, and she clears her throat. "These reminders that I have power over my own choices, it helps. So, I appreciate that."

I kneel in front of her until we're eye to eye, one of my hands resting on top of her thigh and the other one moving up to cup the side of her face. "I may hate you, but I would never wish that kind of treatment on you." I stop and clear my throat, that weird heat in my chest throbbing as I work to push it down so I can continue. Then, I add flippantly, "And what man wouldn't be thrilled to have a fine woman such as yourself using him for sex?"

She giggles, the underlying humor of the situation not lost on her, and I'm glad I was able to break the tension a bit with my general asshole-like personality. "Seriously, Carolina," I say, my voice firm as I hold her gaze. "Any time you have a situation you feel you need to flip your script on, you just say the word."

I release her and then stand, continuing to watch her face as I step back to ensure none of her micro-expressions are showing any type of distress. She gives me a slight smile and says, "Well, we have a safeword. Do we need a new word for some variation of dick-me-down-right-now?"

"I'm generally good to go at any moment," I say with a laugh. "So, it doesn't seem necessary to me. Unless you can come up with a one-word abbreviation," I laugh again, even harder now. "An abbreviation for dick me down."

She's laughing, too, the tears in her eyes now ones of mirth, and once again, I feel that weird pressure in my chest that has my laughter dying down abruptly. She also stops giggling, her brow furring slightly as she asks, "What is it?"

I freeze in place, my shoulders coming up awkwardly as I shake my head and back away from her. "I'm gonna go now, so you can do your thing. Yeah. Okay. Thanks."

I feel her eyes on me as I fumble with the sliding door, and I'm certain I hear her laughing at me as the door shuts behind me.

Chapter Eight

Tony

ANTON MEETS US AT the airstrip. He has a group of people with him, and before I know it, Nettie's rushing toward a man in a pink shirt, hugging him enthusiastically. I look over at Dare as she wanders off with the pink-shirt guy and ask, "Old boyfriend?"

He glares at me, shoving me as he replies, "Not fucking likely." He turns his attention back to her, a smile ghosting his lips as he continues, "They had a conversation in the middle of a gunfight, and he didn't die. In Antoinette's eyes, that makes them practically related."

That sounds like Nettie. She's a bloodthirsty ballbuster, but when she takes ownership of you, good luck. The only way you'll ever shake her is to kill her or be killed.

We walk over to the rest of the group, and Darius and Anton do that bro-hug greeting I generally skip, opting instead for an almost-friendly nod as we walk over to the waiting SUVs. One of Anton's men gets in the driver's seat, and I stand there for a moment, uncertain of what I'm supposed to do since I normally drive. Anton grips my shoulder and asks, "Do you wanna sit up front, Tony?"

I squint at him as I consider his question, and then finally say, "No. No. It's not like I know where I'm going anyway."

I begrudgingly climb in the back, taking a seat at a door where I can easily exit, so I don't feel trapped. Although my line of sight is impaired, at least from my current position, I might see something suspicious before it's too late.

I don't like being in new places, especially when I haven't had time to fully recon every nook and cranny. Maybe that's why I have this deep sense of unease in my chest. I swallow past the sudden lump in my throat, and then jump when Nettie's voice is suddenly right in my ear, asking, "You okay, buddy?"

I crane my head around so I can look at her face, my lips twisting at the incredibly smug expression on her features. "Why wouldn't I be?"

She waggles her eyebrows and shoulders at me and says teasingly, "You seem a little tense. I figured you'd be the opposite right now."

I glance over at Carolina, whose innocent expression doesn't match the tone of her giggles. I give her a stern look. "Really?"

Carolina lifts a shoulder dismissively. "I had to confirm that I didn't welsh on the bet."

"That insinuates that you wouldn't normally talk all the dirty details with each other."

Caroline and Nettie look at each other, then break out into cackles. I roll my eyes and huff, giving them my back as their laughter escalates. Dare snorts beside me, and when I look over at him, he asks, "Girl trouble?"

I scoff, "You damn well know those two are trouble."

He glances back, his eyes softening as his gaze settles on Nettie, and then he shifts his attention back to me and nods.

Anton pipes up from the front passenger seat, "Women will always be trouble, but us men are too stupid to stay away from them—"

"Hey now," Nettie interrupts from behind me. "I don't think you all have any right to be calling us trouble. You guys are all-caps trouble."

None of us bother denying it since we're certainly responsible for our fair share of chaos.

"What's the status, Anton?" Dare asks. "Where we at?"

Anton turns in his seat so he can look at Dare. "We've got some good leads. Agatha went to meet up with Jayme, and they'll meet us at our rendezvous point for a full briefing."

"Did you find her?" Carolina's voice breaks through from the back, sounding hesitant yet hopeful.

I turn my head to look at her as Anton replies dismissively, "We'll do a full briefing once we have everyone together."

Her face falls, and she looks like she wants to say something further, but rather than speak, she snaps her mouth shut and remains silent. My eyes narrow, that increasingly familiar zap in my chest triggering me to turn around and lean in close to Anton and whisper menacingly, "You'll answer her fucking question now."

Anton turns his body and looks back at me, the surprise on his face clear as he then glances back at Carolina. His eyes widen as understanding dawns, and he says, "Not yet. But we will."

She gives me an appreciative smile, then turns her gaze out the window, the tension in her body palpable, and she visibly clenches her jaw. I peek over at Nettie, who's eyeing me with an odd expression on her face. I look at Carolina pointedly and then back to Nettie, who gives me one of those soft looks she typically reserves for Darius, and I repress my urge to roll my eyes. Nettie does what I silently ask of her, easing a little closer to Carolina and taking one of her hands in hers.

Carolina accepts the support without a word, turning her hand up and gripping Nettie's hand like it's a lifeline.

I face forward again, saying nothing else as I look out the window. I feel Dare's eyes on me, burning a hole into the side of my head, so finally, I turn to him, sneering, "What?"

He shrugs his shoulders a bit, inclining his head at me as he sing-songs, "*Oh*, nothing."

I've known this motherfucker for a long goddamn time, and if he's singing, it ain't fucking nothing. I also lack the strength and energy to get into it right now, so I flip him the bird and then go back to staring out the window. I don't feel a need to unpack every action and reaction I have that's related to Carolina. Maybe that's shortsighted of me—maybe avoidance isn't the right path to be on, but right now, that's all I got.

Eventually, we pull up to a gate where Anton's driver stops and stares into a camera until the gate opens. We drive down a long driveway before finally pulling up to a large home with an even larger garage.

One of the garage doors opens, and we pull in, driving up to the door on the far side of the room as the second vehicle pulls in behind us. We all exit the vehicles, and then one of the garage doors a few bays over opens as a lifted 4x4 pulls in. The driver's side door opens, and Agatha jumps out, slamming the door behind her as she rushes toward Nettie. "Toni, you bitch. Get over here!"

Nettie smiles widely, laughing as she meets her sister halfway, returning her embrace as they squeeze each other tightly. They break apart, staring at each other with abject emotion shining in their eyes, and that stupid fucking pain is back in my chest again.

What the actual fuck?

I shake my head and snort at myself in disgust, turning my focus back to our upcoming mission as Anton indicates for us to follow him. We make our way down a long hallway with various sets of stairs headed upwards and downwards until, eventually, the faint smell of bleach has the fine hairs on the back of my neck prickling.

I fucking hate the smell of bleach.

We enter a large room that appears disgustingly similar to a warehouse, and Dare and I look at each other with matching annoyed expressions on our faces as we walk over and join the group of people milling around a workstation in a far corner.

There are a few dozen of Anton's men there, and I look around in confusion when I don't see Carolina nearby. I look back the way we came and see she's standing about twenty feet away, frozen in place, staring at something behind me.

I glance in the direction she's focused on and notice one of Anton's men looking back at her uneasily, so I elbow Darius to get his attention and tilt my head back at her so he'll see what I see. I don't have to say anything further; Dare and Nettie quickly catch on, and Nettie silently moves over to Anton, laughing animatedly, so as to draw attention away from us. She leans in close to Anton's ear, and whatever she says to him is close enough for Erik to overhear because he silently moves around the room until he's standing closer to the staring man.

I take a few steps toward Carolina, keeping my expression neutral as I extend my hand out to her and say, "Come. I got you."

She blinks a few times, her eyes meeting mine as I close the distance between us and grab onto her hand. She squeezes my hand so tightly that the bones grind together, and I pull her body in close to mine, my anger increasing as she trembles against me. I lean closer, pressing my face against her ear, as I ask, "Is he on the first list or the second?"

She presses her face into my neck, her voice breaking as she whispers, "Both. He's one of the ones who was listed as deceased."

That pressure in my chest is back, but this time, it's fueled by white-hot fury. I move to pull away from her, but her hand on my shirt stops me, and I turn back to her as she says, "You can't kill him. He might know something."

I grind my teeth together, knowing she's right, even as I curse the fact. "Good. He deserves the hard way."

She doesn't say anything in response, and this time when I pull away, she lets me. We walk across the room together, but she stops when we reach Nettie, and I keep moving toward Erik, waving to him as if we're old friends and we're about to catch up on old times.

But then, as soon as I'm within arm's reach of that fucking cock-sucker, my arm snaps out, and within seconds, he's on his back on the floor with one of my hands wrapped around his throat and my free hand pummeling him repeatedly in the face.

"Did you touch her?" I hiss the words through my clenched teeth, spittle spraying over him as I don't wait for him to answer. I hit him again, then grit out, "Did you put your hands on her without her permission?" I hit him again and then again, shouting now, "Did you think that you could touch what's mine and fucking live?"

I haven't given him a chance to reply, even if he was capable of speaking through my hand choking him to death. Blood splatters everywhere, all over my hands, arms, face, and chest, but all I see is pitch-black as the pressure in my chest expands to the point that I feel it may render me in half.

Hands grab me, pull me, and then Dare's voice is in my ear, yelling. I gasp for air, my right hand suddenly throbbing, and as I blink, I see that goddamn piece of shit lying motionless on the ground with Anton and Erik kneeling over him. I take a step toward the motionless motherfucker, but Dare's hold on me tightens, and he yanks me back and then pushes me a few feet away. I try to step forward again, determined to make sure he's dead, but a sharp sting against my cheek snaps me out of it, and Dare is right in my face. "Enough. That's enough."

I stand in front of him, staring into his glowing eyes as I take a few deep breaths, my body trembling with adrenaline. I swallow a few times until the lump in my throat eases, and then ask, "What the fuck was that?"

He laughs humorlessly and shakes his head. "If you don't fucking know, I'm not gonna be the one to tell you, but that will be the first and last time that fucking happens on this mission." He gives me a pointed look until I nod in agreement and then adds, "Just think back on all the times that you had to treat me as a loose cannon and use it."

Loose cannon? He just called me a fucking loose cannon. I'm not a loose fucking cannon. Tony fucking Andersen is never a loose fucking cannon.

Nettie laughs, indicating my inner rantings were verbalized, and I look around at the other people in the room and the ones who aren't tending to the motionless man on the floor are staring at me curiously.

Dare doesn't say anything further, so I look at him, and he points across the room to what appears to be a lounge area. I don't say anything, just give a small nod, and then turn and walk away, where I fall heavily into a chair. I lean forward with my forearms resting on my thighs, my head hanging as I stare at the floor between my feet and watch the blood drip rhythmically from my busted knuckles.

I recall every instance where I had to treat Dare like a loose cannon when it came to Nettie. I've had to smack him down on more than one occasion, one time even going so far as busting his nose, so him relating this incident to the unhinged Beast is saying more than I'm prepared to confront right now.

Soft footsteps approach, and then a gentle hand grips the back of my neck firmly. I don't look up, and she doesn't say anything when I reach my hand up, pressing it against the back of hers and pushing it more firmly into my neck.

The fury eases in my chest, only to be replaced by a burning pressure that I'm starting to recognize as something purely Carolina. I grit my teeth together for a moment and attempt to push it down, to kick it out, to reach for that agonizing fury like a lifeline to my old self.

But then her hand squeezes my neck again, the heat of her leaning closer, and she whispers against my ear, "Thank you."

And just like that, I let the warmth in.

Chapter Nine

Carolina

I'M NOT SURE WHAT I expected when I first saw Tony Andersen standing in the hallway, waiting for me, but it sure as fuck wasn't this crazed animal who doesn't actively try to hurt me. Maybe it's the fact I've never had anyone defend me, ever, under any circumstances, but to witness someone revered for being methodical and controlled at all times go completely unhinged in defense of me.

I'm not sure I even have words.

It would've been a setback if he'd actually killed the man, but I wouldn't have been sorry. And while I do feel that Tony has a deep need to avenge the wrongs done to me, I can't help but think there must be something else that fuels his rage.

While everyone focuses on reviving the beaten man, I lead Tony into one of the restrooms in search of a first aid kit. I find one in the cabinet beside the sink, and I work on fixing up his busted knuckles.

He doesn't so much as flinch, but I feel his eyes on me, watching me intently until, finally, I ask, "Do I have mud on my face or something?"

He doesn't say anything, but he makes a weird choking noise, so I up look at him. He has a rather comically pained expression on his face, his lips pressed together so tightly they're white, and I reach my hand up to grab his cheeks between my fingers and thumb and squeeze until his jaw loosens. He growls at me, shaking his head so I release him. Then I ask, "What is it, Tony? Spit it out."

His eyes widen, the look of him a bit wild as he whispers, "I don't fucking know."

I smirk, looking back down at his knuckles and getting back to work. "Well, that was clear."

"I want to fucking hate you. Hating you is easy."

I nod, lifting my shoulders and letting them fall back down as I say, "Well, I can't help you with that. I never wanted you to hate me in the first place."

He yanks his hand from my grip, startling me, and then his hands are on my face, and he pulls me into him and whisper-shouts, "I don't like this."

"This? You don't like hating me?"

"I love hating you."

"You're gonna have to narrow it down for me a little bit, buddy," I say, sighing heavily.

Grunting in frustration, his hands on my face tighten, and he looks so perplexed I finally add, "Why don't you focus on continuing to hate me? And let the rest take care of itself."

His eyes search mine intently, then drop to my lips and back up to my eyes as he leans in closer. His lips barely brush against mine, and he inhales sharply through his mouth, then leans a bit closer, pressing his lips more firmly before he pulls back sharply. "Fuck."

He scrambles off the counter, standing and pushing me to the side as he continues to mutter to himself. I can't quite make out what he's saying, but it sounds a lot like he's cursing, and then he stuffs everything back into the first aid kit, closing it and stuffing it under his arm. He gives me another dirty look, then stalks across the room and yanks open the door, disappearing through it.

I stand there for a moment, staring at the now-closed door, dumbfounded.

Fucking men.

I pick up the odds and ends that he left behind, throw them in the rubbish bin, and wash my hands. I'm standing there, leaning back against the counter, drying my hands, when the door opens, and Darius walks in. "Did something happen?"

I put both my hands up and bark out a laugh. "Your guess is as good as mine. I have no fucking idea what has gotten into that guy."

Dare levels me with a knowing look as he leans back against the door and crosses one foot over the other at the ankle. He says nothing, but he keeps looking at me until, finally, I sputter, "What? What the fuck do you expect me to say?"

He gives me that annoying Darius shrug, then continues to stand there, staring me down. I whirl around to face the mirror, staring at myself keenly as I try to form a word that might actually come out of my mouth appropriately.

Finally, I respond, "I don't have the time or energy to even attempt to unpack all the crazy that is Tony Andersen. Maybe once we get my little girl back, I can switch my focus to something other than her. But right now, I don't have the bandwidth for it." I push off the counter and turn to face him, still leaning against the door, now giving me one of his all-knowing Darius Hughes looks. I kind of want to punch him, but instead, I continue, "But I do have a question. Is it just me and my situation, or has something else happened in the past that made him go so completely unhinged and off the rails?"

"I think it has more to do with you than anything else, but there's definitely something else that fuels his response to innocent people being abused. The only one who can tell that story, though, is Jayme."

"Is he here?"

Dare nods. "He is. You kind of missed it in all the ruckus."

"Oh, right. He was with Agatha, wasn't he?"

"Yes. He hung back because he was stuck on the phone. Or he used that as an excuse to stall, anyway."

"Why would he stall?"

Darius sighs, and his shoulders come up slightly as he responds, "Jayme is one of those simple yet complex people. He comes off as flippant, sometimes even a little silly, but once you break through the superficial armor, he's kind of a stoic protector. Basically, he's probably afraid to face you."

"Afraid of me? That doesn't even make sense."

"It doesn't make sense yet. Obviously, he's not afraid of you physically, but he's been on his own his entire life. His mother was a codependent user, and his father a mean, dictatorial motherfucker. He's been through some shit. And even though he didn't know anything about you until recently, he's still going to be eaten up by guilt that he didn't find you sooner and protect you from all the horrible things you've survived."

"Why would he feel guilty about something he had no control over?"

"He's human? Sometimes, the wounded take on misplaced burdens. They can't heal their own wounds, so they work urgently to protect and heal others. In his hyper-vigilant brain, if he had been around, you wouldn't have suffered at all. In his mind, you have every right to blame him for not protecting you."

I scoff, then laugh bitterly. "As if there would've been anything he could've done. Any kind of offense he would've come up with back before he was fully capable of defending himself would've ended with him being dead. I've been used as a pawn long enough to understand why Vincent chose to impregnate me. He did that intentionally so he could use his own flesh and blood against me to get me to do what he wanted. That's what they would've done to Jayme if he had known about me. And then he would be in no position to help now, if ever."

"I agree. And I think with some soul-searching, he will as well. But for now, he's focused on everything he couldn't do anything about. Our good friend hindsight and all that jazz."

"Well, he's gonna have to get the fuck over it. We have work to do."

Dare smiles at me, then pushes himself off the wall and walks over to stand in front of me. "I was hoping you would say that. But I also didn't want you to get blindsided by him. He can come on pretty intense sometimes, but he means well."

"I guess we'll see."

Darius nods, then reaches out and pulls me closer to him by my upper arms. He wraps his arms around me, hugging me while I stand there stiffly, genuinely perplexed by what the fuck is going on when the door opens, and Antoinette asks, "What the fuck are you doing?"

Darius doesn't release me, but he turns his body so he can look at her as he says, "She looked like she could use a hug."

Antoinette giggles as she enters the room and walks over to us. "Really? Because it doesn't look like she's a willing participant in this hug."

He squeezes me tighter, jostling me around a little until my arms come up to his sides. I half-heartedly give him a little pat, and he says, "See. It's working."

Antoinette laughs again, the easy-going sound allowing me to relax a bit, and finally, he releases me. She steps closer, the fond expression on her face directed at him as she shakes her head. "Have you lost your mind?"

"No. You told me I need to start being more mindful and considerate of the needs of others, so that's what I was doing." He shrugs.

Antoinette turns her smile on me, then leans in, knocking her shoulder against mine. "Sometimes, he misses the mark, but what's a girl to do?"

"Well, I appreciate the sentiment." I return her smile, then the three of us make our way across the room, exiting out into the main of the building. A bunch of people are milling around, but the beaten man is no longer on the floor, and there's no sign of Anton or Tony.

"Where did they go?" I ask Antoinette since she was the last one out there.

"They took him downstairs. I was coming to see if you two want to watch or not."

Darius perks up beside me, a bit of a pep in his step as we walk across the room, and he says, "You know I want to. Where are we going?"

She jabs him with her elbow. "Obviously, you do. I meant Carolina," she says, then turns to me. "You don't have to watch, but if you want to hear what he has to say, you're welcome to. And if you want to be the one to end him, you're also welcome to do that."

"Is there a way for me to watch without him seeing me?"

"We can gouge out his eyes..." Darius says with a certain level of eagerness that should be disconcerting.

"How about something less bloody?"

"Boring," Darius replies, his lip curling in distaste.

Antoinette gives him a patient look and then turns back to me and says, "Yes. There's a two-way mirror in the room they have him in."

"Tony down there already?" Darius asks as he looks around the room.

"He's down there, but he's not in the room yet. He's waiting for you."

"So, it's like that, then?"

"Oh, yeah," Antoinette answers emphatically. "It's like all that I've never seen from him before, so he's your problem."

Darius turns back to her and leans down, nuzzling her cheek before placing a soft kiss on her brow. "Don't worry, baby girl. I got it."

"Oh, I have no doubt. I'll stay in the other room with Carolina, so if she feels she needs to escape, she can. I don't think they're going to need any more bloodthirsty, unhinged maniacs in the room anyway."

Darius frowns at her. "You gonna start with the unhinged thing again?"

She smiles saucily, then turns and flounces away, leaving us to follow her. Darius follows a little more closely than necessary, and I hear him murmur, "Oh, my little minx wants to play, huh?"

She winks at him over her shoulder but doesn't say anything. The growling laugh he directs at her has me shaking my head. "Good to know you two are still disgusting."

This makes Antoinette laugh, and she smirks at me knowingly as she opens the door and indicates for me to proceed her down the stairs. Then, from behind me, she says, "Someday, Carolina, I have a feeling you'll be disgusting, too."

"That'll be the fucking day."

Darius and Antoinette both laugh from behind me, and I shake my head as I continue walking down the stairs, but I hear Dare laughing along with her as he says, "It's a fine line, baby girl. It's a fine fucking line."

Chapter Ten

Tony

I'M FALLING APART.

Actually, falling apart doesn't accurately describe the treacherous ruins of my current existence.

Okay, maybe that's a little dramatic. But it feels as if I have two battling personalities inside me vying for superiority, and my subconscious is there in the middle, playing the middleman while not having a fucking clue about what's going on. Frankly, it's very uncomfortable and disconcerting, and I'm not at all fucking happy about it.

But I digress, and I *never* digress.

After I left Carolina in the lurch in the bathroom, I made my way downstairs, where I knew they were holding that piece of fucking shit douchebag who decided he could put his hands on her. I took one step into that room and did an immediate about-face when I realized I couldn't control my urge to choke the life out of him.

That's why I'm here, in a much smaller bathroom down the hall, leaning over the sink with my face dripping cold water as I stare at my own reflection in the mirror in disgust.

The door opens, and without looking, I know it's Darius. Nettie would've gone to get him, knowing without me saying anything that we have a problem. That's one thing I can say about Nettie, she's very intuitive, and while she has no problem busting anyone's balls, she also knows when to put that away and focus on being helpful.

I certainly had my reservations when she first "joined" our group, but those reservations were quickly put to rest when I realized having a completely different perspective made things better.

I grab a hand towel from the stack on the counter, dry my face, and then toss it in the laundry basket before looking at Darius. He's giving me a small yet still smug smile, and so I squint at him. "Can I help you, Dare?"

He gives me a rather empathetic look and pats me on the shoulder. "I don't know if there's any help for you at this point, buddy."

"What the fuck is that supposed to mean?"

"You're unraveling, man." He stops patting me on my shoulder and squeezes it, waiting for me to meet his eyes before continuing, "You're gonna have to decide what you're gonna do, and then you're gonna have to do it quickly."

I straighten, shaking his hand off as I push away from the counter and start pacing back and forth in the room, sputtering, "It's hard to make a decision when you don't even understand the problem."

"Don't be obtuse, Tony. You know exactly what the problem is."

I stop pacing, whirling around to gape at him. I raise my hands in front of me and shout, "Why can't I keep on fucking hating her."

Dare laughs outright at my nonquestion, throwing his head back until the sound of his laughter echoes around me, taunting me. After a few moments, he quiets enough to get words out and says, "Isn't it grand?"

"Fuck my life. Fuck this goddamn fucking motherfucker shitbag."

He laughs again, and it's like he's laughing at his own inside joke, so I let him laugh, and by the time he stops, he's wiping tears from the corners of his eyes and giving me probably the most sympathetic look he can muster as I stand there with my arms crossed over my chest, glaring at him. Then he sits there watching me, his lips twitching as he waits for me to say something.

"What do I do?" I finally ask in a whisper.

"I can't tell you what to do," he answers softly, most of the humor now gone as he gives me a serious look. "You're the only one who can make that decision for yourself, and even then, it may be a losing battle because you're not the only one who gets to make that decision. And while I won't advise you to be overly cautious, I will advise you to be very clear in your intentions. The last thing that woman needs is a passive-aggressive, indecisive buffoon chasing her tail. So, if all you wanna do is have some fun, and she's game for that, tell her. If it's more, if you come to a definitive conclusion that you want to keep her, then tell her. Regardless of what you decide your overall intentions are, fucking tell her, and then allow her to decide what she wants."

"Keep her? Tell her? Jesus fucking Christ, Dare. I just said I'd rather fucking hate her."

"I can tell you from experience that what you'd rather do makes no difference," he replies, not even bothering to attempt to hide his disbelief. "Obviously, you're still stuck in the denial stage, but knowing you as well as I do, I don't think you'll stay there very long."

A frustrated sound comes out of me that sounds like there's an animal brewing in my chest, and he cackles again. I take a deep breath in through my nose and then exhale out of my mouth, repeating this several times until I feel my blood pressure stabilize. I look up and meet his eyes again, swallowing painfully past the lump in my throat and whispering, "Fuck."

He doesn't say anything as he continues to watch me patiently, likely because he knows where this is going. Which I suppose he does, given his recent history with Nettie. "How did this happen?"

"How does anything happen? Maybe it was like that the entire time, and you used whatever excuse you could find to keep the truth at arm's length. It's now no longer valid, and you're left standing here just like you are now. Wrecked. Destroyed. A tarnished and shattered version of your former self."

I don't bother attempting to make fun of his description; I don't even bother teasing him about what appears to be a romanticized commentary on my current predicament. Instead, I ask, "And how do I fix it?"

"You don't."

"Fuck."

He knows I understand what he's getting at. He knows the meaning behind his words is not lost on me. I may be a dumb fucking asshole sometimes, but I'm not so shortsighted and out of touch with my own thought processes that the sudden deviation in my behavior isn't obvious. And as much as I don't like it, he's correct in his long-winded advice that basically equals it's time to shit or get off the pot. Or, in this case, pin her down or push her away.

"Answer me one question," Darius's voice snaps my attention back to him. "If you were to go out there and see some man with his hands on her, what would you do?"

My lip curls, and the weight on my chest is suddenly crushing as I snarl, "With her consent or without?"

"Does it matter?"

I don't hesitate to shake my head. "Not even a little bit."

"Then what would you do?"

"You would have to stop me from killing him."

I'm not exaggerating. The intense pulse inside me at the thought of someone else touching her makes my skin crawl. I feel physically ill and sweat beads on my forehead trickling down my back. I hold my hand up to find it trembling, and my eyes dart to Dare. "Do you think I'm sick?"

Dare snorts out another laugh, one of his hands slapping his thigh as he says, "Lovesick, maybe."

I step into him, giving him a shove backwards with both my hands. I've really had it with all the laughing. "Shut your fucking mouth."

He only laughs harder, and as much as I want to rough him up, instead, I take a step back and stare up at the ceiling as he gets control of himself. I think back on the last few days, attempting to figure out how the fuck I ended up here, but I come up with nothing. So, I try to say it one more time. "I fucking hate her."

Darius straightens and moves next to me, swinging an arm over my shoulder and giving me a little squeeze. "Sometimes, it's the same exact fucking thing."

I groan loudly, allowing him to steer me out of the bathroom and back into the hallway, where we come face to face with Nettie and Carolina, who are just entering a room across the hallway. They both stop, turning to look at me, so I quickly close the distance between Carolina and me, not stopping until there's barely any space between us. She looks up at me, her gaze unflinching, and right when she opens her mouth to say something, I spit out, "Fuck."

Then I turn on my heel and rush down the hallway, but I hear her say, "What the fuck is wrong with him?"

This question is met with more tittering from Darius and Nettie, and I pause outside the next doorway and turn to give Darius a murderous look as I open the door to go inside. He rushes over, doing a half-ass job at stifling his amusement, and follows me into the room, the door slamming behind us.

The piece of shit I attempted to beat to death is cuffed to a chair in the middle of the room. I take a step toward him before I realize I'm moving, and Darius grabs me, yanking me back and pushing me toward the wall as he says, "Nope. You fucking stay over there."

I push back against him and open my mouth to argue, but his hand comes up sharply, the sting of his palm against my cheek making me flinch away and blink. I'm immediately reminded of the time I had to bust his nose to get him to see reason, so when he says, "Do you hear me, Tony? Do you understand?" I nod, my jaw clenching as I bring both my hands up in surrender and lean back against the wall.

He walks toward the man in the chair, saying something to Anton and Erik that has them changing their position so they're standing between the man in the middle of the room and me. I roll my eyes, amused that the two of them think they could stop me if I wanted to get over there. Of course, most likely, Darius only wants them to slow me down and give him the chance to return the favor for that broken nose.

I trust Darius to get the job done since it's obvious that something inside of me has shifted to the point I can no longer see reason. Not that the fucking piece of shit doesn't deserve to be dead, but we definitely need to squeeze any possible information out of him first.

Darius kneels in front of him, and the man's head comes up, and he peers at Darius with the one eye that he can still barely open. Darius whispers something to him, and the man nods, that one eye glancing at me before looking back at Darius, and he shakes his head in response to whatever is being said to him.

"Anton," I whisper-shout. He turns back and looks at me, and I motion for him to come closer.

"Tony?" Anton's words are directed at me, but his attention is still on Darius.

I answer anyway, "What's he saying?"

"He's giving him a choice," he says as he turns his head to look at me, the corner of his mouth curling up as he continues, "It's the easy way or the hard way—you know what I mean?"

I glance back at Darius, who's still speaking softly to the restrained man whose eye is focused on Dare's face as he nods in understanding of whatever he's hearing. I turn back to Anton and ask, "What's the easy way?"

"Darius is the easy way."

"And the hard way?"

"That would be you." Anton chuckles and then adds, "Cause you're definitely going to make it hurt."

"I guess that makes sense."

Anton smiles at me and then moves back to where he was standing next to Erik as we wait for Darius to finish up and find out what we're doing next.

I lean back against the wall, and my skin prickles. I peek over my shoulder, only to see my own reflection in the mirror. *Carolina*. I turn and stare straight ahead, knowing I'm looking right at her. I feel it in my bones, in the tightness in my chest. A feeling that not even an hour ago was suffocating, but now, it almost feels like a relief. I raise a hand and press it against the glass, and I swear I feel the heat of her hand through the glass as she presses hers against the same spot on the other side.

I inhale sharply, shaking my head at the idiocy of my thought process. Jesus fucking Christ, what's wrong with me? I don't have time for this shit.

I put my back to the wall again, watching Darius continue to murmur to the restrained man, and after a few more moments, Dare stands and walks over to me. "He said he can show us where he thinks they're holding the girl. It was also quite clear that she won't be the only one being held there. So, we're gonna want to take a day or two to get things sorted so we can get them all out."

I grind my teeth together, unable to respond through the rage pumping through me, and he rests his hand on my shoulder and squeezes. He leans in closer to me and asks, "Are you gonna be good for this? Because we can't have you go into the situation and lose your focus."

"Are we going to burn the fucking place to the ground?"

"Of course."

"I'll be good. So long as we can ensure that none of those child-abusing shitbags can breathe when we're done with them, I'll be more than good."

Anton and Erik join us, and Anton turns to Darius and asks, "So, was that guy here to spy on us or something?"

"No," Darius says as he shakes his head. "He's another desperate man having to do desperate things to suit despicable people."

"I'm not buying it," I spit out. "Once Carolina's daughter is secure, he's a fucking dead man."

Dare laughs and knocks me on the shoulder as he replies, "I didn't say he wouldn't pay for his sins; I'm saying that sometimes, sins aren't chosen. That doesn't give them a free pass or anything."

"Kind of like the sliding scale that differentiates between whether you die or if you and everyone you've ever loved dies?"

"Exactly," Darius replies emphatically. "And there are many circumstances where their friends and family knew and did nothing.

They're also culpable."

We move out into the hallway, where Nettie and Carolina are waiting for us. Carolina is leaning her back against the wall, and she asks, "Did he know anything?"

I walk toward her as I reply, "We think so. We're going to do some recognizance and then make a plan." I stop in front of her, taking a step closer to her than is really necessary so I'm infringing on her personal space. She doesn't try to move away; she looks up at me with soft brown eyes so full of deep yearning that my breath catches in my throat. I stroke the backs of my fingers down her cheek, then along her throat and over her collarbone until I'm pressing my palm over her heart. I feel her heart beating as I say, "We'll find her. I promise."

Nettie clears her throat, drawing my gaze away from Carolina, and I raise my brows at her as I ask, "You got a problem?"

She gives me her trademark haughty Nettie grin and replies, "Nope. This is great."

I squint at her and give her a tight-lipped smile that definitely doesn't meet my eyes before I return my gaze to Carolina, who's watching me curiously. I look her over, my eyes traveling from where my hand rests against her chest and up to her neck, along her jawline to her lips, and over her cheekbones and the curve of her brow. Then I meet her eyes again and shake my head, whispering, "Fuck."

With great effort, I step away from her, letting my hand drop to my side and muttering again, "Fuck, fuck, fuck me," as I turn on my heel and walk down the hallway without saying another word.

Chapter Eleven

Carolina

JUST WHEN I THINK Tony Andersen can't be any bigger of an asshole, he proves me wrong. And I can't even pinpoint exactly what he's doing that makes him a big asshole, but for some reason, everything about him is rubbing me the wrong way today.

First of all, he won't stop staring at me. And even when I catch him staring at me, he doesn't avert his eyes like a normal fucking human being and try to pretend that he didn't get caught staring. I've checked my face in the mirror three times, thinking maybe I have something on it, but that's not it.

Apparently, he's a fucking psycho.

Eventually, I decide I need to get away from him, so I move to the other side of the room, and Nettie follows. It's late evening on our second day here, and we all decide to congregate in the game room. There's a bunch of people here, men and women, playing a variety of games, from billiards to darts to cards.

Tony and Dare have been discussing the upcoming plans with Anton, and since they basically keep saying the same thing over and over again, not having to hear it again is ideal.

I sprawl on the sofa, my head resting back with my eyes closed, and Antoinette keeps fidgeting beside me. Finally, I peek an eye open, turning my head to look at her and ask, "What is it?"

She raises an eyebrow and half-shrugs but then giggles. "So...what's up?"

I open my other eye and raise my brows. "What's up with what?"

"Don't play dumb with me, Car," she whisper-shouts and then pokes me in the side with her finger.

My lips curve up in a teasing smile. "Maybe you should be more specific in your interrogation."

She turns her body on the couch so she's fully facing me, pulling her feet up under her so she can lean in close to me. When I turn my head to meet her gaze, she asks, "What's going on with you and Tony? Fucking tell me, already."

I giggle at her question, shaking my head as I ask, "You ever have a close girlfriend?"

"Fuck no," she says with a snort, settling more fully into the couch. "Is it that obvious? Am I being super annoying?"

"No, I just wondered. I've never had a close anything, so I honestly have no idea what's normal and what's annoying."

She waggles her brows at me. "Good, now tell me the truth."

"There's nothing going on. He mostly hates me, but he's being kind enough to help me out with some stuff."

"Tony is not helpful," she sputters, her hand squeezing my forearm as she pulls on me. "And the way he looks at you. There's no way this is nothing."

I face forward again and close my eyes. "I don't know what to tell you. He's probably only helping me because he gets his dick wet in return, but whatever."

"What kind of help are you talking about?"

I sit up, saying nothing for a few moments as I attempt to figure out what to tell her. Finally, I opt for the truth. "I have some trauma issues I need to figure out, and he's basically giving me free use of his body to help me work through it."

"Free use?" she asks, her voice full of wonder. "And how does that help you?"

"I'll give you an example," I say, turning my gaze back to her. "Vincent used to enjoy forcing me to blow him in airplane bathrooms. It didn't matter if it was private or commercial. It was always the same. And if he didn't feel like one, and he was feeling particularly cruel, he'd nominate someone else to test me."

She gasps, her hand once again squeezing my forearm and her eyes wide as she whispers, "And then I dared you to blow him in the bathroom on the plane. I'm so sorry."

I shake my head and laugh. "No, that's not at all the same thing. But it did give me the idea that maybe it would be beneficial for me to actively take charge of my sexual experiences. That's why I went in there and made the *choice* to blow him."

"And you feel like it'll work? That it'll help you?"

I think over the question for a few moments, my lip curling up as I rub my tongue over my teeth. Then I reply, "I do. It was frightening at first, but for some reason, I trusted him to follow my cues. If I'd given him a pinch as he instructed me to, I know he would've stopped, and I know he wouldn't have been mad and wouldn't have tried to punish me for it. I mean, Tony's a huge fucking asshole, but I trust him not to further damage me in that way if that makes sense."

"That makes perfect sense. Tony can be kind of shitty, but when push comes to shove, he's a standup guy."

"Exactly," I say with a sigh of relief. "So, we came up with this deal that if something crosses my mind, and I want to try to flip the script on the experience, all I have to do is tell him, and we'll do it."

Antoinette smiles at me and then lurches forward suddenly, but I flinch back, and she freezes. "I'm sorry, Car. Are you okay? I had an urge to hug you, but I shouldn't have come at you so suddenly."

I inhale sharply through my nose, then swallow the painful lump in my throat so I can reply. "It's fine. I'm feeling a bit raw while discussing it, and you caught me off-guard. I don't have anything against hugs or even spontaneous touching, but in some circumstances, it may take me some time to get used to the fact that I no longer need to have a knee-jerk reaction to everything."

"Did women hurt you, too?"

"Vincent would use anyone and everyone to hurt me if he could. Men, women—it didn't matter." I pause, sighing deeply before I continue, "I haven't the first fucking clue what I truly like or dislike."

She frowns, her hand now tentative on my arm as she strokes me gently. "It's fucking awful that happened to you. Female intimacy is so different—softer, sexier, even. I hate that it was ruined for you."

"Yeah, well, on the other side of that, there isn't anything more vicious than a woman. Which in some circumstances is good, I guess."

She gives me a slight smile and then glances across the room where Dare and Tony are sitting. She turns back to me with a determined expression as she asks, "Carolina, may I kiss you?"

I laugh, shaking my head at her abrupt question. "What? Why?"

"Because I want to help," she whispers, the expression on her face earnest as she adds, "You'll know straightaway if you don't like it, and you can give me a pinch, and I'll back off."

I eye her for a moment, taken aback by her request. She moves closer to me, the hopeful expression on her face almost comical as she waits for me to reply. I look her over, noting every outward reason why Dare would be obsessed with her while also recognizing the countless non-physical reasons anyone would be attracted to her. Even with her being borderline psychotic, she's an incredibly attractive woman.

My hesitation doesn't stem from an aversion to the idea of kissing another woman; I don't mind that at all. It has more to do with my inexperience with my own sexuality, given most of my adult life was spent playing whore to a man who never gave one fuck about my own wants and desires. I was a virgin when I was given to Vincent, and since then, even though I've had more sexual partners than I care to count, none of it was ever for me.

I swallow the lump in my throat, exhilaration running up my spine, a giggle escaping as I lift a shoulder and say, "Okay."

She beams at me, and my giggles intensify at her blatant excitement that I accepted her proposal. She turns so she's seated beside me but facing me, then her hands are cupping my face, and she leans in, her lips brushing over mine tentatively. My breath catches, and I giggle against her lips before clearing my throat and getting control of my nervousness.

This is Antoinette. She won't hurt me.

I relax in her hold, allowing her to angle my head a bit to the side as she presses her lips more firmly against mine—once, twice. Then her tongue comes out, and she licks my lips, inching closer and taking my mouth more firmly as she sighs into my mouth, eliciting a low moan from me as she sinks closer, urging my lips to open for her.

Then, through the fog in my brain, Darius shouts, "Everyone get the fuck out!"

Chapter Twelve

Tony

DARIUS HAS BEEN BORING me for what feels like hours about the finer details of his very anti-climactic interrogation of that motherfucker who put his hands on Carolina. All this talk about micro-expressions, tells, and nuances is enough to make me puke. I'd rather rip out his fingernails and shove them into his eyeballs to get some answers, but Darius says I lack style in my methods.

He can fuck off, but I suppose there's something to be said for variety in the workplace.

He's in the middle of lecturing me on the various reasons why I might need a chill pill when he suddenly stops speaking. His eyes widen, and a look of sheer confusion settles over his features. He tilts his head to the side and mutters, "What the actual fuck?"

I whip my head around to see what has him so flummoxed and immediately do a double-take as I spot Carolina and Nettie on the sofa across the room. Nettie is kneeling over Carolina, her hands cupping her face as she presses her mouth against hers, her tongue coming out to lick over her lips teasingly.

They're already drawing the attention of others in the room, and I whistle, managing to get Anton's attention, who follows my gaze and then immediately barks out orders to his people to avert their eyes.

Dare rushes to his feet and bellows, "Everyone, get the fuck out!"

They all scurry to the door, with Anton and Erik ushering them out, and within seconds, the door is being shut behind them. Silence echoes throughout the room, but neither Carolina nor Nettie took notice of the initial uproar or the current silence.

Dare sits in his chair again, and we look at each other in puzzlement before Dare says, "Don't fucking ask me, man."

"Do you think we should go over there?"

"I don't think this is an invitation or anything," Darius replies. "It's probably best to enjoy the view from over here and not draw attention to ourselves."

I adjust my chair, so I don't have to crane my neck to see what's going on behind me. "Nettie has a thing for women?"

Dare lifts a shoulder dismissively and states, "Maybe. It's never really come up. But Antoinette doesn't do anything without a reason, so I'll sit back and wait till I find out what that is."

"You're not jealous?"

He laughs, shaking his head before giving me a dirty look. "Not at all. Why the fuck would I be jealous?"

I make a face, failing at keeping the confusion out of my voice when I reply, "I don't fucking know. You got all these 'touch her and die vibes', so it's hard to keep up."

"This is a little bit different than some motherfucker putting his hands on my woman without permission. Not that I would give a man permission to put his hands on my woman, but if she chooses to have a dalliance with another woman, I'm not gonna stand in her way."

This is highly confusing for me, which must be evident on my face because he laughs again and then continues, "Listen, Tony. I'm a man. I'm good at many things, but I'm also terrible at many things. I am 100% certain that Antoinette could get an infinite number of things from a woman that I could not provide. And if that's what she wants, that's what she gets." He pauses, glancing over at the two women who are now whispering and giggling, and his features soften, his lips curving up in a small smile. "I'm slightly surprised she's never mentioned it to me before. But I'm sure she has her reasons."

I look back at the two women on the sofa. Nettie turns as if she's going to move off the couch to kneel in front of Carolina, but the re-clined woman stiffens, and Nettie stops moving. Carolina looks down at Nettie, who pats her on the leg and says something that has Carolina visibly relaxing while her hands come up and cover her cheeks.

A pained noise escapes from her lips, and I move to rise, but Dare's hand on my shoulder stops me. "Not unless you're asked, Tony. Antoinette won't do anything to hurt her."

I nod because I know he's right, and then it dawns on me what may be going on over there. So, I say, "I bet this has to do with something that happened to Carolina in the past. Carolina must have talked to Nettie about it, and Nettie wanted to flip the script."

"Is that what you've been doing for her?" Dare asks. "Have you been helping her work through her trauma?"

I inhale deeply through my nose, nodding as I turn my gaze back across the room. Nettie is now kneeling on the floor between Caroli-na's legs, and Carolina is watching her intently, her hands folded across her stomach as they continue to speak to each other.

I'm so enraptured by the scene unfolding in front of me that Dare's bark of laughter startles me. Then he leans in, and whispers close to my ear, "You're fucking jealous."

I jerk away from him, shaking my head and muttering, "I am not."

Darius throws his head back and laughs loudly, drawing the attention of both women. Carolina giggles, embarrassment evident on her face, and then Nettie laughs as she says something else to Carolina before getting to her feet. She walks across the room toward us, and we both straighten in our chairs, not having the first fucking clue why she's coming over here.

She stops in front of me and says, "I need you."

We both stare at her questioningly, and I glance at Dare and then back at Nettie, not knowing what to say. Dare doesn't seem to be bothered at all as he leans back in his chair, watching her with that same small smile and soft look in his eyes. Mostly, he looks proud of her, which seems rather strange to me, but what the fuck do I know about their relationship.

Finally, he says, "Are you being helpful, baby girl?" Nettie beams at him and nods, and then he adds, "Do you need me to go?"

I gape at him and incredulously say, "What do you mean go? You can't go!"

He gives me a bland look and retorts, "I will do whatever Antoinette needs me to do to help her friend."

I'm in an alternate fucking universe right now. That's the only explanation. An alternate universe where Darius Hughes leaves his woman in the same sexual scenario with me–without him.

I shake my head. "This is a terrible idea."

I'm feeling a little panicky, the pressure in my chest increasing, and they both look at me as if I've lost my fucking mind. And maybe I have.

Finally, Nettie leans close to him, whispering in his ear, and whatever she says earns a chuckle from him. "Whatever you need, baby girl. This is your show."

She straightens, then turns away, saying, "Come along, then. Bring your chairs."

She scurries off, leaving Dare and me to do her bidding without any further discussion. Dare doesn't hesitate, rising and picking his chair up to follow her, so with a hearty sigh, I do the same. Halfway across the room, I grab his arm and stop him, and he looks at me questioningly. So, I ask, "Is this a good idea?"

He rolls his eyes at me and sighs. "Sometimes, Tony, you just gotta learn to go with the flow."

He shakes my hand off his arm and walks away, and I watch him as he stops in front of the sofa and places his chair where Nettie points. Meanwhile, I'm still standing there like a fucking asshole, and Nettie barks my name and gives me an annoyed look, pointing to a spot next to Dare.

"Fuck it," I mutter to myself and pick up my chair, taking the same path Dare did as I continue to mutter to myself, "Go with the flow, Tony. Go with the fucking flow."

I place my chair exactly where Nettie pointed, and then sit down and take a deep breath as I attempt not to show exactly how uptight I actually am. Carolina's voice draws my attention, and she says, "Tony. You don't have to do this if you don't want to."

I make a strangled sound in my throat as I choke out, "I don't even know what this is."

Nettie rolls her eyes as she explains, "FF Interlude. We're not really sure where it's going, but it definitely has potential for a little FMF, FFMM, MMF, or even MFM. Or any variation of those, really."

Darius laughs beside me, most likely laughing at me, as I shake my head. "We're back to the book shit again, Nettie. Really?"

She gives me a patient look, then walks over to me, and leans over until she's whispering, "We're helping a girl out. Don't be a cock."

"Fine," I say with far more authority than I feel. "Tell me what to do."

Nettie beams at me, then straightens and pats me on the leg before walking back to Carolina, who's still lying a bit awkwardly on the sofa. "Okay, Car. Give me a rough breakdown of the scene."

Nettie sits beside Carolina, who is now sitting up straighter, and they put their heads together and whisper for a few moments, giggling as they glance back at us.

Carolina whispers something, and Nettie nods and then says in a normal volume, "I don't think we should restrain you this time. No need to get crazy right out of the gate." She pauses, considering her options, and then asks, "Do you want to be spit-roasted?"

Dare and I both choke—Dare more so than me—but he says nothing, so I glance over at him and see his cheeks turning a bit pink. "I bet you weren't expecting that," I mutter, and he glances at me and shakes his head. So, I continue, "Just go with the flow, Dare."

Nettie shushes us, glaring over her shoulder before turning her focus back to Carolina and saying, "Well, technically, we've got two cocks here, so if you want to do that, we can." She stops talking, listening to whatever Carolina is whispering before waving a hand dismissively and replying, "Oh, it's fine. If it will help you, I'm sure Dare will be willing to take one for the team here."

She's lost her fucking mind. I always knew Nettie had the capacity for some seriously fucked-up shit, but this right here takes the cake.

Carolina and Nettie look at each other, and I'm not sure what Nettie sees in Carolina's eyes, but she glances at me over her shoulder, then looks back at Carolina and quips, "Fucking men."

Carolina giggles again, nodding in agreement, and then they go back to whispering to each other. Frankly, I'm a little sick of being in the fucking dark, so I say, "Tell me what you need me to do. I already agreed to help, but you have to tell me what you need."

Nettie smiles at me, and Carolina does the same. That stupid fucking warmth is back in my chest, and I have to suppress my urge to scream.

Carolina covers her cheeks with her hands and giggles almost uncomfortably. I narrow my eyes at Nettie and ask, "Are you sure she even wants to do this?"

Nettie goes to respond, but Carolina interrupts, "It's not that I don't want to. I'm just a little nervous."

Carolina's eyes meet mine, and I recognize the skittish animal in them, making my chest tighten. "Fuck this," I spit out as I rise from my chair and close the short distance between us, indicating for Nettie to move out of my way so I can kneel in front of her.

"Do you want Nettie to touch you?" She nods. "Do you want me to touch you?" She nods again. "And Darius? Do you want his touch as well?" She hesitates, and I see the indecision in her eyes, so I continue, "Regardless of how I feel about another man's hands on you, I would never prevent you from getting what you need. And I wouldn't punish you for it after the fact, either. This isn't about me or my wants or needs; this is about what you need."

Her eyes flit to Dare behind me, and then she turns her head slightly to look at Nettie, who is now seated beside her on the sofa. Nettie smiles at her and says, "Whatever you want, Car. You're in charge here."

Carolina and Nettie continue to stare at each other for a few moments, and then Nettie's lips twitch. "What is it? What are you two scheming?"

Nettie gives me an innocent look and then looks behind me and waggles her brows mischievously and Dare chuckles knowingly. "Oh, you naughty little minx. You wouldn't?"

She smiles broadly, raising a flirty shoulder as she says, "I don't know what you're talking about."

Carolina's giggles turn into a cackle, and I sit back on my haunches, looking back at Dare and asking, "Have we been duped here?"

"I wouldn't say we've been duped, but we've definitely been played."

Carolina and Nettie are both giggling now, and while I'm relieved the tension has been broken, I'm slightly concerned about where this is going.

Finally, Carolina manages to sober long enough to sputter, "Do you think–" She stops as another giggle slips out. "Do you think you two would be willing to make out?"

I give her a bland look and Dare sighs loudly from behind me. I scowl at him. I don't question my own sexuality, and I'm not squeamish about touching other men, but I'm surprised this is coming up now. And also, greatly suspicious. So, I turn to Dare and ask, "This doesn't surprise you?"

"Not at all," he says with humor glinting in his eyes as he watches Nettie. "It seems our girls may be taking advantage of a situation here to get what they want."

I look at Nettie, who now has a suspiciously innocent look on her face, and then at Carolina, who has a matching innocent look. I look between the two of them for several moments before turning back to Darius. "So, we are getting played here?"

"Not entirely," he says with a raised brow. "But my guess is a little minx put the idea into Carolina's head. Not in a malicious way, but still, naughty."

"And this would help you?" I ask Carolina, assessing her face as I continue, "Dare and I swapping some saliva?"

The smile on her face dims, and she lowers her eyes shyly as she thinks over her response for a moment. Then her shoulders lift a bit as she answers, "I'm not sure. But I do like the idea of having two men being in the moment instead of being at odds and treating the entire scene as a punishment."

Nettie has a self-satisfied smirk on her face, and I roll my eyes in response, saying, "Don't you fucking start."

"Yes, Antoinette," Darius purrs from behind me. "Don't think you're gonna get out of your punishment because I still owe you."

"Well, I do like to be punished," she quips, not even a glimmer of remorse on her features.

Dare rises from his chair and slowly walks around me, stopping in front of Nettie, where she's kneeling beside Carolina on the sofa. He delves his fingers through the hair on the back of her skull, pulling her head back and using his other hand to grip her cheeks between his fingers and thumb. He leans down and whispers into your ear, earning a soft gasp from her in response, and then he licks a line over her cheek to her lips.

She attempts to move closer, but his hand is still in her hair, and the one on her face tightens, and he gives her a little jerk, keeping her in place as he growls against her lips, "Don't fucking move. Put your hands behind your back, and don't fucking move, or I'll stop."

She immediately puts her hands behind, and he releases his grip on her face, his hand moving down to dip into her shirt, squeezing her breast. Then his lips claim hers hungrily, and she responds in kind, a low moan vibrating between them.

Carolina fidgets in front of me, drawing my attention back to her, and then I watch her watching them, the desire on her face evident beneath her slight air of uneasiness.

"Do you enjoy watching them?" I ask her as her tongue peeks out, wetting her lips. Her soft brown eyes meet mine, burning with equal parts hunger and wariness, and she nods.

"Do you want to be watched?" I whisper, the shrug of her shoulders matching the uncertainty on her face. "Do you know what you enjoy?" She shakes her head. "Do you want to find out?" She hesitates for the briefest of moments and then nods. "Say it, sweetheart. I need you to use your words."

The breath she takes in is shuddering, and she exhales it slowly before finally saying, "Yes. I want to find out."

Dare and Nettie have paused their interlude and are watching us intently. I meet Dare's eyes and tilt my head behind me, and he gives me a short nod, and then the two of them move off the sofa.

I stand and offer Carolina my hand, which she takes easily, and I pull her to her feet so I can take the spot she just vacated. I pull her between my spread legs and look up at her as I say, "Use the stoplight for this. Not necessarily the green, but maybe the yellow, and definitely the red."

She looks at me warily, "What are you going to do?"

"Nothing too crazy, sweetheart," I say teasingly, grinning up at her. "I'm gonna continue to show you how much I fucking hate you."

That earns me a smile, and she pushes against my shoulder. "Shut up, asshole."

I move to pull her into my lap when Nettie speaks up from behind Carolina. "Take off your shirt, Tony. Actually, both of you take off your shirts."

I lean around Carolina and see Nettie standing there with her hands on her hips, a very serious expression on her face. Carolina looks behind her, frowning. "What?"

"Stop meddling, baby girl," Dare says from beside Nettie. "They may not be ready for your skin-to-skin lecture quite yet."

"Like baby bonding?" Carolina asks.

Nettie gasps in outrage and stomps her foot. "It's not only for babies!"

"Will the two of you humor her, please," Darius says exasperatedly. "Otherwise, her long clinical explanation will bore us to tears, and the moment will be lost."

Nettie's gasp of outrage is louder this time, and she glares at him as she goes to say something further, but he puts his hand over her mouth and pulls her into him. "Shut your mouth and take off your top."

Nettie's eyes light up in excitement, and she nods so he releases her. I turn my attention back to Carolina, who's staring at them curiously.

I pull my shirt over my head and toss it on the other end of the sofa, then tug her hand, drawing her attention back to me. She looks into my eyes first, and then her eyes widen as she sees I'm now shirtless. She scans down my torso, stopping at the waistband of my jeans and then scanning back up before meeting my gaze again.

She licks her lips, and I grin again, sure the look on my face is nothing less than smug preening. I straighten in my seat and pull her closer, turning her around so she's sitting on one of my thighs. "You don't have to take your shirt off if you're uncomfortable. But you should sit here on top of me so I can touch you. Is that okay?"

"Yes," she says without hesitation.

I maneuver her around until she's sitting on me fully, leaning back against me with her head against my shoulder and the sofa behind us. I turn my head and nuzzle her ear, nibbling on her earlobe and down the side of her neck, earning me a shiver. "Keep your eyes on them, sweetheart."

She relaxes back against me, and I run my hands over her hips, up her sides, and over her breasts, circling down to her stomach. I continue this path up and down her body as I kiss, lick, and nibble her neck and shoulder. Her sigh of pleasure sends a jolt right to my cock, and I press up against her ass.

I glance at Dare and Nettie, reassured they're mostly playing, Nettie in her bra and slacks, now seated on Dare's lap the same way Carolina is on mine. I unbutton Carolina's pants, and she moves, allowing me space to wedge my hand inside, a little moan escaping as I slide my finger between her pussy lips, teasing her wet hole before sliding back up and stroking her clit rhythmically.

I use my other hand to tease her nipple, pinching and fondling the tight peak as she writhes against me, her eyes focused on the couple across from us who are keeping pace with my ministrations. Carolina shudders, her body writhing against me as I pick up my pace, rubbing more firmly, wanting to hear her come for me as she watches.

"You like that?" I whisper the question against her ear, enjoying the sound of her breathy moans as I rub her clit. She nods, her head falling back against my shoulder, her face turning into me as her eyes close and her body tenses. I consider stopping, edging her just once to draw out her pleasure, but I don't.

Instead, I increase my efforts, pulling her more firmly against me, twisting my head around and taking her lips with mine, my fingers thrumming her swollen clit a bit faster, pushing her over until she's moaning her orgasm. I take advantage of her open mouth and lick inside, growling as I suck down the sounds of her pleasure, and I barely stop myself from coming from her ass writhing against my dick.

She pants into my mouth, her eyes staring into mine as she catches her breath, and I laugh internally, my initial arguments on how and why I should hate her ringing false in this very moment.

"What in the holy mother of god is going on in here?"

Carolina freezes on top of me, and I remove my hand from between her legs, her eyes curious as she watches me lick my fingers clean. I lean a bit to the side so I can look around Dare and Nettie. Agatha is standing in the doorway with her hands on her hips, a look of disapproving humor on her face.

Nettie cranes her head around where she's sprawled in Dare's lap, smiling broadly at Agatha as she says breathlessly, "Oh, nothing. Just having a little fun."

Agatha raises her brows, obviously used to these antics from her sister, then says, "Well, the fun's done. Fix your fucking clothes, so Jayme can come in without Darius stabbing him in the eyeballs."

Carolina stiffens in my lap, and she moves to sit up. I pull her back against me, pressing my face against her ear and whispering, "Relax, sweetheart." I give her a moment to do so as I adjust her clothing, and she refastens her pants, so she's put back to sorts. "Hear him out."

Carolina clears her throat and nods, then she sits up and turns her head to look at me. "Okay. I will."

Nettie has already made herself presentable, but Darius is still eyeing her like a starved man denied a meal. I unceremoniously dump Carolina off my lap and onto the sofa, laughing as I stand and listen to her sputtering.

Still chuckling, I turn my gaze on Agatha and Jayme, who have walked across the room and are now standing beside Dare and Nettie. Agatha is teasing Nettie about her exhibitionist ways while Jayme eyeballs me in a somewhat confrontational manner. I give him my best condescendingly smug look and say, "Devereaux."

"Andersen." His voice is low, and he narrows his eyes at me. "Is there something I need to know about you and my sister?"

"Excuse me?" Carolina replies from her seat on the couch. "You can shut the fuck up right now with all that sister shit. And it's none of your fucking business."

"I'm making it my business," Jayme responds, his eyes still locked with mine. "I won't stand by and let this fucker toy with you."

A growl vibrates up through my chest, and we both take a small step toward each other, but then Agatha steps between us. She pokes him in the chest. "Take it down a notch," she says flatly. "We don't have time for any pissing contest, never mind this completely unnecessary one."

He looks down at her, his eyes searching hers for a moment, and then he gives a curt nod and steps back. He relaxes some, but the tension in his jaw and fisted hands gives away his continued concern.

I walk over to him, resting my hand on his shoulder as I lean in and whisper, "She's not a fucking toy."

His startled eyes meet mine for a long moment, then he blinks and nods, so I step back. I glance around the room to see everyone staring at me with varying levels of interest. "Fuck off."

I walk back over to the sofa where Carolina is still seated, a sad, almost uncertain look on her face. I move to sit beside her, and she moves over slightly to make room for me, but I still manage to sit close enough to her, so she's pressed up against me, shoulder to hip to thigh. Her hands are folded in her lap, and she fidgets nervously, so I reach out, snag one of her hands, and pull it over, pressing it palm down against my thigh. Her brows raise, and she gives me a surprised look. I lift a shoulder nonchalantly, then lean over and say, "I've got you. You're okay."

Carolina's lips curve up slightly, and her body relaxes while her fingers dig into my thigh firmly. That's all it takes for my cock to harden in my pants again, and I squirm in my seat, thinking of every horrifying scenario possible until I feel the want abate.

Everyone is silent for a few moments, and then Nettie asks, "Well, you broke up the party, so I'm assuming it's for a good reason."

Agatha snorts. "Well, yeah. But I would've interrupted either way, just for fun."

Nettie walks over and gives her a playful shove. "But I was so close. You would've ruined that for me for no good reason?"

"Oh, I definitely would've waited for the two big guys to lock lips if it looked like it was going that direction. But since it obviously wasn't, I figured I wasn't interrupting much."

"What in the fuck?" Jayme says as he pinches the bridge of his nose. "Dare and Tony like to make out?"

"No, we don't. But apparently, these two ladies like to talk about it, especially Nettie. Seems it's pretty high up on her wish list."

Nettie smiles saucily and waggles her eyebrows and shoulders at me, and she responds, "Maybe I do, maybe I don't. I will neither confirm nor deny this accusation—"

"It's probably pretty close to number one," Dare interrupts. "Though it's quite possible she just likes to harass me. And, of course, now she will also use it to harass Tony, so to her, that's a win-win."

Carolina pipes up beside me. "It's not like you dudes haven't been begging women to kiss each other for eons. I don't see any problem with the quid pro quo on a little MM canoodling."

Nettie's eyes widen, and she smiles broadly. "Oh, yes. I totally agree. Do they do MMM ménage?"

Jayme groans as he pulls over an armchair and falls into it heavily. "Don't include me in your guys' crazy shenanigans. I have no urge to kiss a man, never mind these two fucking assholes."

All three women titter, making eyes at each other as if there's an inside joke that we're not privy to. Dare walks up behind Nettie and leans close, speaking quietly into her ear. She turns her head toward him, excitement in her eyes as she says, "Really? Do you promise?"

He nods and leans closer to respond, but Jayme interrupts, "Okay, enough fucking around. You can go back to your weird sex games later. Right now, we have more important matters to discuss."

Dare and Nettie exchange a final knowing look before returning their attention to us. Then Agatha says, "The information our prisoner gave us seems to be legit. We managed to make contact with someone on the inside, who said they will turn the girl over to Carolina, but no one else."

"Let me guess," I respond. "She has to come alone?"

"Yes. That is what they said originally, but I shut that down immediately," Jayme answers. "We won't be able to go in with a full force, but having a handful of people present is better than no one."

I shake my head, my hand over the top of Carolina's, pushing her palm more firmly into my leg as the pressure in my chest intensifies. "I don't like it. Once she goes in the fucking building, anything can happen."

"I'll do it," Carolina says firmly. "I don't care what happens to me. Promise me you'll get her out."

I turn my gaze on her, shaking my head as I say, "No. There has to be ano—"

My words are cut off by a hard pinch to my leg, and she says, "Promise me, Tony." She nips my thigh again, and I yank her hand away as she continues, "Promise me if it comes down to having to choose, you will save her."

She's staring into my eyes with such intensity that the weight in my chest becomes crushing. I grind my teeth together and swallow the lump in my throat as I give her a curt nod. "Okay," I say through gritted teeth. "I promise."

She stares at me for a few more moments, her hand turning over to grip mine as she presses her lips together and gives me a small smile. She nods and then turns her attention back to the people watching us curiously.

They continue to discuss the plan around me as I sit here battling the silent war happening in my gut and chest. I'm so far out of my element I don't even know where to begin unraveling it. Carolina tugs on my hand, and I relax in her hold, allowing her to pull my hand over until she's pressing my palm against the top of her thigh. She rests her palm on the back of my hand, the firm pressure a small lifeline that tethers me to my promise.

She's not paying me any mind as she interacts with everyone in the room, but every once in a while, her thumb strokes the side of my index finger, and with each soft touch, the pressure in my chest eases.

And little by little, I let it go.

Chapter Thirteen

Tony

IT TOOK ME TWO days to pinpoint the location of the little girl.

I was hoping I'd be able to go and retrieve her on my own without anyone else being the wiser, but after a brief conversation with Anton, I realized the impossibility of the scheme. So, begrudgingly, I allow Darius to take the lead on planning the mission, knowing that any hope of keeping Antoinette and Carolina out of it is lost. If nothing else, we can hope to move them both out of harm's way once we locate Flora.

The facility where she's being held is in a remote location, so we decide a small group of us will hoof it in in order to secure a perimeter while Anton and his men wait a safe distance away for us to give word that we're ready for them. We have no idea what we're walking into or what conditions await us. We don't know if there's one child or a hundred or if it's all a trap, and we're all going to die.

I did mention the latter to Nettie and Carolina in the hopes I could talk them into staying behind with Anton, but they weren't having it. I wasn't necessarily surprised by this, just greatly disappointed that they won't see reason.

Anton drops us at the safest location, which is also the shortest distance to our destination, so it should be around dusk by the time we get there. It's a somewhat strenuous hike, but we manage to make good time, and we arrive at the facility shortly before Carolina is due to come for the pickup.

Jayme got them to agree to allow someone to accompany Carolina into the facility, and we knew it would have to be someone less recognizable than me or Dare. Agatha and Erik seemed to be the next best in line, given that we needed Anton to run cleanup crew, and the shortlist of people we trust to be able to roll with various contingency plans is exceptionally short. I'm also hopeful having people with her increases her odds of coming back out of the building quickly and on her own two feet, my recent promise to her lingering in my mind as I consider how easily this could all go wrong.

My normal cool focus is nonexistent, the pressure on my chest increasing with each passing moment. Nothing feels right, and as I watch Agatha and Erik accompany Carolina inside the building, my blood pressure spikes.

As soon as the door closes behind them, their COMS goes out, something we expected but hoped wouldn't happen. There are four exits to this building, and we have been placed on all sides in case anyone attempts to flee.

Suddenly, Agatha and Erik exit out the door they entered, and Agatha comes over the COMS, "They wouldn't let us go up with her, and she insisted we leave. We didn't want to, but there wasn't any choice in the matter."

I curse loudly and look at Dare, who has a concerned expression. "I fucking told you. I fucking told you this was a mistake."

"Her choice," he says calmly. "That was her choice to make."

The door opens again, and a small child scurries out. She stops a few feet from the door, staring at the group of people curiously until Agatha breaks away and walks over, kneeling down in front of her as she asks quietly, "Flora?"

The little girl nods, saying nothing for a few moments as she looks toward the group behind Agatha. "Mama told me to find Tony."

I jerk to attention immediately, pushing off the tree I was leaning against and exiting the wooded area before walking toward her. I stop in front of her, but I don't kneel as I look into her eyes and ask, "I'm Tony. What else did your mama say, Flora?"

She blinks slowly, her throat working as she swallows and then says, "She said sorry. And you promised."

"Oh, she did, huh?" My words are calm and quiet, totally at odds with the rage burning in my chest when she nods in confirmation of the message she delivered. The demon inside me vibrates, threatening to erupt, so I take a calming breath through my nose and exhale it through my mouth.

"Can you do me a favor, Flora?" I ask as I kneel in front of her. Her eyes search mine, and she reaches a small hand out and touches my cheek as she nods. So, I say, "This here is my friend Aggie. She's a real good friend of your mama's. I need you to go with her. Can you do that for me?"

She drops her hand, cocks her head, and then looks at Agatha curiously before looking back at me and giving me another nod. "Good," I turn to Agatha and add, "Get her out of here, please."

Agatha holds her hand out to Flora, who takes it easily, and then Agatha turns back to me and asks, "What are you gonna do?"

"I'm gonna do what I do best," I reply as I pull my favorite leather gloves out of my back pocket and slide my hands inside. "I'm gonna go fuck around and find out."

Knowing where all this is headed, Darius and the rest of the men are already standing with me, waiting to find out what's next. I wait a few moments for Agatha to disappear with Flora, and then I turn to the men before me, switching on my COM to speak to the men surrounding the other parts of the building. "You'll have a choice," I say clearly, wanting them to understand my words for what they truly are—a warning.

"It's highly likely that refusing to allow Carolina to exit the building with Flora is a trap. I'm going in to get her regardless of this fact, but none of you are required to follow me inside. If you do choose to continue with this mission, keep your eyes and ears open at all times, and at the first sign of a problem, you are to abandon the mission. You don't worry about me, you don't worry about Darius, you don't worry about anyone but yourself. You have two minutes to prepare yourself one way or the other."

I switch off my COM, step over close to Darius, and say, "Same goes for you, man. You're not required to follow me into another death trap. Lord knows Nettie will be extra pissed if we both get ourselves killed."

"Seriously." Darius snorts, giving me a dirty look. "And she wouldn't be equally as pissed off if she knew I'd let you go into the death trap without me at your back?"

"So, you're saying there's no winning with her?"

"Yes. She's gonna be pretty fucking pissed either way. But at least this way, she should get to rant at our double funeral. I'll give her a quick call, though. Say my final goodbye so at least she won't piss and moan about that."

"Send her my undying love as well," I say seriously.

I turn away as he pulls his phone from his pocket, hits her number, and then walks a short distance away so I can't hear his conversation. The vans that are supposed to be waiting a safe distance away start pulling into the driveway and then park outside the building. Anton and Jayme exit first, with a steady flow of others quickly joining the small group of men who are already congregated.

Anton and Jayme walk toward me, stop in front of me, and say nothing, so I finally ask, "What part of stay out of sight did you not understand?"

"Did you think I was gonna sit down the road and let you get yourself killed trying to save my sister?" Jayme says.

"And none of us came on this mission to listen to you lot get slaughtered over the COMS. Where's the honor in that?" Anton adds with a shake of his head.

Dare walks back over, sliding his phone into his pocket as he says, "Antoinette says you are an inconsiderate fucking asshole, and if either of us dies, she'll haunt us for the rest of her life."

"That doesn't even make sense."

"She said what she said," Darius responds, shrugging his shoulders dismissively. "You know how she gets. Either way, she fucking means it."

I shake my head, sighing in exasperation as I reply, "Yup, she's a pain in the ass–"

Boom.

The distinct sound of an explosion has us all whirling toward the building. I take a step toward it, but Dare's hand on my chest stops my forward momentum as I yell into the COM, "Any movement? Has anyone left that building?"

My question is met with a constant string of negatives echoing through my ear, and my guts clench, a stabbing pain spiking through my chest and stealing my breath as I shake off Dare's hold and sprint toward the building, his shouts sounding out behind me. His footfalls slap the gravel as he follows closely, but he's not gaining as I close in on the door, his shouts vibrating through my brain without triggering a response.

Boom.

Boom.

Boom.

The whole building vibrates, and the door I was closing in on flies open, the force pushing me back until I'm airborne. Several more explosions follow, shaking the earth beneath me, a sickening reverberation of the destruction around me.

I roll onto my hands and knees, coughing and choking as I attempt to get back my breath. I gain my footing and immediately move toward the smoking building, but Dare grabs me, pulling me backwards and standing in front of me, becoming a human wall every time I try to get to the building. He shouts, "No! It's too late!"

I lean against him so heavily that he's the only thing keeping me upright as this almost all-consuming pain washes over me. I'm shouting incoherent denials, cursing, my hands fisted in his shirt until finally, he pushes me back, and his hands grip my face, forcing me to look in his eyes, and I see the finality there.

I don't believe it. I refuse to believe it. But we've seen the blueprints of this building, and we've studied every possible exit and the entire surrounding area.

I startle as a shout comes from the COM in my ear, and it takes a few beats before I make out the words through the fog in my brain. "Someone's exiting! A woman!"

Dare looks at me, a mixture of shock and disbelief on his face, and then we're both running, sprinting around the building. We come around the corner and run toward the group of men standing over a prone figure in the dirt.

I immediately know it's not Carolina but Dare and I continue to run until we're close enough to get a good look at the figure as it starts to stir. She comes up on all fours, her head bent down as she coughs and gags, and Dare and I both slow as we get closer, stopping several feet from her. Then we look at each other in complete disbelief at what we're seeing, and Dare asks, "Is this a fucking joke?"

I'm speechless.

I shake my head, waiting for confirmation of what we already seem to know, even though it doesn't seem possible. Then the woman turns, still on all fours, and looks over at us, those bright blue eyes cutting me in half as I attempt to speak. But nothing comes out.

Finally, Darius asks, "Lilith?"

She grunts at him, not bothering to deny what's right in front of our face, as impossible as it may seem.

Lilith fucking Ferro.

In the flesh.

What the actual fuck?

Chapter Fourteen

Tony

IT TAKES US A while to clear the scene and head back to Agatha's place. I've had to compartmentalize everything that's happened, which makes me more efficient and methodical but also impossible to talk to. We looked around as best we could, given the amount of damage to the building, and a few of Anton's men stayed behind to do a more thorough search as things cool off enough to sort through.

Dare has been right by my side the entire time, and I can tell he's torn between figuring out how the fuck Lilith Ferro is still alive and making sure I don't go into full-destruction mode.

I think he realizes we need to stay in our own lane and let Nettie handle the Lilith thing. The only one we can think of who might know what's going on is Matt, and of course, he's not answering his phone. With the time difference, he's probably on a shift, which pisses me off even more because the idea that this fucking criminal is a police chief is fucking asinine.

He doesn't even need the damn money. And then there's Mickey, who also isn't answering his goddamn phone.

Those two motherfuckers are going to get it.

Anton loaded Lilith into the medic van, so at least I didn't have to look at her. I'm leaning against the hood of the van, my forehead against my forearms, when a hand squeezes my shoulder, and Dare says, "I'm sorry, man."

I shake him off and straighten, turning to him as I reply, "Sorry for what?"

"I wish there was something I could do. I know how excruciating it is, that feeling of loss."

I glare at him, taking a step closer and pushing hard against his chest. "You don't know what you're talking about. You shut your fucking mouth."

Dare takes the hit without flinching, even stepping back a bit as a sign that he's not going to engage. He says nothing, but the look on his face says everything that he doesn't bother saying, and I grind my teeth as the pressure in my chest reaches a fever point. I bellow with rage, whirling around and putting my fist through the side window of the van, not even feeling the pain of my split knuckles splitting open again.

I turn back to Dare, who's standing there with a helpless expression on his face, and I grit out, "She's not dead. She's not gone."

I gasp in a sharp inhalation as my heart stutters in my chest, almost taking my breath. I pause for a moment, then give him a hard look. "I would know. I don't know how, I don't know why, but if she was truly gone, I would know."

I half expect him to argue with me or, if nothing else, give me a pitying look and ignore the conversation entirely. But he doesn't.

Instead, he steps closer to me and grips my upper arms in both his hands, then leans in so he's looking right into my eyes as he replies, "Then we'll find her."

I search his eyes briefly, recognizing the sincerity of his words, and I manage to expel the breath I was holding as the ache in my chest eases. I shouldn't be surprised, given if anyone knows the agony of never giving up on the one you love, it's Darius Hughes.

He releases me and steps back, looking back toward the van I know Lilith is in. He shakes his head and turns back to me, saying, "Antoinette's gonna lose it."

"Oh, yeah. I have to wonder how deep this treachery goes."

"What do you mean?"

"Matt? Mickey? Who all knows about this?"

Dare grimaces, his features twisting as my meaning sinks in. "I have a hard time believing Matt wouldn't tell us, but I guess we never really know. If he thought it was safer for us not to know, then he definitely wouldn't have told us."

"Did you tell her?"

He winces and shakes his head. "I was going to, but I didn't know what to say, and she's with Agatha and Flora, so I didn't want to agitate her before it was necessary."

"They made it back to Aggie's okay?"

"Yes, they're there. I'm sure she'll come right out when we get there, so I'll have a brief word with her first. See what she wants to do."

The ride back is quiet as we're all lost in our own thoughts. By the time we arrive, my anger has dissipated, and a cold sadness that I am thoroughly not used to is left behind. I push it all down as Nettie walks out into the driveway and then waits as Dare and I walk over to her.

He pulls her close, leaning in and pressing his lips against hers. Her hands clutch his neck, the worry on her face changing to relief, and he pulls back, staring into her eyes as he says, "We didn't find Carolina, but someone else showed up in the chaos."

She frowns, her arms falling to her sides and her hands fisting as she replies, "I swear to Christ, Darius Hughes, if you tell me Vincent or Dimitri is alive, I will lose it."

He barks out a laugh, shaking his head, likely relieved that at least that didn't happen. "No, but it's still crazy, and I have no explanation."

Anton and a couple of the other guys come over, and Anton asks, "What are we doing with our unexpected guest?"

"I was getting to that," Dare replies and then turns back to Nettie. "Somehow, someway, Lilith is alive."

Nettie's eyes widen, but she says nothing. She stares at him for a few long moments, likely waiting for him to make some kind of horrible punchline, and when he remains silent, she brings her hands up to her hips, and her face twists in pained confusion. "Excuse me? What do you mean? Lilith is alive?"

"Before we could get into the building, a bunch of explosives went off," Dare explains. "One person exited from the far side of the building, coughing up smoke and obviously banged up. That person is Lilith Ferro." His roaming eyes pause on her face as a whole kaleidoscope of emotions crosses over her features before settling on what appears to be a mixture of anger and hope. But she still says nothing, so Darius goes on, "We haven't spoken to her at all. She's been in the back of the med van getting tended to. I don't think any of us are equipped to deal with it tonight, but you tell us what you want us to do for now, and we're gonna do it."

Nettie's mouth has been hanging open, and she snaps it shut as the realization of what Dare is saying finally sinks in. Then her eyes narrow, and she looks at Anton and says quietly, "Chain her up in an interrogation room and leave her there."

Anton looks from Nettie to me, then to Dare, and back to Nettie, confusion evident on his face. Finally, Dare says, "You heard the woman."

I'm only mildly surprised Nettie chose the prisoner route. The fact of the matter is, without having any idea where she's been all this time, we can't say for certain if she's friend or foe. I would truly be shocked if she turned out to be a foe, at least with Nettie and Aggie, but she also knows we come as one big, somewhat deranged package at this point.

With a nod, Anton and his men take off toward the van, and the three of us head into the house, making our way toward the living quarters. I'm sure Dare will be headed for some food, but I need a shower and sleep, or else I'll crash at the most inopportune moment and be useless when they need me.

Dare turns to me and asks, "You going to be okay?"

"Yeah," I reply with a snort. "Why wouldn't I be?"

He exchanges a look with Nettie, then refocuses on me as he says, "We're really going with the 'she's not dead' scenario here?" He pauses, his eyes flitting to Nettie again, who's now staring at me wide-eyed, her brow furrowed with concern. Then he adds, "I mean, that's good. We can totally work with that."

"I already told you, Darius. She's alive. I know it."

He nods briefly, and Nettie also nods, and then we continue through the house in silence. I can tell from their demeanor they're not quite buying it, but I don't give a fuck what they believe. She's alive, and one way or another, we're going to find her.

"Where are Aggie and Flora?" I ask Nettie, pausing at the intersection of the hallways between the sleeping quarters and the dining room. She gives a nod to the left in answer, and I turn abruptly and head toward the bedrooms. Most of the doors are closed, so I continue down the hallway until I come to an open one, and sure enough, Aggie and Flora are there.

Aggie speaks softly to the little girl, who gives her a soft smile and nods at whatever she's saying. I clear my throat, and they both look over at me as Aggie says, "Thank goodness you're back. She's been asking for you this whole time."

"Me?" I reply incredulously, turning my gaze on the tiny little human who's staring at me with her mother's eyes. "I'm kind of a mean, old asshole. You'll learn that eventually."

"Well, she didn't wanna sleep until she knew you were here. So, now we know where you are, and she can go to sleep." Aggie helps Flora into bed and pulls the blanket up over her. She kneels and smooths her hair off her forehead. "I'll leave your bedroom door open, and I'll leave my door open, too, so if you need me, take a right," she stops and points to the right so Flora will know which direction and then continues, "And come find me."

The little girl mutters something, and I can't make out her words, but then Aggie laughs and looks over at me as she replies, "Tony is right directly across the hall from you. Don't worry, he won't escape in the night."

She giggles, and the childlike sound of it stabs me in the guts, so I give her a bored look and quip, "You never know. I do like to vanish whenever I feel like it. I'm pretty much a magician."

"Hush now." Aggie glares at me, looks back down at Flora, and says, "He's just playing. Don't listen to him."

I give her an annoyed look and then turn on my heel and walk across the hall to my room, slamming the door behind me. All these goddamn people have lost their minds, including me.

I take a quick shower and pull on some cotton pants and a T-shirt in case I have to make a move in the middle of the night. I finish my nighttime routine then turn off lights and climb into bed, staring at the ceiling as the weight of the situation crashes over me. I know there's nothing I can do about any of it right now, but my urge to get up and do something is a constant ache in my chest. Like I should be out there searching the ruins for her body or razing hellfire all over the criminal world in search of her.

Then there's the fact that this crazy woman entrusted me, of all people, with her daughter. Even went so far as tell a little girl that Tony would protect her. That's a huge statement from a mama to her child, and not something most children would take lightly.

Obviously, Carolina is a raging freaking lunatic.

The door clicks as someone turns the handle from the hallway. It opens, and a small form enters, then quickly closes the door, and leans against it. I slowly turn over until I'm lying on my side, facing the door, watching this tiny human as she creeps closer to me. I close my eyes as she leans over me, her small hand touching my face gently, as if she's making sure it's the same face she touched previously.

Her hand falls from my cheek, and she moves away from me toward the end of the bed, then the mattress dips slightly as she climbs on, the blanket pulling a bit as she wiggles on top of it. She lays beside me silently, not touching me, and sighs.

I move to roll onto my back, but as soon as I move, she audibly sucks in her breath and holds it, so I relax back onto my side-sleeping position. She exhales heavily and makes a quiet humming noise as she wiggles around. She's silent for a few moments, and then she fidgets some more. She does this repeatedly until her small hand presses against the middle of my back.

And that's when I realize that during all of her wiggling, fidgeting, and sighing, she was moving closer to me. She fidgets again until she leans into me, her forehead resting against me, rhythmic little puffs of air warm against my back as she relaxes into sleep.

I'm startled out of sleep by crying. Her small form is no longer pressed against my back as she flails on the bed beside me, her cries wounded and afraid.

I switch on the bedside lamp, so she'll be able to see that it's me then I stand up and walk to the foot of the bed. I reach over to pull her foot, my words as close to calm and soothing as I can muster as I say, "Flora. It's okay. Wake up."

First, she kicks at me, and I immediately release her, saying a bit more loudly, "Flora. Wake up, princess."

She thrashes about on the bed as if she's fighting someone off, then crashes against the wall and sits upright, pressing herself back against it, as she stares at me with wild eyes. I don't make any move to get closer to her; I remain standing where I am, my expression neutral.

Her eyes flit around the room as if she's looking for an escape route. She takes a shuddering breath in, and then exhales on a sob before her eyes move back to mine and she finally recognizes where she is and who I am.

I hold my hand out to her, palm up, and whisper, "I'm here, princess. No one's gonna hurt you."

Her eyes move from my face to my hand, then back to my face and I extend my hand a little further and wait. One beat passes, and then she reaches her hand out, hesitantly placing it in mine. I grip her hand gently; then wait to see what she'll do.

Tears stream down her face, but she's starting to calm, and I open my mouth to reassure her again when she scurries across the mattress and into my arms, where she curls around me, her face pressed against my chest, and then she sobs.

I cradle her small frame in my arms and walk over to the chair in the corner, sitting down with her in my lap. I press my face against the top of her head, whispering, "I've got you, princess. I've got you. It's okay. No one will ever hurt you again."

I continue to hold her, rocking her and speaking soothingly, reassuring her that her nightmares are over.

And at the same time, in the back of my mind, I plot my revenge.

They're all going to die.

Chapter Fifteen

Tony

I WAKE IN THE morning with a dead arm and a stiff neck.

Flora lay against me, crying for an hour before she finally settled enough to fall back asleep. When I tried to move her back to the bed, she stirred, and the low sad sound that fell from her mouth stopped me from trying to move again.

Finally, I reclined us in the chair, and she slept fitfully for the rest of the night.

I manage to deposit her back onto the bed, and by the time I get myself cleaned up and dressed for the day, I exit the bathroom to find her lying there with her eyes open, staring at the ceiling. I stop beside the bed and poke her foot until she looks at me.

"You gonna get up, or you gonna lay there all day?"

She says nothing, so I flip the blanket back and grab her ankle, pulling her down the bed until she squeaks and then laughs. She wriggles around until she's sitting on the side of the bed, wearing what appears to be some small adult clothes that are obviously way too big for her tiny frame.

"Do you need the bathroom?" I ask softly, unsure of the morning routine of any child, never mind a little girl.

She shakes her head, so I hold my hand out to her, and she takes it without hesitation, and then we exit the room and make our way down the hallway toward the kitchen.

Voices float from the room, but as soon as we enter, everyone stops speaking, and they all stare at us. Flora releases my hand and steps behind me, peering around my leg cautiously as she takes in the group standing before us.

Nettie and Aggie both come around and walk over, then they take turns speaking to her until she slowly comes out from behind me and stands next to me, once again gripping my hand.

"How is she?" Aggie asks as she straightens, her eyes still on the little girl.

"A little touch and go," I say, waving a hand dismissively. "But no problem. I got it covered."

Nettie also stands, placing a hand on Flora's head as she gives me a speculative look. "No problem, huh?"

I ignore her, instead asking, "Where are her clothes? These makeshift ones aren't gonna work with her up and walking around."

"I burned them," Aggie says. "One of the men has girls around her age, so he called his wife to bring her some stuff. She should be here soon."

Jayme walks over and stands next to Aggie, eyeing me expectantly, obviously intent on an introduction. I nudge Flora, and when she looks up at me, I nod toward Jayme and say, "Princess, this is your Uncle Jayme. He's kind of an asshole, but he's alright. Most of the time—"

"Tony!" Nettie interrupts, her tone chiding. "Watch your language."

"My language?" I say in annoyance. I turn back to Flora and ask, "Princess, do you have a problem with my language?"

Flora shakes her head in response, and I give Nettie a superior look as I reply, "I think it's safe to say that my language is the least of our problems right now. But I'll keep that in mind."

Nettie glares at me, but Jayme interrupts any further response she may have as he says, "Hello, Flora. How are you this morning?"

Flora stares at him curiously, her brown eyes flitting back to me questioningly. I lift my shoulder in response. She looks back at Jayme as if she's waiting for him to continue, so he does. "I know that's a silly question. But I hope you know we're all here to help you."

He pauses, swallowing visibly, his eyes glancing up to mine before focusing once again on Flora. "I don't know exactly what you've been through, but when I was young, I had something bad happen to me, too. So, I understand, and if you ever wanna talk about it, I'll be right here."

Flora's face scrunches up in concentration, and she takes a step closer to Jayme, her tiny hand reaching out and patting him on the face. "You're okay?"

His features soften, and he puts his hand over hers and replies, "Yes. But do you wanna know a secret?"

She inclines her head as if she's thinking about it and then smiles as she nods, and he continues, "Tony is the one who saved me."

She looks up, her startled eyes meet mine for a moment, and then she looks back at Jayme and asks, "My Tony?"

Agatha and Nettie giggle at her words, and I glare at them, which makes them laugh a little louder. Jayme joins in the laughter and nods, then straightens as he says, "Yes, Flora. Your Tony."

The girls are still having a good laugh at my expense, and I shake my head, rolling my eyes at them as I push between them to get to the food. Flora follows closely behind me, but as I step into the mix of men at the buffet, I quickly realize she's no longer right there. I pivot, and she's standing uncertainly on the outskirts, so I backtrack, scooping her up and carrying her over to the newly vacated seats at the breakfast bar. I set her on a chair and then move around to the other side and grab a plate and a glass. "What do you like?"

She stares at the vast array of food choices with wide eyes, and I take a good look at her, noting how small she is. She's not only small, but she's also almost emaciated, her neglect glaringly obvious, and my anger bubbles beneath the surface. My hand tightens on the glass, and Nettie notices, yanking it from my grasp, then pulling the plate from my other hand before shooing me away, "Go. Sit down. I got this."

Nettie piles one plate until it's overflowing with a variety of foods and then grabs a fork and knife, handing it to me across the table. Then she takes the other plate and adds a little of this and a little of that before walking around and setting it in front of Flora.

She holds the utensils out to her, and Flora takes the fork hesitantly as she looks from Nettie to me to the plate and then back again. I start inhaling my food as normal, and eventually, Flora does the same, though much more tentatively. I observe her from the corner of my eye, taking note of the foods she seems to enjoy and the ones she's not too keen on.

She tries everything on her plate but doesn't appear to consume much as she puts her fork down and pushes the plate away. Then she starts on the various drinks Nettie put in front of her, taking small sips of each one before drinking all of her milk and leaving the rest.

A few of the men work on picking up the plates and cups, and

I push away from the counter, standing and turning to Nettie and Aggie, who are standing by Flora. "So, we gonna do this Lilith thing now?"

"Lilith?" Flora whispers.

"Do you know Lilith, princess?"

"Mhmm," she says with a nod. "She tried tellin' Mama no, but Mama couldn't do it."

"Did she now?" I ask, my tone calm, even though that's not at all how I'm feeling right now. "What else happened between Lilith and your mama?"

She screws her face up in concentration as she thinks, and then she shrugs. "When Lilith and Mama was talkin', everyone got real mad."

"And then what happened, Flora?" Nettie asks.

Flora looks up at her with wide eyes and shrugs again. "Mama told me to find Tony."

Nettie and I look at each other, and she raises a brow at me as she says, "Well, I guess we better speak to Lilith and find out."

I move to walk around Nettie, and Flora jumps to attention, scrambling down from the chair as she comes over to grip my hand. Then Agatha says, "Well, I don't think this is gonna work."

Nettie adds, "Yeah, I don't know if she's ready for our whole fudge around and find out way of doing things."

"*Fudge*," I repeat. "Is this really where we're at already? Fudge?"

Flora giggles beside me, so I look down at her and ask, "Princess. Do you wanna go see Lilith?"

She grabs my hand tighter and nods enthusiastically, so I glance back up at Nettie and smirk at her. "See. It's fine."

We make our way out of the dining room and down the maze of hallways into the basement, where they hold people waiting to be questioned. Lilith is being held in a different room than the guy I almost beat to death, and I'm mostly relieved. I'm not keen on being reminded of the time I lost my cool and went off the rails.

We enter the room to find Lilith seated facing the door, appropriately shackled to a chair. She looks a little beat up but otherwise no worse for wear, and she doesn't seem too bothered about having been shackled in this room, alone, overnight.

The lights come on, and she blinks against the glare, then her eyes settle on Nettie, and her face lights up, her smile bright as she breathlessly exclaims, "Toni! Aren't you a sight for sore eyes?"

Nettie walks across the room, and when she's a few feet from Lilith, she crosses her arms over her chest and replies dryly, "Don't fucking Toni me. You've got a lot of explaining to do."

Lilith smiles almost sheepishly but bobs her head around frivolously. I walk through the doorway, Flora following close behind me, but when I turn to close the door, Flora continues further into the room, stopping in front of Lilith and patting her on the leg. Lilith turns her attention to the little girl and smiles at her fondly. "I see you found Tony like your mama said. Has he been taking good care of you?"

Flora nods, and then turns to us as she points at Lilith's restrained hands and says, "Why she got those? She won't hurt us."

Lilith laughs boisterously, obviously tickled by the little girl's words. "You never can be too careful, Flora. But I appreciate that."

Aggie makes a disgusted sound from behind me, then walks over to Lilith with the keys to the cuffs jingling at her side. She leans over the older woman and unlocks her hands and ankles, then steps back, giving her a cool look. "Don't fucking try anything."

Lilith waves her hand and tsks. "Try what exactly? Regardless of where I've been or what I've been up to, I protect my family. That will never change."

"You protect your family by literally destroying them by faking your own death?" I spit.

Lilith blanches slightly, a grimace dulling her otherwise bright expression. She recovers quickly and says, "That's fair. I can see how you might be salty about that, but in my defense, for a little while there, I was dead. But then I didn't die-die, if you know what I mean."

"No, I don't know what you fucking mean!" Nettie exclaims, her hands fisted by her side in frustration as she stomps her foot. "No sane person is ever dead, but then not dead-dead. Either you're dead, or you're not dead."

"I can see that this is going to take you a moment to get over," Lilith says with a sigh. "But it would be best if you could get over it while we try to figure out how we're going to stop people from coming after Flora."

"Over my dead body is the only way they'll manage to get to her," I snarl.

"You won't stop them from trying," Lilith replies. "With Carolina dead—"

"Carolina is not dead," I interrupt angrily. "There's no way they'd have let Flora go if they planned on killing Carolina. That doesn't make sense."

Lilith thinks over my words for a moment and then nods. "You may be right, but Flora's the heir to an empire. If Carolina is out of the way, Flora is in line to inherit the entire enterprise, so we may as well plan for the worst-case scenario."

"You left her behind," I spit out, while looking down at her. "You let them fucking take her. Why?"

Lilith narrows her eyes at me. "I tried to get her to reconsider making a deal with those snakes. I tried to get her to come with me. She wouldn't do anything to risk Flora."

I give her an assessing look as Flora climbs up and sits in Lilith's lap, playing with her hair familiarly. It's obvious the little girl knows her, that she's comfortable with her, so I ask, "What were you even doing there?"

"Looking for Flora," she says. "I'd only been in there for a few days when you all showed up and fucked it all up."

"Fucked it all up?" Nettie snarls. "You're supposed to be fucking dead. We didn't know we had any other options to get her. Do you think that if any of us had had one inkling of what was going on that we would've jeopardized your mission? That we would've jeopardized Carolina by sending her in there?"

Lilith expression becomes pinched, and she sighs. "Well, there wasn't really a way for me to brief you on the situation," she says, then chuckles as she says, "Kinda difficult for a dead woman to speak."

"Maybe if you'd had the common courtesy to not fucking die, that wouldn't have been an issue," Aggie replies from behind me, her tone pained yet annoyed. "I'm still waiting for you to tell us why you thought that was necessary."

"Because with me around, you would always have a target on your back. Since everyone thought I was dead, it was easier to stay that way. And I figured I could accomplish more being deep underground than I could walking around as normal."

"Who knew about this?" I ask, "Surely, you didn't manage to pull this off all on your own."

She gives me a bored look, and then says dryly, "Don't underestimate me, fuckface. You know I'm not gonna answer that."

"Have you been pulling the strings behind the scenes with The Dead?" Nettie asks, concern showing on her face. "Was Mickey pretending he had everything under control, and it was you handling everything all along?"

Regret passes over Lilith's face, and she looks at the floor briefly before meeting Nettie's eyes. "Mickey doesn't know. He can't keep a secret for shit."

Nettie and I look at each other, then we both say, "Fucking Matt."

Lilith laughs cheerfully. "Oh, don't be like that. Matt's a doll."

"Did you tell him the cat was gonna be out of the bag? Because, conveniently, the fucker's not answering his phone or calling anyone back."

"I haven't spoken to him recently. He might answer me, but if his phone is turned off, I assume he's probably working."

"Matt and his fucking *job*," I snarl. "What a joke."

"I don't know why you get so angry about Matt's day job," Lilith says. "No point in denying a man his dream job."

"He's a fucking criminal."

Lilith scoffs, her hand waving around as she replies, "Oh, pish-posh. So, the man fights crime with a badge, and then drops the badge to fight crime where the law can't reach. Personally, I think it's perfect."

"She has a point, Tony," Nettie pipes in. "He basically has access to the best of both worlds. He uses his above-board contacts to dig up whatever information he possibly can, and then scrubs the bottom of the barrel to see what's missing. No stone left unturned."

"You know what," I say snippily. "I don't care right now. As soon as I see that lying motherfucker, I'm gonna kick the shit out of him. He let you mourn your mother for months. He watched you cry for months. That's unforgivable."

Lilith rolls her eyes at me obnoxiously, then sputters, "Oh, for the love of fuck, Tony. Calm down. You're being very dramatic."

"Dramatic? I'm being fucking dramatic?" I look at Nettie, and then at Agatha, and then back at Nettie and ask exasperatedly, "Am I being dramatic? Do you not fucking care that Matt sat back and let y'all mourn your mother's traumatic death for months when he could've told you she was alive?"

The two women look at each other for a moment, and then turn to me, and Aggie speaks first. "I agree with Lilith that it's likely a lot more complicated than that. Obviously, if I view it from a purely emotional perspective, it's shitty. But I also don't have any great attachment to the woman having never really spent any time with her, so I don't have much of an opinion either way."

Then Nettie adds, "Aggie's right. Emotionally speaking, it's fucking shitty, but we know we can't look at anything from a purely emotional perspective. If nothing else, we know Matt, and if he had any way that he could have spared me the pain of losing her, I believe he would have. Likely the only reason he kept it from you and Dare is because he didn't trust either of you to keep your fucking mouth shut, and, frankly, he's not wrong there."

And now I'm offended that she's insinuating that I can't keep a fucking secret. "Are you fucking serious right now? I'm not trustworthy?"

"You are obviously exceptionally trustworthy; however, sometimes you tend to be a bit of a hothead and shit falls out of your mouth because you're mad. And you would've been really fucking mad about this."

Aggie nods in agreement. "Super fucking mad. You totally would've taken it personally, and whenever Tony Andersen takes something personally, fucking shit happens."

I'm still gaping at them, so I snap my mouth shut and grind my teeth together in annoyance. I want to argue further, but the basis of their argument is sound. I can be a fucking hothead. And they're also correct in the fact that Matt would've made the all-around best decision instead of the knee-jerk-reaction decision.

Sometimes, I fucking hate that guy.

I turn back to Lilith and ask, "So, Matt is the only one who was in on this? The two of you managed to pull off the biggest fake out ever?"

Lilith smiles broadly and nods. "In all honesty, it was mostly Matt. He's a fucking genius. If you ever wanna disappear, he's your man."

I groan loudly, turning away from them and staring at the ceiling as I work on getting control of my urge to punch something. There's a tug on my pant leg, and I look down to see Flora beside me, looking up at me expectantly. I turn toward her and ask, "What do you want?"

She says nothing as she pulls on my shirt with one hand and raises the other one in the air. Then Aggie says, "She wants you to pick her up, dumbass."

I reach down and scoop her up, glaring at Aggie as I mutter, "Yeah, I know that."

But of course, I didn't fucking know that. I don't know the first thing about kids. I was barely around kids when I was a kid, and now, this little sprite is wrapped around me like a spider monkey, and I've got this heavy fucking feeling in my chest, and I want to stab myself in the eyeball.

I'm muttering to myself, and the entire room has fallen silent. I glance around and see they're all watching me. "What? Why are you looking at me like that?"

They all shake their head, and they all say a variation of, "No reason. Nothing."

Flora cuddles closer, her face pressed against my neck, and my urge to run screaming from the building increases tenfold. So, I turn to Lilith and say, "Let's cut to the chase here. You believe Carolina is dead, right?" She nods, and Flora stiffens in my arms. I rub her back and press my face against the side of hers and whisper, "Don't listen to her, princess. She doesn't know what she's talking about."

I turn back to the three woman and say, "We'll go with that theory.

Which means the best way for me to hunt down whoever is responsible is for me to start knocking off the people on those lists she gave me, one by one. So, that's what I'm gonna do. You all have two jobs right now: one, watch Flora—you do not let her out of your sight."

I turn to leave the room, and Nettie yells from behind me, "What about the second thing, asshole?"

I pause in the doorway, looking at her over my shoulder as I reply, "Stay the fuck out of my way."

And then I exit the room with Flora in my arms, slamming the door behind me.

Chapter Sixteen

Tony

CARRYING FLORA, I LEAVE the basement and return to the main living area where Anton's man's wife, Anya, has come with clothing for Flora. She also brought their two children, which is helpful, so once Flora warms up to them, I leave her in their capable hands and head out to the main work area.

I grab my extra special phone and shoot off a message to Matt, letting him know that if he isn't already on a fucking plane to Russia, he better be on the next one. He replies with a middle finger emoji, which I take as an answer enough that it's one or the other.

I find the file Matt sent me with the information he found on Carolina's lists, and then I make myself a game plan on how I want to handle the situation. I still don't believe Carolina is dead, but I also know that time is of the essence, and the more time that goes by, the more likely it is she's going to be dead.

Dare and Anton join me, and we go over the rough outline of my plan, which is me hunting all these people down and hurting them until they're dead.

Dare and Anton feel there's a better way for me to manage the list, given I'm just one person and the lists are extensive and span continents. I'm still convinced I can get to them all within a week, but Dare isn't having it, and I hate to admit that his argument is sound.

"For fuck sake, Tony," Dare sputters. "If we divide and conquer, we could have it all done in thirty-six hours."

"How about we compromise?" Anton adds. "You take the people on her personal list who are closer to this area. Dare, a couple of the guys and I will divvy up the others and get it handled."

I'm not saying they don't have a valid argument; I'm saying I want to kill them all myself. Which I know is completely ludicrous, given time is not on our side, but I'm definitely having a difficult time shaking the urge for murder time.

They're both standing there, looking at me expectantly. Finally, I sigh and say through my gritted teeth, "Fine. But I get to choose mine."

They both nod in agreement, and Dare says, "I'll forward the US list to Mickey, let him take care of it."

"Should we have Matt do it?" Anton asks.

Dare shakes his head, glancing at his watch as he replies, "No. I figure Matt will be here within the next hour to three hours."

"How do you figure?"

"I'm sure he dropped everything as soon as he heard the ruse was up," Darius says. "I wouldn't be surprised if—"

Like clockwork, Anton's phone pings. He reads the message and laughs. "Apparently, we have an incoming helicopter sited a few miles out."

"That fucking show off."

"I wish we had time to fuck with him," Dare says as he rubs his hands together.

"Am I allowed to hit him at least once?" I ask petulantly.

"I think once is definitely called for."

We don't have to wait long before Matt is escorted into the room. He greets Anton enthusiastically, then walks over and gives Dare his normal bro-hug before turning to me. He puts his hands in his pockets and says, "Get it over with."

"I don't know what you're talking about," I say calmly, walking over to him with my hand extended. He takes my hand rather gingerly, suspicion all over his face as I lean forward to give him the same bro-hug he gave Dare. But then, as soon as he leans into me, I change tactics and smash my forehead right into his face.

Matt recoils, his hands coming up to his already bleeding nose as he yells, "Mother fuck, Tony. Goddamn it, you're an asshole."

"Maybe so, but you're lucky that's all you're getting."

Matt glares at me as he takes the towel Anton offers him and presses it against his bleeding nose. "You could've at least given me time to explain before going for blood?"

I raise my shoulder dismissively. "I'm not sure if you unraveling your tangled web is going to help your case. But you can try."

Matt sits down heavily in a chair, leaning his head back with the towel still pressed against his nose as he says, "Ask whatever you want."

"Did you know Lilith was still alive when we met with Mickey that day?"

"Nope," he says. "I left her body with a known contact of mine, who brought her to a morgue he was connected with in the city. It wasn't until the next day I got a scrambled call from someone telling me she wasn't dead-dead and asking if I wanted them to fix that."

"She wasn't dead-dead? What the fuck?"

"Yeah, you're telling me," Matt says with a laugh. "So, I went down there, and sure enough, she still looked mostly dead, but she had a pulse, and they were asking me if I wanted them to make her dead-dead or if we're gonna transfer her somewhere else to make her less dead—"

Dare interrupts, "Why didn't you call anyone?"

"Call and say what? At this point, everyone had already accepted that she was gone. Should I have gotten everyone's hopes up only to possibly have to crush them again? I couldn't do that."

I have to acknowledge the truth behind that statement. Getting Antoinette's hopes up only to have to crush her again would've been a form of cruel and unusual punishment. Still, I ask, "And once you realized she was going to live, why not say anything then?"

"We thought about it," Matt says with a grimace. "But then we realized she could do a lot more good being dead. Because the only person they may fear more than Lilith Ferro would be the ghost of Lilith Ferro."

Anton eyes widen, and then he laughs, his hands slapping the tops of his thighs as he exclaims, "Oh, shit. All that ghost talk was her?"

Dare and I look at each other, and then look at Anton curiously before I ask, "What was her? There hasn't been any ghost activity in New York that I'm aware of."

"No, this was Russia and parts of Europe, as far as I know," Anton replies. "I know some of it was us, but the amount of chatter going through was far more than we could take credit for."

"Yeah," Matt says. "We were on a roll there for a little while. But then we caught wind of Tony snatching Carolina and figured we better fast-track retrieving Flora before her cover was blown. Obviously, that didn't work."

"You guys knew where Flora was this entire fucking time?" I growl, my fists clenching.

He shakes his head. "No, we'd just started closing in on her location at that point. Lilith went in there under the guise of being a human-trafficking mercenary in the hopes she'd be able to locate whoever's in charge of the whole operation while also getting close to Flora to get her out. She'd only been in there for a few days when you guys showed up. Initially, she was going to vanish and allow you to come in, but then she overheard them trying to arrange for Carolina to come alone. She figured something stupid was gonna happen, so she stuck around."

"And Mickey doesn't know?" Dare asks.

"No, he doesn't know. And you're not gonna fucking tell him either. That's between Lilith and him. Mickey's going about his day, taking direction from Antoinette, keeping shit in New York in line. Just let him do his job until Lilith decides what she wants to do."

"I don't like keeping this from him," I reply, my arms crossing over my chest in annoyance. "That man was fucking destroyed when Lilith died. He may as well have lost his own child."

Regret passes over Matt's features, but he shakes it off, shrugging as he murmurs, "I'm aware. But nothing's gonna change that right now."

"You're right. We have more urgent matters to take care of right now," Darius says as he walks over to Matt and hands him the lists we've been working on. "We finally talked Tony into a divide and conquer method. I'll have Antoinette notify Mickey of who he's looking for and how to handle them once he finds them. And Anton will delegate some of his people to handle the outlier destinations. Tony has his shortlist of the more criminally important subjects, and you and I can divvy up the rest—"

"What about us?" Nettie interrupts from the doorway.

We turn our attention in that direction, and all three women stand there, looking as obstinate as ever. I groan, and Darius chuckles, with

Matt and Anton quickly joining in. I shouldn't be surprised, given their tendency to always want to be part of the action, but still, I say, "You guys already have your fucking orders."

"We're not taking fucking babysitting duty, Tony," Aggie pipes in.

"Yeah," Nettie adds. "Flora has already made friends with the kids, and their mum decided they're gonna stay here for a while and help her get settled. Having a bit of childlike normalcy is the best thing for her right now."

"Fine," I relent. "I have the perfect job for you murder triplets."

Three sets of eyes light up, matching maniacal blue orbs that have the hair on the back of my neck standing up. I shake my head at their enthusiasm and then add, "Don't get too excited; you ain't gonna like it."

"But do we get to fuck around and find out?" Aggie asks.

"Stop ruining my line." Nettie giggles. "That's a yes."

I glance at Dare and Matt, who are openly laughing at my pain rather than being at all supportive. I roll my eyes at them, turning and walking out of the room, only pausing to flip them the bird from the doorway.

Chapter Seventeen

Tony

Darius isn't overly excited about the mission I've given the murder triplets.

Well, the murder twins, anyway. Mama murder is currently too conspicuous for the job, so she's going to have to run things behind the scenes. Aggie and Nettie, however, jumped right on the idea of being able to play dress up as mafia bosses.

While having women in positions of power is rare, it's not unheard of, and it didn't take much for Matt to come up with a decent background story and cover for them. And lord knows, they're insufferable enough to pull it off.

I left everyone to their own devices and went on with my merry business in a very particular order. I learned long ago that the best way to get away with something is to begin the farthest distance from the heart of the problem as you can and work your way back.

This is how I ended up with a crybaby as my first mark, out in the middle of fucking nowhere, which was annoying and not at all fun. I tend to take these types out more quickly because the crying gets under my skin, and historically, the crybabies don't know anything, anyway.

My second mark was a blowhard. Those types are the most fun because no matter what you do to them, they continue to talk shit. And while they're talking shit, they're actually giving you information without even knowing about it.

My third mark had a wife who was all too happy to let me in. By then, I didn't really give a fuck who knew I was coming, so once I got done with her piece of shit husband, I didn't bother killing her. She actually thanked me on my way out, which was a little peculiar, but given his reputation, not at all surprising.

Now, here I am at stop number four, leaning against the door jam in the bedroom, watching this fucking asshole humping a woman who's doing her best dead fish impression. And from listening to them, I get the impression that's what he's going for, and the idea makes my skin crawl.

This one is a two-for-one deal because both their names are on that list, and at this point, it seems likely they'll know where Carolina might be. I'm greatly looking forward to our conversation.

I wait for him to finish up, relieved that he didn't bother undressing, and he has his already flaccid dick put away before he turns to face me. He freezes in place, his eyes glancing toward the bedside table, so I say, "Don't bother."

His jaw clenches, then he gives me an obstinate look and spits out, "You're unarmed and outnumbered."

I give him a half-smile and lift my shoulder nonchalantly. "Go ahead," I say flatly. "Try me."

The woman is still lying face down across the side of the bed, un-moving, but I see from the rise and fall of her back that she's breathing. "Get her up, get her dressed, and then restrain her."

"Who the fuck are you?"

"Doesn't really fucking matter."

The woman on the bed stirs, pushing herself up with her hands pressed against the mattress then turning to face me as she says, "An American."

"How perceptive of you," I respond sarcastically. "Cover yourself."

"What if I don't want to?"

"I'll cut off your tits before I kill you. Your choice."

She frowns, obviously thinking over my words for a moment before taking a step toward the dresser. I raise a hand up to stop her. "Nope. You've got clothes on the floor. Use them."

She gives me a dirty look, but does as I say, and soon, she's standing there fully clothed. I toss some zip ties onto the floor at the man's feet. "Get her face down on the floor, wrists and ankles, then secure them together."

I've heard stories about these two, and it's already obvious that the woman is far more of a problem than the man. I don't see this very often, but in the rare cases that I do, you have to either restrain her first or kill her outright because the last thing you want is to have her at your back.

He completes the tasks to my specifications, then opens his mouth as if he's going to say something to me, but I interrupt, "You, stand over there in that fucking corner and don't move."

Once again, he does as I ask, and then I walk into the room and double-check to make sure the woman is restrained properly. She doesn't seem to be in any kind of distress, which isn't surprising, given what I know about her.

I point to the chair in the corner and say, "Have a seat."

He sits gingerly as I walk over to him and remains calm as I zip tie him to the chair. But then he spits out, "I don't know who the fuck you think you are, but you're gonna be a dead man."

I laugh as I reply, "That's where you're wrong, my man. You're gonna tell me what I wanna know, and then I'm gonna kill you."

"I won't tell you shit," the man says belligerently. "You may as well kill me and get it over with."

I roll my eyes, already mentally exhausted, and we haven't even gotten started. "You already know how this is gonna go. Either you tell me easy, or you tell me hard. But either way, you're gonna fucking tell me."

"Who are you?" the woman asks from her position on the floor. "What do you want? What did we do to you?"

"Here's the thing," I say calmly, walking over and standing over her. "Sometimes, when you do wrong to one person, you're actually doing wrong to someone else. And this is one of those situations."

"You're gonna have to be more specific," she replies.

I kneel, squeezing her face between my thumb and fingers and twisting her head awkwardly until she whimpers, and a bit of that anticipatory delight in her eyes dulls. "I hope you're not thinking that I'll go easy on you because you're a fucking woman. I'll take you apart piece by piece the same as any fucking man. You think you like pain, but you're gonna find out you don't even know the beginning of pain."

That light goes out, replaced by nervousness, and I punctuate my statement by showing her my teeth, shoving her face away from me like the trash she is.

I walk back over the man strapped to the chair and ask, "Surely, you remember Vincent."

His eyes widen, his arrogant demeanor instantly changing, but he says nothing, so I persist. "Dimitri? I hear you're pretty good pals with those guys."

He shakes his head, his shoulders lifting as he says, "No one was friends with Vincent and Dimitri. Everyone was their fucking slave until they had no use for you. Their death was something to rejoice over."

"So, you're telling me you didn't revel in the parties they threw, that the two of you didn't enjoy being allowed to take part in such lechery? That you didn't take the opportunity to use and abuse and discard human beings indiscriminately and without question or consequence?"

Excitement flashes across his face, quickly covered by unease as he realizes what I'm talking about. Still, he says nothing, so I continue, "I mean, I've heard stories where Vincent would put his own wife out on the block for the taking. From what I understand, she was a particular favorite of yours."

He swallows visibly, sweat beading on his forehead, no longer looking me in the eye as he squirms in his chair. Nervous energy radiates off him as he says quietly, "I don't know where you're getting your information, but it's wrong."

"Oh, really," I say as I step closer to him and then lean forward until I'm looking him right in the face. "You don't think maybe she would remember correctly? You're saying that her eyewitness account of her own treatment is incorrect?"

His eyes widen further, and he shakes his head. "We didn't do shit to her. From what we saw that little bitch liked it all."

I don't let him speak any further. I pull back slightly and then drive my forehead into his nose, and he shouts in pain as blood spatters everywhere. Then I grind out, "Don't you fucking talk about her, you spineless piece of shit."

The woman yells from the other side of the room, "Don't you fucking touch him!"

I walk back over to her and say, "Or what? If y'all would just answer my question, this would be a lot easier."

"Maybe try being more specific in your questioning, asshole."

"Are you the fucking sadist everyone makes you out to be?"

"I'm that and more, baby." She raises her chin at me defiantly, and I resist the urge to wipe the look off her face with my boot. If this bitch is even half as evil as she's been made out to be, she deserves far worse than a boot to the face. But still, I'm not naturally programmed to beat on women, so I'll put it off until it's the last resort. "You seem to think you're untouchable, that since you enjoy pain, nothing can hurt you. But let me educate you on something, asshole: dead is dead, and there isn't anyone out there who doesn't flinch when they see it coming down the pipeline."

She stares up at me, the haughtiness on her features fading as realization dawns. Still, she raises her chin at me and replies, "Good luck. I don't give a fuck about anyone or anything, me included. So, kill me slow or kill me fast, but just kill me already."

"Well, we will see about that, won't we?"

I stand and look around, asking, "Where is that cute little dog of yours? Muffin or Croissant, or what's her name?"

She gasps, "You wouldn't."

"I guess there's only one way to find out."

She's silent for a few moments and then whispers, "You're a monster."

I laugh outright at this, the fact that this lunatic is calling me a monster is completely fucking asinine. I mean, I wouldn't actually hurt her fucking dog, but she doesn't know that, and I'm hoping she won't call my bluff and will instead give me some damn answers. "I don't think we wanna play a game of who's the biggest monster in this room. But we can if you'd like."

She stares up at me, indecision on her face as she searches my eyes for the lie, but she remains quiet.

I shrug. "Have it your way, then," I yell and move to the door, opening it and calling again, "Muffin! Here, baby!"

She gasps, a sob wrenching free from her as she cries, "No, please!"

I shut the door, stepping back and crouching beside her, leveling her with my most serious face. She stares back at me, her jaw clenched as she contemplates her choices, but finally, she sighs and says, "Word came up a few days ago that Vincent's widow is gonna be up on the block again on the weekend. Her and her daughter."

My eyes narrow. "What do you mean her daughter? They don't have her daughter."

"I don't know who they did or didn't have at the time, but that's what they said. And that information has not changed as far as I know. That will both be there on the weekend as advertised."

I pull out my phone and send out the code to be on high alert, and then look back at the man in the chair and ask, "Anything else you wanna add?"

He shakes his head, spitting blood onto the floor and swallowing before replying, "That's it. You'll find all the relevant information on the phone in the bedside table over there."

I walk over to where he's pointing and yank open the drawer, pulling the phone from it and then walking it over to him so I can use his finger to wake the main screen. I scroll through it, taking screen-shots of what I need and forwarding them to my burner phone before resetting his security features so I can easily attain access without him. I stuff the phone into my back pocket, then head back across the room.

The man speaks up as I'm walking away, "Surely you'll let a dead man have a last wish, right?"

I turn back toward him, smiling as if I'm considering it, but then the smile falls from my face as I bring my arm around and shoot him in the face—once, twice, then a third time for luck.

He falls forward, slumping over in the chair, and the woman on the floor makes a pained noise as I approach her. I stop beside her, and there's no hesitation as I point my gun at her and squeeze the trigger until it clicks—empty.

They're both lucky I'm on a deadline.

I exit the bedroom, shutting the door behind me, and make my way down the hallway toward the stairs. A whine behind me stops my forward momentum, and I turn around, facing two sets of curious eyes staring back at me. "Two fucking dogs," I mutter, sighing as I turn and continue my descent to the first floor.

Toenails tap behind me, and I sigh again as I reach the main foyer and stop with my hand extended toward the handle.

They're watching me.

Slowly, I turn to face them, and this time, they're quite close. They walk over to me and then sit nicely at my feet, as if they're waiting for me to give them instructions. "For fuck sake," I say sternly. "I don't have time for you two shitheads right now."

The bigger one barely manages to control the tail wags, or lack thereof, and the smaller one stares at me calmly, obviously waiting for me to do something.

"Fucking hell," I groan, stomping as I turn back to the door and yank it open. I stand back, allowing the two mutts to proceed me out into the night, then I follow them, cursing all the way.

Chapter Eighteen

Tony

ANTON IS DISPLEASED WITH the dog situation. Of course, I completely ignore him and send a couple of his men off to get some dog supplies while I go in search of Flora.

I end up in the living quarters where a room has already been remodeled into a playroom. She's deeply immersed in a board game, but as soon as she sees me, her eyes light up. She squeals my name as she jumps up, her little legs racing toward me, and that odd warmth in my chest that was so uncomfortable before doesn't feel quite as uncomfortable as she leaps up into my arms. I catch her, pulling her in close as she seems to hug me with her entire body and I laugh "Well, hey there, princess. How's it going?"

She mutters into the side of my neck, and it sounds like she's saying she missed me, so I pat her on the back, and give her a squeeze, suddenly incapable of speech. She pulls back, her little hands coming up to pat me on my cheeks, and she smiles at me and says, "You stay."

I laugh again, jostling her around until she giggles, and then I place her on her feet. "I have a surprise for you."

I walk over to the door I had closed behind me when I came into the room, and sure enough, the two mutts are sitting there waiting for me. I open the door further, motioning them inside, and the larger dog makes a beeline for the group of children, walking through their board game excitedly. They all squeal in delight, their board game completely forgotten as they fawn all over the wiggling mutts, and I pat myself on the back for a job well done.

Nettie enters the room, walking over to stand beside me as she says, "Dare I ask where you acquired these two obviously well-pedigreed animals?"

"Their previous owners ran into some issues and could no longer take care of them."

"Issues, huh?" she says dryly. "But why take them with you?"

I say nothing in response because the answer to that question is obvious, and we stand there in silence, watching the children and dogs play. Finally, I say, "That big dog seems to like kids."

Nettie reaches a hand down as the big dog comes over to sniff her. "Boxers are exceptional family dogs," she says. "They're the type of breed that doesn't understand they're not human. Obviously, there are exceptions, but for the most part, they're mostly bombproof."

The boxer flops over on the floor, lying there on its side, panting, and Flora crawls over and lies down with her head on the dog's shoulder. I smile at the scene, patting myself on the back again for my genius plan as Nettie stares at me intently. I wait a few moments, but she continues to stare, so I ask, "What? Why are you looking at me like that?"

She lifts a shoulder nonchalantly and inclines her head as she replies, "Oh, nothing. You're a really nice guy, Tony."

I wince, my mouth turning down in distaste as I lift my hand and press a finger against her lips. "Keep it down, Net. I have a reputation to protect."

She smiles, and I drop my hand and go back to watching the kids, and after a few moments, Dare and Anton join us. Anton shakes his head at the scene in front of him, but he's also smiling as he says, "I had a boxer dog when I was growing up. He was the greatest fucking dog."

"Your man get the stuff?"

"Yes," Anton replies. "They came back with enough stuff for like ten dogs."

I walk over to where Flora is still lying with the dog and kneel down. "I gotta go get some work done, princess. You name these mutts, and I'll see you later for supper, okay?"

She smiles up at me and nods, but then she raises her hands up expectantly, and I raise my brows at her and say, "You can get up." She shakes her head and raises her hands with more emphasis, so I relent and kneel closer to her so she can hug me. A big wet tongue hits me on the side of the face, and I jerk back. "Damn it, dog. Cut it out."

Flora giggles, and when I look over at the big dog now watching me, I swear she's smiling at me. I shake my head and scowl, and the dog huffs and flops back down as I turn and head out of the room.

Nettie and Anton follow me, and we walk back down to the main work area where we find Dare and Matt looking over some papers, and Dare looks over at me and asks, "You get that listed sorted?"

"Sure did."

Dare smiles a bit dreamily. "Did you get to have any extra fun with any of them?"

I shake my head, a bit let down, but knowing I did the right thing by cleaning up quickly. "Wasn't time for any of that, so most of them got lucky."

"Pity." Dare sighs.

Nettie rolls her eyes and huffs, poking him in the side as she says to me, "Never mind him, Tony. He's been out of the bloodshed too long."

"Where's Aggie and Lilith?" I ask, my gaze scanning the room in search of them.

"They went with Erik to scope out the situation for tonight. That information you sent me seems to be legit, but we don't want to go in completely blind, so they decided to do a little last-minute recon. I said we'd meet them there later this evening for the job," Dare answers, his eyes still on the table where blueprints are strung out.

"Is this the facility where she's being held?"

"Yes," Matt replies, picking up a picture from the bottom of the pile and handing it to me. It looks swanky from the outside, but from what I understand, there are some sub-levels that aren't too fancy."

"So, what you're saying is that we've traded warehouses for basement dungeons?"

Matt snorts and nods. "Pretty much."

Dare sighs and shakes his head. Finally, he says, "Are you ready to go get your girl back?"

"She's not my fucking girl."

"Just keep fucking telling yourself that, buddy," he snarks. "Maybe if you say it loud enough, you'll believe it yourself."

"It's not that simple. You know how I feel about liars," I mutter.

"Yes, I do. But I also know that sometimes, lies aren't as simple as that. Especially when you're put into difficult situations to protect someone else. I see how you are with that little girl. What wouldn't you do to protect her?"

I think for a moment, and my jaw clenches, my hands tightening into fists, as I consider my answer to his question. Finally, I say, "That's not a fair question. There isn't anything I wouldn't do to protect children. Her or any of them. You know that."

"Exactly," Darius says evenly. "So, you can only imagine how that feeling intensifies when that child is your own flesh and blood. So sure, she went into a role with the intent to do harm, but then, at the end of the day, she blew her cover to protect us. She didn't have to do that."

"She lied to my fucking face, man," I snarl.

Dare frowns at me and asks, "What are you talking about?"

I go to respond, but snap my mouth shut and inhale deeply through my nose. He's looking at me expectantly, waiting for me to respond, and I know I've already said too much to avoid the conversation. "I went to see her. Way back when you and Aggie duped Nettie into going to that warehouse so you could talk to her. While you were occupied, I went to see Carolina."

Dare's eyes widen in surprise. "Why? Why would you do that?"

"Because I knew things didn't add up. Her trail was too clean. There was something off about the entire situation, so I wanted to ask her some questions."

He turns to face me, leaning his back against the bench, his arms coming up and crossing over his chest. "And what did you learn?"

"Well, nothing," I bark. "She lied to my fucking face. Even after I told her I would help her. She still lied. She lied and then kept going up to a point where she got some of our people dead. It's fucking unforgivable."

"We all lie, Tony," Dare says. He pauses for a moment, his eyes falling on Matt and Nettie, who are deep in conversation across the room. Then he turns his gaze back to me and continues, "If you don't stop drinking the poison, at some point, you're the one who will suffer. Forgiving people isn't a weakness. Antoinette lied to me, and if I hadn't found out, if I hadn't been able to wrangle the situation and force her confession, who knows what would've happened? Maybe even if she had wanted to save me, she wouldn't have been able to anymore. But that's not what happened. And I forgave her. Do you think I shouldn't have?"

"That's not the same fucking thing."

Dare's hands come up as he asks, "How is it not the same thing? She came into my life with a specific task to take me down. Just like Carolina was supposed to take me down. I guess I'm fortunate that in both cases, they saw something in me that changed their mind. Otherwise, I would not be standing here in front of you right now. We both know that depending on who's doing the looking, I'm the bad guy, and in a lot of scenarios from a lot of different perspectives, I deserve to be dead."

I open my mouth to reply but then snap it shut again as I think over my response. I know he's right in the sense that not all lies are condemning. Any lie that Carolina told me to maintain her cover story was all to protect the little girl whom I'm now protecting. She's not even my own flesh and blood, and there isn't anything I wouldn't do to keep her safe.

"What aren't you telling me?" Dare interrupts my train of thought, his eyes intent on my face, and I do my best not to squirm. "There's obviously more to this than one passing conversation, so spit it out."

"It doesn't matter," I reply with a shrug.

Dare crosses his arms over his chest and lifts a brow at me as he replies, "Let me guess. You actually went to see her because you felt the connection to her before you ever even had any interaction with her. She brushed by you in the hotel lobby. A passing glance while you stood in the audience on the red carpet. The sound of her voice during an overheard conversation that prickled your skin, even though she wasn't even speaking to you. The calming familiarity that you yearned for, even while your brain did its best to keep it at bay.

"And then, when that ache in your chest reached a fever pitch, where you could no longer ignore it, you sought her out, intent on squashing it once and for all. But instead, when you stood in her presence, even knowing the words coming out of her mouth were likely lies, that everything about the situation screamed at you to run for your very life, you remained rooted to the spot because something about her calls to you.

"So, you say fuck it, throw caution to the wind, and you give in to the carnal urges and allow her to wrap herself around you to the point she is the air you breathe. And even though you felt at the time that you could not possibly be any more wrapped up in her, once you've had her, once you've established that intimate connection, you realize the error of your ways because the mere idea of existing in the world where she is not beside you is so stifling that you feel you may never breathe again."

My breath is now trapped in my lungs, every word coming from his mouth a hammer to my psyche. Darius has always been incredibly observant, his ability to read a situation, especially a situation that includes someone he's close to, is incredible. That doesn't mean I'm going to readily admit it, but I don't have to because the look on his face tells me he already knows. "What do you want me to say, Dare?"

He chuckles knowingly and shakes his head as he replies, "Nothing. I just wanna make sure you know that you're fucked."

"How am I fucked?"

"You were fucked before you even went in search of her. You were fucked as soon as you breathed the same air she breathed. And now, if she's dead, you're fucked. If she's alive, you're just as fucked. You may as well let it go and embrace it for what it is because you will never be able to shake her. You will never rid yourself of that painful yearning to be in her presence every moment of your life."

I groan and roll my eyes at his dramatic speech, but then Nettie says from beside me, "You talking about Tony being in love with Carolina?"

And then Matt adds, "Is he finally admitting it?"

I glance at the two of them and say, "You're both traitors."

Dare speaks up, "He isn't admitting anything yet, but he doesn't need to admit it. I know what I know from my own experience, and he is deeply fucked."

"Hey, that's not very nice." Nettie glares at him, reaches out, and pushes his shoulder. "Is that how you think of me, that you're fucked?"

He laughs again and nods. "Deeply and truly fucked, baby girl. I just happen to revel in it, but I've also had quite a bit of time to get used to the idea."

"You're fucked? How about me? I'm way more fucked than you are."

He smiles at her fondly, reaching out, snagging her wrist, and pulling her close as he leans into her and whispers into her ear. She giggles, the inappropriate undertones clear as she swats at his chest and replies, "Promises, promises, baby."

"Would you two fucking cut it out," Matt says humorously. They both look at him and smile innocently, and he shakes his head, his eyes meeting mine as he says, "They never fucking stop. It's disgusting."

Nettie's hand flies out, and she sucker punches him in the gut, and Matt grins at her.

I laugh and then turn back to the table where all the papers are still spread out. "So, what's our game plan?"

Dare turns his attention back to the table and pulls a piece of paper over in front of us. "According to Antoinette and Aggie, this is the closest to the actual layout of the underground of the club. We figured Carolina is being held somewhere down here."

"So, are we going in guns blazing, or what?"

"I figure you can go in with Antoinette and Aggie and likely get access to this area. I won't risk showing my face, but since you didn't sense any recognition from the people you've already taken out, I suspect your identity remains unknown. We'll set up a perimeter and await confirmation that she's there."

"And once we confirm she's there?"

"Then you tell us if we're taking her quietly or not," he replies.

"If she's not there?"

Dare smiles, his eyes lighting up as he says, "Well then, if she's not there, that's when we start asking questions."

The wait to get to the club is excruciating. I manage to have an enjoyable supper with Flora, which meant she spent most of her time sitting on my lap and stealing my food. Nettie made jokes about what a nice change it was to be rescuing someone other than Darius from danger, earning her a dirty look from him, who then told her she'd pay for that later.

Of course, she just laughed.

By the time we make it to the club, I'm a mess. I don't think I'm appearing so on the outside, but on the inside, I'm one big ball of fucking nerves. Luckily, we make it inside without incident, and it doesn't take too much maneuvering until Aggie has someone leading us down into the dungeon.

And when I say dungeon, I'm using that word in a serious manner because this place is horrible. This place makes the dankest warehouse look like the Four Seasons.

The viewing room they bring us to is moderately fancier. It's clean, at least, though very dim, except for a spotlight on the stage. Aggie had to tell them we had very particular tastes in order to get them to bring us down here. Knowing what's coming next turns my stomach, and the fact that I have to stand down until the end has my blood pressure boiling.

Dare and I agree that regardless of whether or not Carolina is here, this place will not be standing by morning. It's disgusting enough that people choose to deal in human trafficking of adults, but those who choose to deal in innocents are beyond reprehensible. Having to sit here and stomach the constant procession of innocent lives has me daydreaming about ripping out spines. Aggie and Nettie take turns giving me a pinch every time they catch me grinding my teeth.

There's an extended pause, and I figure Carolina will be out next for the grand finale, but then the spotlight dims, and people start scrambling in and out of the room.

I watch the group of men gathered by the staging area as another man runs in and seems to deliver a message. The man who's been running the auction spits words at the newcomer, who then runs out of the room, and a bunch of people run by the closing door. I grind my teeth, itching to get up and do something.

Nettie leans closer to me and asks, "What is it?"

"Something's fucking wrong," I reply quietly. "They should've brought her out already."

Nettie and Aggie look at each other, and then Nettie turns back to me and says, "What do you want to do?"

"I gotta go find her. I can't just fucking sit here."

"Then go," Aggie replies, nodding toward the door. "We'll stay here. Act like you're going to the restroom or whatever."

"I can't leave you guys here."

Nettie and Aggie both laugh, and then Aggie says, "Are you worried about the murder twins, Tony?"

She has a point. I give her a nod, rise from my chair, and move swiftly toward the door, exiting the room and taking a left toward where I saw the people running earlier.

There's a commotion up ahead, and then a man runs up to me, pointing in the direction I came from, yelling, "You can't be back here. Get the fuck back where you were."

I don't pause my forward momentum. I run right up to him and yank his gun from the holster, shooting him in the face as I keep moving.

I stop at the end of the corridor, peeking around the corner to get a glimpse of what's in the next room. It looks like rows of cells where they must hold people. There are three men standing in the middle of the room, two of them being berated by a bulkier guy. When I hear the big guy ask them where she went, I don't dick around waiting for answers.

I take him out before I enter the room fully. The two other men stand there gaping at the man on the floor, and by the time they look up, I'm already directly in front of them. I grab one by the shoulder, digging my fingers into his pressure point until he drops to his knees, my other hand pointing my gun at his friend's head.

"Where the fuck is she?"

The guy's eyes widen, and he stutters, "H-he took her."

"Who fucking took her?"

The guy lifts his shoulders, the expression on his face pained as he replies, "The Beast. The Beast fucking took her."

"That's impossible."

The guy kneeling on the floor recovers enough to respond, "That's what I saw, too. And when the Beast shows up, you give him what he wants, or you're dead."

"How long ago?"

"A few minutes, maybe," he replies. "Ran out the back."

I take off in the direction he indicated, not even taking the time to shoot them. I run blindly, recklessly, focusing on finding her before she's in the wind again but fearing I'm already too late. So, I shout, "Carolina!"

I'm making a complete fucking spectacle of myself, and even knowing this, I can't make myself stop. I give up all semblance of the character I'm supposed to be playing and continue to yell, "Carolina! Carolina!"

I burst out the back door into the parking lot, not bothered that there might be someone standing on the other side of it, ready to cut me down. I finally understand every stupid fucking thing Darius ever did in pursuit of keeping Nettie safe.

Of course, there's no one there.

I'm standing a few feet from the closed door, trying to catch my breath as I curse a blue streak. I pull out the phone I have hidden in the waistband of my pants that their piss-poor pat down missed and send the group a message, letting them know I'm out back and Carolina is gone.

After a few moments, the back door pops open, and I whirl around, pissed at myself for leaving myself open to someone shooting me in the back. Lilith stands there, making gun fingers and says, "Bang."

I glower at her as I mutter, "Shut the fuck up, Lils. I don't need your shit right now."

"Our amateur asses didn't have anyone on this side of the building, so whatever went down back here, we missed it."

"Those two fuckers in there said the Beast took her."

She shakes her head and replies, "I can assure you, the Beast did not fucking take her, though it would be super cool if he had, and we could just go home."

I stand there for a moment, staring at the ground as the pressure in my chest becomes suffocating. Then Lilith sighs and asks, "Is it fuck around time, then?"

I toss the gun to the side and pull my leather gloves from my pocket. I slide my hands into them, taking comfort in the familiarity of their grip, and then pull out the two small blades I have hidden in my boot.

"Let's shut this motherfucker down."

Chapter Nineteen

Carolina

SO, MAYBE WHEN I agreed to swap myself for my little girl, I hadn't thought it through. Not that I regret it or anything. Knowing that Flora is safe from this nightmare is a huge relief, though I feel bad Tony didn't get more of a warning. I was relieved, even after my long absence, Flora accepted my instructions and went out and did as I asked without question.

I'm sure Tony handled it just fine, but I'm certain he's probably pissed and back to cursing my name.

Seeing Lilith alive and well threw me for a loop. She tried to get me to come with her, but I was so stunned to see her that I froze on the spot, and it didn't take long for the enemy to realize Lilith wasn't who she was pretending to be. I threw a fit as a distraction so she could get away, but in the ruckus, I got knocked silly and missed our escape.

I suppose I should be thankful to Lilith for providing a small distraction from what must appear to be my demise, as it's not every day a criminal mastermind is resurrected from death. I'm sure once the anger and shock passes, they'll be ecstatic to have her back, and I know they'll take care of Flora, and she'll never have to worry about another thing a day in her life.

That's how I can sit here in this dark cage and not worry about what my future holds. No one's looking for me; there won't be any grand rescue or anyone coming to my defense. No one's looking for the dead woman.

I'm not sure how long I've been in this room, but from what I've overheard, I go up for auction on the weekend. Maybe I'll have stronger feelings about it on the day, while it's happening, but right now, general apathy has taken hold.

I'd say there's nothing left they could do to me that would bother me, but I also know that's tempting fate. There's always something.

Running feet draw my attention to the doorway, and then I hear loud voices arguing incoherently. A lock is thrown, and the door opens as two people are shoved inside. "Open that fucking cage," a man's voice says menacingly.

The room is dark, all light coming from the open doorway, so the faces of the men are cloaked in shadows as the cage door is unlocked and a hand reaches in, gesturing for me to get out. As I move closer, I see the person at the cage door is one of the men who's been coming in and out regularly since I got here. I lean closer, noting the fear on his face, then he hisses, "Get the fuck out here. Now."

With little choice otherwise, I crawl out of the cage, and then remain kneeling on the floor as I stretch my back and get my feet beneath me so I'm squatting, unsure of what's going to happen next.

The man who appears to be in charge has moved behind me, so I still can't make out any of his features. An item is tossed on the floor in front of me, and he says, "Put this over her head."

Then I'm blind as the bag is pulled over my head and tightly secured around my neck. I'm relieved they're not gagging me, or worse yet, drugging me and moving me while I'm incapacitated, but still, my heart pounds in my chest as my hands are pulled behind me and cold metal encircles them.

A muffled bang startles me, and my arms are being pulled as that voice says in my ear, "Can you walk?"

"Yes," I choke out. I clear my throat, my voice coming out more clearly. "I can walk."

The man grasps me by my arm, helping me stand, and then pushes me out of the room down what I assume is a hallway. He's rushing now, the sounds of people rushing around behind us growing closer as I ask, "Who are you?"

He says nothing but hustles me along faster, and when I trip over my own feet, he yanks me to a stop, then his shoulder is in my gut, and he's lifting me into the air. Hanging facedown with my hands cuffed behind my back isn't at all pleasant, but I don't bother wasting time complaining and instead focus on not puking in the hood over my head.

Cold air envelops me as we exit the building, and it's a welcome change after the stifling dank of the dungeon-like basement. He picks up his pace, jostling me even more as I focus on his shoes slapping on the pavement. There's a distinct chirping of a car alarm, then the clank of a latch opening, and the next thing I know, I'm falling with a thud.

I wiggle around, attempting to take some stress off my arms, but then I end up almost face-down. The cloth bag over my head smells faintly of spearmint, and I'm grateful, considering how terrible the trunks of cars can smell, and this line of thought makes me laugh. Either that or hysteria is starting to brew.

There's no lurching or erratic driving, so it appears there's no chase happening. Officially baffled with my current situation, I eventually manage to doze off, the sound of the tires lulling me to sleep.

I'm not sure how much time has passed when I'm startled awake by the car jerking to a stop. Two sets of shoes slap on the pavement, and then the trunk pops open, and two sets of hands lift me from the trunk. They carry me a short distance and set me on my feet, where I wobble for a moment before getting my bearings.

The bag is yanked from my head, and I blink against the glare of light. It feels like an eternity before I make out shapes of unknown faces. A woman is looking me up and down, tsking and shaking her head, but she says nothing. She's slightly older, maybe around fifty and dressed to the nines, which seems a bit out of place.

The two men turn and leave the room, and then I'm standing there with the strange woman who's still looking at me. Now, she's walking around me, looking at me, and then she stops in front of me and says, "We need to get you cleaned up. We don't have a lot of time, so I'll trust you can do this quickly."

The idea of a shower excites me, and I nod my head vigorously. She points to the other side of the room, and I waste no time rushing into the compact bathroom, my clothes stripped off before I get to the shower stall.

I've been in these situations before, but those people were not nearly as kind. I breathe a sigh of relief when I get under the hot water, but I do as I'm told, not allowing myself to doddle in the shower as much as I want to.

All too soon, I turn the water off, and a towel appears in front of me, which I take without comment. I dry myself quickly, and then a smaller towel is handed through, which I use to wrap around my hair. I secure the larger towel around my body and step out of the shower, where the woman is waiting with a rack of clothing, an array of make-up, and toiletries on the counter.

I've never heard of people being dolled up before being sold and murdered, so my confusion is escalating.

She places a chair in front of the mirror, and I sit without having to be told. She removes the towel from my head, then combs out my hair, spraying it with some products before weaving it into an elegant updo. She meets my eyes in the mirror and says, "This is better for traveling. We can't have you looking a mess when you arrive."

"Where am I going?" I ask hesitantly. As expected, she doesn't answer, and I don't press the matter for fear her mood will change.

She applies makeup to my face, keeping it subtle, and then goes over to the rack of clothes and rummages through it until she finds what she's looking for. She motions for me to come closer, so I rise and walk to her. She hands me the clothing and says, "Comfortable yet stylish. You'll look perfect."

I glance at the designer label, my confusion increasing as I quickly dress and then stand there looking at her awkwardly. The smile she gives me is genuine, and she says, "Perfect."

She glances at her watch, her eyes widening and a little squeak of surprise falling from her lips as she shoos me toward the door. We hurry across the room and exit out into a sunlit parking lot where a golf cart is waiting, a man behind the wheel waiting for us.

She directs me to sit on the rear-facing seat and then climbs on next to me. The cart takes off. We move quickly through the cars until the parking lot disappears, and we drive out onto what appears to be an airport runway. Trepidation runs down my spine, and I swallow the lump in my throat at the likelihood that I'm being taken out of the country.

The cart stops in front of a fancy private jet, and the woman helps me down from the cart, leads me over to the stairs, and says, "Go on up. And congratulations."

"Excuse me," I reply with a frown. "Congratulations for what?"

She laughs and pats me on the arm before motioning for me to get moving. With no other choice, I turn and make my way up the stairs, pausing in the doorway and glancing around the extravagant space. Two men are standing in the galley, dressed in nondescript uniforms, and then one nods at me and heads into the cockpit.

The other man steps forward, a smile on his face as he says, "Welcome, ma'am. Your husband is waiting for you, so please join him, and we'll be on our way soon."

I blink, my jaw dropping open, a shiver of fear rolling over me, and I stutter, "M-m-m-y...husband?"

His smile loses a bit of its luster, but he quickly recovers and motions for me to walk further into the plane, toward the seating area.

My feet are heavy as I take a small step, but then I look back at him, and I'm sure the look I have is pleading. He smiles at me reassuringly, giving me a little push. "Go on now. No reason to be nervous."

I nod, then turn, and take another step into the plane, forcing my feet to move as I put my hands into the pockets of my comfortable-stylish pants. Pockets are comforting, allowing me to hide my shaking hands from anyone who might notice.

The man seated with his back to me appears to be reading something in front of him and has yet to give any indication that he realizes I'm behind him. I take another step, wanting to remain inconspicuous for as long as I can, but soon, I have no choice but to continue onward at a more normal speed.

When I'm only a few feet from him, a bit of the tension inside me eases as I note the dark head of hair and the obviously well-muscled arm leaning against the armrest. There's no way this is Vincent. That motherfucker is dead. Fucking long gone, dead, and buried.

I take a deep breath, shaking my head against the wave of nausea the few moments of panic brought on, and then I straighten my spine, walking with surer steps toward the man waiting for me.

I lean forward, attempting to get a good glance at him before I have to face him. He turns his head slightly, and I catch a glimpse of his profile. My breath catches in my throat, and my steps completely falter as I whisper, "Darius?"

He stands abruptly, and I see before he faces me fully that he's not Darius. But the resemblance is uncanny—haunting even. Then he smiles and steps into me, his arms coming around me as he says, "Darling. There you are."

I stiffen in his arms, shocked into silence as I try to process what the fuck is going on here. He doesn't seem to notice his embrace is one-sided; either that or he doesn't care, and after a few moments, he pulls back, the smile on his face seemingly genuine.

I stare up at him, noting each feature that is Darius, but at the same time, isn't Darius. He takes a seat in the same chair he just vacated, indicating for me to take the chair across from him, and I do so on wooden legs, sitting there with my spine ramrod straight and my hands clasped tightly on my lap.

He cocks his head at me and leans closer, resting his forearms on his thighs as he asks, "Are you okay?"

I snort, a laugh bursting out that I quickly suppress by slapping my hands over my mouth. I stay like that for a few moments, pretending I'm not on the brink of a mental breakdown but soon manage to sober, my hands falling back to my lap as I ask, "Who the fuck are you?"

He frowns at me for a moment, but then it's gone, and he's leaning back in his chair, an arm on each armrest as he brings his leg up and rests his ankle on the top of his thigh. "Declan Hughes," he replies smoothly. "At your service."

My eyes widen, and I sigh loudly as I slump back in my seat, unable to form words at this very unexpected turn of events.

In the words of Antoinette: *What the actual fuck?*

Chapter Twenty

Tony

IT'S EARLY MORNING BY the time we make it back to the compound. I go directly to the locker room showers so I won't chance running into Flora in my bloody state. By the time I'm exiting, cleaned up and dressed, Darius and Matt are standing at a workstation, their heads close together, and I can tell from their body language that Darius is pissed, and Matt is flabbergasted.

I give them a few minutes to bicker and then interrupt, "What the fuck is it this time?"

They both freeze and then look over at me wide-eyed, making me doubly suspicious. So, I wait, staring at them intently until finally, Matt says, "I got a notification when I got back that was a little concerning."

I glance at Darius and ask, "Is he referring to his gossip rag again?"

"Yes," Darius responds. "You know he has that thing set up to ping for a handful of people that he needs to keep tabs on at all times."

I roll my eyes and shake my head, then look at Matt and say, "What could your gossip rag possibly have to say that would put you all in such a lather?"

Neither of them looks at me for a moment, and I frown as I wait for one of them to say something. I can't imagine what could possibly have come across the gossip rags notifications that would have Matt confused and Darius pissed off, but then to have neither one of them want to tell me insinuates that it can't be good.

Their silence continues until, finally, I huff and walk over, yanking Matt's phone from his hand and glancing at the screen it's still stuck on. "Declan Hughes elopes in Europe."

I click on the link, raising a brow at Matt as I say, "Keeping tabs on Declan of all fucking people?"

He shrugs but has the decency to look slightly contrite as he says quietly, "Well, in this case, it seems to have worked out okay."

I look at the article now loaded on Matt's phone. I scroll down, skimming the article, when a picture goes by, so I stop and scroll back up.

I grind my teeth, my blood pressure skyrocketing again as I take in the image in front of me. I glance up at Dare, and he has a grimace on his face as he says, "There's no fucking way."

I turn my eyes onto Matt, who's shaking his head. "No fucking way, Tony. I don't know how, and I don't know why, but there's no fucking way."

I look back at the picture, scroll back up to the headline, and then back down to the picture. The pressure in my chest explodes—confusion, rage, and something untenable boiling over—and I throw the phone across the room. "Fuck!"

I pick up the closest object to me and smash that, too. Darius and

Matt scramble out of my way, snagging whatever they can grab as I lose my shit, throwing and breaking anything and everything, I can get my hands on.

I'm standing outside my own body, watching myself going ballistic as a means to show the irrational feelings I can't find words to explain. Darkness overwhelms me, anger, and violence the baseline of an explanation I'm incapable of letting loose beyond the pain radiating in my guts.

Once I've exhausted myself, I stand in the middle of the room, panting and annoyed that I've drawn a crowd. Matt and Darius are leaning back against the wall, their arms full of electronic equipment they rescued from my outburst. Anton, Erik, and a couple of other guys are standing on the other side, obviously having done the same thing. I yell out one final curse as I attempt to push down the unbearable weight that has settled back onto my chest.

Nettie approaches from the other side, presses her hand against my back, and I brace myself for her reprimand. But it doesn't come. Instead, she leans close and asks, "Feel better?"

I give her a dirty look but say nothing, though I do feel a little better. Darius and Matt are approaching, and Matt says to Darius, "See. Now you know what we went through with you."

Darius replies, "Seriously? I wasn't that bad."

This makes me laugh. "Not that bad? Jesus fucking Christ. You make my tantrum look like a baby tantrum."

Matt nods in agreement, and some of the tension eases. I take a deep breath and stand up straighter, and Nettie moves in front of me and rests her hands on my shoulders as she looks me in the eye. "Remember, Tony. Nothing is ever as it seems. There's not a chance in fucking hell that Carolina knew Declan. Shit, I barely knew anything about Declan, and he's related to the asshat I'm stuck with."

"She definitely didn't know Declan," Darius interjects as we walk over to the workstation that has been quickly cleaned up by Anton's men. Darius dumps his armload of electronics on the table, pulls out the tablet, and hands it to me. On the screen is a video of a man tied to a chair in the middle of a dark room. I press play, and the man starts to speak, "I don't know what fucking happened. I think everyone took him for the Beast, and by the time we realized our mistake, it was too late. A couple of guys were knocked around, and then they were in the wind."

I pause the video and look at Darius, who has a grim expression. "So, when did Dec change sides? The whole point of your falling out is that he didn't want to lead our life. He wanted to make music and be a good-time guy making millions of dollars."

"He always liked the whole get-famous idea," Darius replies with a sigh. "We all know he didn't choose a different path than us because he was afraid to kill bad people. He liked being the center of attention too much to take on a life career that took him out of the limelight. Of course, if he's now getting attention because people are confusing him with me, that's a problem. And taking Carolina is a huge fucking problem. The dumb shit."

"He probably did it because he thought it was funny," Matt replies.

"What a stupid fucker," I spit out. "I don't care what you say, Dare. When I see that prick, I'm gonna kick the shit out of him."

"Pretty sure we're all gonna help you."

Dare's relationship with his estranged brother is complicated on a good day. On the other side of the story, it's difficult to call it complicated because the breakdown of the relationship was based strictly on common sense and necessity. There has never been any outward animosity between them; they decided to go in separate directions, and those paths are better off not intersecting.

If anything, Declan might have some bitter feelings, given he never truly understood the life we chose to live. It was difficult for him to accept that attempting to remain in the life of the Beast could be detrimental to his health. It could quite easily cost him his life.

Darius never had any qualms about cutting out people he cared about in order to protect them until Nettie. Sure, he dabbled in that mindset a few times at the beginning of their relationship, but he wasn't able to maintain it for long and gave up.

"Are you gonna be okay with this?" I ask.

"I'll be fine," he replies dryly. "Since he made a public spectacle out of pulling one over on us, it's highly likely someone else might get to them first, though. Of all the dumb-ass shit I've seen in my entire career; this one takes the cake. After the shit he has seen, after the things we have explained to him, he goes and does this. I can't even fucking believe it."

"He must be bored," Matt says. "You'd think the life of a rockstar would be exciting enough for him."

Nettie speaks up from behind me. "Anything in particular I need to know about this guy?"

"No," Darius answers. "He's obviously still an infant. All we can do is hope that his idiocy isn't getting people killed."

Nettie squints at him but says nothing. Then she turns to me and asks, "Shall we leave Flora here?"

"This is the safest place for her, so yes," I reply. "Maybe reach out to Mickey and see if he has anyone closer to Declan's place. Even if we leave within the next hour, it's gonna be a while before we get there."

She's already pulling out her phone as she heads out of the room, and I turn to Matt as he says, "Luckily, the helicopter's still here, so we can get to the airstrip quickly. You should speak to Flora first, though, so let's say wheels up in an hour."

By the time I say my goodbyes to Flora, and we get our equipment together, it's about an hour on the nose when we're boarding the jet. I never ask where Matt comes up with these last-minute flight options, but I'm relieved we're not in the cargo hold of a C-130 because that's never comfortable.

This particular luxury jet is a fancy house with wings. There are two bedrooms with ensuite bathrooms, and then there's a third bathroom and a kitchenette. And with a cruising speed close to MACH-1, we'll be able to make up quite a bit of time in the air.

Nettie and Darius take one of the bedrooms, and when I tell Matt to take the other one, he waves me off, pointing at the table full of electronics he brought.

I shrug and close myself into the other bedroom, taking the time to strip down because if we crash, it won't matter if I'm clothed or not, and I prefer to be comfortable.

While I'm pissed Declan pulled this crazy stunt, I'm relieved to know for certain that Carolina is alive. Part of my anger with him is due to the fact he's likely put her in even more danger than she was already in, especially after basically advertising her location for any bloodthirsty criminal to see.

Pain stabs through my chest again, the thought of having to withstand her being taken from me enough to make me feel panicky. I take a few deep inhalations through my nose, exhaling through my mouth, repeating some of the annoying, positive mantras Nettie's always forcing us to do when things are feeling out of control.

I lie on my back with an arm up over my head, my hand beneath my neck, and I close my eyes with a sigh. Then, I let my mind wander.

Chapter Twenty-One

Tony

Six-ish months ago

I wasn't going to do it. I was going to sit back, mind my own fucking business, and let Dare do whatever Dare is gonna do without any concern for what kind of fuckery he might've gotten himself into.

Lilith and I talked about it and decided the best thing for us to do is to stay quiet and let Dare and Agatha do whatever they're doing while we worry about ourselves. I talked to Matt, and I talked to Nettie, and all of us agreed. It's not our fucking problem.

But here I am, staking out a location where I have no business being because I feel like I have no choice but to confront a possible enemy.

Regardless of how Carolina Tennent presents herself to the public, there's something shady going on there. Her background is too spotless, like it's been staged. Kind of like with Nettie's background back when we first started investigating her, but this one's too polished, too detailed, and there's too much public information for it to be legit.

So, when Carolina contacted Lilith and Nettie with a list of possible locations where they might be able to snag Dare, I already knew what was going to happen.

It was obviously a ruse for Dare to get Nettie alone, which meant Carolina would be alone, leaving me with a perfect opportunity to sneak in and give her a start.

I've been sitting out here for about twenty minutes, watching her movements through the poorly covered windows. No sooner do I see Nettie's text stating she's got eyes on our man than I'm exiting my vehicle and making my move.

Getting access to their apartment is a lot easier than I'm comfortable with, something I'll have to address if they continue to stay here.

I let myself in, closing the door silently behind me, and make my way slowly toward the living area where I last saw her. I remain in the shadows, leaning my shoulder against the door jam, watching her focus on some foreign show on the television. The only time I've seen her before was our brief time on the red carpet.

I won't deny that she's a striking woman and that my dick didn't immediately take a serious interest in her. More annoying than that is the sense of unease that wraps around me, an unusual feeling I can only attribute to my lack of trust in her and her position in Dare's life. There's no way she's some random actress they happened upon while looking for some limelight to draw out our enemy.

It's too convenient—too coincidental—and I won't leave here without some answers.

A few minutes go by before some subtle movement I make grabs her attention, but her response to my sudden appearance isn't the startled scream I would expect from most people. Instead, she cocks her head at me, and her mouth curls up as she says, "Tony Andersen.

To what do I owe the pleasure?"

I narrow my eyes, intrigued by how cool and collected she is while also noting the giant fucking red flag it is. I remain in the doorway, silently studying her until finally, she laughs and turns back to the television as she says, "Come in or leave. Don't be a fucking weirdo."

Now, I laugh and walk further into the room until I'm standing over her. She looks up at me, and there's no fear in her eyes, no concern, no anger—just humor glinting in her soft brown eyes.

My cock twitches in my jeans, and I have a sudden vision of grabbing her by the hair and forcing her head back so I can drive my cock down her throat.

I blink, and she's still looking up at me, her lips now curved up in a knowing smirk. I glare at her. "You got somethin' you wanna say to me?"

She laughs, her brows rising as she responds, "You're the one who showed up here uninvited. You got somethin' you wanna say to me?"

I search her eyes, torn between going easy and going hard, and for the first time in my adult life, I'm left speechless, so entirely caught up on her gaze that someone could easily sneak up on me and slit my damn throat.

Then she says, huskily, "Well, are you going to do something or just stand there all goddamn night staring at me like a crazy man?"

A low growl vibrates up from deep within my chest, and I bare my teeth at her in a humorless smile, but still, she doesn't flinch. I reach my hands out, one wrapping around the hair at the back of her head and the other wrapping around her throat, and still, she doesn't flinch. She doesn't so much as blink, barely even breathing as she remains immobile, waiting to see what I'm going to do.

And I fucking hate it.

I hate her nonresponse. I hate how she seems so calm, cool, and unaffected. I hate how she stares up at me with those soft brown eyes emitting such warmth that I want to wrap her around me and lose myself in her. I hate how she's not afraid. I hate knowing the tiny tremor in her body is from an awakening desire, and the pulse in her neck thrashing against my hand is an indication of her excitement.

I fucking hate her.

I tighten my hand on her throat, watching her face as I slowly cut off her air, and still, she doesn't flinch. I squeeze my hand in her hair, yanking her head back and leaning forward until our breath mingles with each exhalation, and still, she doesn't flinch. I run my nose along hers, painting her cheek and jaw with my breath, moving back around until my lips hover over hers, and still, she does not flinch.

I start to pull back, my grip on her neck and hair easing a bit when suddenly, her tongue peeks out, brushing against my lips tentatively. I freeze, my cock now like steel in my jeans, and the humor in her eyes takes on a muted heat as she pushes forward against my grip, her tongue stroking over my lips with intent.

I pull her close, opening my lips and sucking her tongue into my mouth. Her gasp of pleasure vibrates through me, sending a jolt of lust right to my dick, and all I can think about is mounting her like an animal. Her hands on my shoulders pull me toward her rather than push me away, and for a brief moment, I consider giving in, abandoning my reasons for coming here, and fucking the ever-loving shit out of her right on the sofa.

I rip myself away from her and shake my head, attempting to clear the fog of lust from my brain. I ease my grip on her throat enough so she can take in a panting breath. The low sob that falls from her lips sets off an ache in my balls that has me reconsidering my game plan.

"Who the fuck sent you?" I manage to spit out, giving her a slight shake as she frowns up at me.

Her tongue licks over her lips, and her brow furrows in confused concentration as she replies, "I don't know what you're talking about."

"Tell me who you are, and maybe I can help you."

She laughs at this, her eyes twinkling with mirth as she says, "I'm Carolina Tennent. And there's no help for me."

I stare into her eyes, searching for the lie, but I see none. Not that her statement tells me much, considering the vagueness of my line of questioning.

I open my mouth to ask a more direct question, but the look on her face stops me. She's staring up at me, a mixture of sadness and awe on her face. A strange urge to comfort her overwhelms me, and I have to squash it down.

Instead, I adjust my hands on her neck and in her hair, leaning down and running my nose from her collarbone up her neck to her ear, where I whisper, "What is it?"

She shivers, her head tilting toward me as she twists away with a brief giggle and a gasp. "Is this what it feels like?"

"What 'what' feels like?"

"Desire," she whispers brokenly. "Aching need."

I frown, unsure what she means, but the insinuation is there. "Are you a virgin?" I ask incredulously.

She barks out a bitter laugh. "Not hardly."

"Then how can you not know what desire feels like?"

She's quiet for a few moments, then replies, "I guess I've never truly *yearned* before."

"And you yearn now?"

"Yes," she gasps out, her legs rubbing together as she squirms, blatant desire written on her features.

"You want me?" I ask as I lean forward, my lips a hair's breadth from hers.

"Yes."

"Tell me," I whisper, my lips brushing over hers once, twice before I pull back, staring into her lust-drunk eyes. "Tell me what you want."

A glimmer of fear flashes over her face, but as quickly as it's there, it's gone. She swallows beneath my hand and then says, "I want you to fuck me."

"Is that all?" I ask. "You only want me to fuck you?"

She shakes her head as much as my grip on her allows. "I want you to make me come."

"How?"

"With your mouth," she answers, her eyes focusing on my lips. Then, her gaze moves downward until she's blatantly staring at the obvious bulge in the front of my jeans. "And your cock."

A strangled noise brews in my chest, and I choke it back down, covering it with a cough as I release her and roughly say, "Stand up."

She rises from her seat without hesitation, and I walk around her, taking the seat she vacated. She stands before me, wringing her hands nervously as she waits for me to tell her what to do next. I adjust myself on the sofa, her eyes dropping to my hips as I lift them and move down so I'm sprawled more comfortably. "Use me."

Her eyes jump to mine, and she stares at me for a moment before asking, "Use you how?"

"To come," I reply calmly. "Use my mouth, my cock. Whatever you want, any way you want."

"Are you serious?"

"I'm always serious, sweetheart."

She continues to stand in front of me, staring me up and down, fidgeting from one foot to the other while wringing her hands in front of her. So, finally, I ask, "Would it help if I stripped myself?"

Her eyes fly to mine, and she shakes her head. "I'd rather do it. If that's okay?"

I incline my head at her, spreading my legs wider to make room for her, then motion for her to come closer. She steps into the V of my legs and drops to her knees, her hands gripping the tops of my thighs as I move forward. She doesn't move for a few moments, so I grasp her hands in mine and tug gently, placing them over the zipper of my jeans.

I press my hips up, rubbing my hard dick against her palm, and a small smile forms on her lips. She lowers her eyes as if she's suddenly shy, and I frown, completely baffled by her actions and reactions thus far. So, I snake a hand out and wrap it around her throat again, squeezing tightly and yanking her to me. "Tell me one thing," I say quietly. She gives a brief nod, and I continue, "Are you going to hurt Darius?"

Her brow furrows, but she doesn't look away as she shakes her and whispers, "No."

I search her eyes for the lie, waiting a few extra moments to see if she'll flinch, but she doesn't. Her gaze remains steady on mine, her pulse thrumming beneath my hand. The open vulnerability in her eyes does something to me, something foreign, unexplainable.

"Do you feel that?" she asks breathlessly, her hands coming up and gripping my shirt, yanking me into her until I feel her breath against my lips. "The yearning?"

I say nothing. I can't with my words hung up on the lump in my throat. So, I do the only thing I can think of. I release her throat and take her face between both of my hands, squeezing tightly and yanking her close as I crash my mouth down onto hers without preamble.

It's neither subtle nor slick, neither suave nor sophisticated, and soon, we're eating at each other, our lips, teeth, and tongues dueling for dominance. Her hands grip the back of my neck. I adjust my hands on her head so one arm is wrapped behind her, my hand on her throat, keeping her where I want her.

After a few minutes, I rip myself away from her, forcing myself to lie back, to put myself at her mercy as initially planned. "Use me, sweetheart," I say huskily. "Take what you want."

She's panting, her cheeks flushed, her lips and chin glistening with our mixed saliva, as her gaze moves from my face to my chest and then down to where my cock is pressing against my jeans. She pulls at the bottom of my shirt, and I sit up, yanking it over my head and tossing it aside before leaning back again.

Her hands are on the waistband of my jeans, the button undone, zipper down, and she's pulling on the fabric until I lift my hips, allowing her to pull them down my legs. I lean forward, intent on helping her, but she slaps my hands away, so I sit back and watch her as she removes my shoes and then pulls my jeans off, tossing them to the side.

And then I'm sprawled there, completely nude, with her fully clothed and looking ridiculously pleased with herself. She sits back so she's resting her ass on her feet, her eyes slowly appraising every inch of me, and for a moment, I think she may leave me like that—bare as the day I was born, dick in the wind.

Then, she meets my gaze and licks her lips, and any worry I had that she wasn't going to go through with it vanishes, and I suddenly wish I had a cock ring handy.

She doesn't bother teasing me. She wraps both hands around my dick and takes me deep until the tip hits the back of her throat, and then she's gagging around me. My eyes roll into the back of my head. "Holy fuck."

She gives a garbled laugh, and my toes curl because what she lacks in skill, she more than makes up for in enthusiasm. Saliva runs down my cock, dripping over my balls onto the sofa beneath me, and I buck my hips up, pushing in deeper.

She glances up at me, and my breath catches in my throat at the sight of her with her lips wrapped around my cock. Tears stream down her face, her mascara is smudged beneath her eyes, and her cheeks flush red with excitement, making my balls tighten. I attempt to pull back some, to ease off, but the look of confusion on her face stops me. "You better slow down unless you want me to come like some unschooled teenager."

She does her best to smile around my dick, her eyebrows rising as she gets to work with obvious intent, and I lay back and let her have her way with me. If she wants me to come down her throat, then that's exactly what I'll do.

It doesn't take her long to finish me off, and she remains kneeling between my legs, her hands and mouth continuing to work me. It's fucking torture, and it takes all of my self-control not to pull her off me, the aftershocks of my orgasm zapping through me with every squeeze and pull of her hands and mouth on my still hard cock.

"What the fuck are you doing to me?"

"Whatever I want," she replies, her tongue licking over my tip like a lollipop. "That's what you told me to do—take what I want."

"So, you're going to suck me off all night?"

She smiles around my dick, her eyes sparkling as she licks me a few more times. Then she pulls back and says, "I want to sit on it."

A chuckle vibrates up from my chest at her phrasing, and I reach for her, pulling her to her feet and yanking her sleep pants down her legs, where she kicks them away. I grip her hips, urging her forward, but her hands on my shoulders stop me. "Do you have a condom?"

"My jeans, in my wallet."

She reaches over and snags my jeans from where she tossed them, and I rustle around until I find what she asked me for, then toss the clothing aside. I hold up the foil packet and ask, "You wanna do it?"

She gives me a slight smile, then tentatively takes the packet from me, ripping it open and pulling the condom out almost gingerly. I laugh again, truly baffled by her reaction to something as simple as a common prophylactic. "Have you never put a condom on a man before, sweetheart?"

Her eyes jump to mine, her cheeks reddening in embarrassment, and she raises a shoulder dismissively. But then she lowers her eyes almost ashamedly, a reaction I don't like at all, so I squeeze her with my thighs, pulling her into me as I place two fingers under her chin and press upward until she's looking at me again. "Don't look away, sweetheart," I say soothingly. "There's nothing to be afraid or ashamed of here."

She swallows, inhaling through her nose as she nods in acknowledgment of my words, but she remains quiet. I take the condom from her, placing it at the tip of my dick, and then, with my free hand, I grab one of hers and help her roll the latex down my shaft.

I press my hips up, and her hand tightens around me, her eyes never leaving mine as my breath hitches.

The fucking yearning.

A growl rumbles in my chest, pushing down the sudden tightness that I can't explain, and she smiles at me almost smugly, so I ask, "Are you going to play with me or fuck me?"

Her smile shifts to coyness, and I groan and adjust myself on the sofa, reaching for her, but she moves back and tsks at me. "Nuh-uh. You said I'm in charge here."

I narrow my eyes but drop my hands back down to rest on the cushion beneath me. "I don't think I ever said you're in charge, sweetheart," I murmur. "But by all means, take charge."

She leans in close, her eyes boring into mine as she asks, "Why did you come here, Tony?"

"I have no fucking idea."

She smiles, rolling her eyes a bit as she laughs at my obvious lie, but she doesn't comment. Instead, she rises to her feet and places a knee on either side of my thighs, settling her bare cunt against the hard line of my dick. She rubs her pussy up and down, pausing every few moments to grind her clit against me, her quiet gasps and whimpers making desire thrum through me like a live wire.

Her eyes are closed, her head tilted back slightly, and her brow furrowed in concentration. I'm enraptured by the sight of her. It takes every bit of my self-control not to surge forward, toss her onto the floor on her back, and fuck her into the carpet.

She lifts a bit, her hand holding my dick where she wants it so she can tease her pussy with my tip, each undulation of her hips taking me slightly deeper. She pauses when I'm about halfway inside her, and her breath catches, but this time, it doesn't seem to be from desire.

I put a hand on her naked hip, my other hand touching the side of her face gently. When her eyes meet mine, they're glassy, almost sad. "What is it, sweetheart?" I ask gently, not at all sure what caused the change in her mood.

She opens her mouth to respond but then stops, closing her mouth and taking a few shuddering breaths before trying again. "I'm good."

"We don't have to do this."

"No," she says breathlessly, rolling her hips so more of me disappears into her clutching depths, and I grit my teeth against my urge to shove up the rest of the way. "I want to. I needed a minute, but I'm good now."

I'm torn between letting her be and calling her out for her less-than-enthused demeanor, but the pleading in her eyes makes me take the former option. I pull on her shirt, urging her to remove it, and she does, pulling it over her head and tossing it on top of my clothes.

I cup her breasts, massaging her nipples with my palms as she sinks down onto me until I'm fully seated inside. She grinds against me, then eases up and back down before rubbing against me again, trying to find a rhythm that works for her.

I pinch and roll her nipples with my fingers, then lean forward, taking one and then the other into my mouth, sucking and teasing with my lips and tongue. Her movements become more erratic, her moans and cries more frenzied as she rides me, but soon, the frenzy turns into what sounds like frustration.

"I can't," she gasps. "I can't. Oh, fuck, Tony."

"What do you want, sweetheart?" I ask with effort, my need to come again almost overwhelming my good sense. "Tell me what you need."

She shakes her head, her eyes squeeze shut, but then she looks at me and says, "I need you to fuck me."

She doesn't have to tell me twice.

I surge to my feet, taking her with me, and she shouts in surprise as I flip our positions, and then she's sprawled on the sofa. I pull her hips forward so her ass is hanging over the edge slightly, then push her knees back, spreading her open for me. I dribble saliva on her pussy then slide my cock back inside her forcefully, my growl of pleasure echoing throughout the room.

I snag one of her hands, bringing her fingers to my lips and licking them, wetting them with my spit, and then placing her wet hand on her clit. "Touch yourself."

She frowns, confusion evident on her face, but she does as she's told, rubbing her fingers over her clit tentatively at first. I match my thrusts with the stroke of her fingers, the slow tempo quickly escalating until she's actively chasing her orgasm, and I'm pumping into her with a solid slap on each in stroke.

"Fucking look at me, Carolina."

Her eyes open, and she meets my gaze, her fingers on her clit taking on a slightly different rhythm, and soon, she's struggling to keep her eyes on mine as hers roll back into her head, pleasure washing over her in waves. She moans loudly, cursing softly as she writhes beneath me, her body sucking me in deeper, even as she attempts to push me away.

I continue to fuck her through her orgasm, pounding into her until she's completely satiated beneath me, and then I let go, pushing in as far as I can and releasing deep inside her.

She's shaking beneath me, her legs quivering as I help her lower her knees, so her feet are braced on my calves. She has a dreamy expression, and she whispers so softly I almost miss it, "So that's what it's like."

It's almost as if she's never come before.

This thought has me feeling equal parts shock and panic. She's obviously not a virgin, and while she's several years younger than me, she's clearly old enough to have had various partners before now.

She's staring up at me, her chest heaving, a look of awed satisfaction on her features as she reaches up and touches my face. I don't pull away or flinch. I simply lean into her touch, the warmth of her fingers on my skin easing the tension in my chest.

And that's when it hits me.

I am so fucked.

Chapter Twenty-Two

Carolina

THIS GUY IS FUCKING insane.

And that's saying something, given some of the company I've been keeping over the past decade or so.

Declan attempted to make small talk for the entire flight to California, but I flat-out refused to talk to someone so fucking stupid that he would kidnap someone from a human-trafficking ring as a way to prank his older brother.

And then, we deplane on a paparazzi-filled tarmac to camera flashes and questions about our elopement. At this point, it's a toss-up on who's going to murder him first: Dare, Tony, or me.

Now, we're in the back of a stretch limo, and my urge to bash him over the head with a bottle of Cristal is fierce. I'm so intent on my daydream that his voice breaks through my thoughts. "What the fuck is your problem now?"

My eyes bug out of my head, and I force my body to remain seated across from him rather than jumping over there and pummeling him as he so rightly deserves. "Your brother is going to kick your fucking ass, and I'm going to laugh."

He rolls his eyes, taking a sip of his champagne before replying, "Dare may want to, but he won't."

"How about Tony?" I ask between my gritted teeth. "I bet Tony would kick your ass in a fucking heartbeat."

His eyes widen a bit, his fingers on his champagne glass tightening. "What does Tony have to do with any of this?"

I throw my head back and laugh, tears in my eyes, before I finally manage to choke out, "Oh, you didn't know?"

"Know what?" he asks tightly.

"That I belong to Tony."

He squirms a bit but quickly recovers. "Well, good," he says. "Then they won't waste any time coming for you."

I snort and roll my eyes, my teeth grinding in annoyance. The audacity of this asshat is almost comical. "I didn't know Dare had a brother. Where the fuck have you been?"

"He doesn't have a brother," he replies, practically sticking his bottom lip out. "At least not in the real sense of the word. He made sure of that."

The underlying petulance of his words is not lost on me, and I ignore the urge to reach out and slap him across the face, even though he deserves it. "It's bad enough that you came in and took me, but to then publicly announce an elopement is insanity. People will be looking for me and I don't mean only Dare and Tony."

"It's fine. Those assholes will see the headlines, they'll come to get you, yell at me, and then go about their business, going back to ignoring me for the rest of my life."

"Is this about you not feeling included? Did you want to be part of the merry bandits, and they refused you?"

He laughs and shakes his head. "Not hardly. I chose not to be part of the merry bandits. I chose not to live my life under the radar."

"Is that why they've been ignoring your existence? Because you chose a different path than them?"

"Well, that's what they said," Declan replies quietly. "They said it was too dangerous for me to be associated with the Beast if I wasn't going to be part of the gang. Don't get me wrong, Carolina. I'm not a complete fucking moron, and I do know that they're right. But that doesn't mean I don't sometimes get nostalgic and want to cross paths with my big brother and his moronic friends."

"Well, you picked a really bad fucking time to choose to cross paths with Darius. How did you even know about me? Or where I was?"

"I've been following your name since Dare was spotted with you on the red carpet. I noticed you had fallen off the mainstream newsreels, so I had some people looking for you in other places. When I saw your name go across the dark web—and when I say dark, I mean really dark—I figured I couldn't just leave you there."

"You didn't think to maybe reach out to Darius and let him know you had concerns?"

"What's the fun in that?"

I groan, my fingers moving to my temples and rubbing gently to ease the pain in my head. "So, you thought it would be fun to drop everything, get on a jet to the literal middle of nowhere, break into a large criminal organization facility, steal me, stuff me in a trunk, and then set up this whole intricate ruse to make it look like we're having fun. That's what you're saying?"

He smiles, looking proud of himself. "Exactly. I know Darius would be the first one to say I couldn't pull it off, but I did. I'm just showing him that I still got it. That all these years away from his life hasn't dulled my criminal prowess."

The guy is fucking certifiable. I can't decide if he's genuinely crazy or just incredibly misguided. I don't believe he's as stupid as he comes off. If he was, he never would've been able to pull it off, but his thought that this was a good thing is entirely asinine. "At least you waited until we landed for the big reveal. That gives us a bit more time to get ahead of the other people that might be coming for me."

He gives me a sheepish look, then mutters, "I may have put a couple of hooks out before we landed, but my place is behind some state-of-the-art security. You should be safe there."

Trepidation trickles down my spine, knowing that the wrong people might get the jump on us. "And is the location of your home well-known?"

He smiles broadly. "Oh, yes. It's on all the tourist maps for people to drive by. Sometimes, I like to go out there and wave to give people a thrill. It's quite fun."

Fuck my life. Fuck every fucking day of my life.

Of all the people who had to steal me from the bad guys, he had to be a famous, egomaniac attention-whore. "I can see now why Darius thought it best to distance himself from you. Your whole enjoyment of living life in the limelight."

"It has its perks."

"And its cons?"

He nods, sighing as he replies, "Sure, everything has cons. But in this case, usually, the pros greatly outweigh them."

Declan's phone rings, and he picks it up off the seat where he set it down earlier. Glancing at the screen, he taps it, then puts the phone to his ear. "What's up?" He listens for a moment, then asks, "Do you recognize them?" He pauses, listening to whomever he's speaking with again, then says, "Call the others and see if they can intervene at some point while you try to lose them."

He ends the call and then looks at me with a raised brow. "Seems you were correct, Carolina. We have company already."

"What does that mean?"

"We have a tail."

"Of course, we do," I snarl. "I'm sick and tired of being tossed around like a goddamn rag doll."

"I won't let them take you."

I glare at him. "Yes, you will. As far as I'm concerned, you should pull over and let me out."

"And have Tony skin me alive for not even attempting to protect you? Not a fucking chance."

I stare out the window for a few moments, watching the traffic go by as I contemplate the situation. There is no way Declan and one driver will be able to keep me from being taken if that's the intent of the people following us. "Are you sure it isn't paparazzi?"

"My men would know if it was paparazzi," he replies with a head shake. "They know how to deal with that kind of tail without concerning me."

The car accelerates and then veers sharply to the left. "Put on your seatbelt," Declan says as he secures his own. "Things are going to get wild."

I snort and roll my eyes at his flippant attitude. This guy is determined to get his ass kicked by someone today, and I can only hope it's by Dare or Tony when they finally catch up to us.

I brace myself as the car picks up speed, the tires screeching on the pavement as Declan's driver attempts to lose the tail in the busy traffic. "Are you sure it's not Darius?" I ask with concern, not wanting anyone to be hurt attempting to protect me.

"They would know if it was Darius or anyone closely connected to him," he replies, tension now evident on his features as his driver becomes more erratic. "And it seems these people aren't going to give up easily."

"They won't give up as long as they're breathing," I mutter. "If they were sent on a mission to retrieve me, they won't stop until either they have me in their possession or they're dead. That's how this works, Declan. Bad people doing bad things until someone stops them permanently."

"Well, I can make that happen," he says with a humorless laugh.

The car shutters around a corner and then brakes hard, throwing me forward violently. At least two cars pull up, one on either side of us, and doors open, and slam shut. Voices yell incoherently, and through the darkened windows, I see the car being surrounded by men I don't recognize.

Declan unbuckles and moves to the side, pulling the middle of the seat down and then reaching into what I assume is the trunk. He pulls a duffel through and tosses it on the floor of the car between us, unzipping it and pulling out a handgun. "Do you know how to use this?"

"Yes, but we're downtown L.A., so it's kind of hard to discreetly wave a gun around, even in self-defense."

"This part of downtown won't notice or care."

A man approaches and taps on the window. "Give us the woman. We don't give a fuck about you."

Declan doesn't answer; he just keeps pulling weapons out of the bag. "The car is bulletproof," he says calmly. "We're waiting for the rest of my men to come in and take care of the vermin problem."

He seems so nonplussed by the situation, and I'm unsure if I should be concerned as he hands me two handguns. "Will this be necessary if your men are coming to handle it?"

"One can never be too prepared."

"Why do you have an arsenal in the trunk of your car?"

He gives me an impatient look, then goes back to sorting his weapons as he replies, "*Because* you can never be too prepared."

I make a face at him; then check the guns he handed me for ammunition and safety before setting them on the seat next to me. I've never shot anyone before, and I'm not sure if I can do it if it's only to protect myself, but I'm willing to give it a try.

The men outside are becoming increasingly agitated as they attempt to get access to the vehicle. There's a brief yelling match about explosives, but it seems they have instructions to bring me in alive, so that's vetoed quickly. Thank goodness for small favors.

"How's your aim?"

I shrug my shoulders as I reply, "At a non-moving target, mostly accurate. At a live, moving target? I have no fucking idea."

He gives me a cool, assessing look and then says, "The first thing you need to remember at this moment is that they will kill everyone you've ever loved without batting an eye. They will rape and murder you and sell children off into sex slavery. These fucking people don't give a shit about anyone. So, when you take aim, you think about that."

My heartbeat jackhammers in my chest with every word that comes out of his mouth, and my lip curls up in a snarl. Declan may have been out of the criminal world for an extended period of time, but to look at him now, you wouldn't know it. I see Darius seeping out of his pores, that same excited glint in his eye at the thought of taking out these shitbags.

I look out the windows, taking count of the number of men out there waiting for us to make a move. Then I turn back to Declan and nod. "I can do that."

I pick up both guns, give them another check, and then add, "I'm gonna need more ammunition. For what I lack in accuracy, I can make up for in numbers. Or, at the very least, an annoying distraction."

He smiles broadly. "That's the spirit."

He hands me what I asked for and then pulls out a vest and throws it at me. I laugh and ask, "Is that like the clown car of go-bags? How much more shit you got in there?"

His smile turns magnetic, and he seems incredibly pleased with himself. "I've got everything in here you could possibly need if you ever had to fight off a group of bad guys to avoid being taken alive as a prisoner. So basically, you have to make the decision if you want to be taken alive or not. Worst-case scenario, you blow up the whole fucking thing, yourself included. Best-case scenario, you stick a tracker on your person and hope the people coming to get you can find you."

The mention of a tracker gets my attention. "You have tracking devices in the bag?"

"Of course. The fact that everyone isn't microchipped at birth is beyond me. So many unfortunate events could be avoided if we microchipped ourselves in the first place."

I squint at him, unsure of what to say because in a lot of the situations that have happened in the past, he is absolutely correct. Tracking devices have gotten a lot of people out of a lot of bad shit. "Can I have one?"

His head comes up, and his eyes widen as he asks, "You want one of my tracking devices?"

He seems excited that I'd be interested in one of his little toys, and I nod enthusiastically. "Absolutely, yes. From where I'm sitting, the odds of me getting out of this without being taken alive are pretty slim. Since I don't actually feel like dying today, it's probably better to plan it in advance. Which means you need to stay alive because you gotta track me."

He pulls a small black kit out of his clown car bag and then moves to the other side of the car beside me. "The armpit is probably easiest since we're in a rush."

I don't bother asking any other questions as I adjust my clothing, pulling my arm out of my sleeve and lifting it over my head.

He pulls the skin tight, and says, "Just a little pinch," then jabs me, and I squeak in surprise because it fucking hurt. I ignore my urge to slap the shit out of him, and after a few seconds, the pain dissipates.

He puts the needle back into the little kit it came in and moves to the other side of the car, where he places it into the compartment that's hidden in the seat.

I adjust my clothing, putting myself back to rights, before securing the vest to my torso and picking the guns up. I look over at Declan, who is now sitting there cool as a cucumber, eating a fucking granola bar. "How the fuck can you eat right now?"

"Not eating isn't going to change anything. I may as well not be distracted by hunger pains when the action starts."

"You are certifiably fucking insane," I mutter.

He laughs and tips his head to me. "Why thank you, Carolina. But keep in mind that given the company you've been keeping, I'm small potatoes when it comes to being crazy. I can assure you; my brother takes the cake on fucking crazy. And for all I know, Tony's taking the lead."

"May be a toss-up." I think it over for a moment and then continue, "I can't decide. I'm starting to wonder if Matt is the actual crazy mastermind because you know what they say about the quiet ones."

"Matt should be crazy from the bullshit he deals with from the other two. I can't figure out why he puts up with their shit."

Renewed shouting outside the car draws my attention, and I see one of the men is now lying on the ground, and Declan cheers, "And here we go."

I glance over to him, and then back at the men standing around as another one falls to the ground, but I can't see where the gunfire is coming from. Declan kneels in the middle of a car, pressing the button on the roof, and the glass sunroof starts to slide open as he says, "Get down here, brace your back against mine."

I say nothing as I do as I'm told, double-checking the safety on my gun is not engaged as he says, "Get your feet under you and follow me up after three. You got it?"

"Yes," I say as I get my feet under me, bracing myself against his back. I keep my eyes on the edges of the sunroof, so I don't get hung up and try to lean forward a bit to give him a little more room.

"Three," he whispers.

I interrupt him, "How will I know who's not the enemy?"

"Two," he continues. "If you can see them, they are the enemy."

I don't have time to reply as he says, "One," and I feel the pressure of his body against mine starting to rise, so I follow suit.

In a blink, sunlight hits me in the face, and I don't hesitate. I bring both my arms up, pointing my guns at the closest people I see standing in the way, and I fire over and over until I'm out of ammo. Bodies are strewn around the car, but I don't have time to think about it before I feel Declan behind me, dropping back down inside the car.

We quickly reload, and within seconds, we're rising again, taking aim and firing, while whoever is working in the shadows continues to eliminate the more difficult targets like clockwork. I don't recall there being this many people waiting to retrieve me, but the bodies on the ground don't lie.

My heart pounds in my chest, adrenaline coursing through my body, piquing all of my senses, and I laugh. Declan raises his eyebrows at me as he works to reload his weapons. "Are you okay?"

"I'm great," I reply with another giggle. "I never knew shooting people could be this fun."

Declan makes a face at me and shakes his head. "You're fucking losing it. Just keep your shit together long enough for us to get out of here."

"Where the fuck are we going? Can't we just drive away?"

"Can't drive without wheels. First thing they did was slash the tires, so we're gonna have to vacate the vehicle and hoof it to our new ride."

"Our new ride?" I ask, my face scrunching up. "Where the fuck is it?"

"Probably about a quarter mile south of here."

I stuff more ammo into my vest and sit back in my seat, grinning. "So, should we divide and conquer, then?"

The look he gives me leads me to believe he's entirely sure I've completely lost my mind. "No," he says quietly. "We absolutely will not divide and conquer. Jesus fucking Christ. I give you a couple of guns one time, and now you think you're a freaking vigilante warrior."

I laugh again, the level of absolute euphoria flooding my body at an all-time peak. "I am a fucking vigilante warrior. I like the way this feels. I'm gonna do this more often."

"Fuck sake," he huffs, then rubs his hands over his face. "I go into this thinking I'm pulling an epic prank on my big brother by stealing his movie-actress girlfriend, and I end up with another crazy fucker, ready to knock heads."

I laugh again. "I'm not Dare's girlfriend, you moron."

"Yeah, I get that now. But on a surface level, that appeared to be what you were. I've been getting information about him for quite a while, but I guess this information was incorrect on you being my new sister-in-law."

"You're gonna love Antoinette," I say excitedly. "She's amazing crazy. I totally want to be her someday."

His eyes drop from my face to my hands, still holding my guns in my lap, and he mutters, "Looks like you're well on your way."

I smile proudly at him, holding my guns up in front of me in a completely juvenile manner and saying, "Really? Maybe you should get a picture so I can send it to her."

His eyes widen in horror, so I drop my hands back to my lap and cackle. "I'm fucking with you, asshole. You're so gullible."

He glares at me and says, "We don't have time for your fucking games right now. We gotta move it."

"Tell me the plan, and let's do it."

"We're going to make a run for it," Declan replies. "My driver will cover our backs. Stick close behind me, and my men out there will attempt to take out the enemy as they show themselves."

I nod, remaining quiet as he edges closer to the door, and I'm right behind him as he cautiously steps from the vehicle. A bullet ricochets off the door, and I turn toward it just in time to see a man fall to the ground.

Declan motions for me to exit the vehicle, and when I'm standing beside him, he grabs my hand, places it on his jacket, and says, "Hold onto me and keep close. If something happens to me." He pauses and points up the street. "You run like hell three blocks up that street. Take a left, and a white SUV will be on the corner. Codeword is jackrabbit. You do not pause, you do not hesitate, you do not wait for me. You do not try to save me. Do you understand?"

"I'm not going to—" He grabs my upper arm almost painfully, yanking me close as he repeats, "Do you understand, Carolina?"

I clench my jaw for a moment and glare at him. Then I give him a curt nod and say, "Yes. I fucking got it."

I don't know why all of a sudden, I'm so pissed off to have someone going out of their way to try to save me. Maybe it's because I've devoted myself to the health and well-being of the people I love, and to have someone I don't even know to be doing it so willingly confuses me. I may not be the biggest badass on the street, but I'm not the type to leave people behind to save myself.

Declan must sense my inner thought process because he gives me another little shake, and when my eyes meet his, he says, "I mean it, Carolina. If I'm dead, there's nothing you can do to help me. And if I'm not quite dead, you trying to help me will definitely make me dead-dead. You run like fucking hell. Get to the car. Get to safety."

This time, I nod for real. His explanation makes sense, so I'll do as I'm told. Declan nods in response, then makes a break across the parking lot, and I follow closely behind him. We hit the sidewalk, staying close to the building as we move quickly yet cautiously through the crowd.

We haven't gone very far before a bullet ricochets off the side of the building, sending everyone screaming, which gives us some cover to move more swiftly.

By the time we get to the intersection before the second block, it occurs to me that these are not standard New York City blocks, and I'm wishing the shoes I'm wearing had been chosen for function rather than fashion.

We cross the street without incident, but halfway up that second block, Declan stops short in front of me, and I run into the back of him. I peek around him and see a handful of men blocking the sidewalk.

Declan turns his head toward me and says, "I'm going to distract them. If you go through the door right here on our left, it cuts through to an exit on the other side of the building. You can carry on with the directions I told you—hang a right, loop around, and the car should be there. Got it?"

I want to argue, but I don't bother; instead, I'm nodding in acknowledgment. He steps away from me, and I release his suit jacket as he steps forward, posturing almost gleefully. If I didn't know better, I would think he was Darius Hughes getting ready to make a bloody spectacle.

I don't wait to see what happens. I do as I'm told, ducking into the building as instructed and racing through the hallways. At first, it feels like a maze, but I manage to make it out to the other side quicker than I thought, hanging a right and attempting to rush up the street inconspicuously.

Gunshots ring out, and I give up any semblance of caution and run, just like Declan instructed. I race up the street, spotting the white SUV on the corner, slowing my pace slightly so I'm more speed-walking than running, when the driver-side door opens, and a man steps out. When I get to him, he says, "Slow down, jackrabbit."

A wave of relief washes over me as he opens the rear door, and I jump in, the door slamming shut behind me. The driver moves to get into the driver seat when three men rush over, one of them grabbing him from behind and yanking him backwards. One of the other men hits him in the head with the butt of his weapon, and the driver goes down in a heap, then the new men are climbing into the vehicle, their doors slamming as we take off into the traffic.

I take a few minutes to get my bearings, my heartbeat hammering in my chest as I go over my options. This constant merry-go-round of people taking me is beyond old, and while I'm not sure there's much I can do about it at this very moment, there has to be a way to make it stop once and for all.

The man sitting next to me is smiling at me creepily, and my lip curls in distaste. "The fuck are you looking at?"

His eyes widen, and it occurs to me that in previous situations, I've rarely acted out before. I usually go with the flow of whatever comes at me.

The driver gets on the freeway headed south, and the man next to me places his hand on my thigh and squeezes. I narrow my eyes at him and spit out, "Don't touch me."

He leers at me, his hand on my leg moving upwards as he replies, "I was told I can do whatever the fuck I want with you."

I grab his hand, flinging it off me and sitting up straighter in my seat. "I won't tell you again. Don't fucking touch me."

My heart hammers in my chest, years of pent-up fury overflowing inside me, and then, he laughs. The motherfucker laughs. He's reaching for me again, but now, I'm reaching into my vest, where my gun is hidden. I pull it out, not even blinking as I turn it on him and shoot him in the face.

The sound of the gunshot in the enclosed space has my ears ringing, and the driver in the front is shouting as the man in the passenger seat attempts to come over the middle console.

I don't hesitate. I turn my body, the gun coming with me, and fire a shot into his chest, then another into his head as he falls back against the dash.

The driver's still shouting, cutting off other cars as he attempts to maneuver the vehicle toward the side of the road. We're traveling at high speed, but as the vehicle approaches the side of the freeway, he starts to brake, and I know if he manages to stop and get to me, I'm a dead woman.

I point my gun at him.

Fuck it.

Chapter Twenty-Three

Tony

A CONSIDERABLE AMOUNT OF time has passed by the time we land in Los Angeles. Luckily, the article Matt found earlier was local, and from the timestamp on the latest breaking news at LAX, it appears we aren't as far behind them as we originally thought.

We're driving to Declan's estate when Nettie's phone rings. She answers, listening intently and then saying, "Mickey found Declan. He's going to send the address."

I look at her in the rearview mirror and ask, "Carolina?"

She shakes her head as she listens to what Mickey's saying, and then she ends the call. "Mickey said they're doing a big cleanup downtown. Declan was found a couple of blocks away with a gunshot wound. About a block or so from him, they found one of Declan's men knocked out on the sidewalk, so we assume that's where they lost Carolina. They already checked the cams and confirmed three men got into a white SUV with her and took off south, but they haven't managed to pick it up again, so we're not sure where they ended up."

I clench my teeth, saying nothing as I drive toward the location Nettie gave me. I take a few deep breaths in an attempt to get control of my heart pounding in my chest, but it's not doing much.

Pulling into the parking lot, I drive up beside a large blacked-out van. Nettie is out of the car before I'm fully parked, but she seems familiar with the guy who gets out of the van, and they speak briefly before he hands her an item. She takes it from him, then turns and runs back to us, jumping into the back and tossing the object that she took from him into my lap.

I pick it up, turning it over in my hands and looking back at her questioningly as she says, "Declan's not out of the woods, but he did come around long enough to tell them we can find Carolina on that."

My confusion must be evident because she scoots forward and yanks the device from my hands, flipping it around so the screen lights up, and I see it's not an actual phone but a tracking device.

"He put a fucking tracker in her?"

Nettie shrugs her shoulders, shaking her head as she says, "Apparently. They didn't have a lot of answers other than we gotta follow up on that dot."

I snatch the device from her hands, take a closer look at it, and then frown. "The dot's not moving. Why isn't the fucking dot moving?"

"They said it wasn't moving when they found it. They were going to send some people out to check, but we were so close they waited."

"She's not moving on the side of the fucking highway, Nettie. What the fucking fuck?"

I don't waste any more time talking; instead, I exit the parking lot on two wheels, my knuckles white from gripping the steering wheel.

"He's got a crew meeting us out there," Nettie says as she leans back in her seat and fastens her seatbelt. "They may even beat us there."

I don't say anything else, gritting my teeth as I press my foot down on the accelerator and honking the horn harder at the assholes in front of me. The sickness in my gut is overwhelming, and I'm sweating and incredibly fucking pissed off.

I pull up alongside where the dot is blinking at the same time the crew Mickey sent. Matt's on the phone, handling the local and state police because, apparently, the fine, upstanding citizen has connections everywhere.

We all exit the vehicle, looking around for anything that may indicate where she is in this general vicinity. Darius points out what appears to be fresh tire tracks that begin on the pavement and have left intermittent scars in the turf, so we pick up that trail and follow it down the short embankment to a thicket of short trees and shrubbery.

I'm a few feet from the wooded area when I make out the tires and undercarriage of a vehicle, and my fucking heart stops in my chest as I yell, "Over here! She's over here!"

Footsteps pound on the dirt behind me as I pull myself up onto the side of the SUV and peer into the side window that somehow didn't get smashed when the rig rolled over. I yank on the door, but it's locked or stuck, so I press my face against the glass and peer inside.

Carolina is in the back, behind the driver, held suspended by her seatbelt. Three bodies are sprawled haphazardly—two in the front and one in the rear beside her. I try to open the door again, but it doesn't budge. I turn around, ready to smash my foot through the driver's side window, but then Dare is there, handing me a window breaker. I waste no time busting through the window and unlocking the doors.

I move over to the back door where Carolina is, and Darius pulls himself up, helping me open the door, and then I lower myself inside. I press two fingers against her carotid, a wave of relief rolling over me when I feel her pulse beating strongly beneath my fingertips.

Dare hands me a cervical collar, which I secure gently around her neck, then I position myself beneath her as Dare cuts her seatbelt and, she falls into me. A backboard is lowered down, and I ease her over so she's leaning back against it so I can secure her to the board.

They pull her up and away, and I pull myself out of the vehicle, then follow behind them to the waiting van. Standing outside the open rear doors, I'm at a loss of what I should do next when Nettie squeezes my arm and says, "Go with her, Tony."

I shake my head, opening my mouth to argue, but then Dare interrupts, "She's right, Tony. You go with her. We got this."

I look to Matt, who also nods, and then, after a final nod to Nettie and Dare, I turn and climb into the van.

Chapter Twenty-Four

Tony

WE END UP AT a private medical facility east of the city.

It doesn't take long for the medical staff to assess her injuries, which end up being non-life-threatening. The amount of relief this brings me is insurmountable, and I feel like I can finally take a deep breath now that the weight of her safety has been lifted from my chest.

Unfortunately, that doesn't mean I can get out of asking other questions that may come off as uncomfortable.

"Did you do a rape kit?"

The doctor doesn't flinch at my question as he responds, "Yes, there doesn't appear to be any obvious trauma, but we completed it anyway. It will help if we know anyone to rule out as a possible suspect, though."

"I can provide that," I reply. "Also, you may as well do an STD screening. She's mentioned previously wanting one."

"We run all of that as a standard in these cases," he replies blandly. Then he clears his throat and adds, "We did have an issue when we first did her pelvic exam, though."

"What kind of issue?"

"She had an IUD that was no longer appropriately positioned. I would've tried to fix it, but I didn't want to risk it with not knowing how long it's already been in. Regardless, we should let her know she's no longer protected against pregnancy."

"I'll tell her," I say firmly. "I don't think there's any reason to bother her with that kind of details right now, so I'll inform her when she's feeling better, and she can decide how she wants to proceed with that."

He gives me an assessing look, the corners of his mouth twitching slightly as he asks, "So, you don't want me to tell her?"

I cross my arms over my chest and stare him down as I repeat, "That's right. Don't tell her."

"Don't tell her what?" Nettie's voice cuts in from the doorway, and I inwardly groan.

I give the doctor a hard look as I turn to Nettie and reply, "Nothing. It doesn't concern you."

Darius appears behind Nettie. He smiles, his eyebrows raising knowingly as he elbows her and says, "I bet you know."

Her eyes widen, and she looks from Darius to me, and back to Darius, and then gasps, "No! It can't be?"

He lifts a shoulder nonchalantly and inclines his head toward me as he replies, "He's really the only one who can confirm."

I look between the two of them and drop my hands to my hips as I say, "Seriously, guys? Are you gonna go on one of your book trope rants now? It's not exactly the time."

"Listen, Tony," Nettie says as she walks toward me. "You can basically get all of life's do's and don'ts from a book trope list. I don't know why you have such a hard time with this."

I look over at Darius, holding my hands up in front of me in surrender as I say, "Seriously, man. Help me."

"Don't get me involved in this," he replies with a laugh. He puts his hands in his pocket and leans against the door jamb as he adds, "She usually has our number when it comes to book tropes. And honestly, I don't think they've led me wrong so far, so you might wanna listen to her."

Nettie pokes the doctor in the chest and asks, "What do you have to do with this? Don't you have some kind of ethical standard you have to maintain?"

He gives her a bored look and then laughs. "I provide medical care for a criminal organization. So, I think we use the ethical requirements rather loosely."

She narrows her eyes at him and crosses her arms over her chest as she takes a step closer. "But would you let him harm her?"

"Who am I to say what's actually harmful to her? I don't know her."

"What's your name?"

"I don't think I have to tell you that."

"You don't have to tell her, but I highly advise you do because she's not opposed to stabbing you for fun." Dare's words are laced with humor, but the look on the doctor's face indicates he understands the underlying seriousness of the statement.

Finally, he says, "My name is Ryan Gray."

Nettie smiles approvingly. "You can call me Antoinette. I used to go by Toni with an 'i', but having two of us got annoying, so we killed her."

He returns her smile, then asks, "So which trope are you thinking? Secret pregnancy or forced pregnancy?"

Her eyes widen, and she crows with excitement, "You know your tropes!"

He smiles rather smugly and leans back against the table as he responds, "Oh, yes. I have three sisters who got me into reading with them a few years ago. It's quite entertaining."

She smiles approvingly and then whirls on me and asks, "So which one is it, Tony?"

I cross my arms over my chest again and lift my chin defiantly as I say nothing, and finally, she continues, "Don't even think about it. As far as she knows, she can't get pregnant. You can't not tell her. Jesus fucking Christ, Tony, what the fuck is wrong with you?"

"Nettie, I don't know what point you lost track of the fact that I am a self-centered asshole, but those are the facts. How you can question any completely self-serving agenda I might have is beyond me."

She glares and punches me in the arm. "Don't make fucking excuses with me, man. I know you're a good guy, and technically, you're only a couple of better choices away from being a great guy, and frankly, I expect you to be a great fucking guy. Do you hear me?"

Darius laughs from the other side of the room, and I shoot him a glare and a middle finger. He laughs even harder and says, "She won't stop until you're a great guy, Tony, so you may as well just give in."

"I'm not making any fucking promises. I am who I am, and at the end of the day, I'm gonna get what I want regardless."

Nettie stomps her foot in frustration. "I'm quite certain you can get what you want without any kind of duplicitous shenanigans. You could try just talking to the woman."

I grimace, confused about how she thinks that me talking to a woman will get me what I want. I glare at her even harder, hoping she'll get the hint and leave me the fuck alone, but instead, she steps closer and grabs the front of my shirt in both of her hands, yanking me closer to her until she's mere inches from my face where she whisper-shouts, "She will love you if you give her the chance."

Now, Darius and the doctor both laugh, and my annoyance lessens a bit as I shake my head. "You're a fucking pain in my ass."

She smiles and nods, her hands releasing me as her arms come around my shoulders in a hug. I shake my head again, unable to return her hug even if I want to because she has my arms pinned to my sides. It's her trademark prisoner hug.

She squeezes me for a few moments, then releases me and steps back, and I relax slightly, thinking the conversation is over. But then, her serious expression is back, and she points at me and says, "I'm usually on your side, Tony, but in this case, if you fuck around, I will come for you. And you ain't gonna fucking like it."

Darc and the doctor are both doing a terrible job pretending not to laugh, and I give them each a dirty look before turning my glare on Nettie. "I get it. I promise I won't trap her or anything, okay?"

She leans in a little closer to me, her eye searching mine before nodding and turning back to Ryan. "When can we see her?"

I groan in annoyance, putting my hand up and saying, "Slow your roll, Nettie. You can see her after I do."

Ryan chuckles, obviously greatly amused by the entire exchange. "You can see her whenever you want. She did wake up a couple of times while I was examining her, but I imagine she won't stay out for long if she's not already awake. It's the second door on the left, number three."

I don't wait for him to elaborate. I'm out the door before Nettie can attempt to get a jump on me. I pause outside her closed door, my hand on the knob, pressing my forehead against the cool wood as a wave of emotion cuts off my breath. I give myself a moment to get control of myself and then slowly open the door and step into the room, shutting it behind me.

I stand there, watching her from across the room. Her eyes are closed, and she looks impossibly small, lying prone in the hospital bed. Her hair is a tangled mess, the blanket twisted around her, like she flailed about in her sleep.

I walk to her bedside and gently brush her hair away from her face. I attempt to adjust her blanket without disturbing her, choking on the lump in my throat as I manage to straighten the blanket and pull it up to her shoulders. I glance back at her face to find her eyes open and focused on me as she whispers, "Hi."

"Hi."

"Is Flora all right?" Her question is quiet yet hopeful.

I nod in response and reply, "She's great. She's amazing, considering what she's been through. She's still in Russia with Jayme, Aggie, and the dogs I stole for her. Last I heard, she was adjusting well. We even have a child psychologist coming in to see her, and it seems the biggest concern is long-term neglect. She had a few old injuries but nothing severe. She's going to be fine, sweetheart. Don't worry."

She smiles and sighs deeply, and then we stare at each other for a few moments before she moves over in the bed and pats the mattress for me to join her, but I hesitate. "I'm kind of a mess."

She lifts a shoulder and laughs quietly. "I don't care, Tony. Lie here with me."

I don't argue any further, bending down, untying my boots, and kicking them off. I remove my coat, tossing it to the side before stretching out beside her. She scoots over a bit more, giving me space to get situated, and then she curls into me, one of her legs hooking up over my thigh and her arm wrapping around my torso so she's draped across my body.

I wrap my arms around her, pulling her more firmly against me, and she rolls, turning more fully into me and pressing her face into my neck and inhaling deeply, a tremor running through her body as she exhales, and I squeeze her more tightly against me. She leans back so, in my semi-reclined position, she can look me in the face, but she doesn't say anything. She just stares at me.

Finally, I ask, "Do you wanna tell me what happened?"

"There isn't much to tell that you can't guess."

"The doctor did a rape kit, just in case," I whisper. "Not that they'll be able to do much with it criminally, but it was best to have the whole work up done, so you'll know that you're safe."

She laughs almost bitterly, and I raise my brows in response to the unusual sound. But then she says, "No one touched me this time. One of them thought he was going to, and I stopped him."

She rests her head back on my chest, staring at the wall, and I remain quiet, waiting for her to continue. Eventually, she laughs again and clears her throat. "I shot them. That's why we crashed."

I'm genuinely shocked into silence, but I give her another squeeze to let her know I'm not bothered that she killed a few shitbags. The feeling in my chest borders on pride, which probably sounds fucked up, but in my business, it's a legit feeling.

Her voice is quiet and void of emotion as she continues, "I told that fucker not to touch me. I told him more than once, and he wouldn't listen. By the time I got to the driver, I figured it was fuck-around time because I wasn't letting them take me anywhere where some dirty motherfucker thought he was gonna put his hands on me."

"I understand why you did it, but it was definitely a risky move. You're lucky you got out of that rollover with the minor injuries you have, but you're probably gonna feel like you got hit by a truck for a couple of days."

I press my lips against her forehead as she says, "It's already starting, but it was totally fucking worth it."

The door swings open, and Nettie and Dare are standing there with a couple of people loitering in the hallway behind them. "We have company. Can they come in, or do you want them to come back later?"

She glances toward the door from across my torso, her arm tightening as she meets Nettie's eyes. She nods and says, "They can come in."

I raise my chin at them, indicating they can come in. Nettie walks over first while the group of men hang back.

She kneels beside the bed, taking Carolina's hand in her own, and they remain like that for a few moments, staring into each other's eyes as if they're having a silent conversation that I wouldn't understand.

And I probably wouldn't understand. Being a man is a completely different experience from being a woman, regardless of whether you're an upstanding citizen or a criminal mastermind. But for women in the criminal world, many of them have it worse off because they're constantly being treated like pawns in a losing game.

Carolina inhales shakily, then whispers, "I stopped them. For the first time in my life, I fucking stopped them."

Nettie's lips curve up in a sad smile, but her eyes shine with pride as she replies, "Good. Fuck them."

"How do you get past the shame?" Carolina asks quietly. "The question of whether you could have stopped them all along? That maybe your treatment was deserved, even asked for, or wanted?"

Nettie shakes her head, her lips pressed together as her eyes spark with rage. She leans in close to Carolina, her free hand coming to rest on Carolina's head, and she whispers, "There's no shame in survival, Car. You do what you have to do every single day to survive, and then when you finally have an opening, you take it. And even if you never get that opening—if you never get retribution—you still take comfort in the fact that you survived."

Carolina's body shudders, a guttural sob racking her body as she lets loose what's likely years of pent-up pain and frustration. Nettie crawls onto the bed, leaning into my other side as she presses her forehead against Carolina's, her arm clutching around her shoulders.

Nettie swallows visibly, her voice catching as she whispers, "You gotta let it go, Car. Let it out and let it fucking go."

I wrap my other arm around Nettie, my hand gripping her shoulder as they sob quietly, and I turn my gaze to Dare, who's leaning against the door jamb with his arms crossed over his chest, a hard look in his eyes.

My lips twist as I mouth silently, "*They're all fucking dead,*" and he nods in understanding. Matt appears at his side, and he gives the woman a long look, his lips pressing together in a tight line as he turns to Dare and says something incoherent, but I know what it is.

Fuck-around time.

After a few minutes, both women quiet, then eventually, they're asking for tissues with a watery laugh. Nettie excuses herself to freshen up, and the entourage of men goes with her as Ryan comes back to let Carolina know she's cleared to leave whenever she feels up to it.

Someone brought her a fresh change of clothes, and as I help her, I laugh, earning a questioning look from her, so I explain, "It feels funny to be putting clothes on you when normally, I'm trying to take them off."

She gives me an almost-shy smile, and I finish getting her set to rights in a comfortable silence. Once she's dressed, she sits in the chair to put her shoes on, but I put a hand on her shoulder and kneel to do it for her. She gives me an appreciative look, then reaches out, her fingers stroking along the side of my face lingeringly. An ache blooms in my chest with such intensity that when I open my mouth to speak, the words get caught in my throat.

We remain like that, almost suspended in time, with me kneeling at her feet and her hand on my face until, finally, I manage to say, "I'm really fucking happy you didn't die."

Her eyes widen, surprise evident on her features and then she throws her head back and laughs. I smile in response, laughing at my own idiotic words. I shake my head because that isn't at all what I meant to say, but I'm saved from having to correct myself when her other hand grasps the back of my neck, and she pulls me into a hug, her words a whisper against my neck. "I'm happy that you're happy I didn't fucking die."

She squeezes me once more, then releases her hold on me. I rise, putting a hand out to help her stand beside me. Dare and Nettie are back in the doorway and Dare falls into step beside Carolina as she exits the room, slinging an arm over her shoulder and hugging her to him. He leans his head down close to her, and he speaks to her quietly as they walk down the hallway in front of us.

Nettie jabs me in the ribs with her elbow, and I give her a dirty look. "What the fuck do you want?"

She pulls a piece of paper out of her pocket and hands it to me as she says, "Ryan asked me to give this to you. It's Carolina's test results. You don't have to say anything now, but if I find out you decided to fuck around about this, remember you've already been warned."

I take the piece of paper from her and fold it into a smaller square before stuffing it in the inside pocket of my jacket. "Yes, Nettie. I remember. You're gonna fuck me up."

She gives me a short nod but says nothing further as we walk down the hall and exit the building into the late-afternoon California sunshine. Vehicles are waiting for us, so we all climb inside for the short drive to our rendezvous spot, which is another building on the same property.

Matt is already there, working with a small crew on what our next steps should be. Nettie squeals from behind me, rushing past excitedly. I look ahead in the direction she's running and see Mickey with a big grin on his face. There's no hesitation as they wrap their arms around each other, and Mickey's eyes seem a bit glassy as they speak to each other in their embrace.

Emotion isn't something we're allowed to show freely in this business. Seeing a man like Mickey obviously overjoyed to be reunited with Nettie has that warmth erupting in my chest again, and I look back to Carolina, who's hanging in the doorway. I hold my hand out to her, and she moves closer, gripping my hand between both of hers as we walk across the room together.

We walk over to Dare, and I lean in close to him and ask quietly, "Has anyone told him?"

Dare shakes his head and sighs. "No, but she should be here soon to do it herself, so there's that."

I grimace, and Carolina touches my arm, drawing my gaze to her as she asks, "Who doesn't know what?"

I use the secrecy as an excuse to pull her close to me, wrapping an arm around her waist and leaning in to speak into her ear. "Mickey and Lilith go way back, and he doesn't know that she's not dead."

I pull back, and she stares up at me wide-eyed, her mouth opens in shock. After a moment, she snaps her mouth shut and makes a strangled noise in her throat as she looks back at the older man, who's still speaking to Nettie. "That poor man. I hope he doesn't have a heart attack."

Dare laughs. "If that guy hasn't had a heart attack yet, he never will. He's seen some shit, that's for sure."

Carolina doesn't ask any other questions, but I take a few minutes to give her the cliff notes of the situation, and when I'm done speaking, Carolina shakes her head and mutters, "Sometimes, I forget that there are people out there dealing with even more fucked-up situations than my own. Holy shit."

I nod in agreement. Regardless of how shitty our situation may be, it's highly likely there's always someone out there in an even more complicated and dire situation than your own. It doesn't make your situation any better—it doesn't make it right—but the idea that it could always be worse is quite often true. It goes along with the idea that there are far worse things than death, a common theme you hear in our business.

There's a commotion across the room, and I look over in time to see Jayme come strolling in. He's looking over his shoulder, speaking to someone out of sight, but then, I hear a little voice squealing, "Mama! Mama!" and Flora comes bounding out from behind him, running as fast as her little legs will take her right toward Carolina, who made a beeline for her as soon as she came into sight.

Carolina meets her along the way and scoops her up in her arms, Flora wrapping herself around her mother like the little spider monkey she is. Carolina turns back to me, her eyes meeting mine as she walks over to me, carrying her little girl. She leans her head close to mine and whispers, "Thank you, Tony."

I say nothing in reply, relieved I don't have to, as the overload of emotion in the room tries to get the better of me. I wrap my arm around her back and hug them both to me a little awkwardly, but then Flora pulls away from her mother and catches sight of me, "Tony!"

She leans toward me, her little arm snaking around my neck until she's strangling the two of us, and I raise my free hand and pat her on the back, surprised by how strong she is for such a small thing.

Jayme clears his throat from behind us, and Carolina cranes her head around. She's obviously surprised to see him standing there, and I take Flora from her as she turns to face her brother, stepping forward into his embrace. Her arms come up awkwardly, and I laugh at how stiff she is in his arms, but either he doesn't notice, or he doesn't fucking care. He murmurs something into her ear, and her arms tighten, her hands pressing into his back. Flora giggles in my arms with a big smile as she watches them.

After a few moments, they step apart, and Jayme comes over and shakes my hand as I ask, "Where did you all come from?"

He laughs and shakes his head as he replies, "Lils and I wanted to come over here and help, but when we told this sweet cherub we would be gone for a bit, she threw an epic fit. There was no consoling her or changing her mind, so here we are."

Flora pats Jayme on his cheek, then looks at Carolina and says, "Uncle Jayme said Tony fixed his owie, like Tony fixed my owie."

Jayme chokes and sputters an uncomfortable laugh at her childlike statement. "Well, I don't know if we'd call it an 'owie', but I suppose that's mostly accurate."

Carolina looks between us, a slight frown on her face as she asks, "And what does that mean? Saved you from what?"

"It's a long story."

"I think we've got time."

Jayme looks at me, and I shrug my shoulders. "You tell her whatever you want, man. It's your story."

I whistle sharply, drawing Nettie's attention from across the room, and I incline my head at Flora. She smiles and nods, so I lean into Flora and whisper, "Go see your Aunt Nettie. She missed you." Flora wiggles to get out of my arms, and I set her on the floor, and she races off with another squeal of delight.

We move over to a sitting area in the corner, and Dare joins us.

Jayme sits on the edge of his chair, leaning forward with his arms braced on his thighs. "Where do you want me to start?"

"Why don't you start with the trouble."

The three of us look at each other and laugh, and she rolls her eyes and adds, "Start when the saving-Jayme trouble started. Jesus Christ, you guys are trouble all the way around, I can tell."

I smile at her comment, pressing my hand against her thigh and resisting the urge to pull her into my lap, knowing the story will likely either pull her closer to me or have her running in the opposite fucking direction.

Not that I'll let her go or anything, but that would make it a little more difficult than I feel like dealing with right now.

Jayme pauses for a moment, then takes a deep breath and exhales slowly. Then he begins to speak.

Chapter Twenty-Five

Jayme

TWENTY YEARS AGO

I wake with a start, jerking upright, only to have my head collide with something solid and unforgiving.

I fall backward, cracking my skull on the hard surface I'm lying prone on, cursing as pain explodes in my head.

I take a few moments to get my bearings, taking a few deep inhalations followed by slow exhalations, then I open my eyes and blink into the darkness. My palms come down onto the cold surface and slowly move outward until they come into contact with barriers on both sides of me. My hands move upward, probably not even a full two feet, before I come into contact with the top of what is clearly some kind of box.

My heart jackhammers in my chest, and I close my eyes against the darkness and begin counting in my head, fighting the overwhelming anxiety of claustrophobia. I have no idea how I got here or how long I've been here, but as the fog clears from my brain, I become increasingly aware of the various pains in my body.

I grit my teeth and begin counting again, backward, and forward, multiplication, and even long-fucking-division. I'm not hungry or thirsty, though that could be from shock, and it's impossible for me to assess the damage that's been done or the length of time I've been in here.

I work on controlling my breathing and heart rate since those are the only things I have power over right now. I've trained for this, for deprivation, small spaces, the unknown—these are all things Tony, Darius, and I have spent countless hours training to overcome.

Because we knew this would happen someday.

A loud crack startles me from my meditations, and the darkness through my closed eyelids lightens. I keep my eyes shut and my body relaxed, using my ears to learn anything I possibly can about my current situation.

"Get the fuck out of there," a gruff voice demands. "We gotta clean you up for transportation."

"Why can't we keep him?" another voice snipes.

Hands grab me on both sides, yanking me upward, and then carrying me with my head lolling forwards and my feet dragging on the cold ground. Then, it occurs to me that I'm completely naked.

What the fuck.

They drag me for what feels like forever, then unceremoniously release their hold on me, and I tumble to the floor in a heap where I lay there, biting back a pained groan. Ice-cold water hits me, and my gasp becomes a shout as my entire body recoils in pain, both from the shock of the water and whatever trauma I've withstood since I've been here.

Laughter echoes throughout the room, coming from what sounds like three or four different people, but I refuse to open my eyes and bear witness to anything around me. I choke back another pained noise, absorbing the shock of the freezing water and the sting of the concrete beneath my cheek.

"Somebody's gonna have to get in there and scrub him so that blood and shit will come off."

Someone mutters incoherently, and then someone else says, "Oh, fine, I'll fucking do it. Not like you all haven't contributed to the fucking mess."

The stream of water stops, hands push me onto my front, and a cloth scrubs along my back. I shiver in disgust, swallowing down the retch that attempts to erupt.

"Take your fucking hands off him." The voice is faint, barely cutting through the laughter, but I'd know that voice anywhere.

"Who the fuck are you—" The words are cut off by a garbling sound, and then no sooner do I hear a body hit the floor do I hear people shouting and screaming. I curl in on myself, my hands coming up over my head as fists hit flesh, blades clash, then puncturing and slicing skin, and within a few moments, silence.

A warm hand on my shoulder gives me a shove, and I uncurl myself, shoving away across the wet concrete. My eyes fly open, my defensive position faltering as I look up into the stony gaze of Tony fucking Andersen, covered from head to toe in blood.

"You look like fucking shit, Deveraux."

I choke out a laugh that hurts everywhere, but I can't stop it. I don't know what happened. I don't know where I am. I can't fathom how this kid is in here throwing down with these monsters, and I don't even fucking care.

Relief overwhelms me, and I manage to push myself onto my hands and knees just in time for the bile to come up, and I retch everywhere. My arms shake as I try to push myself up far enough to stand, but my elbows give out, and Tony catches me, helping me to sit up fully.

He holds out a handkerchief, and I take it from him gratefully, using it to wipe my face, as Dare pipes in from the doorway, "Jesus fuck, Tony. You couldn't wait for me?"

"You're too fucking slow, man," Tony retorts. "I couldn't sit back and watch these fucking pieces of shit put their hands on him. God only fucking knows what went on here in the time it took us to find him."

"I'm not going to argue that, but we better hurry the fuck up, or we're gonna end up boxed in here."

Tony is opening doors and drawers, finally coming back with what looks to be a mostly clean towel and throws it at me. I use it to rough dry my hair and body, and then I stand there, shivering, with the dirty towel in my hand, unsure of what to do next.

Dare pulls a pack from his back, opening the top and pulling out clothing that I can only assume is his. I take it from him, quickly dressing myself with minimal help. I've barely gotten the shoes and socks on my feet when a bit of commotion from down the hallway turns our attention to the door. Dare pulls some weapons from his pack and hands them to me, then turns to Tony and asks, "Are you ready?"

Tony nods, a gleeful glint in his eyes as he says, "Fuck-around time, boys. What are we gonna do?"

I check the gun Dare gave me, making sure there's a round in the chamber, then secure the blade in my non-dominant hand. I push back every feeling that's bubbling inside me other than the rage, and then I reply, "Let's find out."

Present day

Carolina is clutching Tony's hand that was resting on her leg the entire time I told the story. She gives me a pained look as she asks, "How old were you?"

I shrug, shaking my head as I reply, "I don't know. Fifteen, sixteen."

Tony gives me a look, then turns to Carolina, and says, "He was barely thirteen. Dare and I were around fifteen or so."

She looks at him in horror, her gaze bouncing back to me as she cries, "What the fuck did they do to you?"

"It doesn't matter. I came to terms with that shit a long time ago."

"Who put you there?"

"His own father," Dare interjects. "We tried to find him as soon as we realized he was missing, but we kept hitting one roadblock after another. So, finally, we said fuck it, and went after the one person we knew for sure was behind it. His shitbag fucking father."

"He tried to tell us he was fine," Tony says in disgust. "That he was out on some learning experience and would be back soon. And maybe in his twisted brain, he thought that was true, but I don't believe he'd have ever come back if we hadn't found it."

"Did you kill him?" Carolina asks.

Tony shakes his head as he replies, "No, but I fucking wanted to. If nothing else, he was so fucking scared by the end of the conversation that he didn't fuck with Jayme again for a long time. We made it clear that if he wanted to fuck with Jayme, he better kill all of us first, or we'd come for him. There would be a whole line of people that would come for him."

"What the fuck is wrong with people?" Carolina sputters, then presses her lips together as she laughs bitterly. "But that's basically exactly what he did to me, except I didn't have Darius and Tony to save me."

Tony stiffens beside her, his eyes going to her face as he moves his free hand to the back of her neck. He leans in and says, "Until now. No one will ever fuck with you again, Carolina. Do you understand me?"

Her eyes search his for a few moments and then she nods, her features softening as his fingers caress her neck before releasing her.

"He's right," I breathe. "No one will fuck with you or Flora ever again. Not as long as any of us or anyone that works for us is still standing."

She presses her lips together and gives a short nod in acknowledgment of my words, and then we sit back in our seats, allowing silence to settle around us.

Soon, our quiet is disturbed by chattering coming from the doorway, and I look over to see Agatha enter the room with Lilith right behind her. All of our eyes fly to Mickey as we rise from our seats and migrate closer to see what his reaction will be.

Agatha stops in front of Mickey and Nettie, and Mickey's eyes light up when he sees her. "Aggie, my sweet girl. So good to see you."

She gives the old man a hug, and it's right as they pull back that Mickey's eyes land on Lilith, who's standing there rather sheepishly, wringing her hands together. After a beat, she gives him a little wave and says, "How about me?"

We all hold our collective breaths, and you could hear a pin drop as we wait for his response.

There's no shock or surprise on his face, no gasp of outrage, no wail of disbelief. The old man crosses his arms over his chest and says blandly, "So you finally decide to raise yourself from the dead?"

All of our mouths drop open, and Lilith looks at Matt and asks, "Did you tell him?"

"Not fucking likely," Matt sputters.

Mickey rolls his eyes and says dryly, "Give me a break, girl. I've known you your whole fucking life, and if there's one thing knowing you has taught me, it's to never believe somebody's dead unless you remove their head and set their body on fire yourself."

Nettie pokes Mickey in the shoulder and says accusingly, "So you knew the whole time she wasn't dead?"

Mickey shakes his head. "No, for a good bit of time there, I legitimately thought she was gone. But then I started hearing different things from Europe, things that sounded a little too much like my little viper queen. So, I started putting out feelers, and eventually, I knew there wasn't a chance in hell it wasn't fucking her causing all that havoc abroad."

"Well, that was anti-climactic," Dare mutters.

Nettie laughs, adding, "You ain't kidding."

"Now that that's over, let's get back to business," Matt says as he walks toward the workstation he was standing at before. He starts pressing buttons and continues, "I've managed to pinpoint some locations around the world where there seems to be hive-like activity in human trafficking. I can't figure out why Carolina is still a target with Vincent and Dmitri out of the way. The only thing I can surmise is that it may be someone closely connected to them who's trying to run a business that they're ill-prepared to run, and since they know that their position may be questioned, they'd feel more secure having her and Flora by their side as collateral." He turns to Carolina and asks, "Dimitri have any other kids? Close associates that he treated like family?"

She shrugs in response, shaking her head as she answers, "Not that

I know of. I spent a lot of time skirting around people, keeping my ear to the wall. Unless directed otherwise, most people stick to their own circle for fear they'll end up with a knife in the back, and rightly so, because that's how that whole organization works."

Matt's mouth twists, his eyes narrowing as he considers his response. He presses a few more buttons on his keyboard, then turns to me and asks, "How about you? Can you think of anyone in particular who'd be a direct connection between Carolina and your dad?"

"I imagine a lot of people know about her since it appears my dad didn't hide her from anyone other than me. It was like his last middle finger before meeting his own end. Honestly, the list of possible suspects is too long to weed through."

Mickey and Lilith join us, and Matt glances over, rolling his eyes as he says, "How about you two? Surely, you must know someone who could be involved in this?"

"We've been working down Carolina's list of names that you sent us, but it's taking longer than we thought because we're being extra thorough. Sometimes, the initial name we got branches off to other persons of interest that we had to follow up on. I think if we continue along that line, we'll probably come up with something soon."

Lilith leans into him, bumping him with her shoulder as she gives him a fond look. "It's so great how well things have been going since I've been gone. You and Nettie have managed to clean up the place."

"Your work over in Europe has been helping as well. It's almost like we've been working in tandem to take out all the vermin. It's been a very exciting time," Mickey replies with exhilaration in his eyes.

And then, Nettie adds, "I was pleasantly surprised with how seamless the transition was. Most everyone jumped right on board with the new business plan. We've been keeping track of a few people who opted out, and so far, they've managed to stay aboveboard."

Matt sighs, poking at his keyboard a bit violently as he brings up some charts on the screen. "Since we have no direct leads, most of the data I've been able to compile and analyze indicates our best option is to head back to Europe."

Everyone groans, and then Tony says, "We have to make accommodations for Carolina and Flora before we go anywhere. I don't think that'll take very long, but maybe we leave in the morning?"

"Let's give it a day since we have to hop a redeye flight back anyway. That'll give me more time to double-check some dates and come up with a streamlined itinerary."

Mickey turns to Tony and says, "I have a couple of families over here we trust implicitly, and they're behind gates most of the time. It'll be good for Flora to be with kids around her age so she can adjust to life as a normal child."

Tony nods and opens his mouth to say something else, but Carolina interrupts him. "Excuse me? Are y'all really making decisions for me right now?"

Tony turns wide eyes on her as she steps closer and says through his gritted teeth, "Yes. I am."

She doesn't even blink, just taking another step into him until she's right in his face. "I don't think so."

They stand there for a few moments, chest to chest, silently staring into each other's eyes. The tension in the room is palpable, and I sidle over to Nettie, motioning for her to hand over Flora, who comes willingly as I whisper, "How about we go for a little stroll? Check out the place."

No one says anything as I turn and walk away, but Lilith and Mickey fall into step on either side of me, and Lilith says under her breath, "What happened to Carolina while she was gone?"

Mickey adds, "Right? I was under the impression she was a meek little mouse."

I glance over my shoulder in time to see her poking Tony in the chest, obviously having some choice words for him.

I turn back to Lilith and Mickey with a laugh. "Seems my sister is going to give Tony a run for his money."

Lilith cackles gleefully. "I can't wait to watch!"

Chapter Twenty-Six

Carolina

I DON'T KNOW WHY these people think they can keep making decisions for me without consulting me, but I'm unbelievably sick of it. Tony has gone out of his way to help me feel empowered. He has reminded me time and time again that I choose, and I make decisions for myself. And now, here we are, standing toe to toe, ready to brawl over a choice that should be entirely mine.

Everyone around us is completely silent, likely sitting back and waiting to see what will happen next. But if anyone thinks I'm gonna back down on this, they're gonna find out they're wrong. I poke him in the chest with two fingers as I spit out, "Nope."

I move to prod him in the chest again, and he grabs my hand, holding it firmly when I try to yank it away, so I continue, "This is my fight just as much as it is anyone else's. You don't get to decide what role I play at this point."

His jaw clenches, and I can tell he wants to argue, but Nettie steps up beside us, resting her hand on his shoulder as she says, "She's right, Tony. I know it sucks, I know it's difficult for you, and you want to keep her out of harm's way, but it's not up to you."

He glances at her, then he looks beyond her to where Darius and Matt are leaning against the table. "Help me out, guys."

Matt says nothing, just giving him a sympathetic look, but then Darius answers, "You know I'd put them all in a safe house until the end of days if I had a choice, but you also know I've had to learn the hard way that that choice isn't mine to make. Even now, if I thought I could get away with sneaking Antoinette, Carolina, and Aggie out of danger, I'd do it. But the fact of the matter is, I don't have that kind of power."

Tony huffs out a breath, turns back to me, and asks, "What about Flora? Don't you think you have a responsibility to her as her mother to not go on a suicide mission?"

"I owe it to my little girl to stand up for myself. Now I know she's safe, that no one can get to her, I owe it to her and to myself to put an end to all of it, so it doesn't happen to anyone else."

His features twist in a grimace, and he looks away for a moment and then looks back at me, saying, "It'll never be over, sweetheart. Doesn't matter how many of them we kill or how many organizations we shut down; they pop up faster than we can take them out."

"So, what? Does that mean we stop trying?"

He looks back over to where Matt, Dare, and Antoinette are lined up, leaning against the desk. "I can't," he says and then chokes, pausing for a few beats before clearing his throat and continuing, "There has to be another way."

Dare shakes his head, his shoulders lifting as he responds, "I'm getting some déjà vu here, man. We've switched positions, but at least now, I can answer that question from experience." He pauses, his eyes moving to Antoinette as he continues, "Visceral agony at the mere thought that something will go wrong because lord knows something always goes wrong. Having to acknowledge and accept how destroyed you would be without her. I totally get it." He stops talking, turns his eyes back to Tony, and adds, "You have to remember that the other option would be living with a demoralized, empty shell of the person you're hoping to save. What right do we have to try to steal their spirit and mold it to suit us? Isn't it their spirit that drew us to them in the first place?"

Antoinette smiles at him softly and mouths, "I love you," to which he appears to reply with, "I know," and she laughs.

Tony clears his throat, and he's shaking his head in denial, so I grab onto his shirt with both hands and yank on him until he stops shaking his head and looks at me. "I may have been your damsel in the past, but you already saved her. Now, I don't need you to save me. Now, I need to save myself."

Both of his hands come up and cup my cheeks as he searches my eyes before finally muttering, "Fuck." I release my grip on his shirt, moving my hands to his wrists, which have relaxed a fraction as he replies, "It sounds like I don't have much of a choice here."

"You have a choice," I reply. "You can stand by my side and help me, or you can get the fuck out of my way and watch me."

A noise from the doorway catches our attention, and we all turn to see who's coming in now. "Well, fuck me sideways. She shoots a couple of people, and all of a sudden, she's a fully trained vigilante."

Declan fucking Hughes—in the flesh.

"Did we ever decide who gets to punch him first?" Dare asks.

Matt laughs and replies, "I was thinking about giving him a free pass for that whole tracking thing. I mean, for a second there, he was acting like a professional."

"Haha," Declan retorts as he walks across the room toward his brother. "Still hanging with the comedian, I see, Darius."

"Still the constant fool, I see, Declan."

The two men stand there, eyeing each other warily for a few moments until finally, Dare laughs under his breath and shakes his head. "You have the worst fucking timing, you know that? Of all the moments to try to pull a prank on me, this is the one you choose." He pauses and then laughs again as he raises his hands and grabs Declan by both of his biceps, giving him a little shake as he continues, "How come you didn't show up six months ago, or a year ago, when I really fucking needed you?"

Declan shakes Dare's hands off him, his face twisting as he sputters, "Why didn't you call me and tell me you needed me? You know I would've come."

They stand there, silently glaring at each other, and I look at Tony, who's standing there watching them with an amused expression. I glance over at Antoinette, who's rolling her eyes in annoyance, but then she finally steps forward, putting herself between the two men with a hand on both of their chests as she says, "You'll need to save your sniping at each other for another day. Either focus on the immediate issue we're dealing with or take your little pissing contest to another fucking room so us adults can get on with it."

Both men look at her, then they go back to glaring at each other, and then Declan asks, "Is this the little hellcat that you risked everything for?"

Dare smiles at him wickedly as he responds, "Oh, yes. Please say more so I can watch her kick your ass."

Declan frowns, giving Antoinette a once-over before raising his eyebrows at Darius questioningly. Dare's smile broadens, and Declan turns his questioning eyes on me. I give him the universal sign for cut it out with my finger across my neck. His frown deepens as he looks back at Antoinette, squinting pensively.

Antoinette pays him no mind as she huffs, "Don't encourage him, Darius. Remember, the longer this takes, the less time we have for that thing you were talking about earlier."

All humor drops from Dare's face, and he instantly straightens and click his tongue. "You heard the lady. Let's get this shit together, so we can enjoy what downtime we have left before shit gets messy."

I walk over to Declan and ask, "Shouldn't you be in a hospital?"

"And miss all the fun?" he replies dismissively, but I raise my eyebrows at him and give him my best-unconvinced look until he finally continues with a low chuckle, "Okay, I probably won't be going on any super missions in the immediate future, but I figured I could come here and see what help I could be. If nothing else, I had to show myself outside of the hospital in an upright position, so the paparazzi didn't go fucking cuckoo."

"As annoyed as I am with your fucking bullshit, it's for the best that you didn't die," I say quietly.

He laughs, leans closer to me, and whispers, "And even better that you didn't die. Not sure exactly what was going on when I came in here, but Tony seems a little committed. It's a good look for him, but don't tell him I said that."

My face heats at his words, and I shake my head in denial. "He's a protective guy in general. He's mostly an overbearing pain in the ass."

Declan looks over at Tony, who's deep in conversation with Matt and Dare, the humor on his face disappearing until he appears far off, like he's stuck in a memory. Then he shakes his head, and it's gone. He looks back at me and says, "You may not want to believe it, but this is different. And frankly, the fact that he heard you out at all says more than anything. But make no mistake, Tony Andersen has braved the fiery pit of hell for the people he cares about, and he'll keep fucking doing it until the bitter end."

He doesn't say anything further; he just gives me a curt nod and walks off, and I look back at Tony to find he's watching me. I give him a small smile, and he winks at me, my smile broadening as he walks toward me. "You okay, sweetheart?"

"I think I am."

He leans his head down so he's looking me directly in the eyes as he whispers, "Do you want to get out of here? Let these fucking yahoos figure it out on their own?"

I smile and nod, so he straightens and then holds his hand out to me. I don't hesitate. I put my hand in his, and then he doesn't say anything to anyone as he leads me out of the room and down the hallway.

Chapter Twenty-Seven

Carolina

Tony leads me down winding hallways and up and down stairs. It seems the facility we're borrowing from Matt's contact has every amenity imaginable…if you can find your room. I was assigned a room on the far side of the building, and although it's not fancy, it looks comfortable enough, and it has an ensuite bathroom.

I expect Tony to deposit me there and then return to take part in the planning, but he surprises me when he shuts and locks the door and then disappears into the bathroom. Water comes on in the shower, and he's back in the bedroom, yanking his shirt over his head while I'm standing in the middle of the room, awkwardly twisting my fingers.

He stops a few feet from me and cocks his head at me. "What are you doing? Strip."

My heart skitters in my chest and sweat prickles up my spine at the thought of showering with him. Which is kind of fucked up, considering we've fucked before. I sucked the man's cock in an airplane lavatory, but being stripped bare under the fall of water without so much as the illusion of a mask to cover my features is scary.

I continue to stand there silently until he narrows his eyes and closes the distance between us. He cups my cheeks between his hands, his fingers pressing into my hairline as he looks into my eyes and says, "You're welcome to shower alone if you're more comfortable, but I figured you might be kind of stiff, and I could help you."

I instantly relax at his words, some of the tension seeping out of my bones at the reassurance that I don't have to do anything I don't want to do. It's not that I believe he'd force me, but the lifelong inclination to constantly bend overrides what I know about the man.

I swallow past the lump in my throat and then reply, "No, it's okay. I was just..." I pause and then stand there with my mouth open, unsure of what to say.

He releases his grip on my face and steps into me until the fronts of our bodies are touching, his arms coming around my waist to hold me tightly against him. "You can use that safeword at any time with me, Carolina. I don't care if I'm offering you a snack that you don't feel like eating or you don't want to watch the dumb, shit show I want to watch. One word is all it takes, and it goes away, or it stops."

I nod, now unable to speak because of the giant lump in my throat, and he searches my eyes for a moment and then releases me. He takes my hand in his and leads me toward the bathroom that's filling up with steam.

I've never been in the shower with someone intentionally. As in, I wanted to be there. I've never known a shower scenario where two people found enjoyment in each other, even if it was just because they were sharing the same space. Tony must recognize something in my face because he comes back and asks, "You're lost. Do I need to find you?"

His words break the last bit of tension in my chest, and I chuckle and whisper, "Yes. I think I'd like that."

"What do you need?"

I pause, contemplating his question, unsure how to answer, when he adds, "Do you want to lead or follow, sweetheart?"

"Follow."

"Do you want gentle?" I shrug, so he adds, "Hard?" I shrug again, and he laughs. "How about a mix of both, then?"

I smile at this, nodding as he pulls my shirt over my head. I'm wearing someone else's clothing sans undergarments, so it doesn't take much work before I'm nude in the middle of the steamy room, and he's frowning at the bruises on my body.

I ignore his grumbling, reaching out and yanking on his jeans until he finally turns his focus back to getting naked. Then he pulls me into the shower, and the last of my trepidation swirls down the drain.

I expect him to push me back against the shower wall and get right to ravaging me, but he doesn't. Instead, he places me directly under the water, his fingers firm as he pushes my hair back from my face, directing the angle of my head so water doesn't trickle over my forehead.

I watch his face as he methodically washes and conditions my hair before grabbing a washcloth and bar of soap, working a lather into the cloth, and then running it over my back and down my arms. He's completely focused on the job, his hand holding the lathered cloth, not lingering as he washes every inch of my skin, and I take the opportunity to stare at him unabashedly.

He leans down, running the cloth along each of my legs, and then kneels and washes between my legs gently before sitting back and allowing the water to wash over me, rinsing me clean. He flips the shower dial until the stream of water from above stops, and then steam swirls around us.

"Just keep staring, sweetheart," he says as he stands, his eyes meeting mine as he rasps, "Having your eyes on me gets me hard. Gives me ideas of what you could be doing while looking at me like that."

"Looking at you like what?"

"Blatant want, desire, hunger," he whispers against my lips, the cloth dropping from his hands onto the floor of the shower. "Like you want to be my sweet little whore for the rest of my life."

My heart stutters in my chest, my breath catching as his arms come around me, sliding over my wet skin until they're locked around my waist, and he's lifting me so we're eye to eye. I go to speak, but he leans close, stopping me with his lips on mine, his tongue entering my mouth without hesitation or gentleness. He takes what he wants, angling his head and pushing me back against the wall so I have nowhere to go but into him.

He kisses me until I'm limp and sobbing into his mouth, my arms around his neck, clutching at him. He drags his lips across my cheek and along my jaw, zeroing in on my neck with a tactical intensity that has me moaning and gasping.

My fingers tangle in his hair, and he moves downward, his lips, teeth, and tongue a hot trail over my shoulder and along the outer curve of my breast. I yank his hair, and he laughs, his tongue lazily teasing my sensitive skin, so I yank again, shoving my breast against his mouth until he closes his lips around my aching nipple and sucks.

The sensation sends a jolt of pleasure to my pussy, and I buck my hips against him, wanting nothing more in that moment than for him to fill the empty ache between my legs.

He pays the same attention to my other breast, kissing and licking along each curve before finally sucking my nipple into his mouth, grazing it with his teeth before releasing it and moving further down my body. He kisses over my stomach, along my hips, and partway down my thigh before moving his focus between my legs.

He kneels at my feet, places a kiss at the top of my pubic bone, then goes lower and presses his face into my pussy, inhaling deeply before lapping at my clit. I tense slightly, suddenly self-conscious about my lack of grooming, but then he looks up at me, and the look of absolute pleasure on his face eases my fears.

He nudges my legs and says, "Lean back, sweetheart. Spread your legs for me and let me show you what it's like to have a man worship you."

I rest my back against the shower wall, lifting one of my legs to rest on his shoulder and then moving my other leg so I'm braced wide open for him.

He flicks my clit with the tip of his tongue, teasing me mercilessly until I'm panting and begging for more. He finally presses his open mouth against me and sucks my sensitive flesh into my mouth, pushing one finger inside me, sliding it in and out, in and out. He adds another finger and does the same in-and-out slide a few times before adding a third finger.

I grip my hands in his hair again, giving up any semblance of propriety, writhing against him shamelessly. "Yes. Yes, just like that. Oh, fuck, Tony. That feels so fucking good."

He growls against me, his fingers inside me pressing up sharply and then pulsing rhythmically as he doubles his assault on my clit with his lips and tongue. I press my head back against the tiles and sob with pleasure as white-hot heat rolls over me. He licks and sucks my clit with fervor, his fingers in my spasming cunt twisting, drawing out my orgasm until I'm a twitching, quivering mess against the shower wall.

I'm gasping for breath, little tremors racking my body as he continues to lick me lazily, his fingers stroking inside me gently. I take a deep breath in, exhaling in satisfaction, and then his mouth latches onto my clit again, and I tighten my fingers in his hair, yanking him away from me as I laugh, "No, no. I can't. It's too much."

He looks up at me from between my legs, the heat in his eyes taking my breath as he smiles and asks, "Are you sure? I'll worship you all fucking night, sweetheart. You just say the word."

"I'm good," I reply breathlessly, my fingers releasing his hair as he leans back and eases my leg to the floor. He stands and places his hands on my arms, steadying me until I get both of my feet under me. Then he turns away, messing with the buttons on the fancy shower until the steam stops and water runs from the showerhead.

He gives himself a quick wash, then flips the taps off and turns to me, shooing me toward the door, where he grabs a large towel and half-dries himself before wrapping the towel around his waist. He snags two more towels, using one to dry my body and then wrapping it around my torso and the other to dry my hair.

He exits the bathroom, leaving me standing there, but quickly returns with a chair, which he places in front of the mirror. He points to the chair, and I sit, watching him rummage around in the drawers and cupboards until he comes back with a hairdryer and brush in his hands.

I hold my hands out to take them from him, but he pulls them back and shakes his head. "I'll do it."

I drop my hands to my lap, twisting my fingers to keep them occupied as he gently untangles my long hair. I watch him intently as he walks around me, using the brush and dryer to smooth out my hair until it falls in a shiny mass around me.

I'm doing my best to keep my eyes on his face, but every time he circles in front of me, my gaze is drawn to the front of his towel and the tool beneath bobbing for freedom. I choke on a little laugh, not averting my eyes quickly enough, and when I look up, he's giving me the most disapproving look.

"Stop that," he mutters almost shyly, and I giggle at the serious expression on his face.

"Stop what?" I ask with fake innocence.

He stops brushing my hair and gives me a stern look. "You know what."

I take my innocent look up a notch and bat my eyelashes at him, and he growls in response, going back to his work without further comment. I smile, continuing to watch him and his hard dick attempting to escape the precariously secured towel around his waist.

After a few minutes, he finishes up and turns to put the dryer and brush away, but I reach out and snag the towel, yanking it loose in one move. He freezes, his eyes flashing at me, and I do the only thing I can think of at that moment.

I run.

He doesn't bother putting the appliances away, and they clatter to the floor as he takes off after me, as if I have anywhere to go, wrapped in a towel, barefoot.

He catches me before I even reach the bed and picks me up from behind, falling with me face-first on the bed so I'm pinned beneath him. I'm breathless with mirth, and he laughs quietly against my ear, rubbing his hard cock against my towel-covered ass as he asks, "Can I help you with something, sweetheart?"

I press myself back against him, turning my head to look back at him as I say, "Seems to me like you're the one in need of some help."

He nuzzles my ear, breathing into it and sending a shiver down my spine, and my hips lift off the mattress instinctively. He makes a pleased sound, a mix between a laugh and a growl, and my insides quiver, a sensation that remains almost foreign to me after so many years of avoiding anything so destructive as desire.

I tense up, and Tony must feel it because he pushes himself off me, and then he's rolling me onto my back, leaving the towel between us as he stretches out on top of me. He braces himself with his forearms on either side of my head, and when I attempt to look anywhere but at him, he grasps my face between his hands and holds my head steady so I can't look away. "Just say red, sweetheart," he rasps, his head dipping forward to brush his lips over mine. "Anytime, anywhere, any reason."

I inhale a sharp breath through my nose, a small sob escaping as my hands come up and press the back of his head, so he'll kiss me properly. I've never been one for kissing, likely because it has never been an overly pleasurable experience for me, but it's different now with Tony. He kisses me like he can't get close enough, his lips, tongue, and teeth consuming me as if he's been starved for a lifetime.

And it's not only what he does with his mouth. His hands stroke over me, his legs moving along mine, and before I know it, the towel is a tangle beneath me, and he's pulling back and kneeling between my splayed legs, his lips damp and hair tousled, that familiar sexy glint in his eyes.

"Your test results came back clean," he murmurs, his eyes lingering between my legs where his bare cock nudges my pussy.

My lips curve up in a smile. My hands move to rest on top of his, where he's squeezing my inner thighs. "That's good news for the rest of night, considering we're probably not at all prepared for safety here."

His gaze flits to mine and then trails slowly down my naked body until he's once again staring between my spread legs. He swallows visibly, his movements slowing until he's kneeling there, unmoving.

"What is it?" I ask quietly, my hands squeezing his reassuringly.

His lips twist, his expression conflicted as he pushes the tip of his cock inside me and then pulls out again. He stares down at me with uncertainty painting his features, then he sighs and says, "They lied to you, sweetheart. About not being able to have more children."

I frown, my heart stopping in my chest at his words. "What are you talking about?"

"You can get pregnant," he says with a shrug. "At some point, they put a contraceptive device inside you, and then made it out like you were infertile."

He slides his bare dick against my pussy, his gaze on my chest as he mutters, "I didn't want to tell you."

"Then why did you tell me?"

He huffs out a laugh as he replies, "Nettie shamed me into it. Initially, I wasn't going to."

"And here I thought Tony Andersen didn't have any shame."

All humor falls from his face, and he searches my eyes for a moment before whispering, "Only with you."

I frown, my hands moving up to grip his wrists as I try to speak, but he continues, "Typically, I don't give a fuck what people think of me. I have my small inner circle, who are a slight exception to that rule, but my people know me and accept me for who I am—thorns and all. I literally don't have any fucks for anyone else, but then you showed up and fucked it all to hell. Because for some crazy fucking reason, I don't just want you to look at me as if I'm the only man in the world. I want you to look at me like there's no better man than me. And I know the only way that will happen is if it's true."

"Are you saying I make you want to be a better man?"

"I wouldn't go that far," he says dryly. "But I definitely wanna be better than the type of man you're used to. I want you to trust me implicitly, to seek me out for every need that you'll ever have."

He settles his weight between my legs, his hard cock resting against my pussy, and I instinctively press my hips up, rubbing against him. He attempts to move away, but I bring my legs up and wrap them around his waist, my heels digging into his ass. His breath catches in his throat as he asks, "What are you doing, sweetheart?"

I smile, my hands moving to his ass as I rotate my hips and grind my slick cunt against him. "Whatever I want."

He growls low in his chest and then groans as I move my hips back at just the right angle so the tip of his cock slides inside me. "That's right, baby." I slide my hands up his back, so my hands are on his shoulders, and then pull myself up to lick and bite his ear. "Do you feel how wet you make me?"

His response is a mixture of a moan and a chuckle, and the sound vibrating against the skin of my neck sends a shudder down my spine, so I rotate my hips again, taking more of him inside me. He licks a path up the side of my neck to my ear and mutters breathlessly, "Oh, fuck, that's good. Holy shit, you're so fucking wet for me."

I hook my feet around his thighs and buck my hips up, gasping as his cock slides in deeper. "You like that? You like sliding into me, knowing there's nothing between us?"

He moves his hands to the mattress on either side of my head, attempting to ease away from me, but I tighten my arms and legs around him, attempting to hold him in place. He laughs shakily. "Hold on, sweetheart. I'm not going anywhere; I just wanna do it right."

"I don't see how there's a wrong way for you to put it in me."

He moves more of his weight back onto his knees, lifting his upper body away from me with one arm braced against the mattress as he uses his free hand to loosen my grip on his back.

I fall back onto the mattress, my arms and legs relaxing as he eases away, staring down at me. "The only way you're getting my cum is if your quivering cunt pulls it out of me. You're gonna have to beg me for it."

My pussy clenches at his words, heat rolling over me as he moves backward until he's lying face-down, flat on the bed, and his hot breath is between my legs. He doesn't tease me or ease his way in. He lays the flat of his tongue against my clit and licks as he slides two fingers inside me, pushing them deep.

Any thought on whether I'll be able to come again leaves my mind as his lips, tongue, and fingers drive me steadily higher. My hands move into his hair, my feet shifting beneath me until I'm rubbing my pussy against his face, shamelessly riding his tongue, moaning, gasping, and cursing until pleasure rips through me.

I'm trembling all over, my hands releasing his hair, and then he's kneeling before me, rubbing his wet hand on his cock, the smile on his face one of wanton self-satisfaction. He dribbles saliva directly onto his dick, smearing it around, and then he's pressing between my legs, sliding inside in one smooth motion.

He grabs my hips in his hands and pulls me up as he says, "Brace yourself, sweetheart. Touch yourself as I fuck you. Rub your fingers on that needy little clit until we get another one out of you."

I do as I'm told, bracing my feet again and lifting my hips so only my upper body is on the mattress. I move one arm out to balance myself and then move my other hand between my legs, rubbing firm circles in time with the hard, measured strokes of his cock inside me. "Oh, god. Oh, fuck. Oh, fuck, that feels good. Don't stop."

His eyes close for a moment, his head tilting back as he says, "No chance of that, sweetheart. Not a fucking chance."

He continues to pump into me rhythmically, intent on pulling that last orgasm out of me, and I'm slightly shocked to feel it right there. Taunting me. "Harder. Fuck me harder."

His eyes open, and he stares down at me, panting slightly as he says through his gritted teeth, "Not yet, sweetheart. You're gonna beg for it. You're gonna beg me to fill you up."

His words send a ricochet of pleasure through me, and I sob as the heat crests, my breath catching in my throat. "Oh, fuck, yes," I sob on a long moan. "Please. Oh, fuck. Give it to me. Give it all to me."

Tony releases his hold on my hips, lowering my ass onto the mattress, his upper body falling forward so his chest is pressed against my breasts. His arms move around my shoulders, so his hands are cupping my head, and then his lips are on mine, and he's moaning, cursing into my mouth with his throbbing cock pushed deep inside me.

I barely manage to keep my eyes open as I shake with pleasure, but he's staring at me, and the look of pure rapture on his face is hypnotizing.

He slides in and out of me a few more times as we both catch our breaths. After a few moments, he stops moving but remains inside me as he presses soft kisses on my cheek and jaw and then down my neck until finally, he presses his face against my throbbing pulse point and sighs deeply.

I huff out a laugh, then get a bit concerned when he doesn't so much as twitch a muscle. He's fucking heavy.

I grunt with effort as I try to push him from our now-awkward position, and eventually, I squeak out, "Can't. Breathe."

His arms immediately move, so some of his weight is removed from my chest, but he doesn't move otherwise as he rubs his nose along my neck. I take the quiet moment to wrap my arms around him, my hands pressing on his back, and I lift my head so I can relax my face into his neck, inhaling the familiar scent of him before licking his damp skin. He doesn't move away, so I lick a few more times before taking a bite, laughing as he jumps.

His head comes around to glare at me, and he mutters under his breath as he slowly pulls away. I continue to giggle as he moves over, so he's sprawled beside me on the bed, one of his hands resting on my inner thigh. Then I laugh quietly and say, "Well, that was reckless."

He's lying there with his eyes closed, but his lips curve up in a smug smile. "But so worth it."

"You're not worried?"

"Not at all," he says with a shake of his head, and the tiny flicker of anxiety in my gut dissipates.

We lie there in silence for a while, neither of us looking at the other. His fingers stroke my inner thigh, and I move my hand to his wrist, my thumb gliding over his pulse point leisurely.

"I don't know how this happened," he whispers.

I turn my head toward him, raise my eyebrows at him questioningly, and ask, "How what happened?"

"Loving you," he says, almost in annoyance. Then he turns his head toward me, his eyes on mine as he adds, "It's hugely inconvenient."

My heart stutters in my chest, my breath catching in my throat. I stare at him, wide-eyed, and then the corners of his lips twitch, and he laughs. It's not awkward or bitter; it's pure, unfiltered mirth, and it's almost as if it's the first time I've truly seen him.

I open my mouth to speak, but he puts a hand up and shakes his head. "You don't have to say anything, sweetheart. I didn't say it to get a response from you. I said it because I felt like it needed to be put out into the universe, for it to hang out there and allow you time to soak it in and see how you feel about it."

I take his hand in mine and place it against my chest. "I've never told anyone I love them. Not even Flora. Showing true, heartfelt emotion was too dangerous because it always gave them a target, and lord knows they had enough of those without me painting bullseyes on people. I'm not even sure if I know how to love in the true sense of the emotion."

He pushes his palm against my chest, moving it until it's pressed against my heart. "I have no doubt that you know how to love. Just like I have no doubt that even if you don't love me right now, you will eventually. I'll make sure of it."

"Oh, you will?" I ask with a laugh. "What happened to you not wanting to railroad me into anything?"

"Well, that only had to do with babies," he says seriously. "That's where it begins and ends. I won't force you to bear my children, but you're stuck with me, whether you love me or hate me."

He appears so blasé about the entire conversation that I find myself laughing again, and then the tightness in my chest eases, and I allow myself to revel in this new feeling—freedom.

A jolt of excitement zips up my spine, and I roll over toward him so suddenly that he startles. I press my face against his ear and whisper, "I love you."

He tenses up, his arm coming around my shoulders and holding me against him for a moment, but then he relaxes, leaning back and meeting my eyes with an incredibly smug look on his face as he says, "Good. That'll save us both a lot of trouble going forward."

I slap at his chest playfully, then lie back down next to him, and he pulls me closer, yanking me over until my head is relaxing on his shoulder, my hand now resting on his heart. "Where do we go from here?"

He tightens his grip on me, his lips pressing against my forehead briefly before he says, "First, we're gonna go fuck around. And then, we do whatever the fuck we want."

I rub my cheek against his warm skin, inhaling the scent of him into my lungs as I smile, relief overwhelming me as I think over his words.

Whatever the fuck we want.

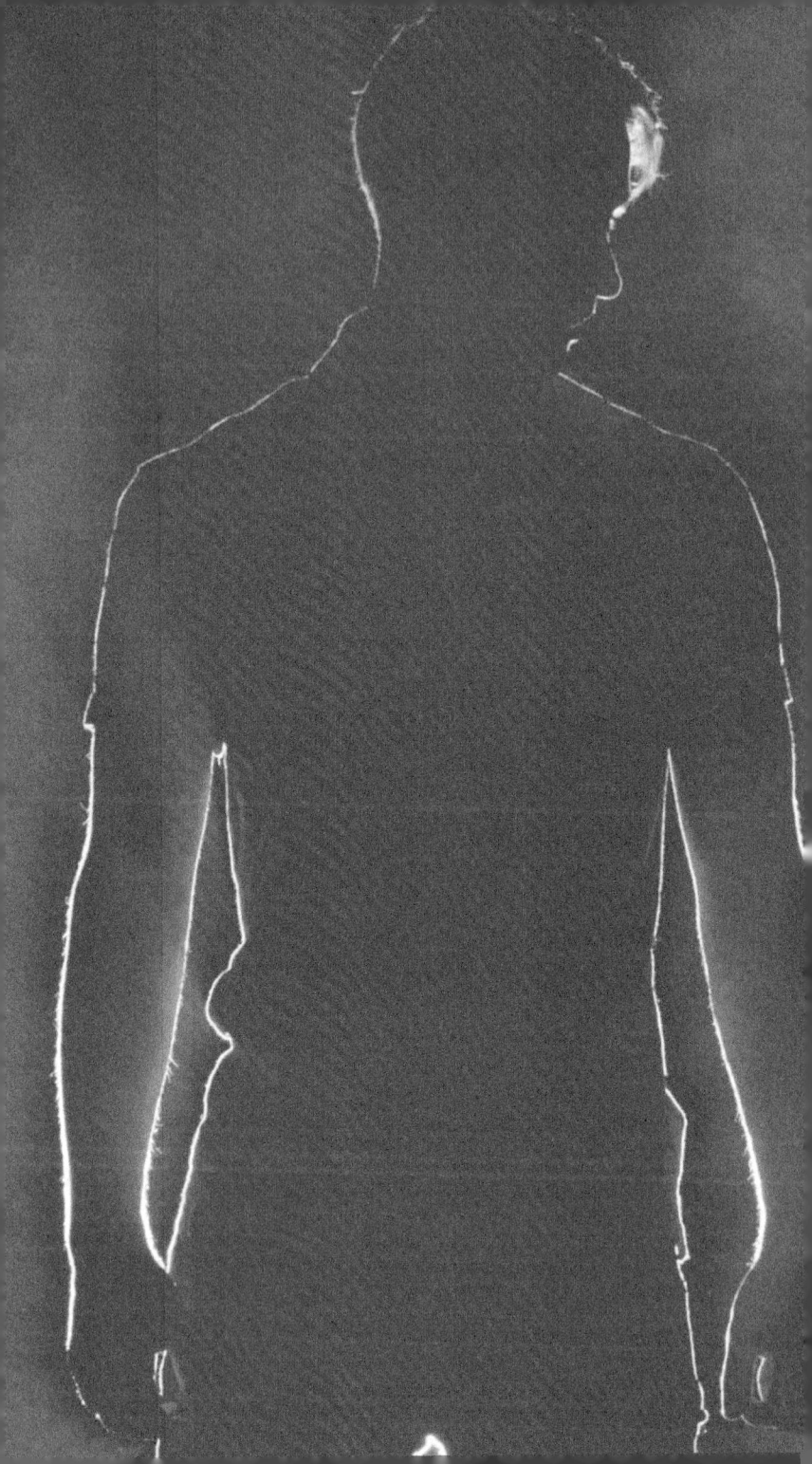

Chapter Twenty-Eight

Tony

I'M NOT SURE IF I'm supposed to be shocked or not, but I am mildly surprised when I roll over in the morning to find Carolina gone.

The alarm hasn't gone off, and a glance at the clock tells me that I haven't overslept, though I would've assumed that she would've woken me up if I had.

I sit up in bed, look around the room, and see that the few belongings that she had with her last night are gone. I narrow my eyes, a little perturbed at her disappearance, but I shake it off and go about getting ready to leave.

By the time I'm showered and dressed and make it back down to the work area, where people are milling around, awaiting further instructions.

But there is no sign of Carolina.

I walk over to Darius and ask, "Have you seen Carolina?"

His eyes widen, and he cocks a brow at me. "She's not with you?"

A shiver runs down my spine, and I grit my teeth as I sputter, "Obviously, she's not with me."

I look around the room until I find Nettie, then I walk over to her, grabbing her arm to get her attention. "Have you seen Carolina?"

She shakes her head, her brow furrowing. "No, I thought she was with you."

I whirl around in the middle of the room and shout, "Has anyone seen Carolina this morning?"

All I get back are shaking heads and murmurs in the negative. A deep sickness settles over me, and I swallow painfully as I look at Matt and say, "Find her." Then I turn to Nettie. "Check on Flora."

Nettie nods, already pulling her phone out and pressing buttons as she walks away. Matt's now staring at his computer, a concerned expression on his face, so I ask, "What is it? Just fucking tell me."

"How long do you think she's been gone?" Matt asks.

I shake my head, shrugging my shoulders as I sputter, "I don't fucking know. Could've been an hour or maybe even up to six or so. I don't know what fucking time I fell asleep. All these goddamn time zones, flying here, flying there, flipping cars, and cleaning up bodies. Jesus fucking Christ, man."

"She must've taken off shortly after you fell asleep because according to this tracker, she's thousands of miles from here. Which means there's 0% chance that we will be able to catch up with her before she lands."

Nettie steps up beside me and says, "Flora's still here. One of the guys said Carolina was there ages ago and peeked in on her and then took off."

I glance around the room, fully baffled by why she would take off, knowing we had a plan. "Where the fuck is Lilith?"

Nettie shakes her head, and Dare says, "I haven't seen her in a while. Or Mickey for that matter."

"Mickey was here earlier," Matt interjects. "He's definitely not with Carolina. But I haven't seen Lilith at all, and lord knows she's fucking wily enough to try and pull some shit, though I have no idea why."

"I'm going to fucking kill her," I spit out through my clenched teeth. Of all the times I've wanted to throttle that bitch, this one takes the cake. That self-serving, overbearing fucking snake.

Nettie gives me a patient and almost condescending look, and I say, "Don't fucking start with me, Nettie. She was a menace in her previous life, and apparently, she's gonna be a bigger menace now. We better teach her a fucking lesson before she gets someone killed."

She inclines her head at me, likely because she can't really disagree at this point, and I look over at Matt and ask, "So what do we do? Chase her until she lands?"

"Difficult to chase them without a flight plan. I mean, it can be done, but it's kind of tricky and also kind of dangerous, not that we give a fuck about that. Probably the best thing we can do is try to guess her destination and hope we don't have to change our course too much once she lands. Or we wait for her to land and then go."

"There is no fucking way we're waiting."

"I figured you'd say that," Matt says. "They're prepping our ride. We just have to decide a rough estimate on flight plan."

"So, we're going to guess where she's headed?" Nettie asks.

"More of an educated guess based on likelihood, given her most recent trajectory."

Nettie gives him a bland look and rolls her eyes. "I don't know what you're talking about, nerdface."

He holds up the tablet that shows Carolina's current location. "These tracking devices don't give constant real-time information—it's more of an intermittent ping. Don't get me wrong; it pings often, so not a lot of time goes by in between, but I can set them up like pinpoints on a map because flight plans don't zigzag. Once I have enough pins in place, I should have enough data to give a relatively accurate forecast on her ultimate destination. It would be much easier if we knew what kind of plane she was on, but we have to make do with what we got."

"How long will it take you to figure that out?" I ask him, feeling my left eye start to twitch.

"I should have a pretty good idea by the time we leave here."

"And if you're wrong?"

"Then we try again," Matt says sarcastically. "We can't be changing our flight plan in the air, Tony. That's not how it works."

"Who says?"

"The fucking aviation government people. Do you want to draw attention to yourself while moving at high speed through the air without reporting it? Depending on where you are and where you're going, you're likely to get shot."

I sigh heavily but don't bother arguing with him. Instead, I turn to Nettie and ask, "Can you make arrangements for Flora?"

"Yes," she replies. "I'll get it sorted and be ready in thirty."

I watch her leave the room and then turn my glare to Dare and Matt. "Do you guys know anything?"

They glance at each other and then look back at me, and Dare says, "No, Tony. I sure as shit don't know anything."

Then Matt adds calmly, "I don't know anything, Tony. And to be clear, not telling anyone Lilith wasn't dead is different than this. If I knew anything, I'd tell you."

I stare at him for a beat, knowing that he wouldn't lie to me when asked outright but annoyed that it isn't going to be that simple. Finally,

I choke out, "Why would she leave?"

"At this point, it's likely instinctive for her to lead the enemy away from the people she cares about," Dare replies. "It's basically what any of us would do if the ball was in our court."

"But she knows I'll go after her. She must know there's no chance in hell I would sit back and wait to see how it pans out. Her and Lilith both know this about me."

"And that's exactly why they got such a head start," Matt replies. "They had the perfect opportunity to get as much distance between them and us as possible before we would even find out they were gone."

Dare walks toward me, stopping in front of me, and placing his hands on my shoulders, leaning in as he looks me in the eye. "And don't forget they're both smart. Carolina has managed to keep herself alive all on her own for this long, and lord fucking knows Lilith Ferro won't do anything she thought would put her in harm's way. Lilith may take risks at her own expense, but she does not take risks at the expense of others."

I inhale deeply, allowing my heart to calm as I mull over his words. I know he's right; both women have been surviving on their own, without the help of any man, for most of their existence. But it doesn't take away my natural instinct to protect them. "It's the man's fucking job to protect the people he cares about."

Nettie snorts from behind me. "Actually, it's everyone's job to protect the people they care about. Not just you short-sighted, tone-deaf fucking men."

Dare hands fall from my shoulder as he grimaces and steps away. "Now, now, Antoinette," he says softly. "You know what he means. No need to attack him when he's feeling wounded."

She's standing a few feet away from me, her arms folded across her chest, giving me a disapproving look. She looks me up and down, then shakes her head as she says, "I'll let it slide this time. But you better fucking watch yourself if you wanna start this 'man is master' bullshit with me. You're not the only one allowed to fight back, just like you're not the only one who feels pain when the people they love are hurt. Sure, you may feel it differently when it comes to Carolina, but she's mine, too, so save your sanctimonious man-loves-best bullshit for another day, and let's go get our girl."

Dare is smiling at her fondly, an intense, proud look on his face, then he turns back to me and says, "Sometimes, we just gotta learn. And most of the time, we gotta learn the hard way."

Matt pipes in, "And sometimes, we have to learn repeatedly. But as long as we learn eventually."

I nod, blowing out a breath as I walk over to Matt. "Okay. We get on the plane for our best guess and, basically, hope for the best and plan for the worst. Am I missing anything?"

Nettie says, "Jayme and Declan will keep Flora at Declan's place since it's secure. The family she's been hanging out with will go with them, so she'll have some kids to play with, and maybe it won't feel so weird. Also, Agatha is missing as well, so it's safe to assume she's with Carolina and Lilith. I sent her a text, but it's currently unread."

I curse, then sputter, "Of course she is."

"I think I've worked out our best-case flight plan. I forwarded the information to Anton. He's gonna send out some of his people to a few different locations that have a high probability of being their final destination. He's gonna meet us in the location with the highest probability that that's where she's going."

"Where is *that*?" I ask.

"Italy."

I raise my brows and make a face. "Italy? Why the fuck Italy?"

He shrugs and responds, "Don't ask me. It's all based on numbers and shit. Do you want me to try to explain numbers to you?" We all shake our heads, and he replies, "Thanks. Fuck."

Dare adds, "Fuck stats."

I tsk Nettie and Dare. "Don't both of you have a bunch of fancy degrees in math?"

They both look at me like I'm stupid, and finally, Nettie says, "And? That's exactly why I say fuck math."

I look over at Matt, who shrugs, so I shake my head again. "So, do we have a ride or what?"

Matt's already packing up a bunch of his electronics and stuffing them into a bag. He smiles at me over his shoulder.

He continues to creepily smile at me, so I ask, "What?"

He laughs, then says, "I was contemplating if it ever gets old."

"If what gets old?" Nettie asks. "The fuck around?"

Matt nods and says, "I don't think it does because it doesn't matter how many times it comes around, those words still fall off the tongue like magic."

"You are truly fucking disturbing," I say, rolling my eyes.

He gives me an incredulous look, his hands going out as he says, "Tell me I'm wrong, Tony. Either say the words or tell me I'm wrong."

I narrow my eyes at him, contemplating telling him he's wrong just for fun, but I can't do it. Because he's not wrong. It never fucking gets old.

I glare at him, then spin around, and walk toward the door. "Let's go fuck around."

Chapter Twenty-Nine

Carolina

Tony must be pissed.

That's basically all that's been going through my head the entire time I've been on this plane. I stopped verbalizing this after about the tenth time I said it for fear that Lilith will stab me in the eyeball, but it's still running through my head on repeat.

In my defense, when Lilith knocked on the door shortly after Tony fell asleep, I had no intention of listening to any grand schemes. But the more she spoke, the more sense it made to me, and I had to accept the shortest path to a resolution was the path of least resistance.

But that doesn't change the fact that Tony must be pissed.

No sooner did I tell the man I love him for the first time, did I scurry off in the middle of the night without a word. For all I know, he's back to thinking I'm the devil and is out to stuff me back in the box.

"Will you fucking cut it out," Lilith sputters. "Tony Andersen may be a hothead, pain in the ass, but he's the first person who understands when it's the right choice to take a road that may appear to be a bit more dangerous. You can't be going into this situation surrounded by your posse because these types of people don't stand up to a posse. They hide in their little fucking hole in the ground until they find a good opportunity to slither out and stab someone in the back."

I say nothing because there isn't anything for me to say. Even if I did decide this was the wrong choice, it's a little too late now. Our course is set, and we're going to stay on it regardless of the forecasted outcome.

"We've got movement," Agatha says as she walks over to where Lilith and I are sitting and takes the empty seat across from us. She slides her phone over to show us the little green blip on the screen.

I look closer, laughing at the label. "That bitch? That's not very nice."

She smirks at me and says, "Have you met Antoinette? It's accurate."

"Is she going to be as pissed as Tony?"

"No," Agatha replies. "She's had to take her own path too many times to be judging anyone else for doing the same thing. She'll probably be glad we didn't tell her and ask her to keep a secret because secrets are not her thing."

"Because she has to tell Dare everything?"

Lilith laughs as she slides the phone back to Agatha. "She's still capable of keeping a secret when appropriate, but she's definitely a full-disclosure kind of girl. She was raised with too many secrets, and now, they leave a bad taste her mouth."

"So, they're like six or eight hours behind us?"

"Probably six to start, but I imagine they'll cut that down, assuming they figured out a relatively close flight plan to ours, and Matt will definitely secure a faster jet. Antoinette has been sending me unamused

GIFs for at least the last hour, so they've had some time to prepare."

I grimace. "They're all gonna kill us. Or at least me. You two will get a free pass for being blood relations. I'm just gonna be dead."

"You'll be fine," Agatha says flippantly. She picks up her phone and points the screen at herself, putting her middle finger in front of her face and taking a picture. She taps on the screen a couple of times, and then laughs as she sets it back down. "That's right, she's gonna love that one."

By the time we land at the private airstrip Lilith secured for us, my stomach is in knots. There are two cars waiting for us, and Agatha walks over to the man standing in front of one of them and takes something from him before coming back to where Lilith and I are standing.

"Are you ready for this?" she asks quietly, holding her hand out to me, a keyring dangling from her fingertips.

I take the key from her and reply, "I'm ready."

She gives me a short nod, then spins on her heel, and walks over to the other vehicle, getting in the back. I turn to Lilith, who's looking me over, but she says nothing and then follows Agatha, disappearing into the vehicle, leaving me there to figure it out.

The GPS of the car is already set for an office building in the middle of Rome. There's a slight chance that the people who keep trying to catch me will make a move before I reach my destination, but we have contingency plans for all likely scenarios.

Of course, Lilith had us fly into a private airstrip outside of the city, so my drive into Rome takes a little longer than anticipated. As much as I enjoy the Italian countryside and Italian drivers, the anticipatory nerves are excruciating. By the time I get to my destination, I'm a sweating, anxious mess, and as I search for a parking spot, I work on getting my shit together.

Once I've moved through the lobby, I get in the elevator and head to the correct floor, finally starting to feel a little better, but the sense of dread of walking into the unknown still hangs over me.

I exit the elevator and step out into reception, walking over to the desk and giving the woman my name. She motions for me to go in, and I don't bother dragging my feet. I march over there, pull the heavy glass door open, and walk into the room with my head held high, having no idea who I'm going to see on the other side.

I strut over and stand in front of the giant hardwood desk in the middle of the room. The chair is turned away from me, so I can't see who is seated there, not that I expect I'll recognize him anyway, since as far as I know, he's just a man Lilith believes will most likely be able to fix my problem.

I clear my throat, shuffling from one foot to the other as I wait for the chair to turn, and when it doesn't, I say, "Hello? Am I in the right place?"

The chair slowly swivels, and an older man looks at me with an amused expression on his face. He's probably in his fifties, his dark hair graying some at the temples, the fine lines on his face just starting to deepen.

His lips curve up in a smile, and he cocks his head at me in acknowledgment and then says, "Yes, Carolina Petrov. You've come to the right place."

I glare at him and snark, "Don't fucking call me that. That is not my name."

His smile broadens, and he laughs, "So, I see the rumors are true."

"Rumors?"

"There's been some chatter about the ever-accommodating wife of Vincent Petrov suddenly becoming a lot less...accommodating."

"How could anyone possibly know that? It happened like two days ago, thousands of miles from here, and all the witnesses are dead."

His shoulders rise, and his hands come up to flutter in the air dismissively. "In our world, there's no such thing as secrets. There's always someone around to tell the story; it's whether the story is accurate by the time it gets to me, which, apparently, this one is."

I say nothing. I just stare at him blandly until, finally, he motions to the chair beside me. I shake my head. "I'll stand."

"Stubborn, too, I see," he says good-naturedly. "I shouldn't be surprised if you're hanging out with the likes of Lilith."

"So, you know Lilith well, then?"

The humor falls from his face, and his lips twist as he replies, "You could say that."

I wait a few moments to see if he's going to elaborate, and when he doesn't, I ask, "Do you think you're gonna be able to help make all this shit stop, or was this a wasted journey for a pointless conversation?"

If he's offended by my words, he doesn't let on. "The best thing you can do in your current predicament is to take the estate and affairs of your late husband off the table. No one wants you in particular; they want what you hold."

"Can I just give it away?"

He shakes his head and leans back in his chair, leveling me with a serious look. "The only way out of this kind of obligation is death."

"You're saying if I die, it'll end?"

He laughs and shakes his head. "It would end for you. But not for your daughter."

My stomach drops at his words, and I whisper, "How do we save her?"

"Marry someone more powerful and scary than the people you're going up against," he says seriously, then he looks me up and down before continuing, "You're attractive enough, so I don't think it would be a difficult sell. There are certainly enough powerful and scary people out there who wouldn't mind taking you on. I would do it myself, but you seem a little young, and I don't need that kind of aggravation or gossip."

"Age gap," I say distractedly.

He raises an eyebrow in confusion. "Excuse me?"

I shake my head and laugh nervously. "Nothing."

He leans forward in his chair and rests his forearms on the top of his desk as he sighs. "I know the situation is absurd. You'd think in this day and age, power plays would no longer be made using marriage contracts, but the fact of the matter is that both legal and illegal transfers of power are still dictated by bloodlines. The only time you'll see that transition of power change from one bloodline to another is through complete slaughter. Yours is almost there. If they were smart, they would've already killed you and taken the girl, and for all we know, that's what their plan is. So, now, you have to decide what lengths you're willing to go to protect her."

"Anything," I reply without hesitation. "I will literally do anything to protect her. I *have* done anything to protect her. You tell me what I have to do, and I'm gonna fucking do it. Doesn't matter if I like it, if I enjoy it, or if it's gonna be a great, happy life for me. As long as I can provide her with the best life possible, then I'm gonna do it."

He looks me up and down again before pushing back from his desk and standing. He leans forward and grabs a pen and a piece of paper, then jots something down. He tosses the pen onto the desk and picks up the paper, walking around his desk to stand in front of me. Folding the paper in half, he hands it to me and says, "Be at this address in three hours. We'll get it sorted. Try to keep yourself out of trouble in the meantime."

He pulls his phone out of his suit coat pocket, presses a button, and then puts it to his ear. He gives me a wink and then walks out of the room, leaving me standing there with my mouth wide open. After a few beats, I come to my senses and turn to the door and yell, "Wait! Who are you?"

My words fall on an empty room, and I roll my eyes at myself in annoyance for not being smart enough to find out who the fuck I'm even making super-crazy life plans with.

Having no other choice, I'll be meeting Mr. No Name in three hours, wherever the fuck this address is.

I leave the office and take the elevator back down to the ground floor. I don't have a phone to call anyone and don't know anyone's number to be able to borrow a phone. Basically, all I can do is hunker down and wait for my next rendezvous time.

I step out onto the busy street and look around the area. I spot a nice café a little way down and head in that direction.

I figure there's a fifty-fifty chance I might die later, so it's the perfect time for a cappuccino and pistachio croissant.

Exactly three hours from the time Mr. No Name gave me the paper with the address on it, I'm standing outside a large brick church. The ever-familiar dread is circling in my guts, but I ignore it and walk up the stairs, where a woman is standing, apparently waiting for someone.

I move to try the door when she stops me. "Carolina?"

Her voice is heavily accented and melodic, and I smile in response.

"Yes. I'm Carolina."

She beams back at me, then opens one of the enormous wooden doors and motions for me to proceed her inside. "My name is Amalia. I have a very simple yet beautiful dress and also a few accessories to help make this day memorable for you."

I frown, stopping in my tracks as I ask, "Memorable for what?"

She raises her meticulously shaped brows at me, her smile no less bright as she replies, "Come now, dear. Let's get you ready."

I dig my heels in for a moment and then relent, knowing in order for me to figure out what's going on, I have to follow the path to the end. But I'm getting the impression that Mr. No Name was taking his marriage contract lecture a bit too seriously.

We enter a small room off the narthex, and the first thing I see is the simple yet beautiful dress she was referring to. It's not pure white but more of a champagne color, and it shimmers in the light. I frown at it, and when I glance at Amalia, she's giving me a confused look. I quickly smile and say, "Thank you. This was very kind of you."

Relief flashes across her features before being quickly replaced with her bright smile. "I'll leave you for a few minutes to get dressed, and then I will help you with your hair and makeup. Nothing too extravagant—just a little touchup."

She scurries out of the room, shutting the door behind her, and I exhale a breath, my hand rubbing over my face in frustration. I can't even fathom what kind of fuckery I've gotten myself into here, and the fact that I have no way of notifying anyone of the current state of events does my head in.

I take a deep breath in through my nose and then let it out through my mouth, muttering to myself all the ways everything is fine and will be fine. Everything is fucking fine.

I stop stalling and quickly change into the dress Amalia brought for me. It's a perfect fit, the bodice hugging my torso nicely while the skirt floats around my thighs to just below my knees. It's a classical, timeless style reminiscent of the fifty's glamour, and under different circumstances, I'd be more than pleased to be wearing it.

I'm attempting to zip it when there's a sharp knock in the door. After a brief pause, the door opens, and Amalia peeks her head in to say, "Are you ready?"

"Yes," I reply. "I could use some help with the zipper."

She enters the room, shutting the door behind her and walking over to finish pulling the zipper up my back. She moves to stand in front of me, a smile on her face as she says, "You're a beautiful bride."

My stomach turns at her words, but I manage to keep the smile on my face. "Thank you. I'm not sure much can be done for my hair at this point."

"Oh, I'll put it up in a simple twist," she says as she pulls the chair out and motions for me to take a seat. She grabs a comb and a spray bottle, then waits for me to be seated before spritzing and combing my wild mess into submission.

Once she's finished with my hair, she trades her tools for makeup, which she applies quickly yet professionally. Before long, I'm staring back at my own reflection and nodding approvingly. "Well done, Amalia. I can only imagine the magic you're capable of if you have a clean canvas."

She laughs as she packs up her stuff. "Clean or not, you're a beautiful canvas. Your groom is going to be breathless when he sees you."

My smile falls from my lips at her words, sadness blanketing me as my breath catches in my throat. My groom. My fucking groom.

"Are you all right, Carolina?"

Amalia's question startles me out of my racing thoughts, and I nod, pasting the smile back on my face as I reply, "Yes. I'm fine. I'm ready."

She studies my face with a furrowed brow but then nods. "They're waiting for you. Out the door and to the left, and you'll come to the aisle you're looking for."

I swallow the lump in my throat as I open the door and walk out into the hallway. I turn to the left and slowly make my way toward the narthex of the congregation, intentionally dragging my feet even more when I spot a man standing at the altar with his back to me.

He seems familiar from this angle, and the closer I get, the more curious I become, my heart doing the occasional pitter-patter in my chest.

He appears to be dressed in an off-the-rack suit that isn't quite ill-fitting but also obviously not tailored—almost like someone purchased it in a hurry. I find this odd, considering if I'm going to be entering into a union with someone who has the power and balls to protect me and Flora, they would likely dress the part.

I stop a few feet away from him, clear my throat, and choke out, "Hello?"

The man spins, and my breath catches, anger building up inside me as the realization hits, and my mouth falls open in shock. My heart pounds in my chest, exhilaration, and happiness bursting inside me as I begin my walk down the aisle, my eyes focused on the figure waiting for me at the end.

But then, the figure turns, and I catch sight of his profile, and my steps falter, but it's too late. I've already been spotted, and he turns to me fully, glowering at me. I swallow, painfully recognizing my error too late, so I straighten my spine and continue forward to what appears to be my future.

Chapter Thirty

Tony

By THE TIME WE land in Italy, we're quite a few hours behind Carolina. We made up some time when they decided to land in a more obscure area, and somehow, Matt managed to secure us landing much closer to Rome. Our transportation is waiting for us right on the tarmac, but that doesn't save us from the traffic and Italian drivers.

We're slowly closing in on Carolina's location when one of Matt's many devices ping, and he pulls one out, looks at it, and then frowns and mutters, "What in the fuck?"

We all look at him, and I ask, "What?"

He gives me a resigned look and replies, "I don't know what the fuck is going on, but I got a ping on Carolina's name for a marriage license dated five days ago."

My blood runs cold, and my heart jackhammers in my chest. "And who the fuck is she marrying?"

Matt gives me an incredulous look and replies, "I think the bigger question here is, how is there a marriage license backdated five days? She wasn't even fucking here."

"Tell me who the fuck it is," I snarl, making a grab for his phone, which he quickly pulls out of my reach. "I swear to fucking Christ, Matt. If you don't tell me who the fuck it is right now, I'm gonna come over there and chew your throat out."

I look at Matt expectantly, and finally, he says, "I don't know who it is, Tony. It doesn't say. I'll get someone working on it, but we're probably gonna find out with our own eyes before we get the information back electronically."

"How are we gonna do that?" Dare asks.

Matt holds out his phone that's now showing a clear map. "She's at a church. And I can't imagine she's going to confession."

Now, my stomach drops right out of my fucking body. "I swear on everything holy, whoever he is, he's a dead man. She's gonna be a widow twice."

I'm sweating, a little nauseated, and completely at a loss of what I'm supposed to do to fix this. Whatever the fuck 'this' is supposed to be. I throw my hands up in disgust. "Are there any guns in this fucking car?"

"This may not be the place for guns, Tony. You'll probably have to old-school it."

"You better be fucking kidding me," I snarl.

He laughs, then looks at the driver and asks, "You got a gun?"

The driver says nothing but points to the glove box, which Matt opens, pulling out a small handgun. Taking it by the barrel, he hands it back to me, and I happily take it as Matt says, "Don't wave the fucking thing around, Tony. We're not in America, all right?"

I check that it's loaded and operational, then flip the safety on and put it in the inside pocket of my jacket. We're less than a kilometer from her, but we're moving so slowly it's gonna take days to get there, so when the vehicle stops again due to traffic, I say, "Fuck this shit," and open the door and step out onto the street.

I take off at a run, the sounds of slamming car doors and footfalls behind me, and I know that my people are following my lead. Matt is right behind me, yelling directions, and soon, we're standing in front of a large brick church with a black fence around it. We easily get over the fence then run up the stairs to the enormous wooden doors which are locked.

"What the fuck, Matt?" I whisper-shout. "This place isn't even open?"

Matt checks the map again then looks around as he replies, "She's here, Tony. We just have to find a way in."

I snort but step back and attempt to get control of myself as time ticks by. After a few moments, Matt walks off, motioning for us to follow him, and we hurry a short distance around the corner and find a side entrance.

Luckily, the side door is open, and we walk in quietly, and then slowly make our way down the hallway, peeking into rooms as we go. About halfway down, we come across a man in a collar, and although he seems startled to see us, he's calm as he asks, "Are you here for the ceremony?"

"Are we not too late?" Nettie asks mildly. "I was worried we'd missed the official man and wife moment with all the traffic here."

"You haven't missed the church vows," the man replies. "But it's not the church ceremony that makes it an official union. That takes place when the marriage certificate is signed and filed, so, technically, they've been legally married for days."

My blood boils, and Dare yanks at my arm, then shoves me down the hallway. "We'll go find a seat then and wait for the big event."

We continue down the hallway and end up in the main congregation. We move through the pews to the main aisle, and that's when I see her, and my heart stops in my chest. She's standing at the top at the altar with a man who is not me, and they're deep in conversation, his hands gripping her shoulders, her hands locked on his wrists.

Jealousy and rage surge through me, fueled by despair, and for a moment, I remain frozen to the spot, completely paralyzed by the overwhelming emotions churning through me.

We ease our way closer to the altar and to the couple who, at a glance, are sharing an intimate moment before declaring their undying commitment to each other in front of God. I grind my teeth against the urge to run up there and bodily rip that motherfucker away from my girl and then take him apart limb by limb in front of her.

I can't see her face or make out any of the words they're saying to each other, but they seem to be filled with emotion, and then that motherfucker's hands move to her arms, and he's pulling her closer. A growl bubbles up from my chest.

Dare steps in front of me, his lips moving, but I can't make out what he's saying over the roaring in my ears. I'm already reaching for my gun, pushing him out of the way.

Fuck all of this.

I've only made it a few rushed steps when Carolina shoves the motherfucker away from her and screams incoherently at him. I leap onto the pews, hurdling toward them like a madman. Some other men appear behind her, and the motherfucker standing before her pulls a gun and points it at her threateningly. I shout as I become airborne, seeing the whites of that motherfucker's eyes as I fly into him, my arms tight around his neck, and I use my strength and momentum to twist as we crash to the floor together.

I roll to my feet and whirl around, quickly closing the distance between me and the man attempting to sneak up behind Carolina. His eyes barely have a chance to widen in recognition before I drive my fist between his eyes, and he drops like a sack of bricks onto the floor.

Carolina's eyes move behind me, and I wait a beat. then pivot, putting my weight into the turn as my fist connects with the approaching man's throat with a satisfying crunch. He lands at my feet, and I meet the next man head-on, grabbing him by the head and squeezing as I lift him until he's on his toes. He's howling in pain as the base of my thumbs dig in right below his temples.

His hands grip my wrists, his toes barely keeping him upright as I shake him, and then I stop and lean in closely until all he can see is my face as I bare my teeth at him and snarl, "Shut your fucking mouth."

He immediately stops howling, but his eyes are rolling in fear and pain, and I feel his galloping heartbeat in his temples as I squeeze a bit harder for sport. He winces but remains quiet, and I look around briefly, taking stock of what's happening around me before turning back to the trembling man whose head I want to remove from his body.

"Do you know who I am?" I ask menacingly, and the man nods in my grip, so I nod at Dare and continue, "And do you know who he is?" He nods again, this time with more vigor, his gaze now frozen on Dare, so I give him a little shake to bring his attention back to me. "Any of these motherfuckers your boss?"

He shakes his head and squeaks out, "No, they were all lackeys like me."

"You go back to your boss and tell him Carolina is with us now, and if he doesn't cease and desist with any plans he may have to take her or harm her, we will hunt him down and make him wish he was dead."

The man's eyes widen as my words sink in, and then he nods, and

I ask, "Do you think you can do that?"

He nods again, more forceful this time. I release him, and he almost collapses to the floor, but he manages to keep himself upright by bracing his hands on my chest. I raise a brow at him in amusement as he yanks his hands away. He gives me a wary look, then glances at Dare briefly before slowly moving away from us.

He bumps into Matt at the first pew, who snaps a picture of him and then pats him down, coming back with his wallet. Matt takes a picture of his ID, then hands the old leather back to him, and he snatches it up as Matt says, "We better never see your face again."

The man tips his head in acknowledgment of his words and then scurries away, wasting no time in running down the aisle and out the exit beside the main doors. Matt's still looking at his phone, and after a few moments, he smiles and puts the phone back into his pocket. "Ready, set, go."

"You chip him?" Dare asks.

"Yeah," Matt replies. "Never hurts to have a human road map leading the way." He pauses, turns to me, and adds, "Good work, Tony. Nice to know you haven't lost your touch."

"I kept it old-school just for you," I say flatly, and Matt laughs, then shakes his head as he looks at the scene before him.

Carolina is standing there, silently twisting her fingers, nervous energy radiating off of her, and I step closer to her and ask, "Are you all right, sweetheart?"

Her eyes jump to mine, and her lips curve up slightly as she nods. "I'm all right."

"What the fuck happened here, Carolina?" I ask hesitantly. "Were you really going to marry a man who wasn't me?"

She grimaces and squirms a bit but then takes a shaky breath in and spits out, "Not on purpose!"

I raise my brows at her, one hand rubbing over my face as I wait for her to explain further, and finally, she says, "Lilith had me meet with Mr. No Name, who explained to me that the best way to secure power, even in this day and age, was through strong marriage ties. Then he told me to meet him at this address in three hours. I had no other explanation, and I didn't have any other options because our backup plans had to do with him, so when I showed up here and a woman was waiting to help me dress, I was more than a bit anxious as to what it meant. But the only way I could find out was to go through the motions and not draw attention to myself. And then, when I got into the main congregation and saw a man standing at the end, and well—"

She abruptly stops talking and looks down at the ground, so I prod, "And well, what?"

"I'd rather not say," she whispers to the ground.

I laugh softly, shaking my head in confusion. "Why not?"

"Because it's embarrassing," she mutters under her breath.

"What's embarrassing?"

She makes a face, her eyes flitting around the room as she actively avoids meeting my gaze. She closes her eyes and takes a deep breath, then opens her eyes, and looks up at me, her face twisting as she visibly swallows, then she exclaims, "For a split second, I thought he was you!"

Her hands come up to cover her face as her cheeks redden, and that familiar warmth is back in my chest. I gently pull her hands away from her face, then cup her cheeks in my palms and tilt her head back so she has no choice but to meet my eyes as I ask softly, "Are you saying the only reason you walked down that aisle in the wedding dress was because you thought you were walking toward me?"

She winces but nods and says, "I was so angry when I realized it wasn't you, but by then, it was too late, and I had no choice but to confront the issue."

"I'm sorry," I murmur, my eyes searching hers as I adjust my hands, so one is gently gripping her neck and the other slides down the silk of her dress to her hip.

"Sorry for what?" she whispers.

"For not being the first guy you walked down the aisle to today," I answer roughly, pulling her close so I can lean in and brush my lips over hers. She doesn't so much return my kiss as allow it to happen, so I pull back and add, "But I'll accept being the last man you ever walk down the aisle to, if you'll have me."

Her breath catches, and a broken laugh escapes, her eyes suddenly glassy as she stares up at me. "What?"

"You heard me, sweetheart," I respond clearly, pulling the front of her body flush with mine. "You got one more aisle walk in you today?"

Chapter Thirty-One

Carolina

I'M AT A LOSS for words. Of all the conversations I thought I might have today; this is not one of them.

He wraps his arms around me, and I press closer as the amused look on his face is replaced by one of yearning, and he murmurs huskily, "You know I'll protect you and Flora with my dying breath regardless, but you'd be doing me a great favor if you'd put me out of my misery now and say you'll make it legal."

"Doesn't that take a bunch of paperwork, planning, and stuff?" I ask breathlessly.

"Is that a yes?"

I can't speak through the lump in my throat, so I nod, and he smiles then leans forward and places a kiss against my lips before wrapping his arms around me fully and pulling me against him.

"We'll have to manage the whole marriage license nonsense since somehow there's already one filed with your name on it," Dare says. "But if you want to get married here, I think it'll only take a few days once the other one disappears."

"Who the hell filed a marriage license in my name?" I ask as Tony releases me and steps away. "I sure as shit didn't sign anything."

Dare shrugs and replies, "Could have been anyone, really. It's not difficult to forge and file government documents, and marriage licenses are rarely looked at after they've been indexed—"

"Um, guys," Matt interjects. "As it turns out, you can get married right now if you want because it appears that Tony is the man listed on the marriage certificate that was filed five days ago."

Silence falls over the room as this news sinks in, and then everyone starts talking at once until, finally, Tony's voice cuts through the din, quieting everyone down. "How is that even possible, Matt?"

"That was me," a voice says from behind me, and I turn to see Mr. No Name standing there, looking a little worse for wear, Lilith, and Agatha on either side of him.

"Well, it's about time you showed up," I snark, thoroughly annoyed I almost ended up shackled to another idiot just because this guy doesn't own a watch.

He gives me an impatient look, walking closer with an obvious limp, and Agatha moves closer to him, letting him lean on her a bit. "My apologies, Carolina. Between securing your wedding wear and attempting to locate an appropriate suit, I was set upon by thugs and left in an alleyway."

Lilith pipes in from behind him, "Fucking moron thinks he can walk around the city on his own without even one person watching his back. He's lucky he's not fucking dead."

"No one asked you, Lilith," he sneers over his shoulder. They glare at each other for a moment, and then he turns back to me and says,

"As I was saying, I was set upon by thugs and incapacitated, and once I came to, I realized how late I was, so I called Lilith. Luckily, she was close by, and here we are."

"And who the fuck are you?" Antoinette asks from beside me.

He turns his gaze to her, his eyes lighting up as he says, "Antoinette, darling. What a pleasure to finally meet you."

She gives him a dirty look, then looks over at Lilith with a stony expression. "Do we know this yahoo?"

Lilith sighs heavily, making a face as she mutters, "This is Antonio Rossi. Your father."

Antoinette's mouth falls open in shock, but then quickly snaps it shut as her eyes spark with anger. "Excuse me?"

Lilith sighs again, looking anywhere but at Antoinette as she says more clearly, "This man is responsible for half your DNA. Whether or not he ever has a future role as your father is entirely your decision."

You could hear a pin drop in this church right now. I look at Tony, who's staring at Antonio intently. Dare has moved closer to Antoinette but says nothing as we all wait to see what will happen next.

After a few long moments, Antoinette's mouth twists, and she murmurs, "Of course you are," then turns her focus back to me and asks, "So, are we having a wedding or what?"

I blink at her for a few beats, then look at Tony, who's also staring at her like she's lost her mind. Tony recovers first and says, "Sure. I don't see any reason to wait." He turns to Antonio and asks, "Do you think there's a decent chance whoever thinks they're going to steal her away for the power they'll gain will rethink their plan?"

"Yes," Antonio says with a nod. "Otherwise, I would've put some-one else on that marriage license."

I gape at him, but Tony laughs again and says, "Well, thanks for that, I guess," before turning back to me with a questioning look.

"Are you sure you want to do this?" I ask seriously. "You don't have to. There's really no rush; everything will work out regardless."

"I'm sure," he replies easily. "And if you're having second thoughts, I'm going to warn you now that I am all for Nettie's forced marriage trope."

Nettie laughs beside me, and I give him my best-unimpressed look, though I have a good idea that he's likely not entirely joking.

"I'll go get the priest," Dare states helpfully, then turns and walks off in search of the man responsible for making this a done deal.

"I'm not Catholic," I say awkwardly.

Tony smiles down at me. "I am," he says nonchalantly. "And if the priest asks, which I doubt he will, lie to him."

"You want me to lie to a priest?" I exclaim. "In a church!"

"Sweetheart. After the events of these past few days, I think lying to a priest is the least of your worries. Actually, you should maybe consider taking a spin in one of those confessionals to get it out of the way. Start our wedded union with a clean slate."

I roll my eyes at his teasing, but I'm saved from having to reply by the arrival of Dare and the priest, who appears a bit flustered but mostly ready to get on with the show.

He smiles at me and then at Tony and asks, "Would you like the traditional vows, or would you like to say your own?"

I open my mouth to tell him traditional is fine, but Tony beats me to it and says, "I'm ready with my own."

I grimace, not because I'm worried about what he'll say but because I have no fucking idea what to say, given this entire scenario was sprung on me, and my tendency to speak nonsense when nervous is a real problem.

Tony takes both of my hands in his, and the priest rambles on about

God, marriage, and holy stuff, and then, before I know it, he turns to me and asks, "Would you like to start?"

I freeze, my eyes wide and mouth open, gaping like a goddamn fish out of water, and after a few beats, Tony saves me. "I'll go first. Don't want to put the lady on the spot or anything."

I smile at him gratefully, but then my stomach knots up in anticipation of what he could possibly say at a ceremony that is one step down from a shotgun wedding.

He smiles down at me, his fingers tightening on my hands, and he leans forward and places a soft kiss on my nose. He straightens and clears his throat, his expression serious as he stares into my eyes. "Carolina, you've been a giant pain in my ass since the moment I laid eyes on you. Even before we met, when all I knew of you was a passing glance on a red carpet, I was completely obsessed. And then, we had that brief moment in Paris, and even though I was briefly deterred by what I assumed was your great treachery, my initial feelings about you never once faltered, hence why I felt driven to hunt you down and stuff you in Dare's box." He laughs at this, and everyone in the room who knows the story laughs with him, and surprisingly, the priest doesn't appear at all concerned.

"I know you've been through a lot," Tony continues, his serious face back in place. "And you have a lot of healing to do, but I hope you trust me to be there for you every step of the way, regardless of whether you need me to lead, guide, or follow."

He pauses for a minute, blinks a few times, then clears his throat. "I guess what I'm trying to say is, wherever you need me, whether it be behind you, beside you, or in front of you, I'll be there. I'll never waver or cower, and I'll make you kiss me goodnight every night, even on nights where you'd rather slap me through the mouth than kiss me, deservedly so, I'm sure. I won't pretend to be capable of perfection, but I will promise to try my damnedest every day of my life to be the man you choose to have by your side."

I swallow past the lump in my throat, completely choked up and shocked by his words and the heartfelt honesty behind them. I try to speak, but a quiet sob comes out, and I press my hand against my lips to prevent myself from completely embarrassing myself.

I look back up at Tony, and he's smiling at me, obviously exceedingly proud of himself, and I'm suddenly torn between kissing him on the mouth and slapping him through the mouth—wow, I guess he was right.

But then, he squeezes my hands again, leans in, and says, "Green or red, sweetheart? That's all I ever need to know."

I clear my throat and manage a grateful smile as I reply, "Green."

He smiles and nods, then leans in, and presses his lips against mine, totally breaking wedding protocol by not waiting to be told to kiss his bride.

He pulls back, keeping one of my hands in his, and we turn toward our small beaming audience. Everyone claps, and Antoinette, who appears a bit glassy-eyed, is practically bouncing on her feet, clapping louder than the rest.

Tony looks back at me and winks. "Shall we get out of here?"

I nod, happiness bubbling up inside me, and for a moment, if throws me off from the sheer intensity of such an unfamiliar emotion.

We all walk back down the aisle and then spill out on to the sidewalk, strolling through the gate onto the street before turning down a side street. Everyone's chatting and laughing, enjoying the odd moment of calm in an otherwise chaotic existence.

I feel the shift in the air before I hear the gunshots, I hear the pedestrians screaming before I see the enemy coming, and then I see them pulling Tony away from me before I can adjust my grip and keep hold of him.

I move toward him, intent on grabbing him, but then I'm knocked backward, pushed to the ground by the force of another body. My ears ring, and I roll to my hands and knees, looking around wildly, but he's gone.

He's not there.

Chapter Thirty-Two

Tony

THAT MUST HAVE BEEN what romantics meant when they said their hearts were full.

That's all I keep thinking about as I lie here in my current predicament.

I've watched enough crime thrillers and epic mobster dramas to know how this shit works. Just as soon as you think everything is going well and everyone's gonna get a happily ever after, some crazy shit goes down.

Because the old adage that love is blind is true.

That's the only excuse I can come up with for missing all the signs that something terrible was going to happen.

In my defense, we all missed it. We all sashayed out of that church, all smiles and cheer, completely unprepared for the hellfire about to rain down on us.

Dare tried to yell a warning, but it was too late, and before I could even react, I was being ripped away by more hands than I could reasonably count. When the gunfire started, I couldn't tell who was hitting the ground for cover and who was falling to the ground, dead.

And as I was being yanked away, dragged, kicking, and fighting—the number of men on me more than I could overcome—Carolina made a move to grab me, only to be knocked back mid-motion, the champagne silk of her dress floating around her.

At that point, I fought harder, unable to look away as I watched everyone I know be cut down, completely unable to save them.

Now, here I am, impotent and immobilized, likely to be tortured and killed in the obscenest fashion, or perhaps their torture is to leave me to die in this box.

But if they're all truly dead, do I even care?

A trail of warmth slides from the corner of my eyes into my hair, and I curse at myself, taking a deep breath and shoving it back down.

In the meantime, if this box opens and they give me so much as a sliver of opportunity to gain my freedom, I'll take it.

All I need is a second. One second. One misstep. The nearest margin of hesitation to give me an opportunity to fuck around.

And then, every one of these motherfuckers is gonna fucking die.

I manage to doze off briefly, and I'm jarred awake by an obnoxious creaking sound. I blink up into the darkness, and it takes me a few moments to recall where I am, but as soon as I do, that crushing weight is back on my chest.

I listen intently, taking stock of varying voices, tones, and footfalls in an attempt to assess what will be waiting for me when they finally crack this fucker open.

I'm not a huge fan of enclosed spaces, but I don't have any problems with claustrophobia like a lot of people do. I've intentionally slept in smaller places than this, though, I suppose the intentional part makes it a little easier.

I work at controlling my breathing, pushing down that edge of despair that attempts to pull me under and lock me there. I know my mind is telling me the people I love are dead, but I also know you can't trust the stressed mind. You can only trust what you see with your actual eyes, and until I see some bodies, I have to believe that they're all alive and likely pissed off.

The scraping of stone on stone draws my attention above me, and I crane my head back at the initial crack of light blinding me. I squeeze my eyes shut and relax as the lid slides open loudly, and I try not to think about the fact that they've been storing me basically in the fucking ground.

I pretend to be asleep, passed out, knocked out, or whatever the fuck will give me an opportunity to kill someone.

I lie there, waiting for a few moments, and then a voice says, "There's no point in pretending not to be awake. You're not gonna get any openings to escape either way."

Hands grab onto me and pull me up and backward as they drag me out of the box. I contemplate remaining a deadweight, then figure no good can come of it, so I get my feet under me and stand as I open my eyes and look around, taking note of the swarm of men surrounding me.

Not ideal, but also not impossible.

I yawn, and the same voice speaks again. "Are we boring you, Mr. Andersen?"

"Maybe bored isn't the right word. How about underwhelmed?"

I look up and see a bearded man around my height and build standing a few feet away, his arms crossed over his chest, and he snorts and says, "I won't lie and say your reputation does not proceed you.

That's why there are more men in here than you could ever hope to defeat on your own rather than the handful we would normally have in this situation. Now, we can do this one of two ways. Either you move on your own two feet where we want to take you, or we put you in chains and take you there anyway. You decide."

I squint and say, "If my reputation truly preceded me, you'd already have me in chains."

His arms drop to his side as a corner of his mouth curls up in amusement, then he shakes his head. "You're gonna end up in chains, eventually, but I was saving us the hassle of having to take them on and off. But we could do them now if you prefer."

I put my hands up in mock surrender. "Nope, that's quite all right. Lead the way."

He's correct in his belief that I couldn't take out this many people at the same time. Maybe if I got my hands on some weapons, preferably a gun, but a knife would also work, I'd be able to take out enough of them to persuade the others to switch sides. But even then, unlikely.

He leads the way out of the room, a group of men falling in behind him, and then the rest around and behind me. It feels silly, but I applaud the man for thinking ahead, even if a good many of these men look like boys who would piss their pants if I said so much as boo to them.

We walk down a narrow hallway, and I make note of the old stone surrounding us, as well as the narrow, high windows, leading me to believe that we're partially underground.

We go down a narrow, stone staircase into another stone room, but this one is windowless, and there's a drain in the middle of it. The man turns to me and asks, "You gonna strip yourself, or you gonna make us do it for you?"

I don't even blink as I quip, "Aren't you gonna buy me dinner first?"

"So, the rumors about you are true, I see," he replies blandly.

I throw him my trademark arrogant smirk but say nothing as I pull my shirt over my head and throw it into a far corner in the hopes it stays dry. I kick off my shoes, shove my pants down my legs, and throw all of it to the edge of the room.

I stand there completely nude, wishing I had some pockets to put my hands in, when he nods to someone behind me, and a whirring noise draws my attention above me. A chain with a hook on the end of it lowers, and now I do grimace because being left with your arms above your head for an extended period of time sucks ass, especially since it appears they're gonna leave me here naked, wet, and cold, a game that is not at all my favorite.

On the other side of that, there's a slim chance they won't secure me appropriately to the hook, and I'll be able to get myself out of it, so I pretend to be a little more distressed than I am about my current predicament.

"Looks fun, doesn't it?" the bearded man asks pleasantly.

"I still think you should've bought me dinner first, but I guess it is what it is."

I don't bother struggling as they walk me forward, so I'm standing beneath the suspended hook. I hold my hands out in front of me help-fully, intentionally holding my hands at such an angle that it makes them a tad wider than they really are. They pull my arms over my head, securing a chain between my shackled wrists and hanging it from the hook. Then the whirring clank of it being lifted above me echoes around the room until I'm suspended appropriately in the air.

And it sucks just as much as I remember.

He nods again, and some other people come forward with their fucking buckets, and I'm quickly drenched, sputtering from the bucket of water I took to the face.

Bearded man steps in front of me, looks up at me, and says, "It's supposed to be a nice and balmy -5 degrees Celsius. I hope you enjoy your stay here because the real fun will start tomorrow."

"Looking forward to it."

He turns to leave, and I ask, "Can you tell me what this is all about, so I have something to fret over while I'm waiting?"

He stops mid-stride, turns back to me, and replies, "Let's just say the boss is annoyed you stole his bride. The only way he can have her now is to make her a widow, and, unfortunately for you, he thinks you should suffer first."

"I didn't know she was promised to anyone else. Surely, we can discuss this little misunderstanding in a civilized manner."

He throws his head back and laughs and then replies, "I guess it's a good thing your reputation does proceed you after all."

Saying nothing further, he turns around and exits the room, his swarm of men following behind him, leaving me here to consider my options.

One of the fun games I like to play in these situations is making a list of all the things they did wrong as a future reference to myself to not make those same mistakes if our roles were ever reversed.

Most of the time, the first mistake people make is they talk too much. Every time they open their stupid mouth, they're giving more information on what's gonna happen, giving their enemy more information to plan around. Sure, sometimes the stuff they're spewing is bullshit, but usually, you can pick out the pertinent truth when you need it.

Since I know they plan on leaving me here all night to freeze to death, that gives me plenty of leeway to come up with an escape plan.

My biggest concern right now is knowing that a lot of these underground strongholds are intricate mazes, and once you get lost, you may never get out.

I wait a few minutes longer than is probably necessary, then twist and swing my way free of the hook. My hands are numb, and my arms scream from being pulled over my head for so long. As soon as I land on my feet and lower my hands in front of me, the pain starts. I know it'll be short-lived, considering the brief amount of time I hung up there, but it's still agonizing.

I scan the room for cameras, and though I don't see anything obvious, there's still a high likelihood that cameras are hidden within the crevices of the rocks that I wouldn't be able to see.

I move to the outer edges of the room and grab my clothing, quickly dressing and then finding my shoes. I'm surprised they didn't take my stuff with them, but that's how things go when people get complacent and start thinking they're untouchable.

Kind of like how I got here.

Feeling slowly returns to my arms as I gradually make my way to the doorway, pressing against the wall and peeking around to stay out of sight of anyone coming down the hallway.

I listen intently, closing my eyes and focusing on my surroundings.

Clicking. Dripping water. The faint clearing of a throat. Even more faint sounds of traffic.

Once I'm reasonably assured there won't be any immediate surprises, I enter the hallway and continue downwards, knowing the direction I initially came from leads to a dead end.

That stairwell curves down onto another level into darkness, and I hesitate for a moment, not keen on forging ahead where I can't see anything. Knowing there are no options behind me, I cautiously move along the wall, dragging my fingertips along the icy stone.

I stop every few steps and listen intently, circling the room down one side and along the other, trying to keep the growing map in my head as I move.

The darkness thins the longer I stare into it, and eventually, I'm able to make out the faintest of shadows. I turn the final corner and end up back on the wall where I began,

and there's a break directly next to the door that I entered.

The danger of pitch-black stairwells isn't lost on me, and if given any other option, I would avoid it, but I'm out of options.

I drag the toe of my boot along the floor and let it slowly fall until it touches down on the first step. I continue to do this over and over, leading with my fingertips along the wall and following with my foot along the step until, finally, I end up on another level.

I feel around, then turn the corner, and a faint light emanates from the far side, and I squash down my urge to hurry toward it. I'm sweating with effort in the cold room, and I force myself to slow down and take my time as I walk along the wall to the other end.

I stop and listen again, this time noting more silence echoing silence. The dimness of the next room feels bright to my aching eyes, and I'm able to move more swiftly, though still cautiously. I take the first stairwell I find that leads upwards, and it circles me up and around, so I feel like I'm doubling back on myself.

With each stairwell comes more light; at first, there's only a dim lightbulb, then two, and three, and then I'm hanging back in a doorway that opens into a large room that's bright in comparison to what I've just been through.

I take a step into the room, scanning for people and staying along the wall as I look for cameras. I circle along the far side, moving with more assurance now as I make out a large bay door that's open, and my heart jumps in my chest at the glimpse of freedom.

Part of me wants to watch and wait and leave a pile of bodies in my wake, but I've learned from experience if you find a way out, you take it and then come back later for the kill.

I take a step toward the door, preparing to make a break for it when shadows cross in front of it, and I stop, pressing myself back against the wall. I make out what sounds like mostly chitchat, as no one appears alarmed, and then a woman laughs, and a chill goes down my spine.

There's no fucking way.

I pull away from the wall, knowing it's a mistake, but I can't stop myself. I have to see with my own eyes, witness this treachery for myself, so that I'll truly accept it for what it is.

A group of people walk in and make their way into the middle of the room where a desk has been set up. At first, all I see is the men, but then one of the men laughs, and they all laugh, and I hear her laugh again.

I take another step forward, and then I see her.

At first, all I feel is relief that she's alive.

Then confusion. Anger. Understanding.

Then that weight that I haven't felt on my chest for so long is back, crushing the life from me.

Anguish.

I watch her speaking to the group of men animatedly, familiarly, and my guts twist painfully. Then I hear her say excitedly, "Victor? No way, that's crazy!" and the man says something I can't quite make out, but she replies clearly, "I wish he had told me all of that years ago. Would've saved us all a lot of fucking trouble."

And I give up any semblance of hiding and step right out into the middle of the room and say, "Are you fucking serious right now?"

The whole group freeze, and her eyes fly to mine, wide with shock. Her mouth snaps shut, and then she raises her chin and says, "I thought you said that fucker was in chains."

My eyes widen, my jaw goes slack, and I shake my head as the meaning behind her words sink in. "So, it was all a lie then? Everything you said was a lie?"

I'm quickly surrounded by men, ending up in the same position I was when I first came out of the box, and I don't fucking care.

My eyes never leave Carolina's face as she steps closer, stopping when she's a few feet from me, and she tilts her head to look up at me and asks, "Don't you read what they say about me in the gossip rags, Tony?"

"What?" I ask helplessly.

She smiles that delicious smile that I yearn for and coldly replies, "I'm a hell of a fucking actress."

My stomach drops, and I grind my teeth together as I use that split second of surprise to my advantage and lurch for her, managing to grip her throat in my hand and yank her to me as I squeeze.

Her eyes light up in surprise and a little glimmer of what looks to be relief, as I manage to grind out between my teeth, "And I just loved you."

Then the swarm takes me down, and it's lights out.

Chapter Thirty-Three

Carolina

They pull Tony off of me, and I bend over, choking and coughing at his decent attempt at crushing my throat.

The group of men are actively working on incapacitating him, though he already appears incapacitated, and a familiar voice behind me pipes up, telling them that's enough.

The men move away, leaving Tony collapsed on the floor, knocked-out cold, and I groan in frustration, my hands massaging my throat as I straighten and turn to see with my own eyes the man standing behind me.

I blink a few times, my memory zapping at seeing this face after so long, and I frown as the past and present collide.

Thinking back, I always knew, deep down, that the one nice bodyguard didn't make sense in the grand scheme of things. And seeing him here now only proves my theory that no good deed comes without conditions.

I squash down my initial knee-jerk reaction to tell him exactly what I think about his two-faced bullshit, and instead, paste a tentative smile on my face as I say, "Victor. What a surprise."

He turns his dark eyes on me, skimming me from head to toe and back up again before finally meeting my eyes and replying, "Carolina. Looking delectable as always."

I cringe inwardly, calling upon every ounce of theatrical training I've ever had to keep the warm smile on my face and shining from my eyes. I probably shouldn't be surprised, but part of me is disappointed that his being nice had nothing to do with human decency and under-standing. Like everyone else in my life, it was all for his own gain—all for him wanting me for himself because he wanted to be king of the evil kingdom.

He walks over to the men hauling Tony up off the floor, speaking to them quietly, and then they're dragging him away, and I'm left unable to even stare after them.

Victor looks me up and down again, then creepily smiles and says, "You were supposed to compromise their fucking organization, not marry one of them."

I shrug my shoulders dismissively, working hard to school my fea-tures at learning he was the one keeping tabs on me after Vincent and Dmitri were killed. "I didn't sign any papers. Surely, you can make them disappear as easily as they made them appear."

His smile broadens. "It won't matter once he's dead. There's no waiting period to remarry if you're a widow."

My heart stutters in my chest, but somehow, I manage to keep my wits about me as he walks closer to me, puts his arm over my shoulder, and pulls me against his body. I lean into him and look up at his face, a face that always held kindness for me in the past. But now, I see the same monster that was Vincent and Dimitri and countless other power-hungry assholes who've come in and out of my life.

I'd like to assume that he wouldn't treat me as poorly as Vincent did, but I also know that in this world, all it takes is the need for one more pawn on the board for all of that to change.

"What are you gonna do with the asshole?" I ask, keeping my voice blasé and my expression bored. "Are you going to have some fun torturing him later?"

He smirks and pulls me tighter against him. "Not worth the risk. I told them to take him down to the incinerator and get rid of him. When it comes to people like Tony Andersen, you need to cut them off at the neck before they have time to retaliate or regroup. Otherwise, you're a dead man."

Thinking about Antoinette and her opinions of men leading with their dicks and their egos, I smile broadly, my eyes shining as I wrap my arm around his neck, pulling myself up closer to him and purring, "Aw, Victor, you were always so nice to me. I wish you'd told me of your plans at the time. Maybe we could've taken him out together and avoided all of this craziness. At least now, we can focus on us and our future."

I rub myself all along his body, raising my leg up in offering, and he takes it, grabbing behind my knee and pulling it up to his hip. My hands move down between our bodies, his eyes closing in anticipation as I fumble along the waistband of his pants. He's so consumed with anticipation that he doesn't realize that only one hand is in his pants while the other is reaching down into my boot that he made accessible to me.

I wasn't lying when I told Tony that I'm an excellent fucking actress.

You just never know which part I'm playing until it's too late.

I move my hand from inside Victor's pants to his hair, and at the same time, I pull the blade from my boot, whipping it around and jabbing down viciously into the side of his neck. He attempts to jerk away, but I tighten my grip on his hair, my foot lifting so my leg around his hip squeezes him closer. I quickly yank the knife out of his neck and jab it back in once, twice, three times in quick succession.

I push back from him, and he blinks at me, his jaw working as he tries to speak, his hands coming up to clutch at his throat. And then, he stands there and fucking bleeds.

Blood gushes with every pump of his heart, and I don't flinch; I don't look away. He sags to the floor, and I push him over, taking the bloody blade still in my hand and stabbing him in the heart, ignoring the vibrating ricochet that runs up my arm.

I spin around and run back toward the stairwell, where Victor's men disappeared with Tony. A shadow crosses the doorway, and I pause for a split second as Darius comes into view, Matt right behind him, and I don't falter in my steps, yelling over my shoulder, "They're gonna kill him!"

I've only been in this facility a few times, and I attempt to focus my mind on the correct path, knowing that one wrong turn means he's that much closer to death. I swallow down the fear and anxiety as I fly down the stone steps, likely faster than is wise, but I don't hesitate. I continue forward, knowing Dare and Matt are right behind me.

My steps stumble as we walk into pitch-blackness, but then a glow behind me pushes me forward, Dare's words behind me moving me faster. "We're gonna make it. We have to make it."

I choke down a sob, pushing forward, knowing the three of us will be moving more swiftly than a group of men who think they're not running against the clock, men who are likely bragging over what they feel they're about to accomplish.

Over my dead fucking body.

The rooms are lightening as we move through, and I burst out into a room I know is two staircases from their final destination. I make a sharp left and barrel up the stairs, coming through the second-to-last door right as the unmistakable vibration of a 2000° inferno roars to life.

I stumble into the room, my eyes on the short set of stairs that lead up to the incinerator, and I lose my footing on the slick stone, stumbling a few feet as I try to get my feet back under me. I scream, "No! No!"

Hands grip under my arms, dragging me to my feet, and we're all running toward the doorway now aglow with fire, blinding and ominous. Final. I stumble again. This time, a guttural wail falls from my lips as I crash to my knees on the stone, Dare and Matt flanking me helplessly. I lie there on the cold stone for a few long moments, my broken sobs uncontrollable as I choke and gag on what feels like a lifetime of pent-up rage and fear pouring from my body.

Hands press against my shoulders and my back, and Dare is there whispering words I can't make out through my sobs. Both of my hands are braced against the floor, tears, snot, and spit splattering on the stones beneath where I'm kneeling. I squeeze my eyes shut and take a deep breath in an attempt to get control of myself.

I take a few deep breaths and then open my eyes as two booted feet come into sight, walking right up to me. I whimper, not daring to look up.

Dare releases me, and new hands grip my upper arms, forcing my eyes to rise with my upper body, and there's Tony, bloody and knocked around, looking at me with a resigned expression on his face as he says clearly, "I was gonna let them take me, but then I decided I didn't even wanna die without you."

I choke out a laugh and sob, "I fucking hate you so much!"

He pulls me into him, and I wrap my arms around him, his breath against my ear as he replies, "Same, sweetheart. Same."

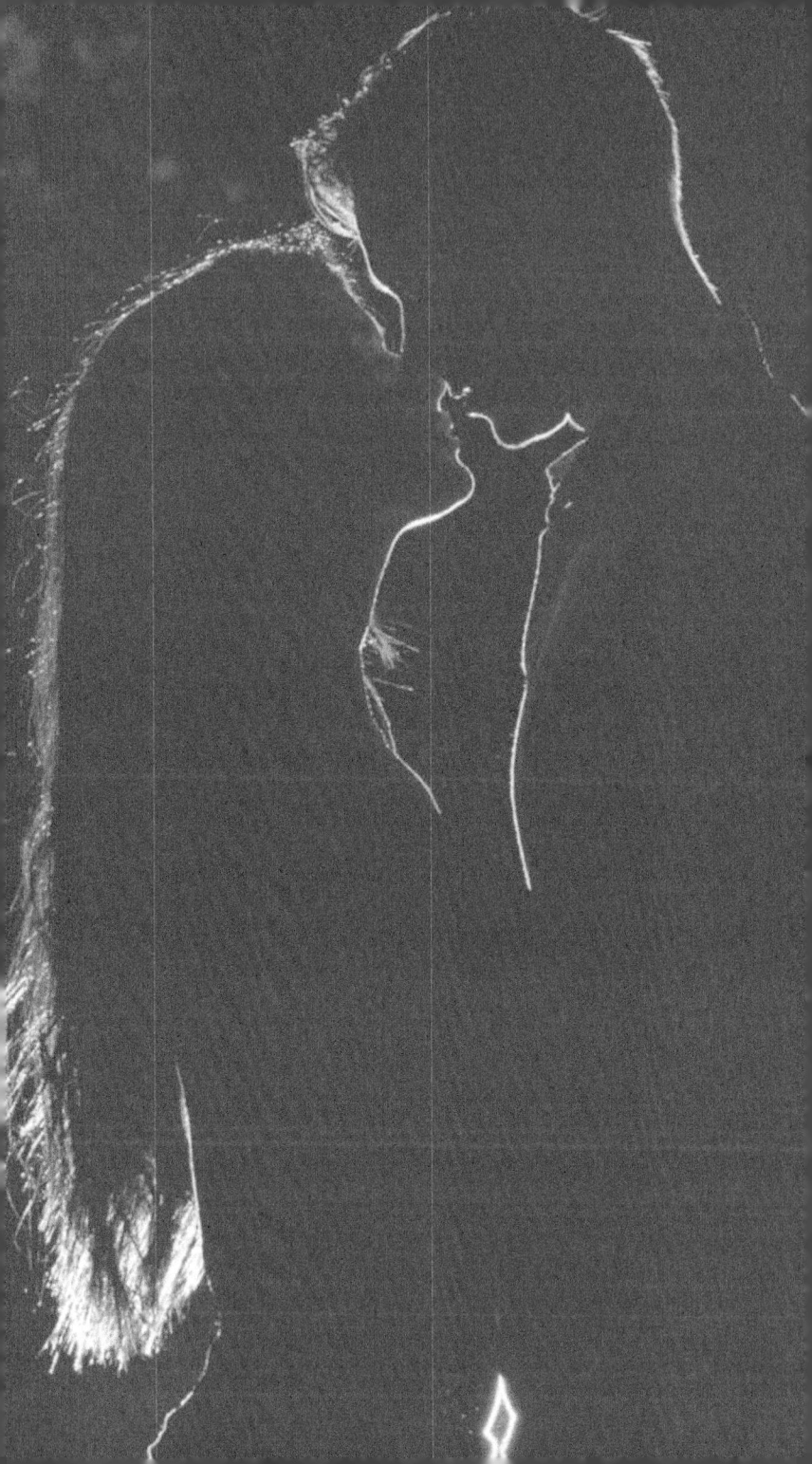

Chapter Thirty-Four

Tony

IT TAKES A GOOD ten minutes for me to calm Carolina down enough that she'll release me. I would've carried her out, but I sure as shit would've gotten us lost, or our necks broke falling down the stone steps, so I let her take her time coming around.

Even now, as we're working through this shithole, I keep catching her looking at me, an odd mix of pain and relief on her face. And a few times, she sought me out just to put her hand on my face and then walk away, as if she's proving to herself that I'm truly there.

She's been relaying as much information about Vincent, Dmitri, and their business as she remembers to Matt, and we're setting up a final extermination of Dmitri Petrov's bloodline and loyal associates.

As Nettie likes to say, we're going full Wyatt Earp on their asses.

It sounds far more sinister and complicated than it is, but we have to make sure that anyone who may have eyes on any enterprise run by

Dimitri, Vincent, or Victor never sees the light of day again.

Dare relays as much information as he can on what happened, but he doesn't know a lot so that still leaves big holes in the story. So, this time, when Carolina sneaks over to touch me, I snag her hand and yank her to me, caging her with my arms. "Why didn't you tell me, sweetheart?" I ask softly, my words worried yet resigned.

"There wasn't time," she replies. "Lilith came to me with an idea on how to flush out the enemy once and for all, and I felt I had no choice but to go along with it. And she was right that I couldn't bring a whole posse with me because rats don't stand up to an army. And then, the whole church thing threw me off, and you actually wanting to be married to me, and there was like a whole five-minute span there where I truly felt everything was going to be fine. But then, not even a hundred feet from the church, gunfire brought me back down to reality. And you were gone, so any plan I had to flush out an enemy had to be accelerated because we didn't know what would happen to you."

"So, you weren't just acting?" I ask, mostly rhetorically but still wanting her to answer. "With me, I mean."

She shakes her head and laughs softly. "Never. Not even for a second."

I smooth her hair back from her face with one hand, my fingers spearing into the hair at the base of her skull. I tighten my grip and pull her head back so she's looking me in the face, and her mouth opens slightly as her eyes soften. My lips curve up, and I lean forward, press my cheek against hers, and whisper, "For a moment in time, I thought you had truly betrayed me, and I wanted nothing more than to squeeze your throat until you stopped breathing. But that was when I realized that I love you too much to kill you. I would rather live in a world, knowing that you're my enemy, than in a world where you didn't exist."

I pull back and meet her eyes again, and she sighs. "But did you ever really believe it?"

I think over her question for a few moments, allowing myself to relive an event that happened only a short time ago but already feels like a lifetime ago. "I don't know. My initial reaction was knee-jerk to the shock of the situation, and when I came to on the long trek to my doom, I thought fuck it, let them kill me. I deserve to die anyway. But no sooner had they dropped me on the floor, thinking I was out cold, then I was on my feet, ready to fuck around. I think if there had been any more of them, I'd have been in trouble, but I made it out by the skin of my teeth. All I could think about was finding you and making you pay but also fearing that something would happen to you before I could get to you. But I came flying down the stairs, and there you were."

"Don't remind me. I'm going to have nightmares for the rest of my fucking life," she replies.

"Dare said we didn't lose anyone at the church. I'm thankful but also shocked."

"Antonio was grazed by a bullet, but he's okay. That means either we were blessed, or they have really bad fucking aim. Maybe both."

I'm quiet for a moment, part of me not wanting to talk about it anymore, even though I know I need to know what happened. So, I ask, "How did you find me?"

"Purely luck, like usual," she answers. "Anton showed up in the middle of everything going down. Antonio reached out to some of his contacts to help clean up with the local authorities, and in the meantime, Matt checked the location of that shithead you released out into the wild. Turns out he didn't waste any time scurrying back to the snake's nest. Since we knew where we had to go, we just needed to find a way in, and I figured, if nothing else, a few of Vincent's old men would recognize me and at least get me access to the building. I had no idea Victor was the man in charge. That fucking prick was always nice to me when he was playing bodyguard, but I had no clue who he actually was until I came face to face with him again."

"Who was he?"

She raises her brows at me, her features twisting as she says, "Vincent's younger brother. Seems the estranged brother shit is going around. At least Declan is entertaining."

I snort, wanting to argue but unable to because she's not wrong. Declan is a lot of things, and entertaining is one of them. Hence his multi-million-dollar entertainment enterprise. Then she continues, "Anyway, Victor couldn't inherit the whole bullshit empire because it wasn't left to him. No living will exists, so everything automatically goes to me. What's super fucked up is he could've kept on running shit with no one the wiser, and it wouldn't have mattered. But he had to make a play for legitimacy and ended up dead."

"Good job on that."

She beams at me, no remorse or shame evident as she replies, "Thank you. I learned a lot from Antoinette in a very short amount of time."

I smile down at her, allowing relief to settle into me as I look around the room. "Did Lilith know what Antonio planned with the whole marriage license thing?"

"No fucking idea, and they all fucked off before I could get any answers out of them."

"Where are they?"

"Matt said they're getting a head start on razing Europe of its criminal problem."

I snort, shaking my head as I ask, "Does that mean we're on that list?"

"Nah," she answers seriously. "Basically, if you stay out of human trade, you're almost safe."

"I'm surprised Dare let Antoinette go without him."

"As if he could stop her. I had no idea how wild Antionette was, but sometimes, I think she might be the craziest one out of all of you."

"Come on now," I say with a laugh. "You know it's a sliding scale. We all take turns with the crazy."

She gives me a soft look, then sighs. "Is it really over?"

I raise a shoulder noncommittally, then reply, "Is it ever really over?"

"So, you're saying there's zero chance you want to retire and come live with me in the suburbs with a white picket fence, a dog, and a passel of kids?"

My eyes widen, and I try to keep the horror out of them, but then her lips twitch, and I realize she's fucking with me. "Just for that, I should keep you pregnant for the next decade and see how much you enjoy hanging out in the kitchen."

"You can try, but remember, I don't cook, so joke's on you."

"Nah," I reply smugly. "Joke's on you 'cause you're stuck with me, and you haven't caught on to the fact that one way or another, I get what I want."

"Oh, really?" she asks with raised brows. "And what is that?"

"Only you, sweetheart. Only you."

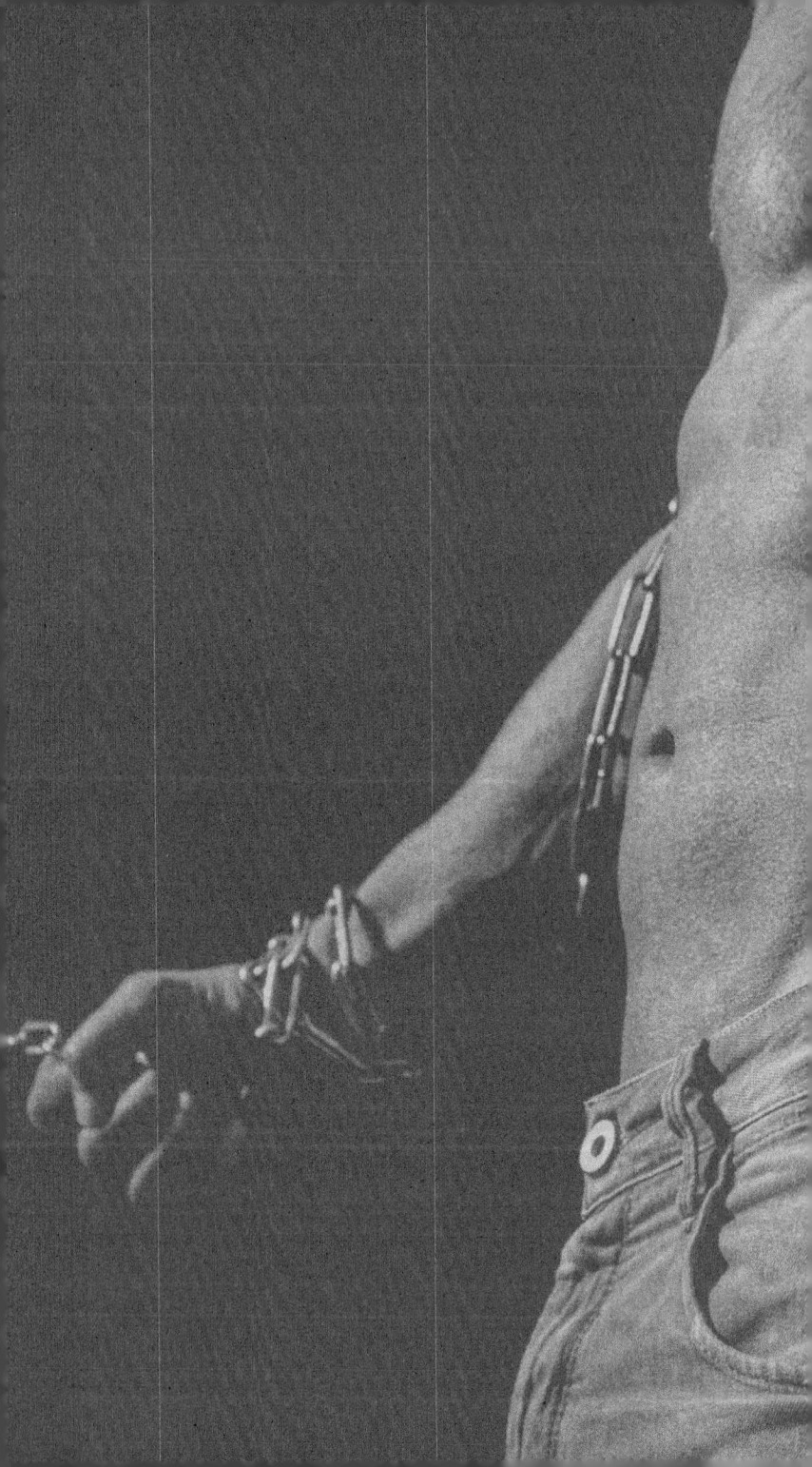

Epilogue

Tony

Two months later...

If anyone had ever told me that one day, I would be married with children, I would've laughed in their face.

But here I am, a married father of one, constantly contemplating impregnating his wife.

Just that word "wife" heats my blood and speaks to that purely animalistic part of me that I didn't know existed.

That being said, no one ever explained to me the many restrictions of having a small child around all the time. Not that I'm complaining, but the distinct lack of privacy is a problem when you want to stick it in your wife twenty-four-seven.

Until now, I never realized how easily a man can be edged, and the fact she doesn't even have to put her hands on me to twist me around to the point I'm a throbbing, reckless animal, entirely focused on destroying her pussy or her mouth or her ass, basically any part of her that I can get my dick into, is hilarious.

For example, right now, she keeps looking at me, licking her lips like I'm a tasty snack, and she knows damn well there's nothing we can do about it until Nettie gets here to take the cock-blocking child off our hands for a few hours.

What she doesn't know is that Nettie and Dare are keeping Flora overnight, so I have a full twenty-four hours to torture her. The first thing I'm gonna do is spank her, then stuff her full of my cum, and then I'm going to stick her in the box and let her cool off for a few minutes...or maybe an hour.

In the months since our impromptu wedding, things have remained mostly quiet. Nettie has been in sporadic communication with her father, though she still refers to him as the sperm donor, and I suppose that will go on until she decides he's earned the right to be called anything different.

So far, all the chatter regarding Carolina has died down. It seems our cease and desist or else message was received and believed.

That doesn't mean there isn't still a threat. We can't let our guard down entirely, but the more we dismantle the organizations that these people want to acquire, the less likely they are to bother.

And we've been very busy on that part. The extensive network of illegal operations that Vincent and Dimitri were operating was extreme. Carolina has helped with a few of them, but for the most part, she's been happy to sit back and allow us guys to take care of it for a while. It's the first time in her life she's been able to sit back and not worry about what comes next, and though it took her some time to acclimate to this new mindset, she's been settling in nicely.

I'm in the process of cleaning the kitchen when she enters the room after seeing off Flora. She's standing on the other side of the large island, and I ask, "You mind pushing that pan over to me, please."

She eyes me suspiciously, but she places her hand on the pan and leans forward, pushing it in my direction. I reach over the pan and snag her wrist, quickly cuffing it before she can snatch it back. Her eyes light with excitement, but she frowns at me. "Really, Tony? This is how you're gonna play it?"

"Take off your shirt, sweetheart," I reply as I release her cuffed wrist. "And then give me your hands, and I'll show you exactly how I'm gonna play it."

"My shirt?"

I nod. "Take it off or I'll cut it off."

She cocks her head at me, and I can tell she's considering making it difficult for me, which is perfectly fine with me since it doesn't matter what order she goes in the box as long as she ends up in the box.

She waits a few beats and then pulls her shirt over her head before holding her hands out to me so I can cuff them, and then I pull her until her upper body is flat on the counter and secure her to island with the ropes I had hidden in the cupboard.

Once her hands are secure, I go around to the other side and yank her pants down over her hips and down her legs, pulling them off and tossing them to the side. I flip the trim boards on the sides of the kitchen island, pulling out the restraints I have hidden there and securing both of her ankles. I adjust the length of the ropes, placing her legs apart exactly where I want them. Then I step back and look at my handiwork and the vision she makes, sprawled face-down with her ass in the air.

She looks at me over her shoulder, her tongue peeking out and licking her lips, her eyes sparking with excitement as she asks, "What are you doing?"

I give her my most smug smile and reply, "Whatever the fuck I want."

"And what makes you think you can do that?"

I step in close, my palm coming down on her ass cheek with a resounding smack, and she jumps. "I can do anything I want, sweetheart. Don't you ever forget it."

She chuckles low in her throat and wags her ass at me. "What if I won't let you?"

I smack her other ass cheek. "I see you're a comedian tonight. Let's see how much you're laughing when you're in that box, begging to come with my cum leaking out of your needy cunt."

Her eyes widen as she gapes at me for a moment before, finally, she whimpers and whispers, "You wouldn't."

I laugh, massaging both of her ass cheeks with my hands as I lean forward and kiss and lick up her spine until I reach her shoulder where I bite down and suck, leaving a mark on her. Then I pull back and whisper, "Here's what I'm gonna do, sweetheart. I'm gonna give you a couple more spanks, and then I'm gonna get my dick out, and I'm gonna fuck that weeping pussy right up until the point you're about to come, and then I'm gonna stop. And then I'll do it again. Later, once you're humping the counter in frustration, I'm gonna fill you full of my cum while withholding your own orgasm. And then, I'm gonna put you in that box and let you think about that sassy fucking mouth of yours."

She rubs her ass back against me and whispers, "And then what?"

I run my nose over her ear, growling a bit as I think about it all. "I'm gonna take you out of that box, and I'm gonna eat my cum out of your pussy until you gush all over my face. And then I'm gonna put you face-down on the floor and fuck you raw until your screaming for it."

"Oh, fuck," she says breathlessly.

"Do you like that? Is this plan okay with you, sweetheart?"

She nods and pushes her ass back on my dick in invitation, so I pull back and stand, my hand immediately coming down on her ass cheek, and she yelps.

I find a rhythm of spanking and massaging her ass cheeks, while intermittently licking between her legs, and before too long, she's a writhing, pleading mess, begging me to fuck her.

I unbutton and unzip my jeans and push them down far enough that I can get my dick out, then I rub the head between her legs, dipping inside and sliding back to rub over her clit. Her hips buck, pushing back and trying to force me deeper, but her range of motion is too small, and she groans in frustration.

I put my fingers in my mouth, dragging them along my tongue, and then sliding my wet fingers along my cock before I slowly push into her pussy, pulling back slightly, then thrusting back in as she moans.

I set a nice, easy pace, teasing her until she's cursing for more, and then I pull out and slam back in, crashing her hips against the counter. I stop and ease her back, snaking my arm around her front so my forearm is braced between her and the hard granite. I bring my other hand around, adjusting my stance so I can hold her steady and rub her clit while I fuck her.

I know she'll try to sneak an orgasm if I don't watch her closely, so I pay close attention to her body, her breathing, her moans as she attempts to not give away how close she is. Of course, if she comes before I want her to, I'll have to punish her more. But still, I have a plan that I'd like to stick to.

It doesn't take long for the tension in her body to indicate her orgasm is looming, and I thrust into her two more times, and then cease my movements, my hand pressed against her stomach, my cock pushed in deep. I remain motionless as she twitches, using my arms to keep her from riding my cock to her desperate orgasm.

After a few moments, she quiets, but she's cursing me under her breath, and I laugh. "That's right, sweetheart. Wait your turn."

I let her curse me, enjoying her enthusiasm as I resume the teasing strokes of my cock in tandem with my fingers on her clit. I know this time, it won't take long since she was right on the edge, and within a couple of minutes, the tension escalates once more. I move my hands to her hips, leaning my body away and pulling my dick from her tight cunt. She wails, cursing and thrashing, and I'm disappointed I'm not sure the cameras in this room are recording.

I give her a few minutes to settle down, contemplating if I've edged myself enough to be able to come quickly. As soon as I shove back inside her slick pussy, I know I'm there, and then I fuck her, rutting into her like a man possessed.

She doesn't normally orgasm from penetration alone, but I feel the cues of her body kicking in, and I'm torn between following through on my promise and feeling her pussy pulling the cum from my balls. But then she looks back at me over her shoulder and grins as she says, "That's right, baby. Make me come as you fill me up. You know you can't help yourself."

The smug look on her face puts me back on the original plan, and I push into her all the way and stop, and she freezes, anger sparking in her gaze as she realizes what I'm doing, and she moans, "Fuck. Oh, fuck."

I pull out a couple of inches, then slide right back in, my pelvis slapping against her ass as my dick pulses, and I come deep inside her. "That's right, sweetheart. Take all my cum. Take it and keep it right where it belongs."

She whimpers and rubs her body on the counter, lying there limply as she mutters under her breath, and I chuckle and ask pleasantly,

"What's wrong, sweetheart?"

Her body thrashes, and I step away and laugh some more. "Here I thought you liked the box."

She squirms on the counter, panting, but she says nothing, so I climb up on the counter, straddling her hips on the edge as I unhook the cuffs from the ropes that are attached to the kitchen island, and pull both of her arms behind her, connecting both wrists together.

I lean forward and kiss between her shoulder blades before jumping off the counter and kneeling down to unhook her ankles. It only takes me a second to realize the error in my order of operations, and the next thing I know, I'm pushed backwards as she makes a break for it.

I roll to my feet easily enough and take off after her slower than I could because I know she likes to think she's winning. It's not lost on me that she's running closer to the box, and when I finally catch up to her on the second floor and pin her face-down in the hallway, she's pushing her ass up, begging me to fuck her, and I know I've made the right decision.

I haul her up off the floor so she's standing, then put a shoulder under her stomach and scoop her up in a fireman's carry. She's still cursing, her hands tied behind her back, so there isn't much she can do to escape, but it also wouldn't be the first time she's bitten me in retaliation. I jostle her around on my shoulder so her teeth can't make contact with my person, then continue walking to the bedroom, locating the remote I keep on top of the armoire, where no one else can get a hold of it.

This box is similar to the one Dare has in his hideaway in the woods, except this one is far more high-tech. I push a button, and the drawer slides out, nice and smooth. I appreciate the technology as I kneel and none too gently topple her inside. She attempts to sit up a couple of times, but my hand pushes on her shoulder. "Stay down or I make it extra uncomfortable for you."

She glares at me, practically hissing, and I lean down and lick across her cheek, then whisper in her ear, "Just lie in there and think about your reward, sweetheart."

She quiets down, and I move her a bit to make sure she's clear of the platform before I press the button that slides the drawer back under the bed.

I'm not sure how long I'll leave her in there, so I walk down to the kitchen and finish cleaning up, wiping everything down. I listen for any signs of distress, though I did have the box outfitted with a red panic button in case she needs to call the scene. She's only ever had to use it once, but that once gave me a fucking heart attack, and now I have it wired throughout the whole house to be sure I'll hear it.

I finish cleaning up and stash my ropes back in their hiding place. I peek at my watch, surprised only about twenty minutes has gone by. I contemplate finding another little project that needs tending, but then reconsider, figuring I've tortured her long enough.

She's in there, ready to get dicked down right now, all the waiting and anticipation, along with the cum I left inside her, means she'll be dripping wet for sure.

I start to undress, then change my mind because she loves it when I fuck her with my pants on. I remove my shirt and toss it on the bed, then push the button to reopen the box.

It slides out smoothly, and she's lying there with her eyes closed, but I know she's not asleep by the erratic rise and fall of her chest along with how she squirms, her hips rocking as she rubs her thighs together. I pull my phone out of my back pocket and say, "I'm taking a picture of you, sweetheart. So, I can show you how perfect you look later."

She rolls on her side, more of her ass tilting toward me, and I see my seed oozing from between her pussy lips and down between her thighs.

I kneel, corkscrewing two fingers into her cunt, pushing my cum back in, and she gasps at the sudden intrusion.

I remove my fingers from inside her and use my other hand to roll her on her back, so I can lean over her and push my wet fingers between her lips. She moans around them, sucking and licking, a groan of pleasure coming out of her mouth.

I take my fingers from her mouth, my hands bracing on both sides of her as I lean down and capture her lips with mine. I push my tongue inside her mouth, my cock like stone in my pants at the taste of us, and I growl in approval, suddenly more than ready to give her reward.

I push myself up and away, then turn and hook an arm beneath her cuffed arms, pulling up enough so I can lift her out of the box and onto the floor. I ease her onto her front and position her, so her head and chest are flat on the floor, her ass in the air, presented to me.

I tease her first, breathing against her sensitive flesh with the occasional flutter of my tongue against her clit until she's panting and moaning, her hips bucking as she attempts to ride my face.

I stop playing with her and dive right in, tongue-fucking her, and then replacing my tongue with three fingers as I press my tongue against her clit. I lick and suck, occasionally grazing her with my teeth, and she presses back against me insistently, likely worried I'll stop and edge her again for fun, but I'm not going to. I want her to come on my face, and then she's gonna come again on my dick.

I reach into my unbuttoned jeans with my free hand and get out my dick, giving it a couple of strokes as I continue to eat her. It doesn't take long before her body becomes taunt, and her breath stops, then she gasps, "Fuck, yes, don't stop. Don't stop. Don't stop. Please make me come. Please, please, please make me come. Please, fuck, let me come."

The cresting tension breaks, and her sounds of seeking pleasure echoes throughout the room, her pleading curses switching to relief as she orgasms. Her pussy clenches around my fingers, and she pushes back against me. I don't move, allowing her to take what she wants, what she's earned.

Soon, her moans become quieter, and her body sags into the floor. I sit back, leaning over and reaching into the drawer of the bedside table beside me and pulling out a small vibe. I disconnect her hands and place the vibe in one of them, telling her, "Press this against your clit, sweetheart. Don't take it off until I tell you, or I'll stop and put you back in the box and start over."

Sometimes, this isn't a threat to her, and she would do it on purpose, but I don't feel she will tonight. She seems more intent on coming some more, so that's what we'll do.

I slide my dick between her legs, rubbing the tip between her pussy lips before pushing inside a few inches. She's relaxed and dripping wet, and I ease myself in slowly until she's taking all of me. I pump in and out a few times, but then I notice her hands by her sides, and I stop the press of my cock inside her, my hand coming down hard on her ass cheek. "Put it on your clit, sweetheart. Now."

This gets her attention, and she presses the button on the end of the vibe, and her hand disappears beneath her, and I feel that vibration in my dick. I groan and pull out slowly, pushing back in forcefully and grinding in as far as I can, and she groans loudly as I hit her just right inside, and she gushes.

She presses the vibrator more firmly against her clit, the vibrations of the small device running up into my balls, and it's my turn to curse. "Fuck, sweetheart. You feel so fucking good. Are you gonna come on this big fucking dick? Say it, sweetheart. Tell me what you're gonna do."

She remains incoherent, moaning and pushing back against me insistently as her next orgasm builds, so I slap her on the ass again, and she whimpers, "I wanna come on your dick, baby. Please. Fuck your little cum whore."

I'm gripping her hips with both of my hands, and I pick up the speed and intensity of my thrusts, holding back becoming an increasingly difficult endeavor. And then, her other hand moves beneath her, and I know what she's going to do before her fingers touch my balls, and I spit out, "Fuck, sweetheart. Is my little whore trying to steal my cum? You want it that bad?"

She sobs, her grip on my balls tightening as she pulls, just the way she knows I love it. I release her hips, my hands going to the floor on either side of her as I fall on top of her, driving my cock into her over and over, my head falling forward so my lips are right by her ear as I grunt out, "Take it, sweetheart. Take all of my fucking cum. You can have it; it's all yours."

She chokes, then sobs again, her body shaking with her release as she pushes back against me, and I snarl like a fucking animal, my dick pulsing my release inside her, and she moans, "Fuck. Fuck. Give it to me. Please."

I lie on top of her like that for a few moments, nuzzling and kissing her ear and her neck. She sighs and then laughs, and finally, I manage to push myself up off of her, pulling myself from her body and sitting back on my knees. I look down at her and this new picture she's made for me, and I snag my phone from where I left it on the floor. "I have another picture for you, sweetheart. You're gonna love this one."

I snap one of her lying face-down on the floor, her ass in the air with my cum leaking out of it, then I push two fingers into my mess, and snap a picture of that, too. I turn the phone off and toss it over on the bed, then I continue to kneel there with my fingers still inside her, my other hand stroking her ass as I say, "You still haven't told me."

She cranes her head around, giving me a lazy smile, her brows raised in question, so I continue, "If you went on birth control or not. I never know if I'm breeding you for sport or for real."

Her lips curve up in a smile, and she laughs softly. "I'll never tell."

"Oh, you naughty little whore," I reply teasingly. "That's because you like how excited I get at the thought."

Her smile broadens, but she says nothing, so I lean forward and say, "Let's get you up, sweetheart. Get you cleaned up."

She sighs contentedly and allows me to help roll her over, but when I attempt to scoop her up, she slaps me away. "I don't need you to carry me. I'm fine. I'm great, actually."

"I like to carry you," I mutter, but I help her stand on her own two feet anyway. "Do you wanna take a bath?" She shakes her head, so I ask, "Shower?" She shakes her head again, and I stare at her with raised eyebrows until, finally, she replies, "I like smelling like you."

My eyes widen, and I make what can only be described as a purring noise in my throat. "Now you're speaking my love language, sweetheart."

She grabs a robe from the back of the door then turns to me, her brow furrowed in confusion. "Your what language?"

I give her one of my most self-satisfied smiles and reply, "My-wife-smelling-like-my-cum love language."

She throws her head back and laughs, then shakes her head at me and slaps me on the chest as if I'm joking. She should know better, but I'll let it slide, and when she goes to walk by me, I stop her and lean in to place a kiss at the corner of her mouth before I ask, "Seriously, Carolina. Am I breeding you for real?"

She raises her brows and tilts head teasingly as she smiles mysteriously. "I don't know Tony." She pauses and continues to walk out into the hallway, turning in the doorway and looking back at me as she says with a wink, "Only one way to find out for sure." Then she turns tail and runs down the hallway, laughing.

"Oh, we're gonna play it like that, then, huh?" I call after her, but I'm smiling like a Cheshire cat as I do the only thing I can do.

I go after her.

THE fucking END.

Well, I did it. I wrote three books. And this one was, by far, way more difficult than the first two. Combined.

No, for reals, though: I quit writing at least 436739467306 times while writing this book. Depression, chronic illness, being a 200-year-old perimenopausal woman with a job and a family—writing three books in one year may have been a bit more than I should have taken on. But I did it. I fucking did it.

Here's just a tiny sample of all the people I need to thank:

To you, the readers: thank you for taking the time to read this book (and any of my books), and for taking the chance on a new author (or sticking with me since the start). Yes, I continue to poke fun at negative reviews, but I still appreciate everyone who takes a chance on my books. Continue to read what you love, and love what you read.

My family: (you read it anyway) - for continuing to put up with my self-imposed writing deadlines, and supporting my efforts even if my books aren't exactly your thing.

My Non-Book friends: (JESSICA!!!) I promise at least two trips this year. And to everyone who supported me by reading, and those who don't read, but bought it anyway because I wrote it.

Layla Towers: Declan is gonna fuck around like no other. I keep saying that I wouldn't be here without you, and it is a freaking fact. Thank you for putting up with me. ILY4E.

Jay: The past year has brought so much change, and I can't wait to see what's next. Keep being amazing. ILY.

The Spicy Book Nook family: LA Ferro and LM Fox. <3

Still Censored: Carolina Jax & VR Tennent — *Why are we like this?*! Lamp. ILY.

Matt and my KGQ family: Amanda, Dani, Heather—what a fucking year. Honored to know you. Love you 4-eva, my OG bitches.

My Bookish Sisters: Issa Marie and April—so many things. Like why? How?! ILY. Never stop being fabulous.

Britt: Tears are a salve that dilute the grief so we may find comfort in memories. ILY.

Kayla: So, I guess this means you're going to stick around for book 4? ILY.

Sam: You know I'm too stubborn to let that dumb clock app win. We got this! <3

Stacey: So you wanna fuck around, too? Welcome and thank you! <3

The Bookish Girls Services: Always a pleasure. Keepin' it red flags...

vo.EROS & my Egirls: Tamora, Katarina, Goldie (twinner), Jane Apatova, Amy, Denise, Abby, Elle, LadyT, Erin, Candy, Kytana...to name a few. GTPLPOTBFD. All love.

My CABG crEw: Aimee, Ashley, Krystin, Mags, Manda—even if I'm silent I think of you, taking comfort in the fact you're there, like a safety net. I may fall, but not for long. ILYSM.

Big thanks to the BookTok/Bookstagram worlds for showing me love even when the apps (TT) don't really like me overly much.

My ARC team: Thank you for continuing to show up, and for always being game for whatever hairbrained survey or poll I may have. The group sex thing isn't totally off the table...

Extra shoutout to those I see constantly throwing my name out into the universe: Suzanne, Nancy, Cami, Stef, Gabby.

Kirsty McQuarrie with **Let's Get Proofed** for humoring my insanity and then stepping in when I came to my senses and added 15k words in the home stretch. It's fine. Everything is fine.

And to my brother, Jason.

Do you know what I do when this cape don't fly?

I dance. I love you.

Made in the USA
Las Vegas, NV
31 December 2024

15615983R10223